THE BAD LANDS

A NOVEL AS BIG, BOLD
AND RICH AS THE WESTERN
FRONTIER IT DESCRIBES

"I LOVED EVERY PAGE OF IT."
—Peter S. Prescott, *Newsweek*

"Reading this novel is like watching a classic Western film."
—*Philadelphia Inquirer*

"A SOLID, SATISFYING STORY."
—*Chicago Tribune*

THE BAD LANDS

a novel by

Oakley Hall

FAWCETT CREST • NEW YORK

THE BAD LANDS

THIS BOOK CONTAINS THE COMPLETE TEXT OF THE
ORIGINAL HARDCOVER EDITION.

Published by Fawcett Crest Books, a unit of CBS Publications, the
Consumer Publishing Division of CBS Inc., by arrangement with
Atheneum Publishers

Copyright © 1978 by Oakley Hall

Map Copyright © 1978 by Anita Karl

ALL RIGHTS RESERVED

ISBN: 0-449-23966-7

Alternate Selection of the Book-of-the-Month Club

Printed in the United States of America

10 9 8 7 6 5 4 3 2 1

This one for my daughter

BRETT

My gratitude to Herman Gollob, whose idea this novel was, and whose enthusiasm and counsel sustained the long task of writing. My apologies to Theodore Roosevelt and the Marquis de Morès, of the historical Badlands.

THE AUTHOR

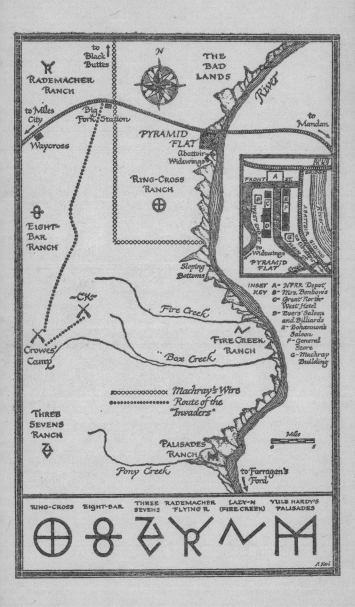

Prologue

Andrew Livingston's father had likened the various lives a man leads to railroads. "One must make some sort of running arrangement on every railroad," his father had said.

Andrew had made many such arrangements in his life, as a pianist, a banker, an artist, a rancher, and a politician. Ultimately his only continuing arrangements had been with politics, that profession of which its practitioners were at once so proud and so defensive. Like a good many of his colleagues in the Senate, he would not have traded his membership in the nation's most exclusive club for the even more exclusive occupancy of the large, white house visible down H street.

"If you are to stop but five minutes for refreshment at the art station, you must have those five minutes clear," his father had said. He could not often find more than five minutes to stop at the art station anymore, but he did make it a point to keep the minutes clear when he looked at the drawings he loved: the Raphael red chalk, the Hogarth in blue and red, the sweet little Veronese that was his wife's favorite, the Watteau sketch of the barefoot girl asleep on the couch, and the Blake color monotype of Nebuchadnezzar in his madness, on hands and knees with tormented face. In his study he would also consider two of his own paintings: a Bad Lands vista of bottomland sloping to the river half concealed behind cottonwoods, with grazing cattle; and a friendly pronghorn, Rufus by name, head attentively turned toward his limner.

In those few minutes he would also go out onto the little enclosed porch that served as his studio. On the easel stood his last painting, which he knew he would never finish, although still from time to time he would take up brush and palette and bend to it, perhaps only to tone down the yellow slant of sun he had inserted in a previous effort to lighten the somberness of the mood. Although he could not say why the depiction of a man's death should not be somber.

The bed in the painting had a scrolled brass foot that caught a little light from the window, which was draped in heavy folds of dark red. The figure filled the bed, a big man in a white shirt. In actuality that white fabric had been bandages, but he had chosen to show it as an open-throated, By-

11

ronic shirt. The man's arms lay at his sides. His head was thrown back on the pillow so that his features could not be seen. The throat was muscular. Beside the bed a woman was seated in the patient aspect of grief, all in black with thick black hair shaped like a cowl, and the pale triangle of her face driving down toward the torso of the dying man with a dynamic force that fascinated and repelled the artist. The colors were chunky blotches: the religious and unrelieved black of the woman's costume; the gray wall behind her; the whites of the bed and the man's shirt; the dark red of the draperies. Amid all this the scrollwork of the bed end appeared merry, almost frivolous; and, although this was not right, neither was it entirely wrong.

As the years passed and the porch reverberated to the sound of passing automobiles rather than the clipping of hoofs and the scrape of carriage wheels, that painted scene continued to challenge and entreat him. Behind it in his memory loomed yet another image, one he had never been able to bring himself even to sketch—the hanged boy like a limp question mark, with attendant figures in perfect formal arrangement. And behind that still other potent transparencies, like a parade of ghosts invoking the violence and the poetry, the bad acts and the good, the questions posed and wrongs pleaded, that, he knew now, he would not live to see answered or righted.

Book One

1883

1

Andrew sat straight-backed on the little mare, watching the sun spreading and sinking behind a cluster of round-topped buttes that glowed chalky white with the blaze behind them. Gold-bottomed clouds spread out from the horizon like a religious glory in a Renaissance painting. A thin spike of smoke rose into the golden space, the campfire of another Bad Lands hunting party, or a vein of lignite, ignited by lightning, burning underground.

The starkness of this country, which had at first appealed to his bitter mood, had, in three weeks' time, changed to a fairy tale landscape of fantastic turrets and cupolas stained with exotic colors, like these back-lit western buttes with their terra-cotta heads.

Below him, by a pool that gleamed like beaten copper, Joe Reuter squatted stacking twigs above a flickering of flame. The guide's father, old Sam, was hunkered down beside him, hands stretched out to the warmth. These two had been engaged for him by the correspondent in Mandan of the Manufacturers and Grain Bank of New York. They had met him in Pyramid Flat when he stepped down from the westbound. At first, he knew, they had thought no more of him than he had of them, but during three weeks of hunting certain accommodations had been established.

He watched the sun spread into a thin line across the horizon, to vanish like bright liquid sucked into the earth. He tethered his mare with the other animals and carried to the campfire his bedroll and rifle, his sketch pads and saddlebags, finally his saddle. The fire was blazing now and he unrolled his bedroll beside its heat.

Supper consisted of three curlews Joe Reuter had shot, dry meat on fragile bones that crumbled to be spat into the fire, and biscuits hard as rocks which the old man grumblingly pushed into the side of his mouth where a few remaining teeth evidently met. The water of the pool was like thin jelly, slimy even when boiled with coffee. They ate in silence, leaning against saddles while the animals stamped and whickered outside the circle of firelight. Frogs racketed around the pool, falling into a tense quiet as, far off, a lynx screamed. Darkness shrank the space around them.

The old man squatted close beside his son, seamed face in shadow beneath his hatbrim, and Andrew reached for his sketch pad to limn the grouping, the firelight and the dense shadow, the tense but reposeful postures. Among the pages of the sketchbook were the three elk grazing among the cotton-woods, one with head raised alertly; the wolf at dusk on the ridge three nights ago; a prairie dog haunched up, forearms crossed over his belly, for all the world like some plump and comical fellow lounging before a country store; the mountain sheep with that astonishing heft of horn parted like a bar-tender's toupee, and the yellow eye with its vertical dark stripe of pupil. The light of life fading visibly from that eye hung indelibly in his memory.

"You've set yourself to shoot one of every kind of game in the Bad Lands, have you, Mr. Livingston?" the old man said in his rasp of a voice.

"Shoot them and then draw them in that book there," Joe Reuter said.

"I would certainly like to shoot a buffalo," he said, and watched Joe shake his head with a negative cluck. There were few of the great beasts left in the Bad Lands, his guides claimed—maybe none; he liked to fancy himself on the trail of the last buffalo.

"Had one Englishman out here with a big rig tryin to make photygraphs of everything," the old man said. "If that wasn't one big damned clutter of a mess to pack around!"

"I understand there are a good many Europeans taking up range hereabouts."

"Thicker'n ticks on a elk! That big Scotchman's got himself a township! Fenced! The Ring-cross. And there's a Frenchie over in the slope country with a big spread. *And* English. *And* Easterners. After them big profits they've heered about. Haw! Me'n my sons been runnin cows in this country for a bunch of years, and if there's any profit besides tough beef for dinner I'd like to know it."

"I'd say about half the big outfits out here was foreign-owned or foreign-backed," Joe Reuter said. "I won't say the Scotchman is the biggest, but he is sure the most *ambitious*."

"Built up Pyramid Flat to a regular city," the old man went on. "Big brick building for offices—offices!—and a

16

slaughterhouse goin up looks like he could provision a army outten it. And a regular castle up on the bluff there. Ruinin the country!" he said, and expectorated copiously into the fire.

Leaning back against his saddle with his sketchbook in his lap, Andrew said, "But they must be finding it a good business proposition." The two looked at him, Joe sideways, the old man with the brim of his hat tipped down over his eyes as though against the starlight. "Raising cattle," he added.

"Mebbe if you run more'n thirty head," the old man said. "These big outfits do pretty good from the look of them, but they're runnin three-four-five thousand."

"Bad Lands catching a hold on you, are they, Mr. Livingston?" Joe drawled. "Well, they'll do that to a fellow."

There was a silence, sudden and total. Then distant wolves began their weird chorus, complex as part singing. At first that music had kept him awake, sweating and reaching for his rifle. Now nothing kept him awake. At first his guides had tried to haze the tenderfoot with what were no doubt traditional tales of the dangers of the Bad Lands: the wolves, rattlers, and grizzlers, the quick sands, the horse thieves who would run off your stock to leave you stranded and starving, Cree braves prowling off the reservation with bloody mischief on their minds.

He felt the hairs prickle at the back of his neck as he recognized a kind of tune in the wolf howls. Then the sound separated, came louder—a mouth organ. As the music swelled, he stared into the black bowl of night pierced with stars. The melody seemed so beautiful and so sad that tears burned in his eyes. Tears overwhelmed him easily these days.

With a pad of hoofs and a clink of harness a horseman appeared, tall against the sky. The music ceased. "Howdy, gents."

"Evening," Joe said, lounging back against his saddle, while the newcomer slid from his horse and, spurs jingling, approached the fire. He was a round-faced youngster with a fuzz of pale mustache.

"Evening," he said to the guides. "Evening," he said, nodding to Andrew, breath smoking in the cooling air. He squatted and spread his hands to the fire. "Comin on chilly," he said.

"That was a pleasant sound you were making."

With a grin the boy whipped his mouth organ from his

17

pocket and, with flourishes, began to play. Andrew recognized "Little Mohee." Finished, the musician knocked the spit from his instrument, beating it against the heel of his hand.

"Nighthawk, I expect," Joe said casually.

The boy nodded with exaggerated motion. "Playin a harp sure do keep them dogies quiet!" His smile, as he glanced from face to face, was sly but beguiling, with a raffish gap between his front teeth. When Andrew rose to warm his hands at the fire, he said, "Say, you got your chaps on backwards, mister!"

The guides laughed and Andrew grinned down at his corduroy riding trousers with their leather seat. The old man said, "Can't offer you any grub, young feller; we're cleaned out. Plenty of coffee, though."

"Anything that'll slide down. My stomach thinks my mouth's fell off."

The coffee was put on the boil again while the young cowboy played another selection, the old man keeping time beating a fork against the coffeepot. From time to time the boy would fondle a gold, heart-shaped locket, like a girl's, that hung around his neck, as though seeking musical inspiration there. Andrew was aware of happiness as a palpable thing; it seemed marvelous to him that life could be so simple that this young man with his mouth organ playing by firelight produced such pleasure.

The cowboy shuddered and pulled a face as he sipped coffee from the cup the old man handed him. "I ain't eat for so long I feel like about two pounds lighter'n a straw hat." He rubbed his locket between his fingers, glancing from face to face with a raised eyebrow. "Hunters, huh?"

"Bound for buffalo," Joe said.

"Seen tracks," the boy said, flipping a hand to indicate the direction from which he had come.

"Fresh ones?" Andrew asked, leaning forward.

"Believe so."

"Who'd you say you worked for?" Joe inquired.

"Worked for the Eight-bar awhile, but me'n that high-pockets foreman of Lamey's couldn't get on. Thought I'd look in on the roundup. Who's runnin the show, anybody know?"

"Johnny Goforth," Joe said. "That's the Scotchman's super."

The boy's grin reappeared like a sleight-of-hand trick. "Say, that big fellow is one trump card, ain't he?"

18

"Ruinin the country!" the old man said. "Fencin! Runnin wire everywheres!"

"Well, he don't want any scrub bulls gettin to his fancy cows," Joe Reuter said. "I don't blame him, but my how he makes some folks mad."

"I remember the old days drivin up," the old man rasped. "It was Bozeman Trail or Bridger. Bozeman was good grass and water all the way, and fight Red Cloud. Bridger was poor grass and bad water and Shoshones that wouldn't fight. So we come Bozeman. Now these damned foreigners come in here on the railroad like a picnic outin, bringin a bunch of fancy cows and wire till you can't see the end of it."

The boy played another song. Beating his palm with his mouth organ, he asked where Andrew was from.

"From New York State."

"What do you do there, mister?"

"He does pitchers," Joe Reuter said with his candid gaze of mock innocence. "Shoots himself one of every game we have got out here and draws pitchers of it. Mr. Livingston is an artiste."

"Make your living doing pitchers?" the boy said, gaping at him.

He said he was a banker. Art was his hobby.

"Young for a banker," the old man said, squatting with his sharp face thrust out like an ax blade.

"Married, are you, Mr. Livingston?" the boy inquired.

"A widower," he said. The wolves seemed to have moved farther away but their long wails were still audible like a tingling of the skin.

"Young for a widower," the old man said. "Who's that Alice you was yelling after the other night? That your wife?"

"No, my little girl," he said, his face feeling taut as a skull.

"Say, you gents hear the story about the granger and the punkin vine?" the young cowboy said after a time.

"Grangers!" the old man said. "Crowdin in! Ruinin the country!"

The cowboy told his story: "This here nester gets hold of a punkin seed and plants it, see? He's goin to have punkin pies for his wife and kids for Christmas, just like back home. Well, he nurses the little squib that comes up, and waters it, and it grows just like a punkin vine's sposed to, big and green, buds all over it, all proper. But no punkins. So his neighbor comes over and tells him why. Seems a cow punkin vine has to have a bull one along by, for a crop of punkins.

19

Punkin vines're that way. And that granger gets mad! 'Why, goldurnit!' he yells. 'I will be goldurned if I will pimp for a goldurn punkin vine!' "

The boy shouted with laughter, Andrew and the guides laughing as much at his delight as at his story. Then he began to play again, and Andrew brought out his flask and parceled out his precious supply of whiskey, a half inch in each of the four coffee cups.

Presently the boy rose, wiping his mouth on the back of his hand, thanked them for their hospitality, and said he would be on his way.

"Welcome to bunk down here," the old man said.

"Believe I'll head on over toward Hardy's, thank you kindly."

"Roundup's the other way," Joe said.

"That Johnny Goforth's stricter'n a schoolmaster," the boy said, fingering the gold locket. "Other folks I'd rather see," he added with a wink.

When he had departed they sat listening to the sound of the mouth organ fading into the vast dark. The throaty music, which had been merry by the campfire, now seemed infinitely sad. The frogs recommenced their converse.

"Folks he'd rather see'd be Hardy's daughter, I expect," Joe Reuter said. "Couldn't keep his fingers off that locket he had, I noticed."

"Pleasant young fellow," Andrew said, grunting as he pried off a boot.

"Known for it," Joe said.

"Matty," the old man said. "Matty *Gruby*—couldn't recollect his name while he was here."

Joe rose and disappeared, to return leading his horse, whose halter he made fast to his saddle horn. The other horses were also brought in close, as they were each night, a precaution against horse thieves.

Andrew slipped under his quilts and, drawing the tarp over, lay staring up at the stars. He listened to the guides preparing for the night, the restless movements of the stock, the frogs, the wolves' faint wailing parley. He felt himself falling asleep like gliding down a long slide, like slipping from a float into deep water. It had been many nights since he had wakened himself crying out the child's name, but this night he surged in familiar horror out of the deep pool of his sleep, shouting a warning. Awake, however, he discovered that he had not uttered her name aloud.

He was in the Bad Lands because of Rudolph Duarte. Duarte had been professor of geology at Harvard, a part-Portuguese, part-Italian New England blueblood, red-bearded, an elegant miniature in his person, but not in his spirit or experience. Duarte's lectures and his books of reminiscences were filled with zest for everything in nature, for science and the "adventure of observation," as well as for poetry, music, and painting. He referred to the "exaltation of the pursuit," and loved to regale his admirers, Andrew among them, with tales of the wildest sorts of experiences among the Indians, in explorations of the Rockies, hardships on "the old Yuma trail," and hunting in the Dakota Bad Lands.

Harvard had not held Professor Duarte long. He had become a geological consultant to the great capitalists and had made and lost fortunes making fortunes for others in the copper mines of Arizona, the coalfields of China, and the silver mountains of Mexico. But he had scoffed at money to audiences of New England young men, who, after the Civil War, had come to look upon the Far West as financial opportunity incarnate. "Money is of no importance!" he had said. "Adventure is all, and enthusiasm is the vehicle of adventure!"

It was Duarte's small, bright, excited face with its burning bush of beard that hung in Andrew's mind through that long afternoon after he had buried his wife and his daughter and, his son given into the care of his sister and the empty house unbearable to him, sat alone in a hotel room watching a summer rainstorm battering against the window. His wife's death had at the same time freed him to search for some meaning in a life out of which all enthusiasm had vanished, and burdened him with the absolute necessity for that search.

So he had come out to a tamed and settled Bad Lands eleven years after his mentor's expedition, as though by retracing Rudolph Duarte's steps he could repeat his adventures. He had his sketch pad and his journal to record observations and his rifle to shoot game, whose trophy, taken, would become proof of the adventure. Although he realized that his careful banker's premeditation had probably doomed his pursuit to defeat, still he must maintain that he was pursuing life, not fleeing death, as he trod the flamboyant footsteps of the only man he knew who lived life not merely in dread of its exigencies, but in the joy of its possibilities.

2

With the rising sun warming his left cheek, he held himself in the saddle as though too much motion might shatter his chilled body. Beside him Joe rode with his collar turned up around his face. Behind, the old man grumbled at the pack animals, two of the packs jagged with trophy antlers. Andrew breathed the burning cold air deep and exhaled a milky vapor as the sun climbed and shrank.

Joe halted them with a raised hand and pointed down to the chalky gray clay, a chain of cleft hoofprints there, some clearly cut. The track was easy to follow, crossing and recrossing a dry creek bottom, then climbing the side of a coulee where it faded to infrequent scuffings. For an hour they rode up the ravine, Joe Reuter in the lead with Andrew close behind, Winchester gripped in his left hand, butt resting on his thigh.

At first he thought the buffalo only an oddly shaped butte. But it was the almost legendary animal itself, shabby-looking, with thick curly hair covering head and shoulders, and short-haired, skinny hindquarters, as though two animals of different species had been joined together, like a cameleopard or a griffin. As soon as he had realized what it was, it was in motion, as though it had been awaiting recognition, scrambling at speed over a bank and across a patch of broken ground. He sat frozen and gaping on his mare, panting with emotion. The old bison had looked like something out of a nightmare, of ridiculous construction but awesome also.

"Little buffler fever, there, Mr. Livingston?" the old man called, cackling. Joe had also halted. A quarter of a mile away the animal turned to gaze back at them, something leonine and regal now in its posture. Then it galloped off. They followed its track for miles without catching another glimpse of it.

At noon Andrew shot a jackrabbit. They broiled it over a fire in the shade of a clump of scrub cedars, gnawing the bones in discouraged silence. He made a number of quick sketches from memory, and one of these caught some of the combination of quickness and clumsiness, strength and fragility, and the arrogance of the buffalo's backward gaze.

Licking his fingers, Joe said, "There's a yellow spot right behind the shoulder you aim for, for a heart shot. If we catch up with him."

"Not likely to catch up with him now," the old man said with satisfaction.

"Maybe we will," Joe said. "If Mr. Livingston's lucky."

"That big feller's stayed alive this long not letting anybody catch up with him."

"Got to die sometime," Joe said.

In the middle of the afternoon they glimpsed the old bull again, grazing in a grassy bottom half a mile away. Dismounted, Joe and Andrew slid down a rocky slope, sometimes on hands and knees. Joe blundered into a bed of cactus and cursed in a whisper as he wrenched spines out of his hand with his teeth. Andrew continued to scramble downward through the brush and boulders until he was within fifty yards of the grazing animal. He slowly rose, laid the rifle butt to his shoulder, smooth stock against his cheek, and took a deep breath to steady himself. The bead of the front sight danced, then steadied; he could make out the spot behind the animal's shaggy shoulder. The butt slammed back. Dust flew from the curly hide; he heard the smack of the bullet into flesh. Tail up the buffalo dashed over a low rise. He almost flung his rifle down in disappointment.

He glanced back to see Joe sucking on the heel of his hand, the old man riding toward them, leading the string of pack animals through the rough ground. "They are some hard to kill," Joe said.

Mounted, they loped off on the trail again. Now and again they caught glimpses of their quarry far ahead, and once Joe pointed out drops of blood dotting the spiky brown grass.

The red sun was deflating against a turreted horizon when they came upon the buffalo once more. There was a shout from the old man as the hairy hump rose beyond a sandy ridge. The bull appeared to be galloping on a parallel course. Joe was shouting instructions Andrew did not hear as he slapped the rifle up to fire, lever and fire. The ridge flattened, and the wounded bull charged straight at him. The mare squealed and fled. When he managed to wrench her around the buffalo was chasing Joe. He spurred after them, the mare floundering and panting in rough terrain. At fifty feet he fired but thought he missed. Now no amount of spurring would move the mare faster. The buffalo lumbered over a rise and vanished. Joe had halted, his horse panting and steaming.

"I just can't understand why we are runnin in such luck," Joe said mildly. Shadow rolled over them; the sun had gone down.

Andrew clucked and teased the tired mare over the rise. The old bull stood facing them, hoofs braced apart. Blood streamed from his nostrils. He lurched forward in a charge, but his forelegs crumpled. He toppled over on his side with a ground-shaking thump.

As Andrew dismounted his own legs almost collapsed beneath him. He knelt beside the dying animal to clutch a hand in the hair as coarse as wire. He could feel the warmth beneath. He was aware of his guides standing deferentially twenty feet from him, the old man with his hat in his hand, watching as he buried his face in the beast's shoulder, his hand tugging and wrenching at the fleece as the heat of life cooled.

That night at the campfire, after they had gorged themselves on slices of buffalo tongue braised over the fire, he sketched the dead animal, remembering when his father had once paid this same homage. The big red setter, Poody, with more and more gray in his muzzle, moving more and more slowly, at last could only lie on his worn quilt in the kitchen corner with his head on his paws and his feathery tail pat-patting when anyone came near. One morning he was gone, and the quilt gone.

Then in the library his father had held his two hands and looked into his face while he told him about death, and explained, to his tears, why death had to be, the rest that rounded off a life.

The setter was buried with pomp beneath the rosebushes where he had loved to sleep, with a wooden marker: POODY GOOD DOG. And on his next birthday his father had presented him with a watercolor of the big red dog, hale and erect, head and tail up proudly, although with the gray muzzle of his last years. What had happened to that painting in its gold frame that had hung over his bed for so many years?

That night he wrote to his sister:

"Dearest Cissie:

"I know you are terribly worried about me, but I have not written until I had something positive to report. Well, I said to you that my life was over, you told me I was wrong, and of course you were right. The words 'why me?' no longer troop through my brain in egocentric refrain, and Cissie, I have not had an asthma attack since I arrived in the Bad Lands!

"I have now killed one of every variety of game of the Great Plains, including a mountain sheep, a 'royal' elk (meaning an animal of seven points or more), and a buffalo, the only exception being a grizzly bear, which my guides claim have vanished from the Bad Lands, due to the many hunting parties. On our own hunt we have met or heard of at least a dozen other parties of either English or eastern hunters. This great hunting ground is becoming overcrowded!

"I am sure few of them have had the success we have had. This is mainly because most 'tenderfeet' insist on hunting from horseback, much the least laborious way. My guide and I have hunted every day on foot, following game into the deepest and most inaccessible ravines, or on horseback for many miles.

"So I have had good sport, which has been most salutary for me. There has been enough excitement and fatigue to prevent meditation until I am prepared to deal with painful rumination in a sensible and positive manner.

"I suppose it is a sign of returning health that I have fallen in love with the Bad Lands. Now I find quite beautiful aspects that earlier seemed grim and ugly. I love the evenings when the hard, gray outlines of the buttes soften and empurple (and encarnadine!) as the sunset flames and fades. And the dawns! I never miss one of these colorful displays. There is a light 'that never was on land or sea' I would love to ride alone for hours on end through rolling prairies or broken 'Bad Lands.' I have never feared loneliness.

"I think I will never again be content to spend my days figuring interest at three per centum.

"Please give Baby Lee a kiss from his 'Daddy,' and whisper in his little ear that I think of him often.

"*Your loving brother,*
"*Andy.*"

3

By first light the dead buffalo looked deflated, as though he were sinking into and merging with the earth. The old man broiled more slices of tongue while Andrew sketched the animal in detail, the wicked little horns half hidden in coarse fleece, the lumps of ticks on the skinny haunch, the surprisingly delicate hoofs. He filled many pages before he was satisfied, and it was late in the morning when, after exhausting labor, they had stripped the hide from the carcass.

In the afternoon the heat bounced in waves of haze off the bony ridges and the pale flanks of the buttes. A horseman congealed out of the haze, a cowboy who galloped straight toward them, to halt in a smoke of dust. He tipped up the brim of his hat from a sunburnt, dusty face in salute.

"You're a Back East fellow from the look of you, mister," he said to Andrew. "You know boxing?"

Puzzled, Andrew said he was familiar with boxing, why?

"The lord'll put on a show for us if we can find him boxing partners, you see."

"The lord?"

"Lord Machray," the cowboy said, with a sweeping gesture indicating breadth and height at the same time. "We got him a English fellow, a hunter, that said he could box, but the lord set him down like that!" He snapped his fingers. " 'N then we heard there was hunters over this way. You'll come box with the lord, now, won't you?"

"All right," Andrew said. He saw that the old man was scowling ferociously; Joe wore his habitual expression of mild surprise.

"Oh, that's fine!" the cowboy said. He jerked his head at the laden pack animals. "Got yourself some trophy, I see. Knock the lord down, maybe you can get his kilt offen him!" He guffawed.

Joe asked where the roundup was.

"We're over on this side of the divide—up by Black Buttes."

They headed north and in the late afternoon came into a broad basin, with buttes like huge, burnt stumps along the northern rim. The basin was crowded with grazing cattle, for the most part shorthorns bearing the Ring-cross brand. Among them were a few sleek, long-haired animals.

"Ruinin the country," Andrew heard the old man mutter.

"Looks like that buffer of yours did him some stud bidness, Mr. Livingston," Joe commented.

"Them's the lord's Highlanders," the cowboy said. "Look like they'd take a hard winter goin away, don't they?"

Andrew could see riders out among the clumps of cattle. Yelps and yodels rang in the dusty air. They approached a little settlement of tents and wagons, and passed a cavyyard of saddle stock, a thicket of curious heads slanting out to examine them. Beyond, branding was in process—squawling calves, stink of burnt hair and flesh, men shouting, convulsions of furious motion. Andrew could feel the excitement like a galvanic charge.

A giant of a man loped away from one of the fires to intercept them. He was barelegged in a red kilt and filthy khaki shirt, thick woolen stockings rolled down around dusty shanks. He had a clean-shaven, scarlet sweating face and a mop of yellow hair.

His hand swallowed Andrew's in a steaming grip. "Machray," he said. His eyes were green as emeralds. "Found a taker, did you, Ben?" To Andrew, who had identified himself, he said out of the side of his mouth, "These hard-working laddies are crazed for entertainment, and nothing entertains them so much as seeing members of the upper classes pounding away at each other. Done some boxing, have you, Mr. Livingston?"

"At college," he said. He did not think he would be able to stand up long against this outsize Scotsman.

"Well, we will go right to it while there is still light," Machray said, as he dismounted. "If you will forgive us for being a bit peremptory."

Men were running up, calling to others. A din of metal pounded on metal began. There were yells of delight. Machray's hot hand rested in friendly fashion on his shoulder as they moved forward together. Excitedly, the sweating men of the roping and branding crews fell behind them. From a cook tent came a delicious damp smell of boiling stew.

Nearby was a boxing ring, ropes strung to three fence posts and a stunted cedar. Padded brown gloves hung from a branch.

"Brought along a set of gloves to enliven matters out here," Machray explained. "Afraid I didn't realize I'd have to be the principal performer." He held up the rope for Andrew to duck under.

With the familiar excitement of adrenaline singing in his veins, Andrew stripped off his shirt and pulled on one of the gloves and then the other. They smelled of cocoa butter and sweat, cool and damp to his hands. He held them out to Joe Reuter, on the other side of the rope, who stared at them blankly before he began to tighten and knot the laces. Machray had also peeled his shirt from a chalky white torso like monumental marble; Andrew winced to see the shocking scarlet sunburst of a scar on his right shoulder.

Cowboys crowded two deep along the side of the ring closest to the cook tent, and newcomers arrayed themselves along the other sides as well. The din of crashing pan lids had ceased, and now the cook appeared at ringside, white cloth tied about his head like a gypsy's scarf, the two lids raised like cymbals.

Gloves on, Machray assumed an old-fashioned stance with his fists held low. He milled in a backward-leaning posture, striking out with rights and lefts, the cowboys cheering. Andrew also feinted some practice blows. The cheering increased in volume. He flexed his shoulder blades, tucked his chin in his right shoulder, and chuckled at the mysteries of life in the Bad Lands. Punching out jabs, he felt drunk with excitement.

The cook slammed his pan lids together, and Andrew and Machray stepped to the center of the ring to touch gloves. Again the side of the Scotsman's face convulsed in the vast wink. He towered a head above Andrew.

Jabbing at Machray's chin, he sidestepped away. Immediately he had to block a right so hard it drove his glove back into his face. Cheers echoed in his ears. He jabbed and retreated. Presently he found his range and exulted to see the yellow head knocked back. With his elbows he blocked another powerful swing to his belly. He jabbed and retreated. Stalking him, the Scotsman's glistening torso swung from side to side, the scar tissue angry red against the white flesh. His nose was reddening also. One of his fists caught Andrew in

28

the ribs just as the pan lids beat again for the end of the round.

In his corner, where Joe hailed him holding up a dripping sponge, he leaned against the fence post pressing an elbow to his aching ribs. The cheering continued raggedly, interspersed with laughter and shouts.

"You are doin just fine, Mr. Livingston!" Joe said enthusiastically, sponging his face. "He is getting a beak on him like a rose blossom!"

"Say, you are some fancy box-fighter, Mr. Livingston!" the old man said. It was the first approval he had ever heard from that quarter, and he grinned and closed his eyes against the sponge. It seemed only seconds before the metal din began again, and he and Machray advanced from their corners.

He continued to jab and retreat. He blocked an uppercut, knocked another aside, and lunged straight in to plant his right. Backpedaling, he congratulated himself to see Machray standing with his glove to his face like a child with a bumped nose. The cheers rose to a roar. When they engaged again, Machray's nose was dripping blood.

He blocked a mighty right that drove his defense back, blocked another and another as the Scotsman wheelbarrowed in pursuit. He lashed out with his right again, but this time took another blow to the ribs that made him gasp. His legs were quivering as the round ended.

He leaned panting on the corner post while Joe sponged his face and the old man chattered. Over his shoulder he glimpsed his opponent in identical posture, but with face raised as his second tended to his nose.

When the pans clanged again, it seemed important that he reach the center of the ring before Machray. Blood smeared on his cheek and cotton wadding visible in his nostrils, the other came rearing out of his corner with a flourish of gloves. Andrew jabbed, drove in a straight right, and pushed Machray on back, jabbing, ducking, blocking that right that drove for his ribs. He planted another right on Machray's nose. The cheering was continuous as the Scotsman backed away. Surely Machray's legs must be as tired as his own. When the round was over he knew that he had won it.

Next round Machray did not pursue him but stood with his feet braced apart, swinging his shoulders from side to side. nose immediately beginning to drip blood, a dogged dull expression on his face. Even his kilt seemed wilted. Andrew jabbed, crossed with his right, pushed in, jabbing, his right hand cocked—

Next thing he knew he was lying on his back gazing up into Machray's worried face. He laid a glove gently against his jaw and moved it from side to side. Joe Reuter's face joined Machray's at a great height above him. The Scotsman knelt to work a glove under his neck and lift his head. Machray's blood dripped onto his bare chest.

"All right, there, Livingston?" More faces crowded over him. "Believe you let your guard down a bit in view of your successes," Machray said.

He sat up. With Machray supporting him under one arm and Joe the other, he rose to his feet. Cheering came from very far away. He saw cowboys waving their hats. They knew him by name. There was a complicated business of removing the gloves. Joe brushed the dirt from his bare back and helped him into his shirt. Machray was gripping his nose between his thumb and forefinger.

"Will you take some whiskey with me, Livingston?"

He was still dizzy as Machray accompanied him through the thinning ranks of cowboys. The sun had gone down and there was a chill in the air. "Well done, there, Mr. Livingston!" a beard-stubbled, dirty-faced cowboy called; and another, "Scratched out some blood, anyhow!"

"You lasted an eternity longer than I out there, my dear fellow," said an overcultivated voice. This was a stout young Englishman in a checked shirt, with sidewhiskers which he stroked in an affected manner. "The fellow laid me out in the first round!"

Andrew was ushered into a tent with flaps rolled up all around, along with the Englishman, who continued to talk: "Yes, yes, there I was spreading some terror among the local fauna when I was summoned here to be soundly pummeled. Seems to be a local custom for all passersby to be mauled by the Green Knight here." He laughed shrilly, showing rabbity front teeth.

"Deserve to be mauled for false pretenses," Machray said. Shirtless still, he wandered around the tent in a disoriented way, head hunched as though used to low ceilings. "Fellows travel about the country pretending to be hunting animals. Actually they have their eyes peeled for business opportunity. But it is too late! All the opportunities have been snatched up."

A leather chest stood at the foot of a cot with coverlet

drawn tight as a drumhead. There was a field desk on crossed legs, and two camp chairs. Andrew plumped down into one of these while the Englishman took the other. Machray located glasses, and produced a brown bottle from a cubby of the desk. Holding a glass to his eye he measured golden whiskey, passed the glass to Andrew, poured a second for the Englishman, and a third for himself. With a grunt he seated himself on the cot. His jutting knees were red and sharp-boned.

Just then a man strode into the tent, clean-shaven, with close-cropped hair—Machray's second. He was holding a khaki shirt with a disapproving expression.

"Ah, Dickson—" Machray said.

"Put your shirt on, now, Captain; you'll take a chill," Dickson said. Clucking, he helped Machray into the shirt. He opened the chest, and took from it a folded canvas jacket, which he spread over Machray's shoulders. Then he squatted to peer at the cotton stuffing Machray's nose.

"Takes care of me," Machray said, when the man had departed. "To the absent ones!" he said, holding up his glass. The liquor burned down Andrew's throat to vein his belly with warmth.

"Ah, that's very good, sir!" The Englishman said, pulling on his whiskers.

Machray made rubbery sounds of enjoyment, punctuated by a popping sigh. He squinted at Andrew. "You may know, Livingston, that Edward the First of England was known as 'the hammer of the Scots.' Felt I must be facing Sassenach Edward out there this evening! You have given me a very tender proboscis!" Gingerly he touched his cotton-stuffed nose.

Andrew said he would trade noses if a badly used jaw and ribs could be included in the transaction.

Machray raised his glass to sip again. "Thank Providence it is nightfall, or those chaps would be out kidnapping more boxing partners. And how are you feeling, Sir Charles?"

"Pains are easing rapidly, sir!"

"You are a hunter, also, are you, Mr. Livingston? And how has the Bad Lands treated you?"

He said he had killed a buffalo yesterday.

"Really! Rare fellows these days." Machray addressed himself to Sir Charles. "Do you realize there were upwards of three hundred thousand of those grand beasts in these parts not three years ago? Wiped out for their skins, for their tongues, for the pleasure of the killing merely! Shot down out of train windows! Good meat left to rot!"

Andrew felt himself flushing as though from personal criticism. Machray set down his empty glass and braced a huge hand on either knee. His green eyes were hard, his lower lip thrust out. "You'll pardon me if I sound captious. Less than elevating experiences with hunters. Where do you hail from, Livingston?"

To his host's probing, he answered that he was a New Yorker, a city man, although his home was Long Island, a product of Harvard College, a banker, a Republican, and that his expedition to the Bad Lands was as much for the purpose of sketching as bringing home trophies.

"We'll see some of these sketches after we've supped, if we may," Machray said.

"Fearful scar you have there," Sir Charles said, who did not share Machray's interest in Andrew.

"Tel-el-Kebir," Machray said, wincing as he touched his shoulder. "The pasha's laddies would come loping toward you four or five together, all spears and flowing robes so you couldn't make out what was which, and just when you thought you had laid them out there'd be one more loping in. Close thing it was," he said. "Dickson blew the fellow's brains out in the very nick."

He rose to pour whiskey into their glasses again. They toasted the Bad Lands.

"I say, I can't understand the country's appellation," Sir Charles drawled. "Beautiful terrain, it seems to me. Like a sculpture garden."

"French termed it on their maps '*Mauvaises terres pour traverser*,'" Machray said. "The name stuck, though some fancy fellows have tried to rename it Pyramid Park. Vide our metropolis Pyramid Flat."

"I understand you are building an abattoir in Pyramid Flat, Lord Machray."

"No doubt you saw the chimney stack when you came through. Damned great pintle of an affair. Yes, if does seem a silly business to ship livestock to Chicago so they can ship us back dressed meat. To the great benefit of the railroad."

"The local ranchers will be selling their cattle to you rather than shipping to Chicago?"

"And at a more favorable price. You see before you a public benefactor, Mr. Livingston; and universally suspect as such fellows always are. But I will see the Bad Lands bloom like a rosegarden! Cattle! Sheep! Hogs! Plantations of crops! A city in the midst of it. Cheerful herdsmen, navvies, clerks, the lot, bustling about their business, while their liege lord keeps prosperity bounding!"

Machray laughed again but there was a set to his face that convinced Andrew he was not entirely joking. In a moment he continued:

"And now disputations with the railroad convince me I may have to purchase my own refrigerator cars. Perhaps I will have to acquire my own railroad! Ah, the cries of rage and pain from Glasglow, where my jew backers reside, counting their ill-gotten lucre. Think of their squealings rising from that foul city to become the very music of the spheres!" Again he burst into laughter, beating his leg with his hand, and Andrew and Sir Charles laughed with him.

A voice called from outside, "Lord Machray?"

"Come in, come in, Johnny."

A thin man entered, carrying a canvasbound book, which he handed to Lord Machray. He was introduced as Johnny Goforth, a name Andrew recognized from Joe Reuter's conversation with the musical cowboy. Like most of the natives of the Bad Lands he had met, the super had a young face under a kind of rough bark. There seemed to be no middle-aged of the breed, only young men or old ones like Sam Reuter. A hand like a bundle of taut wire shook his hand, and pale eyes he thought would not forget his face looked into his. Machray was paging through the book.

"Tally book," he said to Andrew. "Shows you how many less head you have than you thought you had."

Goforth chuckled politely.

"Theft is a problem, then?" Andrew said. Sir Charles was twiddling his thumbs over his thick middle.

"Yes, sir," Goforth said.

"Large ranchers out here became very suspicious of the smaller ones mavericking," Machray said. "That is the process of applying your own brand to another man's unbranded calf. Or simply leading the animal home. Grangers also tend to shoot range stock as though it were game, a practice that causes the ranchers irritation. O' course, the buying of land and fencing of it turns them absolutely livid."

"Every cow should have her calf, you see, sir," Goforth said to Andrew. "Instead you will find some small spreads hereabouts where a cow has two or three calves, while we have come up short."

"But aren't the winters fearful?" Sir Charles asked.

"Creatures seem to thrive on them," Machray said. "Although the wolves will take a few." He closed the tally book with a slap and returned it to Goforth. "Well, these chaps out here will praise free range, free grass, to the skies, but I say it brings out the worst in men. Cupidity, mendacity, resentment of newcomers, suspicion of your neighbors. So I have fenced my own land and retain my serene temperament."

"If I remember my history," Sir Charles said, when the super had departed, "it consisted of those wild men, your ancestors, screaming down out of their mountains to frighten half to death those peaceable farmers, mine, and run off their kine."

"It wasn't your kine they were after but your women," Machray said. "And so we are all brothers beneath the skin." The familiar iron clamor came again, "Ah, the chef calls!" Machray said, rising.

"We are to eat with the rank and file, are we?" Sir Charles said.

"Believe it useful to break bread with those you expect hard work from on the morrow," Machray said. "Lesson well learned in Her Majesty's expeditionary forces." He winked at Andrew. "Are you in good appetitate, Livingston? I believe the menu calls for a local delicacy known as slumgullion."

Waiting to be served in the cook tent, Andrew was introduced to a number of men called "reps," representatives of other big outfits on hand to keep an eye out for their brands. All ate squatting or standing around the campfire, some seated on wagon tongues or pieces of equipment, spooning meat, carrots, and potatoes into their mouths and soaking up gravy with hard-crusted chunks of bread. The cook passed among them with a tall, blackened pot of coffee. Andrew asked Goforth how many ranches were represented at the roundup.

"Eight or nine," the super said, counting on his fingers. "There's the Three Sevens, the Lazy-K, the Eight-bar—" He continued with his list, which meant nothing to Andrew.

He asked how many head Lord Machray possessed.

"We're hoping to find that out up here," Goforth said. "About eight thousand, in round numbers."

"And he has the largest holdings in the Bad Lands?"

"There's a few others with near to that many."

"How many head would a prospective rancher need to purchase to have a paying proposition?"

Goforth's cool eyes regarded him for a moment. "Why, no more than a few hundred head, I'd say. But that is beside the point out here. There is a difference that is more than numbers between a man that runs a thousand head and one that runs a hundred."

"What is that?" Andrew asked.

Goforth's teeth showed beneath his mustache in a thin grin. "The bigger fellow thinks the smaller one is a thief, and the smaller one thinks the bigger is a bully."

Around them spoons scraped in empty bowls; there was a dense low mutter of talk.

"Give us some poetry, lord!" a voice called out. Others took it up, and Machray rose, stuffing the last of his bread into his mouth and wiping his lips on his sleeve.

"I'll give you a poem that will cause you to mend your carefree ways, my lads. This one has got some Latin in it for your especial edification, but I must warn you I have forgot some of the verses and don't always have the rest in proper order. 'Lament for the Makaris' she is called."

He struck a pose, one hand on a kilted hip, the other extended. Now his accent was thick:

"I that in heill wes and glaidnes
    Am trublit now with gret seiknes,
    And feblit with infirmitie;
        Timor Mortis conturbat me."

"Any man here understand the old Scots?" Machray called, leaning down to take up his cup.

"Nary a word!" a voice called back. "But she do sound grand!"

"Nor the Latin either?"

"Fear of death perturbs me," Sir Charles said. Machray struck his pose again.

"Our pleasance here is all vain-glory,
    This false world is but transitory,
    The Flesh is brukle, the Fiend is slee.
        Timor Mortis conturbat me!"

"Unto the dead go all Estatés
    Princes, Prelates, and Potestatés,
    Both rich and poor in all degree.
        Timor Mortis conturbat me!"

The heavy voice beat in Andrew's skull as again Machray paused. "Enough? This one may poison your spirits a bit, lads!" Someone called back, "Enough!" but others raised the cry of "More! More!"

Andrew sat with his fists clenched and aching as Machray said, "More, then." He stood a massive figure, looming against the fire, and the men clustered about him listening.

> "He has done piteously devour
> The noble Chaucer, of Makaris Flower!
> The Monk of Bury, and Gower, all three!
> *Timor Mortis conturbat me!*"

> "Good Master Walter Kennedy,
> In point of death lies verily!
> Great ruth it were, that so should be!
> *Timor Mortis conturbat me!*"

> "Sen he has all my brethren ta'en
> He will not let my life alone!
> Of force, I must his next prey be!
> *Timor Mortis conturbat me!*"

Andrew was grateful for the darkness as, through the damp that burned like acid in his eyes, he watched the giant figure that, by some Highland clairvoyance, had known exactly the words to strike to the heart of his guest's soul's sickness, as he had pierced his boxing guard with a right hand like a maul. Surely it was too much coincidence that he, Andrew Livington, should flee the sly Fiend halfway across the continent only to find himself royally summoned to a boxing match, knocked senseless, and then overpowered a second time by this articulation: *Timor Mortis conturbat me!*

The guttural voice continued inexorably:

> "He spares no Lord for his puissance;
> No Clerk for his intelligence!
> His awful stroke may no man flee!
> *Timor Mortis conturbat me!*

> "He takes the knightes in the Field,
> Enarmed under helm and shield!
> Victor he is in all melee!
> *Timor Mortis conturbat me!*

> "Sen for the death remeid is none,
> Best is that we for death dispone,
> After our death, that live may wel
> *Timor Mortis conturbat me!*

The **voice** ceased. There was silence for a moment, then a racket of spoons beaten on bowls, of hard hands clapped together, cries of, "More! More!"

> "He takes the Champion in the stour!
> The Captain closed in the Tower,
> The Lady, in bower—

"Ah, I can't remember any more of it, friends!"

The clamor rose again. "The butt and ben one, Lord Machray!" someone called.

Machray paced, waving a hand above his head for silence. "There are some here who will not know what this one is about, then. It seems that not so long ago in the great city of Edinburgh, there was a traffic in cadavers."

"There goes *another* one!" a voice cried out. "Look out, it's gettin away!" Amid laughter a second voice called, "Say, what's a traffic in cadavers, anyhow, lord?"

"Called bodysnatching," Machray said. "They must be dissecting bodies at the Medical College for the benefit of the young sawbones, but the procuring of the corpses was illegal in that benighted time. So the head of the College paid grave robbers to bring him new-buried bodies. Burke and Hare were these men, and here is the doggerel:

> "Up the close and down the stair,
> Butt and ben with Burke and Hare.
> Burke's the butcher, Hare's the thief,
> Knox the man that buys the beef!"

He had then to explain the meaning of "close," "butt," and "ben," and repeat the verse by universal demand. Afterwards he announced in a solemn voice. "Hanged for their crimes, you know—Burke and Hare. Taking beef that wasn't theirs and selling it at a profit." He clapped his hands together and said that three *ante meridiem* by the clock would be upon them before they knew it.

Still there were cries for just one more poem, until he bellowed, "But when's a mon to take his beauty sleepit!"

"In winter like the rest of us!" someone shouted back, to laughter.

Andrew rolled his bedding out beside that of the Reuters, father and son, and lay awake gazing up at the designs of the cold stars, which a poem had likened to the brain of heaven. He listened to the soft sounds of moving cattle and, far off, a night herdsman singing. He was remembering his father, that almost complete man, his foot bruised in a riding accident in Central Park, the skin hardly broken—cheerful and bright in the terrors of lockjaw. Hour by hour while his muscles strained rigid, his mind had remained lucid. He, who had once lectured his son on death, had faced his own end bravely and even gaily, yielding slowly to the Fiend, surrendering only under the extremes of torture. When he had died, screaming in convulsions, he had no longer resembled a human being, much less a man of courage, wisdom, and great personal style.

If Andrew had lost his religion watching his father die, he had almost lost his reason when he had been called out to the green lawn beside the pool—whose water was nowhere deep enough that he could not stand with his head above the surface—to view the two bodies in their white dresses. They had been pulled from the pond by the hired man, the one so small, the other, it seemed then, not much larger, lying gray-faced and still, in their wilted fabrics.

He wakened to the clamor of metal on metal, so soon it was as though he had not slept at all, in pit darkness. He spent the morning sketching scenes of action, cowboys riding, turning a herd, roping, branding; many sketches of his host's furious activities. At the midday meal Machray joined him briefly, wolfing down bread and jam. Andrew asked how he had come to ranching in the Bad Lands.

"Usual manner," Machray said. "Hunting with a friend of mine from Cambridge—James Freling—has an enormous ranch out in western Montana, size of Belgium, I believe, lives like a feudal lord. Liked the country, decided to settle in, went home to drum up some capital, etcetera, etcetera. Sad and repetitious story!"

Andrew admitted that he had also been looking around him in that way, and Machray whooped with laughter, slapping a hand on a dusty bare knee.

"Madness!" he cried. "Debts! Contention! Fingers to the

bone! The absolute, utter contrariness of cattle and everything to do with them. Come and see me in town when this affair is over, and we'll discuss the matter over a bottle of claret. Do my best to dissuade you from a suicidal course."

Machray stuffed the last of his bread and jam into his mouth and loped back to the branding fire. As Andrew and the Reuters took leave of the round-up, he announced casually to them, too, that he was thinking of getting into the cattle business.

Neither of his guides seemed surprised, although Joe Reuter may have raised an eyebrow a quarter of an inch.

"Would you be lookin for somebody to run a outfit for you, then?" the old man asked.

"I wouldn't be here all the time, of course. Yes, I'd have to have a manager."

"Better talk to Chally," Joe said.

"Who's Chally?"

"That's my other boy," the old man said. "Oh, he knows cows, all right. He can tell you what you'd be gettin into, gettin into the cattle bidness."

4

Challis Reuter was a taller, leaner edition of his brother, with a high-shouldered, bent-forward, hurrying walk, a tense handshake, and, Andrew suspected, a violent temper under strict control. They sat in the kitchen of a neat, white-washed cabin with a sod roof and beaten earth floor, beneath the tinted photograph of a grim-faced woman with black hair gathered into a dozen tight little buns. A florid clock on the mantelpiece ticked portentously. Challis drummed fingers on the tabletop and shot glances at Andrew out of the corners of his eyes.

"Well, you don't buy land out here," he said. "You just find some range that's not took up already, and get on a piece of it claimin your quarter section. Where you want your headquarters camp. You want your hundred-sixty on as much water as you can get to, and you figure about twenty-five acres a head on your range. How many head was you thinkin of runnin, Mr. Livingston?"

They discussed costs, settling on an initial herd of five hundred, to be doubled next year if the operation proved successful. Challis had a small herd on his own, which would be included.

"Now, Mr. Livingston, you had better understand this is hard country out here. There is old-timers that think they own the range. But they don't own it. Some of it is railroad land that ain't even been surveyed yet, and Machray has got his great lot, but mostly it is government land. One person has as much right clamin range as another. But we will probably have to put up with some roustin. It'd be a while before they'd get *used* to us. We'd be ridin drag at first."

"What does that mean?" he asked.

"Eatin dust," the old man said.

"What does rousting mean?"

Joe Reuter leaned in the doorway, rolling a cigarette. "It means they plain don't want anybody else takin up range out here, and might turn mean," he said.

"How mean?" Andrew asked. None of them spoke. Scowling ferociously, Challis scratched at his cheek. "But you wouldn't be afraid to go into this?" Andrew asked him.

Challis' expression turned scornful. "They wouldn't scare me!"

"All right then, they won't scare me, either. I'd think Lord Machray might be friendly."

The three Reuters assumed identical skeptical expressions. "Hah!" the old man said. "Maybe," Challis said. But he knew a place south of Machray where they might start looking, he said.

Leaving the old man and Joe behind, he and Challis rode northeast through the buttes toward the river. Their destination was an old stockade shack near the mouth of Fire Creek. The shack had given shelter to hunters, served as a line camp for cowboys wintering, and a family of grangers had perched there briefly before abandoning the Bad Lands in defeat. The log structure was slightly tilted and appeared sunken from the weight of winter snows.

They forced the door open against an accumulation of baked mud. There was one large room with filthy walls, which, Challis said, could be papered over with newspapers for insulation, and whitewashed. There was one broken chair in a corner. The floor was packed earth, the roof needed attention, but the shack would do very well for a while.

Andrew strode through the thick grass down toward the

creek, swinging around from time to time to gaze back at the shack, where Challis squatted in the shade, smoking, and the two horses grazed. He felt a premature pride of ownership, and already many of the arrangements of the half-completed house on the hill at Prester Head had become incorporated in the house he planned to build on Fire Creek, although in much reduced scale. The trophies of his hunting trip would hang on walls in the Bad Lands, where they belonged.

He wandered farther, toward the river. A fish leaped in a pool where the creek had formed a lagoon, and he startled a doe, which high-tailed off among the cottonwoods. Challis grinned at him as he returned, obviously pleased at his pleasure. Behind the shack was a kitchen garden, half dead and run to weeds, but promising. Beyond this was a horse corral, the poles of one side tumbled into a jack-straw stack. A cowshed adjoined, with a stove-in roof covered with morning glories.

The view from the cabin door delighted him. Sloping, irregular balconies covered with thick grass and sagebrush fell away to the lagoon, with a show of moving water where the creek emptied into the river. Not many creeks still ran at this time of year, Challis advised him.

To the north was an amphitheater bounded by buttes, and, beyond, the river swung out in a wide arc, mud banks gleaming. He planned a painting of this scene, perhaps by that Bad Lands dawn light that had so entranced him, or in the blaze of noon with a doe turning to peer back at him from the harsh shadows of the trees. Whenever he counted over the paintings he had ahead of him from the store of his sketchbooks, he felt excitement prickle.

He trudged to the river and back again, spotting the matted grass where a buck had made his bed in a tangle of brush. To be able to shoot the week's supply of meat from his doorway! He would retire here frequently from the life he must eventually try to rebuild for himself in the East. Or must he?

"Suit?" Challis inquired, squinting at him when he returned.

"Suits."

"What I think we ought to do is set on range to the next river crossing north—right up to Machray's wire. And south to Grassy Creek. That's about as far as we can go without treadin on Hardy's toes. He's the next outfit south. And west to the head of Fire Creek and Grassy. Some of that's range I been usin, but Hardy and Machray'd be our main neighbors."

"How many head would that graze?"

"A thousand easy. And we ought to be all right up against the wire like that. The Scotchman fenced himself in when he fenced everybody else out."

"Do we have to fence?"

"Better not if we don't want real trouble! They have about got tired of cuttin Machray's wire and him patchin it back, but they surely wouldn't take kindly to any more."

He asked what kind of trouble might be expected.

Challis pushed his hat back on his pale forehead, scowling. "Mr. Livingston, I just don't know. Might be no worse'n just nobody speakin to you in town. We will just have to sit tight and see. First thing, though, I will go into Mandan and sort out this quarter section with the Land Office. I'll bring the claim papers back. Now: Will you be wanting to put your stock in now, or in the spring?"

"Is it too late in the year?"

"I'd buy down in Iowa and drive up very slow and easy so they don't get gaunted out. Then they ought to take a Bad Lands winter all right. Joe'll come along with me, and we'll need a cook and a couple—three hands. We ought to buy saddle stock down there, too. Well, Mr. Livingston, you sure you want to go ahead with this?"

"I'm sure."

Challis' face reddened. "I'll be needin money before I go into Mandan."

"How much all together?"

This required a great deal of calculation with paper and pencil, while Andrew crossed to the corral, where the horses were nibbling at the morning glory vines, and returned with a check from his kit. "I guess I could bring you back some out of six thousand dollars," Challis said.

He wrote the check to Challis Reuter in that amount, and, in the lower left-hand corner, the name of the correspondent bank in Mandan of the New York Manufacturers and Grain Bank.

Holding the check, Challis said, "Well, I guess we are in business, Mr. Livingston."

"Andy," he said, and they shook hands. Together they set out for Pyramid Flat, Chally to take the train to Mandan to file on the quarter section on which the shack stood, and Andrew to purchase supplies, tools, and utensils with which to set up housekeeping.

42

5

*Two days after he had returned from town he was sitting out-*side his shack in the morning sun, on the chair he had managed to repair with cord and wire, working over one of his roundup sketches, when he heard the jingle of harness. Two horsemen sat regarding him from fifty feet away.

"Who are you?" one of them demanded.

He said his name was Livingston. The two rode closer, the one who had spoken a darkly handsome man with a black mustache and intense black eyes, the other an ugly little bull-dog with an undershot, beard-stubbled jaw.

"Camping here?" the first one said.

As they approached their shadows fell over him. He said he was claiming land here. "Chally Reuter and I."

"Chally Reuter!" the smaller man said. "Huh!"

"Homesteading?" the other said.

The fact that these two frightened him angered him. Rising, he folded his arms and nodded.

"Planning on running some stock, then?"

He nodded again.

"Huh!" the smaller man said again. He dismounted with a clinking of spurs, and dropped his reins to the ground. The dark man continued to sit his saddle, staring at Andrew with a quality of total absorption.

"You are not welcome here," he said.

His partner had moved close, to peer into Andrew's face. Then he sidled on past to stand, hands on hips, looking down at the sketchbook open on the seat of the chair. He wore a holstered revolver at his waist.

Andrew tried to speak clamly. "I do not accept that. This is public land."

The dark man's nostrils flared. "It happens I've been think-ing of claiming this place."

"Challis Reuter is in Mandan claiming it."

"I had it in mind first."

He shrugged in irritation, more at the pressure he felt from the man's stillness than at his insistence on claims. "It is a le-gal matter, then," he said.

"No, it is a matter between you and me."

"Say, this is the artist-feller that was up on roundup," the little man said. "He is some fancy box-fighter, I heard." He confronted Andrew again, his raised fists rotating rapidly. "Show us some fancy box-fighting, will you?"

He could feel his face burning. He cursed the fact that he had left his rifle inside the shack. The dark man continued to stare at him.

"You *hear* me?" the smaller man said. He plucked his revolver from its holster. "Tell you what you do, you just do some fancy posin and struttin for us. That'll be just fine."

A cool voice in his head told him to do whatever was demanded. These men, whoever they were, were entirely capable of doing him harm, but not, he thought, without provocation. It was provocation they were seeking. He ignored the little man and his revolver.

"What do you want of me?" he asked the other.

"You guess," the dark man said quietly.

He was knocked off balance by a blow on his shoulder. The little man held the revolver pointed downward. His lower jaw was jutted, brown teeth exposed. "I said you will do some struttin for us! Now you do it or I'll blow a foot off!"

His head felt swollen tight, as, fists raised, he shuffled, feinted with rights and lefts, swung away, swung back, contrived to stumble, dropped his shoulder and brought his fist up from his side to slam it against the tip of that undershot jaw. With a stifled yell the little man toppled over flat on his back. He leaped for the revolver.

"Hold up!"

Panting, he straightened, and turned. The dark man was aiming a revolver at him.

"Get up on that horse." He motioned with the firearm. When Andrew did not move he cocked it with a loud click.

Andrew mounted the horse. The little man was sitting up now, cursing and working his jaw from side to side. Picking up his hat and jamming it back on his head, he rose, grunting and staggering. "Tie his hands," the other said.

"Jesaminit," the little man said. "Knocked my teeth all out of whack," he grumbled. He wandered aimlessly for some moments, before arriving beside Andrew. "Just get your hands back of you before I break your arm," he said.

Andrew's hands were bound behind him. He was jerked roughly as each new loop of rope was pulled tight. "Sneaky son of a bitch!" the little man grunted.

The dark man rode ahead, leading the horse Andrew straddled, while the little man tramped behind, holding the end of the rope that bound Andrew's hands. He gripped the saddle with his thighs to try to keep his balance as the sun glared into his eyes and waves of faintness swept over him. He couldn't believe this was happening to him. *Probably have to put up with some rousting at first*, Chally had said. He couldn't believe they meant anything more than that. The dark leader was heading for the cottonwoods along the creek. He had taken the roll of lariat from his saddle and wore it over his shoulder.

He halted in the shadow of the trees, and tossed the loop of the rope over a branch. The rope hung down, still retaining the curves of the coil. The dark man turned, having caught the loop, and Andrew involuntarily hunched his shoulders as it fell over his head. It lay loosely there with a kind of alive pressure. The dark man sat, half-turned, staring into his face.

"I guess that will be enough," a new voice said.

This was a man seated on a big gray horse in the underbrush across the creek, a rifle laid over his forearm. He wore a greasy buckskin jacket and a battered hat, beneath which was a face so deeply wrinkled it appeared to have been clawed by an animal. He motioned with the rifle barrel.

"Get the rope off that feller, Jake."

"This is none of your put-in," the dark man said.

"Get it off! Bob, you free up his hands!"

Cursing under his breath, the little man began to jerk at the rope that bound Andrew's hands.

"If any man'd ride by here and watch you two stringin a fellow up and think it wasn't his put-in, I'd say the human race had pure gone bad," the newcomer said. His hands free, Andrew clutched the saddle horn.

"Expect you are only bluffin him, but just the same I hold it is my put-in. You just hop down, now, young fellow, and let Bob get up there. Then these two'll be on their way."

When Andrew swung to the ground his knees gave way and he almost fell. The little man mounted, both of them facing the third man, behind whom empty pack saddles and the backs of horses were visible.

"You have interfered where it was none of your business, Bill," the dark man said, without apparent heat.

"Haven't I just been tellin you this kind of dirty business is every man's business! I remember a time if a fellow was

45

caught by redskin devils every man knew it was his put-in to get him out. Let me tell you! These two introduced themself to you, mister?" he said to Andrew.

He shook his head.

"Good-lookin one's Jake Boutelle, and the little fyce one Bob Cletus. So you'll know them if you see them again."

"You will," Boutelle said, and the obsidian eyes flashed at him briefly.

"I will be watching for you next time," he said.

"It won't do any good," Boutelle said.

"Oh, my, you had better stop this dirty business, Jake," the newcomer said. His tone, like his expression, was only half jocular. "Or I may stop talkin to you in town. And dogs'll start barkin at you when you go by them. And babies go to cryin. I am the voice of sweet reason *tellin* you, Jake. And Bob Cletus, ain't you just pure *ashamed* of yourself?"

"You have got the drop, Bill," the little man said. "So I guess you can say what you want."

Boutelle swung his horse away and, with Cletus following, trotted north through the bottom. The smaller man's back was caked with dust from his fall.

The newcomer rode splashing across Fire Creek, trailing his string of unladen pack animals.

"I am very grateful to you," Andrew said.

"Expect you are at that," the other said, grinning. He was almost comically ugly. "Bill Driggs," he said, reaching down a big, gnarled hand.

"Andrew Livingston. If you'll come up to the shack I'll give you some whiskey."

"Don't think that'd be out of my way," Driggs said. He dismounted, and they walked together up to the shack, Driggs leading the seven animals. He was as tall as Machray, with an easy long lope of a walk. He was a hunter, he said, just headed out to shoot game for the railroad dining cars. Andrew told him what had happened.

"Trying to scare you off the range. Don't believe they'd done more than run a bluff, unless you started somethin."

"I'd knocked the smaller one down."

Driggs contemplated that information silently. Finally he said, "Bob Cletus is just not a feller that's easy to like. But Jake Boutelle—" He shook his head. "These old bufflers. They are fell on hard times. Used to makin buckets of money without laboring dawn to dark and year in and out to do it,

46

and run themselves out of business. What do they do now?" He shook his head again. "Dirty business," he said.

Striding along beside him, Andrew felt strangely light on his feet. His head felt light. He had never been so frightened, nor so relieved. He said he thought he must make a complaint to the sheriff.

Driggs seemed puzzled at the idea. "What for? You'd have to go a hundred miles to Mandan to do it, and you don't think old Cece'd come out here for some triflin affair like this, do you?"

"Who were those men acting for?"

"I have heard the Stockraisers Association's pretty exercised about range overcrowdin. Might be it. You and Chally Reuter's takin up range here, are you?"

"That is our intention."

Driggs grimaced, shrugged, and nodded, all at once.

At the shack Andrew measured out two large portions of whiskey, and he and Driggs squatted against the wall outside. The liquor calmed his fluttery stomach.

"Might come along with me and meet Yule Hardy," Driggs said, holding up his glass and squinting judiciously at the level of the liquor. "He is south of here a bit. If he'd take up your side there'd be no more trouble with Association fellers. I usually stop there for supper anyhow. Pleasant folks. How're you feelin?"

"Shaky."

"Well, you was puttin on a pretty good show of it, there. Rope necktie and all."

"Thanks. I wasn't feeling much confidence, I'm afraid. And now I must be on the lookout for Boutelle."

"Well, I see you are not thinkin of runnin home east," Driggs said and laughed. Then he said, "We'll go see Hardy, and fix it so's Boutelle won't bother anymore. But I would tread light with him. He is a hard customer. If he'll let be, you let be."

"I'd like nothing better," Andrew said, and they both laughed and drank whiskey.

6

His first glimpse of Yule Hardy's Palisades Ranch was from the bluffs above the river, an L of low buildings, squared-off logs separated by pale horizontals of chinking. Baked-clay roofs sprouted dried weeds. The ranch house was shaded by cottonwoods bunched on a promontory that extended out into the sluggish gray of the river. Beyond were horse corrals and barns.

A trail threaded down the eroded pyramidals of the bluff. In the grassy bottom a buckboard with a canvas top awaited their approach, the occupant Hardy himself, a small, stout man in his late forties, with steel-rimmed spectacles and a fringe of graying chin whiskers. He greeted Driggs with a surprisingly sweet smile which vanished as he nodded to Andrew.

Andrew dismounted to shake the rancher's hand, while Driggs, leaning on his saddlehorn, explained his interest in the Bad Lands, and told of the encounter with Boutelle and Cletus. Hardy listened to this expressionlessly. He invited Andrew to ride with him, whipping up his gelding in the direction of the ranch house, while Driggs, leading Andrew's horse along with the pack train, headed for the corrals.

On the veranda several rawhide chairs were ranged with a prospect of the river, and Hardy led the way to these in a scuttling walk, as though crippled with rheumatism or old wounds. He settled into a chair with a groan, and directed Andrew to the one next to him.

"So you are determined to make a life in the Bad Lands, Mr. Livingston."

"At least for part of each year. Bill Driggs tells me you are the best man to advise me on my prospects in the cattle business."

"It is a hard business, Mr. Livingston," Hardy said. He had a trace of British accent. "I have pursued it for many years, here and in Virginia before coming here, and I can tell you that much." He lipped his cigar and gazed out at the river.

"I am a businessman, sir," Andrew said. "Not a dilettante." He did not like Hardy.

48

"That may be so. Nevertheless, if I am called upon to advise a stranger in the matter of raising cattle, I can only say that it is a hard business. It has been overpublicized as an extremely profitable one."

Andrew was distracted by a vision in the open doorway of the house, a slim girl in blue so like his wife in the bloom of her life that for a moment he could hardly catch his breath.

He leaned back in his creaking chair. "I would like to learn more of the two men who were evidently sent to harass me. Bill Driggs suggests that the local cattlemen's association might have been responsible."

"If that were the case, I would know of it!" Hardy snapped.

The girl he had glimpsed through the doorway appeared on the veranda. She carried one hand in the other, as though bearing some precious object. Color was high in her cheeks.

"F-father, would you and the gentleman care for tea?"

"Ah—my Mary," Hardy said, swinging around. "Of course we would! This is Mr. Livingston. My daughter."

"How do you do, Miss Hardy," said Andrew, who had risen.

The girl, with a slight ducking of her head, gave the impression of curtseying. Dimples streaked her cheeks when she smiled, and her short upper lip curled delightfully. She did not look at all like Elizabeth; it was only that she was young, and slim. She withdrew, still holding one hand in the other.

"You have a very pretty daughter, Mr. Hardy."

"No doubt you noticed that she is crippled."

He had not noticed.

"Her right hand," Hardy said. He made a brusque gesture with his cigar. "I approve Creation in most things, but not in all."

Standing beside his chair, Andrew found his discomfort strangely physical. Hardy stared out at the dull sweep of river with his mouth set like a scar.

"I cannot encourage you in your interest," he continued, after a moment. "It is unfortunate that you did not speak to someone more knowledgeable before you took whatever steps you have taken with Challis Reuter. This range is public land. In effect, of course, it is free for all, and no way has been found to discourage newcomers from crowding in—although one of our winters is usually sufficient to finish a granger trying to prove his quarter section. We can only refuse cooperation, without which range cattle husbandry becomes impossible. No doubt those men you encountered were over-aggressive toward what they consider an interloper. But this is a hard place, and cattle raising a hard business. As I have already said."

Miss Hardy returned with a lacquer tray laden with tea things, and he observed that she held the tray with her left hand, steadying it against her right wrist. Her right hand was pale and perfect, with long, graceful fingers, her left work-reddened and muscular. When she had put down the tray she grasped the crippled hand to her again, flushing beneath his gaze.

An older woman joined them. Mrs. Hardy was as plump as her husband and also equipped with steel-rimmed eyeglasses. Seated stiff-backed, she poured the tea while the girl vanished inside once more. Presently the notes of a piano sounded, quiet as a brook over stones; Schubert. Hardy glared at the river while Mrs. Hardy wore a set smile wreathed in double chins.

"The child plays very well, does she not, Mr. Livingston?"

"I wonder if I might be permitted to join her at the piano, Mrs. Hardy."

"Do you play, Mr. Livingston?"

He said he did, and, without waiting for permission, stepped inside. In a dim room the girl sat at an upright piano, left hand flowing over the keys. She glanced at him as he seated himself on her right. He held his right hand extended over the keys of the upper register as she continued to play. He heard the small exhalation of her breath as he joined her. It was a strange sensation playing merely the right hand part, but quickly he took the lead. She followed him like a dancer. An elation ached behind his eyes, and once Miss Hardy gave him a swift smile.

They had finished before he realized that the Hardys had come inside, to stand in curiously similar attitudes—Hardy with fingers touching the knot of his cravat, his wife with the palms of her hands pressed together beneath her chin. With them were Bill Driggs and a shock-headed boy of about fifteen.

"That was lovely, Mr. Livingston," Mrs. Hardy said. "I used to play the right hand with Mary, but we haven't done that for so long!"

Miss Hardy was bending forward with her hand fluttering above the keys.

"You will take supper with us, won't you, Mr. Livingston?"

Mrs. Hardy inquired. Hardy introduced the boy, Mary's brother Jefferson, who shook Andrew's hand with stiff good manners, regarding his sister with a rolling eye. Bill Driggs was grinning.

He seated himself again. "I love Schubert," Miss Hardy said, in a flat voice. She struck a chord. They began to play.

Hardy spoke a lengthy grace, invoking, Andrew noticed, Creation, the Deity, and Nature's God, while net curtains bellied and slackened in the breeze through the open window, filtering the late sun. At table were the Hardys, Andrew, Driggs, and three of the Palisades cowboys. Mrs. Hardy served the plates from steaming bowls, her daughter distributed these with her good hand, and the cowboys shoveled down their food and immediately excused themselves. Andrew mentioned that he had met Lord Machray on the roundup.

He was conscious of a pressure he did not understand, everyone gazing at him expectantly except for Mary Hardy, who busied herself dicing a carrot with her knife and fork.

"You are friendly with Lord Machray?" Hardy asked.

He said that he had liked the man very much. Driggs was scowling as though he had committed a social error. "I gather that that is an unpopular sentiment," he said.

"Yep," Driggs said.

"Perhaps I could be informed why that is the case."

Driggs and Hardy exchanged looks. "Guess it is up to me, Yule," Driggs said. He leaned forward on his elbows, his deeply graven face thrust toward Andrew.

"To begin with, he comes out here with something called scrip, that no one else's ever heard of. Entitles him to grab land wherever he wants to grab it. Next thing, he has fenced him a piece of ground half the size of the Territory, it looks like, and got claims and range rights out on more besides. He has fenced some fellers in, and some out. Some he has fenced out, like me, has been makin a living here for twenty years wolfin or shootin game for railroad crews. He has got him a fence across the only route a man can take downriver without fordin deep water or fightin quicksand in the spring. And maybe you haven't seen yet what wire can do to a pronghorn, or a cow either, that gets messed up with it.

"He has just about bought up the town of Pyramid. He is oversize and prideful, and just the way he rides around in his shiny buggy with a cigar stickin out of his face can make a fellow mad." He grinned at the table at large. "You will notice I don't mention the fact that he is buildin himself a *palace* up on the bluff there. Or how his slaughterhouse will *stink* when it's workin, if it ever does. Or the way those clerks of his in that brick buildin go around with green *eyeshades* on. I won't even stoop to mention *those*."

"Those are strong sentiments, Bill," Mrs. Hardy said.

Driggs said to Andrew, "I do guess I sound a hateful man. Maybe I am that. I was wolfin out here when a feller had to carry a extra dose of strychnine for his personal use, beat the torture stake in case the redskin devils caught him. I hate a Sioux. Grizzly the same. And now if I don't think Lord Muck-a-muck beats all!"

Mary Hardy whispered, "F-father—"

"I will speak, if you don't mind, my dear," Hardy said. He gazed at Andrew over the tops of his spectacles. "I have been in love with free institutions all my life," he said, and paused weightily. "I came here from England at an early age because I considered my life there little better than slavery, and I gained citizenship in this country fighting for the Union against slavery. Freedom has obsessed me, Mr. Livingston! And the freest section of this freest of countries is here in the Bad Lands. Which Lord Machray would turn into his personal fief. It is what this nation rebelled against one hundred years ago!"

He leveled his forefinger. "I consider him my enemy. He is the enemy of the particular freedom of the Bad Lands. Of free range, free cooperation, free institutions. With his contempt for lesser men, and his schemes to enrich himself at their expense!"

"His plans sounded to me as though they would be to the benefit of anyone raising cattle in the Bad Lands," Andrew said.

Mrs. Hardy glanced at him sideways and he thought she agreed with him, although she did not speak.

Hardy glared. "I would rather Chicago commission men of the vilest stamp reaped the benefits of our industry than such as Lord Machray!"

There was a silence. Hands against her breast, Mary Hardy watched her father's face. Beside her, her brother sat hunched uncomfortably, his protuberant ears flushed dark red.

"What is this scrip that Machray acquired?" Andrew asked.

"Some of it is called 'soldiers' scrip,'" Hardy said. "It was

52

given as a reward to soldiers, so they could acquire public lands. Some was given the Choctaws in exchange for their lands. And I believe there is other that came from the appropriation of the Spanish land grants in California. All has fallen into the hands of speculators, of course. Who make enormous profits from it." He sighed and said, "In addition, Lord Machray purchased a great deal of land from the railroad. Nine thousand acres, I believe."

Driggs laughed. "Mostly," he said. "Nobody wants to buy land when they can have the use of it for nothing. Free grass!"

Hardy leveled his finger again. "The range here, Mr. Livingston—like the great world itself—was made for the benefit of all. But throughout history men who consider themselves better than the common lot have preempted land to their own use. Conquered it, connived for it, bought it—all the same thing. Thus other men are demeaned and disenfranchised, and the high opinion of themselves of these few reenforced." He paused, sighed, and said in a quieter tone, "Well, I must not mount my hobby horse, to the distress of my wife and daughter."

"Horse was rocking along at a fine clip, there, Yule," Driggs said grinning, as Hardy daubed at the corners of his mouth with his napkin.

"I know, I carry on. But I see so well what this country should be—should have been! Free men. Free land. Every man cooperating with his neighbor to ensure Nature's blessings. I suppose I sound a visionary, Mr. Livingston."

"Lord Machray seems to be a visionary also," he said.

"In a different way. In a very different way." Hardy sat polishing his eyeglasses with his napkin. His son was staring at him as though he had been listening to Holy Writ. Mary Hardy broke the silence.

"You play the piano beautifully, Mr. Livingston!"

"I return the compliment, Miss Hardy!"

"You must have studied for many years."

"With a strict old gentlewoman named Mme. Lester," he said. "Who would rap on my hands with a ferrule when they did not behave."

Mary Hardy slipped her crippled hand into her lap with a glance at her father, who, in the act of returning his spectacles to his nose, gave Andrew a glare out of pale eyesockets. He felt his cheeks burning at his gaffe.

But the girl's smile flashed reassuringly when he inquired with whom she had studied. "Oh—with my mother!"

"You must be a fine artist yourself, Mrs. Hardy."

Long dimples, like her daughter's, creased Mrs. Hardy's cheeks when she smiled. "Oh, once, perhaps. I had a career once, but the war came, and I married." The dimples vanished, to be replaced by her set, amiable expression. Abruptly she rose. "We will clear the table now, Mary." To Andrew she said, "My husband does not believe in servants, you see, Mr. Livingston. Therefore it is the women of the house who perform the work."

Later, Andrew and his host stood alone on the veranda at dusk. He ventured the opinion that his savior, Driggs, was a man of violent opinions.

"I hold him the salt of this particular bit of earth," Hardy said. "And would rather be possessed of his good opinion than that of any European Junker." It seemed a rebuke.

Hardy paced the veranda, hands clasped behind his back. Finally he inquired if Andrew was an educated man.

He said that he was educated enough to know that he was uneducated.

"That is educated!" Hardy said, nodding approvingly. "When I spoke of aristocracy just now I did not mean to imply that it is indigenous to Europe. This country's eastern seaboard has its own aristocracy." He cleared his throat. "Tell me something of yourself, Mr. Livingston."

"I suppose my family is of that class you mention," he said. "We have always been active in politics in the State of New York, and bankers for generations, although my father chose to become an architect. I was educated at Harvard College. I am a widower. My employer before I came to the Bad Lands was the Manfacturers and Grain Bank of New York City, and I am a vice-president of that city's Republican Club."

He had thought Hardy might be offended by his response, but his host only nodded, watching a flight of birds sweep low over the river and climb, beating, to disappear over the buttes.

"So you are political, Mr. Livingston."

"It is expected of members of my family."

"And do you always do what is expected of you?"

"Up until a month ago."

54

Hardy offered him a cigar, which he declined, and lit one himself, shaking the match out. He puffed aromatic smoke.

"Mr. Livingston, I will admit to not having been as forthright as I like to consider myself. The fact is that I have every faith in cattle raising as a business proposition. As Cato the Elder says in *De agri cultura* in answer to the question: What are the wisest uses of land? First, profitable cattle raising. Second, moderately profitable cattle raising. Third, unprofitable cattle raising. Fourth, to plow the land.

"The increase of your herd becomes a kind of natural interest, Mr. Livingston. Moreover, the grass is especially nutritious in the Bad Lands, and the animals survive our severe winters well, seeming more robust, if anything, for their privations."

"But the range is already overcrowded, you say." It occurred to him that he and Chally had become a kind of buffer state between his host and Lord Machray.

"There are such feelings, as you have learned today. There are many possibilities of friction. It is inevitable that your stock will wander onto a neighbor's range, and some of his onto yours—that is why we hold roundups in the fall and spring. Cooperation is an absolute necessity in cattle country. As to overcrowding, there is still range enough for all if simple rules of human intercourse are observed."

"I'm afraid it has been my experience that such rules are observed just so long as it suits human nature to observe them."

"Apparently my experience with human nature has been superior to yours," Hardy said coldly.

"My experience earlier today confirmed all my worst opinions," Andrew said. "But since meeting Bill Driggs, and the Hardy family, I have become more optimistic."

Hardy smiled his sudden, sweet smile, "Mr. Livingston," he announced, extending his hand, "we will be friends as well as neighbors!"

*When Chally, returned from Mandan with the homestead pa-*pers, learned of the visitation at Fire Creek, Andrew thought he had never seen a man so angry. Chally paced up and down, slapping a hand against his leg, his face a stiff mask.

"Why, that damned bushwhacker!" he said through his teeth. "Well, I will guarantee he will not trouble us here again!"

"It was Bill Driggs' advice that we let be if he lets be."

"He had better let be!" Chally said, pacing, cuffing a hand against his leg. "By God, he is lucky I wasn't here!"

Clearly his own performance had not impressed his partner, but he did not wish to fuel Chally's wrath by objecting. "I think we've been rousted and that's the end of it," he said. "Now we seem to be in the good graces of our neighbors to the south, and I foresee no difficulties with Lord Machray."

"That damned landgrabber," Chally said. He seemed unable to stand still. "Well, that is fine if Yule Hardy is friendly." He continued pacing. "Jake Boutelle had better let be, all right, or him and me is coming to it!"

"When will you be leaving for Iowa?"

"Leavin tomorrow, if Joe's scared up that cook. You'll be all right here, will you?"

He had been staying at the Hardys', coming up every day to do a little work on the shack. And now he kept a rifle close to hand. He said a little stiffly that he would be all right.

An hour after Chally had departed he started back for Palisades Ranch for supper. Crossing a bottom he saw three horsemen approaching, heat-hazed. One wore a canvas jacket, another a blue-checked shirt, the third what appeared to be a blanket. Their faces were dark and moon-shaped beneath braided hair and eagle feathers.

With an almost scientific interest he noticed that fear was a little quicker to tickle in his veins since he had met Jake Boutelle. He reined his mare to a halt, feeling the hard beating of his heart and the dry flicker of breath between his lips. He laid a hand to the stock of his rifle. The three Indians continued their approach until he drew his rifle and propped the butt on his thigh. They halted twenty yards from him.

"We bring no harm!" one of them called. "We wish only to speak."

"One of you come forward."

The young man with the blue shirt spurred ahead of his companions on a brown-and-white spotted pony. He reined up before Andrew, staring at him with slitted eyes, his mouth slicing down at the corners.

"We seek our stolen ponies, white man!" He spread filthy fingers, dissolved the hand into a fist, and repeated this three times. "Twenty!"

"I've seen no ponies."

"White men have stolen them!"

He said he was sorry to hear that, and the Indian grunted as though it had been a confession. "If it is true," he added.

"It is true!" the other said. He swung his pony away, continuing to turn his head to gaze straight into Andrew's face until with a yip he spurred to a trot to rejoin the other two. The three of them passed, and he resheathed his rifle and rode on also. It took all his will power not to glance behind him.

Near Palisades, with a pounding of hoofs, Jeff Hardy and one of the Palisades cowboys caught up with him. He told them of his encounter with the Indians.

"Crees," the cowboy said contemptuously.

"No need to worry about them, Mr. Livingston," Jeff said. For all his jug ears, snub nose, and cowlick of colorless hair, he habitually wore a serious expression. "They'd be pleased if they scared you, but they are not apt to *do* anything."

"It seems a shame that white men are stealing their ponies."

"They will just turn around and steal themself some others," the cowboy said, and spat a brown gout of tobacco juice. "They have got no respect for another person's property."

"Palisades Ranch,
Dakota Territory
October 15, 1883

"Dearest Cissie:

"Thank you so much for the bundle of newspapers and magazines, which I and my hosts have been devouring. It was brought down from Pyramid Flat by a visiting cowboy, the grapevine having spread the information that I am in residence at Palisades Ranch.

"I have spent a most pleasant week here with my new friends, the Hardys, while awaiting the wagonload of supplies and appurtenances I have ordered for my new house! In actual fact it is not a house, but the meanest of shacks. It is to be the headquarters of my ranch! Cissie, I have made a very grave decision. I am determined to stock a ranch here with my own herd, and to divide my life between New York and the Bad Lands. I have engaged a stalwart fellow as my 'factor,' and he is now in Iowa, purchasing our livestock.

"I have made this determination despite a thoroughly unpleasant experience last week. Two ruffians accosted me at the aforementioned shack and threatened me with their six-shooters. I knocked one of them down, whereupon I found myself in quite a serious predicament, which was most fortunately relieved by the advent of another new friend, a hunter named Driggs. It seems they were trying to frighten me into abandoning this shack, which they coveted.

"On the more pleasant side of the ledger, the Hardys, my hosts, are cultivated, friendly people. I play Mendelssohn and Schubert with the daughter of the house before supper, and argue various ethical points with Hardy during the meal. His philosophy is composed of great chunks from Tom Paine, Matthew Arnold, and von Humboldt. He is an Englishman by birth, but so in love with America as to make me feel weary and cynical. He is a perfervid Democrat in national politics, but in local matters violent on the subject of 'rustlers, horse thieves, and squatters.'

" 'Junkerism' on the one hand and 'Fenianism' on the other are Hardy's hobgoblins: unjust authority and anarchy. The grangers, some of whom are indeed 'Fenians' in that they are of Irish extraction, fill this latter bill of disapproval. Their acquisition of their quarter sections may be legal, but for Hardy it violates some higher law of the free range. That they do slaughter cattle belonging to others is incontestable.

"Hardy's definition of 'Junkerism,' or 'aristocracy' seems to embody extremes of personal liberty heedless of others, arrogance, bullying, insistence upon privilege, etc. Personification of all this is Lord Machray, a large, florid Scot whom I met on a visit to the roundup, and a man who reminds me very much of Rudolph Duarte at Harvard, all exuberance and 'pursuit,' spouting poetry the while. He also reminds me of the Marquis of Karabas, in 'Puss in Boots,' for a great deal hereabouts seems to belong to him, an enormous fenced acreage, some eight thousand head of cattle, a great deal of the town of Pyramid Flat, including the slaughterhouse, incomplete as yet, & etc. You would instantly like him. Hardy detests him.

"Machray's announced intentions are in aid of progress, while it is Hardy's claim that progress equals destruction. In his passionate arguments there is a good deal of rationalization, that very human desire to close the gate of the promised land—lest it become overcrowded—just after we ourselves have squeezed through.

"I must not forget, however, that Hardy has held that gate open for me, whatever his motives. . . ."

8

He had been camping at Fire Creek for a week when Mary Hardy and her brother came to call on him, the girl in blue gingham and a deep bonnet, sidesaddle on a chestnut, her brother following her, a wicker hamper strapped behind his saddle. Beyond them heat haze swam over the mud banks of the river.

He handed Mary Hardy down, reaching first for the wrong hand but swiftly changing the course of his own. She plumped to the ground beside him, pink-cheeked. Jeff passed down the hamper.

"Mother thought you might be hungry for some fried chicken!"

"We've come to see your sketches, Mr. Livingston!" Mary Hardy said.

They admired the watercolor on his easel, and paged through his sketches of animals and Machray's roundup. Jeff looked embarrassed, as though he considered art an improper occupation for a man. "Didn't draw any grizzly, I guess," he said finally, handing the sheaf of drawings to his sister and standing with his thumbs hooked in his cartridge belt.

Andrew said they hadn't seen any grizzly.

"Not so many left in the Bad Lands, I guess," Jeff said. "I *hate* grizzlies. I used to dream about grizzlies coming after me, and I'd wake up *bawling*."

"I used to dream I was riding along a wide road on a powerful black horse," Mary Hardy said, holding one black-net gloved hand in the other. "I didn't know whether it was running away with me or not. And behind me there would be a great company of men all galloping too. Maybe they were soldiers—in silver breastplates and those helmets like Cromwell's men. I was never certain whether they were chasing me, or I was leading them." She flushed painfully.

He saw he was expected to share a dream of his own as a kind of earnest to the confessions of these children, but he could think of nothing. "Do you know," he said, "I've not had a single dream since I've been sleeping in this place?"

"Really?" Mary Hardy said faintly. Jeff had stepped outside to gaze down toward the river, spraddle-legged in his chaps.

"Wait'll you see how the ice gorges up down there when the river breaks up in the spring."

"So I've heard."

"You said once that you would like to sketch me, Mr. Livingston," Mary Hardy said, putting down the sketches and pressing her clasped hands to her neat bosom.

"I will insist on it. I know exactly how I will pose you—seated, leaning slightly forward with crossed arms. Do you know Fra Angelico's 'Annunciation'?"

She shook her head. "What's 'Annunciation'?" Jeff asked, turning back.

"When the angel announced to that other Mary that she was to bear the Christ child."

"That's Catholic stuff," Jeff said, scowling.

Andrew said he was very interested in that fried chicken that Mrs. Hardy had sent.

The blanket was spread in a shady place beside the creek, and the blanket, the hamper, the hamper's contents, and the cool shade were very like summer picnics by the pond at Prester Head, lacking only the little crooked dock and the canoe tied there. Her bonnet pushed back from her face, Mary Hardy passed plates laden with golden pieces of chicken, cole slaw, biscuits, butter, and wild plum jam. Jeff built a fire of broken bits of dead wood, and forced into the ground an iron spike with a hook for the teapot handle. When he had eaten he took up a post on the creek bank not quite out of earshot, reclining against a tree trunk with his hat tipped over his eyes and a fish line dangling into the water.

Andrew was able to establish Mary Hardy's age as nineteen. She had mentioned that she was four years older than Jeff, whose age he inquired. Their father was worried about Jeff, she said in a low voice; Jeff had set himself against books. She herself was a great reader. He asked about her reading.

"*Lorna Doone, Wuthering Heights, Jane Eyre*—" Her smile flashed. "Precisely what a young woman out here on the moors could be expected to read. And I do enjoy Harriet Prescott Spofford, though Father disapproves."

She leaned forward to pour tea into their cups. Her collarbone was fragile as a bird's. He could see blue veins there, and her pulse beating just where the sun-browned flesh turned milky. "Actually, father disapproves of novels. I tell him that the only way a person can learn to conduct herself is through reading novels."

"But he thinks you should learn to conduct yourself reading the philosophers?"

"Plato instead of *Pamela*," she said, laughing. "There is a little taboret in the hall just outside my room, and I find there the books I *should* be reading. I did rebel at *The Republic*, Mr. Livingston!"

"Good for you!"

She brought her teacup to her lips, her eyes meeting his over the rim, and dropping quickly away. "Everything is so *brown* here, now," she said. "It was so green in the Shenandoah Valley where I was a girl. I will never forget those different hues of green!"

"You were happy in Virginia, then?"

"No, we were not. We were uncomfortable in many ways. They considered F-father a carpetbagger, you see, though he would like to think that his difficulties were those of an educated man surrounded by bumpkins."

"He is a self-educated man?"

"Oh, he went to quite a good public school in England, Ruthvens Hall, near Manchester. Though it must have been terribly strict. I know he believes now that he came to this country as a pauper, but my mother says that he and a number of other young Englishmen, who came here together just before the war, had some funds. They farmed together in Pennsylvania, but they had a falling out. Mother is from Pennsylvania." As though that was enough of that subject, she asked if it was green in the State of New York. On being informed that it was, she said, "I know you are a widower, Mr. Livingston, but I have never learned if you have children."

"One boy of three years. His aunt is caring for him."

"And do you love him very much?"

He did not say that he was determined never again to love very much, but answered conventionally.

"Here comes Matty!" Jeff called.

It was the young cowboy who had visited the hunting camp, approaching at a quick trot; he dismounted to squat beside Mary Hardy and accept a cup of tea. Jeff also rejoined them, and the three youngsters laughed and joked together with easy familiarity from which Andrew felt excluded, finally realizing that the exclusion was contrived. Matty Gruby combed his sparse mustache with his thumb, fingered his locket, and ignored Andrew, who did not know how to reassure the young cowboy that he had no designs on his fair lady. He leaned back on his elbows listening to the music of the mouth organ and to Mary Hardy singing along in her small, rather sweet voice, and tried not to think of the picnics at Prester Head.

The three of them left together, Mary Hardy insisting that Andrew return to Palisades soon. Her father loved good argumentation, and she their duets on the piano. Even when they had disappeared down along the river he could hear the faint, sad music of the mouth organ.

He had told Mary and Jeff Hardy that he had not dreamed at Fire Creek, but that night he dreamed, hearing in his head the distant sweet music that was not a mouth organ. He came again to the great Palladian house at Newport, with its white columns, its arbors and hedges of roses and myrtle run wild, its bowers, the ruined summerhouse, the intersecting paths; and found Elizabeth Darcy there, both memory and dream. How small had been her little gloves, how high the heels of her little boots, how electric the flutter of her snowy skirts! How they had talked, that summer, of art, of love, of their souls. They had experimented with nitrous oxide and with laudanum, and read aloud the poems of Elizabeth Barrett Browning. How could they have been so ill-prepared for life—and death?

Lying with his eyes tight closed, he thought that it must be June, with a hint of chill in the breeze off the water. The music softly, insistently played. The colored lights swayed. Hand in hand he and Elizabeth ran along the paths between the hedges, the music fainter and fainter. Now they ran on among the tall, narrow-trunked trees of the old Quaker graveyard, where Death must have observed them in their pleasure, and consulted his watch.

9

Next day he locked the shack with the padlock and chain he had borrowed from Hardy, and, with a pack animal, set out for Pyramid Flat for mail and supplies. He headed north by way of the ravine through which Boutelle had disappeared.

Though he had known he must encounter Machray's fence, it was a shock when he came upon it, three strands of glinting, twisted wire zigzagging from tree to tree on the north slope of a broad swale. Farther along posts had been set.

He rode along the wire, noticing where it had been cut and patched. He felt a prickling at the back of his neck and glanced up to see a horseman watching him from the top of a butte. It seemed important that he ignore the guard as he rode on east toward the dull gleam of the river. His anger seemed to him disproportionate, and was physical, like a cold in his head; he realized that this was what Hardy and Driggs had been trying to express. He had been unable to understand why the Scot was so hated, but the fence and its guard violated some deeply held and sacred sentiment of which he had not even been aware until he had encountered Machray's wire in its arrogance.

The river was very low and fording it easy enough, the silted water washing up over the horses' fetlocks. He continued his way north along the eastern bank.

He was watching for Machray's mansion, but it too came as a surprise. Suddenly it was riding a bluff on the western side of the river like a warship, decked with broad verandas, masted with chimneys. The mansion seemed, like the fence, aggressive and arrogant; he had to remind himself that he had liked what he had seen of Machray at the roundup.

He recrossed the river on the planked-over railroad bridge in the wake of a wagon with a high-hooped cover of dirty white canvas, a black and white spotted cow trailing with her stiff-legged gait. A galvanized washtub thumped rhythmically against the side of the wagon, and from time to time a rear wheel shrieked. When he rode past the wagon and its team of mules he nodded to the grangers, a thin man with a burnt-black face, a woman in a poke bonnet, children peering at him. The man nodded curtly in response. A half-grown boy with bare feet and matted fair hair rode one of the lead mules.

Pyramid Flat clustered along the railroad, its center a yellow and brown clapboard station with a cupola and a flag hanging limp from the pole. Frame buildings of one and two stories were ranged on a T of streets. The powdery dust of the main street prickled in the sweat of his face. From the shade of wooden awnings townspeople watched him passing. A shirt-sleeved storekeeper sat tipped back in a chair, two men in town clothes strolled arm in arm, and a cluster of roughly dressed men guffawed on a street corner, the object of their humor a woman in tawdry finery and a pink parasol parading past them.

He inquired for Fat Jenny and followed directions to a tar-paper shack at the end of town, where a toothless, mountainous squaw apologized that the buffalo hide Joe Reuter had left with her was not yet tanned, extracted money on account, and promised a robe of transcendent softness within a week.

Returning, he again passed the town's most substantial building, of yellow brick with intricate cornices, and now he noticed a name set in relief above the double doors: MACHRAY. He passed the granger's wagon again, he and the driver nodding in exactly the same aloof recognition as before. He left his horses at the livery stable, engaged a room in the Great Northwest Hotel, and had started to cross the street in search of a saloon when a red and yellow buggy drawn by a prancing sorrel bore down upon him.

In the buggy was Machray, cigar between his teeth, soft hat on his head, tweed-suited, with a four-in-hand cravat in which a diamond stickpin caught the sun in a stroke of fire. Machray raised a whip in greeting and reined the buggy to a halt. He looked large, scrubbed, prosperous, and impervious.

"Livingston! Do I hear rumors that you have made the plunge without my advice?"

Andrew admitted that it was true. "I will be bringing in a herd to take up range to the south of you."

Machray's face turned to stone. "How large a herd, sir?"

"Five hundred head."

The big man stared at him, squinting, his jaw bunched; for a moment it occurred to him that Machray was going to strike him. Then Machray's mood seemed abruptly to change. "Come along," he said. "I'm going out to the abattoir for a look-see."

He climbed into the buggy, refusing the cigar proffered him. He was still shaken by the violence of Machray's displeasure.

"Day of celebration for me!" Machray said. "Eight pounds of bairn born to my wife. Anthony Ernest Balater! Names for his grandfather, who is ailing. Lady Machray's come through her ordeal with flying colors—ah, she is a wee slip of a thing for such a calving!"

"Congratulations!" He and Machray grinned at each other, and Machray ticked the sorrel's rump with his whip. Blue ribbons had been braided into the animal's tail. Townsmen and cowboys watched from the boardwalk's shade, the townsmen nodding or waving, the cowboys more reserved, some with wooden faces.

Cigar and hat set at jaunty angles, a sweep of yellow hair decorating his forehead, Machray pointed out the vacant site beyond his office building where he hoped to build an opera house. "We'll have good music in Pyramid Flat one day, mark my words, Livingston. Opera singers with fine bosoms! Ah, but a public benefactor has man's suspicious nature to combat at every turning, it seems."

"Not everyone in the Bad Lands is enthusiastic about progress, I understand."

"Ah, once we are in operation the suspicious gentry will begin to see the benefits," Machray said. "We are also planning abattoirs in Miles City and Billings, you know. Offices and storehouses in St. Paul, Duluth, Chicago, and Portland. And icing stations! We shall cover the northwest with a great net, Livingston."

"I would think Swift and Armour would be less than enthusiastic about your great net."

Machray's laugh boomed out as the tall chimney stack of the slaughterhouse loomed ahead. "So long as I can keep a pack of jews in Glasgow satisfied I think I need not worry myself over old Armour's displeasure!"

The buggy rattled over a wooden bridge spanning a dry creek bottom, Machray flicking his whip at the sorrel's rump. "Our intention is to be in a position to buy all the cattle, sheep, and hogs that come over the railroad, slaughter them here, and ship dressed meat east and west. If we encounter resistance from the great meatpackers we will plan to establish our own retail outlets. What do you think of that, sir?"

"Impressive plans!" he said, and Machray laughed fatly.

"Wife complains about bringing a butcher's son into the world," he said. "But we shall see. We shall see!"

They followed alongside a spur track, and presently a sprawl of buildings at the base of the tall, yellow brick stack came into view. One of these showed only bare studding, the other was walled and roofed. The two were connected by complex, overhead framing.

"I'll be purchasing cattle for slaughter next June," Machray said. "Possibly by May, if it is a mild winter. Ah, but there is still much work to be done!"

They rolled on under an elevated pipeline on a trestle that ran off the bluff behind the slaughterhouse. A guard with a rifle made a gesture of salute, which Machray returned.

"Water under pressure," he said, pointing up to the trestle. "Takes a devil's own amount of water." He waved a hand ahead. "Cattle pens out this way. Takes a devilish amount of land as well."

In the larger building the blows of hammers reverberated. They left the buggy and ascended a long ramp to enter a vast interior, very dim. Men were at work at the far end, voices echoing.

"Slaughtering room," Machray said. "Here the beasts will be poleaxed as they enter. Simplest to separate the edible from the inedible parts by gravity, you see. Beasts arrive here by their own motive power." They moved on along, Machray pointing out where the overhead track was to run.

"Here the hide is removed and dropped through this opening into a chute to the hide room. Next the inedible portions of the carcasses are snipped away and drop to the rendering room. Soap, fats, fertilizer, etcetera. Next the viscera-separating departments. Then we move along to the cold rooms. The body heat must be removed promptly from the edible portions, you see. Here the carcasses will hang from overhead

66

rails, and the edible organs will be spread out on trays."
Machray illustrated the processes at each area of operation.
A carpenter in a leather apron stood listening to the flood of
words, his hammer frozen in his hand.

"You know a great deal about your business," Andrew
said, when Machray had ceased for breath.

"Consulted with experts," Machray said. "Had the best advice available. At first we considered a much more modest
operation, but I was able to convince my backers it was false
economy. For twenty-five head a day one would still need an
engineer, a foreman, bookkeeper, hide man, tallow man,
blood man, cooper, guards, draymen. Such a crew can as easily process two or three hundred a day. Still, the plenishing
will be monstrous. Ochone, the bills!"

Andrew was relieved when they had made their way out
into the sunlight again. The sheer size of the place was op-
pressive, as was Machray in his enthusiasm. They leaned
against a railing built of green lumber still dripping pitch.

"And the frustrations!" Machray continued. "I am not a
man built to withstand many frustrations, Livingston, and it
has been a bitter blow not to be able to open this fall. But in
the spring we will begin slaughtering very early. I am assured
that, because of the excellent qualities of the stem-dried
grasses of the Bad Lands, beef fit for the market can be
slaughtered as early as the end of May—when beef commands an *excellent* price!"

"Will grass-fed beef command as good a price as corn-
fed?"

Machray scowled. "That is an objection that we've considered. And we have a plan to meet it. Buy up the Pacific
coast hop crop, sell it to the Milwaukee brewers on the agreement that they return the resultant malt, which is known to
be the most concentrated and fattening food to be had. Far
better than corn!"

He waved an arm. "We'll build individual feeding pens—
thousands of them! Then we can hold fat cattle for the best
market, year round if need be. Run the place at maximum
volume."

He stood spread-legged with his chin thrust out as though
at the helm of a great ship surging through treacherous seas,
gazing out on the thousands of individual feeding pens as
though they already existed by the sheer power of his will.
Pacing, hands behind his back, he continued:

"Agent in France talking to some high-command fellows

there. Prospect of furnishing beef soup for the army. We'd put it up for them here. Great soup eaters, the Frenchies."

Andrew said that was well known to be the case, and Machray took his arm as they moved on through the premises. "Dealing with quartermaster people is something I could manage," he went on. "Family's been soldiers since the dawn of time. Two grandfathers at Waterloo. Father served in Afghanistan. But wars aren't what they used to be, Livingston. Nothing's what it used to be, alas."

When they returned to Pyramid Flat Machray ushered him through the office building, where clerks were at work, introducing him to the chief clerk, a steely-eyed, chin-whiskered little accountant named Marston. In his own office a tiger's head adorned the wall, huge yellow eyes glaring down on Machray's untidy desk. The walls were crowded with dozens of framed and glassed photographs, reflecting each other and the glass-fronted bookcases packed with volumes.

Machray waved him into a chair and produced a whiskey bottle. He poured two large portions and, standing, offered a toast to a large, oval photograph—a sepia girl with her neck gracefully bowed, a blossom held to her nose.

"To Lady Milly! A wee, lovely woman with hair as red as gold—steady as Castle Rock, Livingston! And to the little laird!"

They drank. Machray squinted at him. "Livingston, you must sup with me this evening—see my house. Great, empty barn of a place, but what a prospect! Say you will!"

That evening at six he rode up the well-brushed-out road that climbed the bluff to present himself at the mansion, turning Ginger over to a cowboy who met him in the yard, and pausing to gaze out on the limitless, violet prairie before mounting wooden steps to the veranda. The soldierly-looking fellow he had last seen attending to Machray in his tent at the roundup appeared, colorless hair parted precisely in the center of his head.

"Good evening, Mr. Livingston. My name is Dickson, sir. I believe I had better advise you that the Captain is having another guest for dinner also. Her name is Mrs. Benbow. Perhaps you already know the lady?"

He said he did not.

Dickson's hazel eyes met his calmly. "She keeps a house in town, you see, sir. I must say that she is not exactly a lady, but she is a great friend of the Captain's, if you take my meaning."

"I understand, Dickson."

Dickson ushered him inside. A cavernous great hall reminded him of the slaughter room at the abattoir. Walls decorated with antlered heads ran up into high gloom above, and there were brick fireplaces at either end, each with its blazing fire. A staircase mounted to a second story, with, midway, a sort of mezzanine. The place smelled of dust and sawdust. Machray appeared through a far doorway, wearing kilts, stockings, and a short woolen jacket with captain's pips on the shoulder flaps.

"Ah, Livingston! I've asked Mrs. Benbow to take supper with us, a bit of feminine companionship makes for ceremony, don't you think? Come along, and I'll show you round the place."

They toured the mansion—bedrooms, nursery, library, office—a few of its barren rooms stacked with leather trunks. In the dining room another fire burned, and the table gleamed with white napery, silver, and crystal.

"There will be some changes when Lady Milly comes with the child next summer," Machray said. "Unwilling to have her out to the Bad Lands until we had some semblance of order here. Can hardly be called marital life, seeing your lady only by winter. I've had house plans sent her, and she intends to have a model made. She'll purchase furnishings in New York. Fancies that sort of thing." He laughed. "A case-hardened fancy, she has! Named the place, too, from a photograph I sent her. 'Widewings.' "

They stood looking at each other. Machray grinned sheepishly.

"Not inaccurate," Andrew said. "Perhaps a little . . ."

"Yes," Machray said. "For the Bad Lands." He sighed. "Whim of adamant," he said. "You're not a married man, Livingston?"

He said he was a widower. Machray looked at him with such consternation and pity that he felt his eyes fill. He heard himself explaining that his wife and daughter had drowned in a boating accident.

"Why, that is terrible, man!" Machray said in a gentle voice. A big hand kneaded his shoulder. "Come, let us take a glass of whiskey together."

Back in the great hall Machray poured liquor from a decanter, and arm in arm they moved out onto the veranda with its view of the prairie, the slaughterhouse, and, a mile or two to the north, the T-shaped huddle of buildings that was Pyramid Flat. Machray pointed out the buggy twisting its way up the road from town, varnished surfaces gleaming in the late sun as it came out on top of the bluff. They strolled back along the veranda as the buggy halted in the yard. The driver handed the occupant down, a big woman, generously curved, all in black and wearing an immense, shaggy black hat.

Machray introduced them. "Mr. Livingston's taking up land in the Bad Lands, my dear. More demented gentry crowding out here in search of ruination."

Mrs. Benbow's face was marred with old smallpox scars that gave it a curiously blurred quality. Dark eyes regarded Andrew comprehensively.

"Will you be wintering in the Bad Lands, Mr. Livingston?"

He said he would be returning to New York for the winter.

She nodded. "Winters are very hard here."

"You must come with me in my private railway car, Livingston," Machray said. "You'll find *Aurora* most comfortable. In about a month? I believe I am to embark on the *Carolla* for England the twenty-sixth of December. I will keep you informed."

At dinner, with the candle flames making trembling spots of purple on the linen through the wineglasses that Dickson replenished regularly, Andrew sat on Machray's left and Mrs. Benbow on his right. By candlelight her pocked face appeared only pale and soft, framed by wings of thick, dark hair. An invisible Dickson played squealing, sentimental selections on his bagpipes, reappearing from time to time with a wine bottle.

Andrew complimented Machray on the claret.

"Ah, the Scots are fanciers of fine claret," Machray said. "At one time more claret was drunk in Scotland than anywhere else. That was before Union. Thereafter we had port forced upon us—wine of England's oldest ally and all that." He held up his wineglass before him as though it were a heavy goblet, squinting at it as he declaimed:

"Firm and erect the Caledonian stood.
Old was his mutton, and his claret good.
Let him drink port, the Saxon cried!
He drank the poison, and his spirit died."

70

He grinned to their laughter. Mrs. Benbow asked what "Union" was. "Like the War Between the States, Machray?"

"Not a war, but a business of trick and treaty merely," Machray said. "A beautiful girl dragged into marriage with an old bachelor of putrid habits; 1707 was a black year for Scotland! They tell a story of it that will amuse you, my dear." He leaned forward, tenting his hands together with his green eyes fixed on the woman.

"In olden times, for some reason I cannot remember, treaties always used to refer to the Kingdoms of England and Scotland and 'His Majesty's good town of Berwick-upon-Tweed.' And a mean little hole it is to be included in such company. These words were used in the Union, and still in the declaration of war with Russia. They were dropped, however, sometime before the Crimean treaty, so Berwick-upon-Tweed is still at war with Russia. It is a way I often feel myself."

"At war with Russia?" Andrew asked.

"With whoever threatens my borders, let us say," Machray said.

There was a silence. Andrew pondered on whether or not that had been a warning to him. He watched Mrs. Benbow's white hand smoothing at the tablecloth.

"Well, you are proud of your country, Machray."

"Ah, yes!" Machray said. "Soldiered for her quite a bit, you know, as have all the Machrays."

"I imagine a title gives a certain stake," Andrew said.

Machray grinned and nodded. "My pater is Marquess of Strathgorm and Cairnsporran, Earl of Sorby, and so on and so forth. I can remember as a lad trying to count the quarterings of the arms on the hammercloth of the old coach which was rolled out of its hibernation, creaking fearfully, upon certain state occasions. There was a groom who loved to tick them off for me. Without fellows like old Joby the peerage could never keep track of itself."

"I don't even know what quarterings are, Machray," Mrs. Benbow said.

Machray explained. "You must not be impressed by all that," he said, patting her hand. "It is all a great humbug. You are much more sensible in this country."

"These matters are very mysterious in this sensible country," Andrew said. "You will become the marquess when your father passes away?"

Machray nodded. "Landlord of a great drafty ruin of a

castle—Cairnsporran castle, a place unfit for human habitation; Lady Milly positively refuses to live there. And of several hunting lodges and countless disreputable cottages connected to rocky acreages that cannot be made to pay without grinding the poor tenants exceedin' fine. It is my responsibility to restore the family fortunes, you see."

Dickson was passing a service dish, spiced steaming smell of meat as he uncovered it for Mrs. Benbow. She sniffed suspiciously and helped herself to a small serving.

"You are proud of your country, though, Machray," she said. "They are not so proud of this one anymore."

"Some of us are," Andrew said. "Perhaps it is more love than pride, these days." He watched her watching Machray; it did not seem that her dark eyes could keep away from his face for long.

"A toast!" Machray said. "A toast to America!"

He raised his glass. "To America! Bordered on the east by the Atlantic Ocean, the north by Canada, the south by the Monroe Doctrine, and the west by Manifest Destiny!"

Machray chuckled, but Mrs. Benbow did not look amused. She said in her rather coarse voice, "Well, I don't know many men that love their country here. They just love money."

"Not purely an American trait, my dear," Machray said, serving his own plate from the dish Dickson held for him.

"I had a professor at Harvard whose belief it was that the proper American pursuit was pursuit itself," Andrew said. "That at its worst this turned into the crass pursuit of money, but that even so we are not so much in love with money as with the getting of it."

"It is the same thing!" Mrs. Benbow said spiritedly.

Machray shook a finger at her. "But men do love the *idea* of a thing, you know, my dear."

"Oh, yes, I have heard men out here claiming they love the *idea* of free range! Such a fuss over foreigners coming in and fencing!" She shook a finger back at Machray. "What they love is the idea of their own land, without the expense of buying or the trouble of fencing!"

Machray laughed, and Andrew watched the tug of small muscles at the corners of Mrs. Benbow's mouth. He was seeing something of the motive force of the origins of noble families—an ability to command fierce loyalty. The obverse was the ferocity of the enmity men such as Machray could arouse. He laughed to himself to think that what had been

72

aroused in Mrs. Benbow was not loyalty to an aristocratic principle, but love.

"I will tell you a curious matter in regard to land ownership," Machray said to him. "When Scotland was an independent kingdom, her monarch was known as 'king of Scots,' not as 'king of Scotland.' He was the chief of men merely, and the land belonged to the people."

"We have a chance in this country yet," Andrew said. "There are bills before Congress in regard to the public domain—for instance, Powell's bills increasing the homestead acreage on nonirrigated land to twenty-five hundred and sixty acres. And parceling by topographic basins."

"Ah, Major Powell of the Geographic Survey. I have met him, Livingston. But is even twenty-five hundred acres sufficient out here?"

"It is better than a quarter section, which is worse than nothing."

Machray was shaking his head. "I believe I chose the right course, and would do the same again. Although it was expensive!"

"Because it is expensive it is a course hardly available to homesteaders. Or to most ranchmen."

"Well, that is bad luck for them, isn't it?" Machray said cheerfully. "Your fine land bills will never pass anyhow, you know. The land rings will defeat them. And the western senators, who pretend they are favoring the little man, but instead are favoring the speculators."

Dickson began piping again outside the door. Machray saluted Mrs. Benbow with his glass. "Here is to good company, madam! I will tell you a story. There was a fine, small convocation of Scotsmen, good whiskey, a fire on the hearth, the hour late. Each of these fellows was well pleased with the others, until one noticed a bit of quietness—" He slipped into a thick accent:

" 'Wha gars the laird o' Harscadden look sae gash?' 'Oh, he slippit awa' tae his Maker twa hour syne, but I dinnae like to disturb good company by mentioning it!' "

Andrew laughed longer than he intended until both the others glanced at him curiously.

Mrs. Benbow said, "We must toast your child, Machray."

Machray raised his glass. "To the wee laird, then!"

They drank. Andrew watched the bloody spots reflected on the table trembling, and Mrs. Benbow's hand smoothing at the cloth.

"We shall hail the mother as well," Machray said, and they drank again.

There was a silence in which the pleasant mood seemed to be draining away. Andrew proposed a toast to the Bad Lands.

"Aye, to the Bad Lands!" Machray said. "Bordered on the east by the rising sun, the north by the aurora borealis, the south by—the precession of the equinoxes. And the west by the course of empire!"

He slapped his hands together triumphantly at their laughter, rising. "Shall we stroll a bit upon the veranda while Dickson clears the table? It will be chill!"

They strolled on the veranda, Mrs. Benbow with a heavy cloak thrown around her. It was very cold, their breath steaming. The stars were small and clear as diamond chips. To the north were the lights of Pyramid Flat, to the east only darkness, the sweep of the continent toward the Atlantic Ocean and the rising sun. Staring east, he wondered if he still loved his country, as he had avowed, in which he no longer felt the pride that he wished to feel.

"A shooting star!" Machray cried, raising an arm to point. Andrew glimpsed the fiery arc. Immediately another curved across the black universe.

"One for sorrow," Mrs. Benbow said breathlessly, in almost a child's voice. "Two for joy!"

Another flash came, and another; a storm of falling stars. "Three for marry," she continued. "Four for die. Five for silver. Six for lead. Seven for fire. Eight for ice. Nine for children. Ten . . ." Her voice trailed away.

Watching her head incline to Machray's shoulder and his arm swing around her, Andrew felt a quickening in his throat and a longing he had pretended had withered in him.

10

"Fire Creek Ranch,
October 26, 1883

"*Dearest Cissie:*
"Thank you so much for your long letter, with news of my little mite of a son and of all of you. It is

74

frightening to learn he has been so ill without my knowing of it, but I am grateful that he has come safely around and is again his cheerful and healthy self.

"I am waiting with a great deal of impatience for the arrival of my herd from Iowa. Meanwhile I make watercolor sketches of the surrounding vistas, read in the shade at midday, and ride out in my range in the early mornings or late afternoons. I am brown as a walnut. The days are hot, the nights cold. Thunderheads built up swiftly, to produce brief, violent downpours.

"I have a new friend, whom I have named Rufus after a politician of my acquaintance, a gentleman similarly bold and evasive. Rufus is a pronghorn, handsomely striped. He is a connoisseur of art, for often when I set up my easel outside the shack the fellow will work his way closer and closer, until he is all but peering over my shoulder. One abrupt move on my part and he bounds off, to halt gazing back at me from a butte half a mile away.

"These days great Vs of southbound birds cross the sky, but the thickets near the shack and the groves along the creek are still loud with bird music. I have identified thrashers, wood thrushes, meadowlarks, robins, bluebirds, and song sparrows. At night I can hear the whippoorwill's boding call, and the little owls calling to each other in tremulous voices.

"Most nights I sleep outside the shack, wrapped in my buffalo robe, watching the stars and the steaming of my breath in the frigid air, listening to the night birds, to the snorting and stamping of a deer and, more distantly, coyotes wailing. I glory in my loneliness among these sounds that once were strange and fearful, and now are so familiar.

"I have, however, neighbors with whom I do not wish to become familiar. Yesterday, riding near the headwaters of Grassy Creek, I had an experience that will cause me some bad dreams.

"I had dismounted to lead Brownie along a narrow track in an area of tumbled slabs of hard, bluish clay where a butte had collapsed, when a buzzing began. The disquieting sound rose in pitch and volume like some vast quantity of liquid rapidly filling a container. I had blundered into a garden of rattlesnakes.

"The serpents were coiled upon every flat surface

75

within sight, heads erect and all pointed toward me, tails all raised and vibrating. The heads resembled flattened hands bent from scaly, brown-diamonded forearms. I stood there transfixed, with the reins jerking at my hand. The sound seemed to fill my head, and at the same time I was almost drawn on by some terrible fascination and yet so repulsed that icewater seemed to be coursing through my veins. At that moment Brownie began to buck violently, and I backed out of that venomous place with my heart beating like a triphammer.

"I feel that that city of snakes was a reminder to me that there are human 'snakes' also in the Bad Lands, two of which I have already encountered...."

In those days when the herd was trailing north, he finished each afternoon's ride on the top of the highest butte to gaze south for signs of it, squinting his eyes into the sun-hazed distance to see nothing. But on a Sunday morning there was a thin, tan dustcloud, like a cocoon, and he yipped with excitement.

He galloped out to meet Joe and Chally, and tried to assist at the river crossing, riding in tight arcs to head the stubborn, lowing, lurching brown and white animals that appeared to him fat as butterballs—his herd. They managed to funnel the cattle toward a narrow way between treacherous mudbanks, and across the shallow stream on a shoal of firm footing. He waved his hat, shouting, "Hoo!" and "Go there!" along with the Reuters.

On the western bank he watched with pride as the herd, attended by noise, dust, and confusion, spread out to graze on the brown-grassed terraces between Fire Creek and the river. Challis came to sit his wiry little pony beside him, dirty-faced above the paler mouth and chin where he had worn his bandanna.

"Moved them slow to keep the flesh on," he said. "Can't see they have gaunted much of any."

"They are fine-looking animals, Chally," he said. His face ached with his grin. They rode together to the site he had chosen for his house, Chally nodding in agreement to his plans. He and Joe would get to work on it first thing in the spring. Now they would be busy preparing for winter.

Joe was bringing in the saddle stock that had been purchased along with the herd, shooing along the fifteen cleanly trotting animals with his hat. "Look at the nose on that one!"

76

Andrew said. "We'll call him Cicero!" He heard himself, as though from a distance, laughing inordinately.

He had designed a brand, an *A* and an *L* with a common leg, which he had had the blacksmith in town make up into an iron. He was disappointed in the result, which resembled a badly made *N*. Chally said it would be called the "Lazy-N," as Machray's Ringcross had immediately become the "Puckered-A," and they might just as well start off calling it that themselves.

The next four days were dawn-to-dark hells of roping and branding, dust and heat, bruises and blisters. Each morning he ached so that he didn't think he would be able to rise and eat again the cook's flannely pancakes. But rise he did, before dawn, to eat and saddle up his cow pony again. He had never learned so much so quickly.

The day after they had finished the branding he was sitting on the corral fence watching Joe Reuter breaking one of the new horses when Joe jerked his head to indicate something behind him.

Machray was trotting toward them on a tall, white-faced stallion. He wore a round-crowned hat with a leather band, a leather jacket with fringed sleeves, gauntlets, and a red and yellow kerchief knotted at his throat. Cradled on his arm was an over-and-under gun, a revolver in a holster rested on his thigh, and the stock of a rifle or shotgun protruded from a scabbard slung alongside his mount's neck. His face was a mask of shadow beneath the broad hat brim.

Andrew swung off the fence and went out to meet him. Machray reined up his stallion.

"Understood you'd brought your herd in, so I came down for a look-see," he said in an unfriendly voice.

"You are welcome," Andrew said. This was a very different man from the affable host at Widewings, and he felt a twisting of resentment as he stood at his caller's stirrup, a kind of historical inferiority of a man afoot to one mounted.

Machray said, "I must tell you that I do not accept your claim to range rights on the pastures south of my fence. I am used to grazing livestock there."

"I do not accept your objection," he said, folding his arms. Machray stared grimly down at him. Joe Reuter, who shied at any sign of contention, had contrived to disappear.

"Some hired bullies came here to try to frighten me from

this range," Andrew went on. "I did not suppose that they could have been your men."

"They were certainly not!" Machray said.

"I must tell you that I am here to stay."

Red-faced, Machray grimaced and slapped a gauntleted hand on his thigh. There was a silence. Machray peered toward the shack. "Is that an easel I see, Livingston?" he said in a milder voice. "Perhaps I could see some of your work."

"Fine," he said, retreating as the big man dismounted. Still carrying his armament, Machray followed him to the shack.

By the dusty, quartered light ray through the window glass, Andrew showed his guest his sketches of deer, elk, antelope, and mountain sheep, the many renderings of the buffalo, and the water-colors he had been doing lately. The sketches of the roping and branding at the roundup especially interested Machray. He leaned the long gun against the wall and braced both fists on the table top, studying one drawing of himself and two cowboys in almost a Laocoon grouping, his legs with the rolled-down stockings straddled, trunk turned, a thick arm raised beckoning, mouth open to shout a command.

"Very fine, this," he said. "Like to buy it."

"It's yours as a gift."

The green eyes squinted, the jaw stiffened and lengthened. "I said I'd buy it. Name your price, man."

"It's not for sale."

"I won't have it, then!"

"Very well!" he said. He shuffled the sketches back together and returned them to their portfolio. Machray swung around to examine the half-completed watercolor on the easel just outside the door.

"Colors are quite monotonous just now," he said gruffly. "In the spring you see some color, but the endless duns and tans and grays of this season are wearing. Ah, it is a damnable place in so many ways!"

"I assume you like it or you wouldn't be here."

"Oh, aye, I like it here. But here don't seem to like me." Machray removed his hat, poked a finger through a hole in the crown, and wiggled it. Andrew whistled.

"Just now?"

"Not an hour ago. That is number eight."

"Holes in your *hat?*"

Machray barked a laugh. "Bullets whistling by." He continued to wiggle his finger in the hole. "This one was the closest yet. Of course they are not seeking to do me damage. Or so it appears. But there is always the thought that this laddie may try to cut it too fine."

"Who is he?"

"Ah, I don't know that. More than one, I suspect. I am not popular with my neighbors, you know. They object to my person, my land, my fence, even my abattoir, it seems. It is a puzzle. You'd think they'd see that what's to the benefit of the Bad Lands is to their benefit. Well, I have stopped trying to understand them."

"I understand their objections to your fence."

Machray replaced his hat and looked at him coldly. "Do you, now? Well, you had better get used to it. You are all going to have to follow suit, you know, or one day soon you will have grangers settling on your range thicker than crab lice in a tinker's crotch. How many head did you say you are running?"

"Something over five hundred."

"And thinking of putting in more, I imagine, if my own experience serves. Wait until you see how *your* neighbors object to that." He glared at Andrew, then stepped back inside the shack to open the portfolio again. "I *would* like this sketch very much, you know. Like to take it to my wife."

"Please have it."

"Well, I believe I will, then. Thanks."

Outside, blinking in the bright sun, Machray carefully rolled the sketch, and picked up his long gun.

"By the way, Livingston, *Aurora* will be coupled onto the eastbound on December 15. I repeat that you are welcome to accompany me to New York, if that fits in with your plans."

"I'd like that very much. Count me in."

"Very well, then." Machray took his leave, and Andrew stood watching his neighbor ride off into the northern buttes on his tall stallion, the rolled sketch fastened by thongs behind his saddle. He did not tell Chally that Machray has disputed their claim to range rights on the pastures they called "Sloping Bottoms."

11

"Dearest Cissie:

"The enclosed bills are all correct and I should greatly like them to be paid, if they could be got to Uncle.

"I will be seeing all of you very soon, for I leave here on the 15th with Lord Machray in his private railway car. None of the large ranchmen out here will winter in the Bad Lands if they have the means to go elsewhere, and Machray will embark from New York for Scotland to spend the ensuing months with his wife and newborn son. I am looking forward to the journey as well as my destination, for Machray is an amusing companion when not in a black Caledonian mood. He is a changeable man, certainly, for he and I were involved in what might have become a bitter quarrel over grazing rights. Yet he appears to harbor no grudges.

"It has been storming, and we have had a first snow-fall. The Indian-summer haze lifted to higher altitudes, so that there came a kind of gauzy curtain between the earth and the sun, which lost its halos and the brackets of sun dogs we had become used to. Then the sky turned green, the wind began distantly to moan, and snow to fall. The wind howled closer and closer until it was gusting around our tight little shack, blowing bits of snow as sharp as glass. It was very cold. Now everything is white.

"Suddenly I am feeling an anxiety to be gone, lest I be trapped here, that is comical in its intensity. After all, I have been repeatedly warned that wintering is hard in the Bad Lands—meaning that it is hard for 'greenhorns.'

"I believe I will go into Pyramid Flat in a day or two, and put up at the hotel. The Bad Lands in this season seems a rather forbidding place. . . ."

The eastbound, with Machray's private car Aurora *coupled* behind, drove across the prairies in a dreary, sleeting rain.

Machray was very proud of *Aurora*. "It is the only decent way to travel, Livingston," he said. "My backers disapprove thoroughly; my wife as well! But a man of my station simply must have such a convenience or expect shabby treatment in many other respects!"

They awaited a morning through-train to New York in the wetly gleaming maze of tracks of the Chicago yards, and at dinner in *Aurora*'s mahogany and brass interior toasts were proposed while Dickson piped and poured burgundy.

"By God, it is a blessing to a man to have his wife and bairn awaiting him!" Machray said. "You will be seeing your own lad much sooner than I, Livingston. They will be fine friends one day, those two. Grow up with some space around them!"

Machray confided that he had got himself into a "fearful pickle" once when he came through Chicago in *Aurora*. "Consequently it seems best to celebrate right here where we are. Not at my best in cities, you know." And he declaimed:

"I see the City in a thicked cloud.
 Of business, than of smoke; where men like Ants,
 Toil to prevent imaginary Wants!"

When Dickson had left the car on some errand, Machray said to Andrew, "I am determined upon fidelity during this journey. It is the only course I will allow myself!" He went to bed early.

At the other end of the car, Andrew lay awake listening to the clanking, the hissing of steam, and chuffing of trains coming and going. The bones of his skull ached from the red wine he had drunk. He was thinking of his own son. He had forgotten the boy's fourth birthday, and the neglect seemed to him unforgivable.

Aurora was not coupled to an eastbound express until the next afternoon. Andrew read copies of months-old magazines in an easy chair as they rolled eastward through the twilight, Machray having disappeared forward. All at once a chattering company trooped into the car, small, dark, lively men and women in formal attire, very noisy in an unfamiliar language. Machray brought up the rear, waving his arms to shepherd them inside, half again as tall as his charges. He called to Dickson to open a case of Monopole.

The newcomers, Italians, swarmed around Andrew, filling the car, handling its accoutrements and pointing things out to one another admiringly. Two small, mole-spotted men came to stand with him, smiling, bowing, and handshaking. A taller, big-bellied fellow of great dignity also joined him. Several of the young women were of striking appearance, and one was beautiful, tall and statuesque, with a remarkable bosom. Dickson hurried to ice champagne, while Machray, smiling and courtly, made his way through his guests.

"Livingston, imagine what I have happened upon! This is the Petrocelli Opera Company of Rome!" Introductions were performed, with more smiling, bowing, and handshaking. The impresario, Petrocelli, was one of the small, mole-spotted men, wearing rings, it seemed, on every finger. Signor Vacelli, the leading tenor, was big-belly, and the lady with the magnificent bosom Mme Martini-Andrescu. The diva wore her black hair in long ringlets against her white shoulders, and possessed flashing eyes and an eagle mannerism of presenting one profile and then the other. She had a beauty mark on one rouged cheekbone.

"I am going to contract for them to open my opera house in Pyramid Flat!" Machray announced excitedly, and Dickson brought champagne on a tray, to a shrilling of enthusiasm from the ladies.

The empty green bottles accumulated on the mahogany counter as toasts were proposed to Machray's opera house as though it already existed, to the Petrocelli Opera Company, to Rome, to the United States, to Mme Martini-Andrescu, Machray, and finally even Andrew Livingston. A young singer with huge dark eyes hung on his arm and questioned him about himself in atrocious English. When Andrew mentioned that he had toured Italy two years ago and had fallen in love with Florence, she cried out, "Beautiful Florence!" It was her beloved home! She presented him with her calling card, violet scented, and he promised to call on her when next he visited Florence. He drank more champagne than he knew to be good for him.

Machray and Mme Martini-Andrescu were conversing in French on the subject of the opera to be selected for the opening of the opera house, the choice seeming to be between *Norma* and *Lucia di Lammermoor*, both of them Mme Martini-Andrescu's finest roles. Dickson replenished his glass again. The young soprano had been replaced by one of the mole-spotted men, who questioned him rather closely on Machray's resources. "Was the gentleman capable of all he was promising?" More than capable! "Was it safe to sign a contract with the milord?"

"Safe as opera houses!" he said, gesturing with deprecation. "Money is of no importance!" he continued. "Adventure is all, and enthusiasm the vehicle of adventure!" Professor Duarte's dictum did not seem to satisfy the Italian.

Meanwhile a harmonium had appeared, and a small, gray-haired man with waxed mustaches seated himself at the keyboard with a flourish of coattails. Music surged through the rocking car to cries of approval. The Petrocelli Opera Company reminded Andrew of a flock of exotic birds.

After considerable urging, Machray took up a pose beside the harmonium. A wrangle ensued, the gray-haired man shaking his head and helplessly holding up his hands. "Livingston!" Machray cried. "Can you play 'Green Grow the Rashes'?"

He could; he made his way to the harmonium and, bowing and excusing himself, replaced the gray-haired man. He pumped and played, while Machray sang, in a loud, tuneless voice:

"Green grow the rashes, O;
　Green grow the rashes, O;
　The sweetest hours that e'er I spend
　　Are spent amang the lasses, O!"

There were bravos and smacking of palms, but Andrew noticed at least one covert glance of dismay as Machray continued:

"There's nought but care for ev'ry han',
　In ev'ry hour that passes, O;
　What signifies the life o' man,
　　An' twere na for the lasses, O!"

"Join me, Livingston!" Machray commanded, and so he lent his voice to the choruses. After several verses, Mme Martini-Andrescu also joined in. They concluded to resounding applause, and he abandoned the harmonium to the gray-haired man and went to refill his champagne glass. Another young woman attached herself to his arm. This one spoke no recognizable English whatsoever.

Mme Martini-Andrescu now stood beside the harmonium, with her large eyes sparkling, body drawn up erect, and

83

hands tugging together before her bosom. Cords stood out in her white neck as she burst into song:

> *"Regnava nel silenzio*
> *Alta la notte e bruna . . .*
> *Colpia la fronte*
> *Un pallido raggio di etra luna—"*

Signor Vacelli joined her for the ensuing duet from the first act of *Lucia*. Another copule presented themselves for the quartet from *Rigoletto*, as big-belly sang:

> *"Bella figlia dell'amore*
> *Schiavo de' vezzi tuoi—"*

They finished to a storm of applause. Machray's face gleamed like a polished red apple as he urged more singing. Dickson came past with another champagne bottle. . . .

Andrew wakened at first light in the jolting, keening car, with a headache like a steam drill and a desert for a mouth. Outside his cubicle the mess of empty and half-empty glasses, champagne bottles, and ashtrays overflowing with cigar butts was depressing in the extreme, and he saw from a disarray of clothing on the divan that Machray had not been able to hold his determination upon fidelity on this journey. He went back to bed again.

But last night's beautiful songs still rang in his head, and he remembered Machray seated beside him for a moment as he reclined in his drunkenness within that whirling company of bright birds, saying:

"What can a man do, Livingston? What's there to do when the best of life comes up to grab you, and give you a good shake? Can a man pass it by? *Can he?* I say he had better not!"

12

A week after he had seen Machray off on the Carolla, Southampton bound, on a bright, brisk, end-of-December day he walked arm in arm with his sister up the hill that surmounted Prester Head, on the metaled road winding between the dark trunks of locust trees. Sometimes the "house on the hill" would come into view in fragments between the tree trunks—tall stone chimney, windows boarded over with gray planks, broad verandas. Lower down, among the treetops, were visible the chimneypots of the old house, where he and his sister had been born, and his father and uncle before them. Beyond, the waters of the Sound gleamed in brilliant sunlight.

They had already agreed several times that it was a beautiful day, this day of his return to Prester Head. Now they mounted the curving road in silence. Soon the pond would be visible.

He listened to the beating of his heart as they came around a bend and it lay beneath them, round as an eye and glittering with the gold coins of sun, the rickety pier with its green-mossed piles unchanged, the boats put up for the winter. On the brown-grassed bank where the dripping bodies had lain, plump Miss Connell sat in a striped canvas folding chair. The three children, all in white, played around her, the two cousins teasing the brown spaniel, Lee squatting alone intent upon something between his feet.

His heart seemed softly to fold upon itself as the small figure, hair so fair it appeared white, rose and scampered on plump legs to show something cupped in his hands to the nursemaid, small bright face thrust close to hers. Dodging, ears swinging, the spaniel yapped thinly in the bright air. Lee glanced up to where his father and his aunt stood, and waved. He waved in return.

"I can never thank you enough," he said to his sister.

"He is a happy child," she said.

"In two or three years, when he's old enough for his own pony, I'll take him back to the Bad Lands with me. I will be fascinated to watch him grow up there."

As they walked on, Cissie said, "So you really will make your life there."

"I have told you so!"

"It upsets James so much!" she said, laughing. "I believe he takes it as a reflection on our own staid lives, Andy! He brings it up in the most curious connections, so I know he thinks of it a great deal. Always disapproving, of course."

"When I asked him to come out for a hunt next fall he was very vehement. He would as soon make a trip to Cochin China!"

85

"Well, Andy, you are a bit righteous, you know. 'Filthy air of the city'; sky of iron and brass, and all of that!"

"I'll try harder to conceal my righteousness," he said, patting her hand. Once he and Elizabeth had loved to stroll up this path at sunset. Now he considered himself shallow that he felt so little emotion, remembering.

"Nevertheless, I believe I've found my true place," he continued. "There is a feeling of every man with an equal chance, no one better than another. Perhaps we must always go to the frontier to find the fellowship that the nation's Founders intended."

"Can it be such an Eden?" Cissie asked quietly.

"Of course not. There is contention, and I've been badly frightened. But perhaps so were our original ancestors." Then he laughed. "Oh, I see what you're getting at. You think I *endow* too much. Places. People. The Bad Lands an Eden. Elizabeth a saint."

They plodded on. "You do read my mind, Andy, dear."

"That if I hadn't endowed her with sainthood, I would not have taken her death so hard. Turned against our new house, the bank, politics, my life in the East, the East itself, my life itself! Almost against my country! That is quite an endowment!" He managed to laugh again. "Poor Elizabeth!"

The house came into sight in its entirety. For a moment her hand urged him on, then desisted. "I think this is as far as I shall go this time, thank you," he said. The chimney was hazed with the sun's bright glisten.

"It is so sad to see it this way," Cissie said. "You must finish it, Andy." She had detached her arm from his and stood before him, smiling. She had a strong, angular face that he knew resembled his own, although she was a pretty woman. He regretted that his disapproval of James Brewster's life was so easily discernible, which life, although James was a lawyer and not a banker, was almost exactly the same as his own had not been long ago.

"What would you have done if you had discovered that Elizabeth was not a saint, poor thing?" Cissie asked. "For of course she was not. No one is, Andy."

Staring past her at the shimmering lines of the house crouched upon its hilltop, he said, "Maybe I did realize it. When she died in such a foolish accident."

"I wonder if she would ever have grown into an adult woman," Cissie said softly.

"Why would she, when she was such an adorable child?

When she so loved to be treated as an adorable child?" His throat had swelled to choke him.

She took his arm again as they started back down the hill. When he could trust his voice again, he said, "I suppose I overendow the Republican Party also. The only hope for progress and reform! Yet before we can carry the fight to Tammany we must do battle with the Bourbons of our own party! The dragon Holdfast is everywhere! I suppose he will even turn up in my Eden!"

They came in sight of the pond again. Miss Connell and the children had returned to the house.

"Herman diGarmo is in despair that you will not involve yourself in politics again," Cissie said.

"I think neither he, nor you, dear sister, believes that I intend to make my regular life in the Bad Lands."

"Well, I do believe Papa would have approved," she said." But Andy, you really must call upon poor old Mr. Darcy."

"I know I must not proscrastinate any longer."

"I believe he took it harder than you did. Perhaps she really was a saint. Perhaps that is what I always resented in her."

"I don't believe you ever resented her, or anyone! You yourself are too much a saint for that!"

"Oh, no, I am not! And the first person who will tell you so is James!" They walked on down toward the old house, invisible behind the chestnut trees, where lunch was waiting, laughing and easy together again.

In the greenhouse of the tall old house on Washington Square, Kermit Darcy sat in his wheelchair with a green plaid robe covering his knees in the steaming heat. Surrounding him were lush, fat-leaved plants, brilliant flowers, dwarf fruit trees and, radiating off behind him, corridors in which shelves bore still more thickets of greenery. Hunched and scowling, he watched Andrew cross the coco-matting runner, tucking his spotted, skinny hands under his robe as though to insure there would be no question of shaking hands. His bitter old jaw made him resemble a moray eel.

"How are you, Mr. Darcy?"

"Well as I look," Elizabeth's grandfather snapped, in his duck quack of a voice. "You may take off your coat. I'm told it's too hot in here for anyone alive."

"Thank you, sir." He removed his jacket and hung it on the coat rack. Kermit Darcy flipped a hand to indicate the white wicker chair, and he seated himself, mopping his brow with his handkerchief.

"Heard you'd gone off to Dakota Territory to drown your sorrows killing wild beasts," Darcy said.

"Yes, sir, something like that. I—"

"Prefer to drown mine making things live."

"I've become a stockraiser in the Bad Lands. I—"

"What've you come here for?"

"Sir, I don't know how I have offended you, but I would like very much to make amends." He mopped his steaming forehead again.

"Promised to care for my granddaughter and sent her out in a leaky boat."

He gasped as though he had been struck in the belly. "That's unfair!"

Darcy shrugged. In the open collar of his robe his Adam's apple bounced in his scrawny neck. He rubbed at an eye with a gnarled hand. "That lovely girl. Her parents dead, and now she's dead. And I'll be dead soon enough."

"I loved her too, Mr. Darcy!"

"Didn't say you didn't. Said you were careless. If you love something you should take care of it. Guard it. Kiting around with a bunch of politicians leaving her alone out in that great barn of a place."

Carefully he leaned back in the wicker chair. "I believe it is my politics you disapprove of, Mr. Darcey."

"Pay no attention to politics," the old man said. "Little men squabbling. People trying to get something for nothing. When I'm told I have a troublemaker in the family, I say you are no part of my family. Got no family. No friends either. Nobody's friend to a dying man, afraid it might be catching. Well, it is catching all right, they have already caught it, and not from me!" He shot his jaw out.

Timor Mortis conturbat me. Pity dissolved his anger at Darcy's unjust accusation. "You have a family, sir, whether you recognize *me* or not," he said.

The muddy old eyes with their yellowed whites stared ferociously into his.

"He is a beautiful little boy, four now. I believe you could not help but see Elizabeth in him. I'd like to bring him to you."

Darcy swung his chair and propelled it toward one of the aisles of greenery, then halted and swung back. "Why would you want to bring him here?"

"I would like him to have known an ancestor whose grandfather signed the Declaration of Independence."

"Before it's too late, eh?" Darcy quacked.

"Yes, sir," he said. "Because I believe it is important that he be aware of the line of continuity back to the Founders. In times when we forget what we are about."

"I'm told your politics are irresponsible," the old man said. "No politics anymore myself, except the politics of heaven and hell."

"I'd like to bring him to see you next week, sir," he said.

"Well, bring him along, bring him along then, if that's what you want," old Darcy said. "I'll try not to frighten the lad."

He sat across from Herman diGarmo in a German lager-beer saloon on Sixth Avenue, to which he had been summoned.

"I hear you are joining the Free Trade Club," Herman said, scowling. He shot his cuffs as he raised the pitcher to fill Andrew's glass, a rather dandy little man with a perpetual shadow of beard on his sallow cheeks. He wore a fashionably cut suit and clean linen; he had the courage to appear a "dude" when his fellow politicians tended to be rough, ungrammatical, and none too clean personally. He was a product of New Jersey slums, had attended a small Roman Catholic college in Newark, and had found his vocation as a political boss in an era of bossism, but not of reflective, progressive bosses.

Andrew replied that what he had heard was true.

"You must not do that."

"Why not, if I am an advocate of the reduction of duties on raw materials?"

"Another Harvard idea," diGarmo said with a sigh. "You are a Republican, Andy, and one of the party's principles is high tariffs."

"Nevertheless—"

"I am trying to prevent your past from ruining your future. If you wish to work for the reduction of duties on raw materials, your work will not be effective unless you work within a party framework. What party will you work within, then, the Democratic?"

He didn't answer.

"What is more important to you?" diGarmo asked. "The reduction of duties on raw materials, or civil service reform? I believe a man should not scatter his powers unnecessarily."

Andrew glanced in irritation around the saloon. The bartender was drawing a beer for a man in a black overcoat and a black derby hat placed squarely on the top of his head. Outside cabs passed in a gloomy street.

"Herman," he said, "I don't have any future in the Republican Party."

"Ah, well," diGarmo said. "Then you are not going to be effective in the cause of free trade or civil service reform or anything else, are you?"

"Maybe some day a new party will be established—a party of principle."

"Some people would just have to dig in and work for *that*, wouldn't they?" DiGarmo beckoned to the barkeep; pickled eggs were brought on thick white crockery saucers. Andrew watched diGarmo peeling his egg with neat fingers, flicking aside the bits of shell, as precise in this as in everything he bent his mind to. He skinned his own egg and munched the sour flesh, washing it down with draughts of lager.

"I don't understand why you think I have a political future in the state," he said. "I have high ideals, which are baggage a practical politician can hardly carry along with him. I am stuffy by nature; I don't mix well. I am not fond of Irish-Catholic politicians, although I hope my prejudices do not show. I—"

"Wouldn't have to worry about Irish-Catholic politicians in the Twenty-first," diGarmo said.

He was struck silent. The Twenty-first Assembly District was the one most apt to take his fancy, half "diamondback"—the fashionable Madison and Fifth Avenue purlieus where blue-bloods were supposed to feast on diamondback terrapin—and half West Side slums, more German than Irish. So that was why he had been summoned here.

"Now, just a minute, Herman—"

Smiling as though to deprecate his gratitude, diGarmo said, "You can have your cake and eat it too. Assembly term is January to late spring, so you can go on playing Far West rancher. Bingham's got his eye on larger things than the Assembly."

A bite of egg stuck dryly in Andrew's throat as he shook his head. Appearing theatrically stunned, Herman closed his eyes and also shook his head. He took a long swallow of beer. Finally he said, "But oblige me by not joining the Free Trade Club. That would be *very* heavy baggage to carry when you begin thinking of moving on to larger things than the Assembly. Now: Who do you favor as the party's candidate for the presidency in June?"

"Nobody."

"Nobody!" diGarmo echoed, and tossed up his hands in disgust.

"Nobody who has a chance. I believe that the nation suffered as great a loss with Garfield's assassination as with Lincoln's. And the party. For now we have General Arthur. I assume he will be renominated."

"No, he will not be. Not because the public won't vote for him, which it wouldn't, but because he has continued Garfield's patronage policies. He will not be forgiven that. He is not a bad man, Andy."

"I'm afraid I remember him as the member of Conkling's gang who was forced to resign as collector of customs for the Port of New York."

"Men change," diGarmo said with a shrug. "Nor James Blaine either, then?"

"If the party is mottled with corruption, surely Blaine is one of the darker spots. Letters have been published that prove it."

"You disclaim Chester Arthur and James Blaine, but your ideals are too high to work for anyone else. You'll have no complaints, then!"

"Oh, I'll have complaints aplenty," he said, grinning.

"Complaining to a bunch of cows. Or are you thinking of entering Dakota politics when the Territory gets its statehood?"

"Maybe," he said. "The air is cleaner out there."

"Exciting times are coming in Albany, you know. The Independent Republicans are in a *very* interesting situation. A balance of power. As you know, we're already getting some things accomplished in the way of civil service reform, playing the 'Stalwarts' against the 'Half-breeds.' "

"No, Herman."

DiGarmo squinted at him. "What would you think of running for city comptroller, Andy?"

"Herman, no!"

DiGarmo shook his head dolefully. "Hard to make responsible citizens face their responsibilities. So difficult. Sometimes I think it is a hopeless case." He continued to shake his head. Finally he asked offhandedly what Andrew thought of Edmunds of Vermont.

"Straightest man in the Senate!"

Nodding, diGarmo bent his attention to the saucer, driving the untidy flecks of eggshell into a compact pile with deft proddings of his little finger. "I believe the Independents will be backing Edmunds for the nomination," he said and rose, pulling down the tabs of his vest over his neat little belly. He produced a cigar and lit it.

"What's all this about Edmunds?" Andrew demanded.

"Maybe you'd better come up to the convention in Utica and find out," diGarmo said.

In the third-story room of the Commercial-Grand Hotel of Utica, Andrew sat in the smoky air watching diGarmo on the bed, vest unbuttoned and cravat tugged askew, glancing down a list of names with a grim expression. Around the table, upon which was centered a metal water pitcher beaded with cold, sat the rest of them. Charley Fletcher of Otsego County, Carl Schroeder of Niagara, the others all assemblymen from New York City districts, except for himself, the vice-president of the New York Republican Club. They were the Independents, who carried the balance of power between the adherents of Chester A. Arthur and those of James G. Blaine at the state convention.

DiGarmo passed the list back to Fletcher, who was acting as secretary. He lit a cigar and waved smoke from in front of his face as Andrew said, "I believe we can play the Arthur men to support Edmunds by threatening them with Blaine, but not the Blaine men by threatening Arthur. Isn't that an advantage, anyway?"

DiGarmo closed one eye in contemplation. "*You* look those numbers over, Charley."

Fletcher totted down the page with the eraser of his pencil, grimaced, shrugged, nodded.

"What'll we have to give up?" Schroeder asked.

"There are the Reform Charter Bill, the Aldermanic Bill, the Bureau of Elections Bill, and the Tenure of Office Bill that we have gone on the line for," diGarmo said, ticking the bills off on the fingers of his hand. "The Reform Charter is probably safe. The Bureau of Elections will be in danger. We'll get the Aldermanic, but if the governor vetoes the Tenure of Office, which he can safely do if we don't bring it in with a good majority, the Board of Aldermen will not be much affected. No question but that we will be giving up something by taking the New York delegation in for Edmunds. Who will go no further anyhow."

"I don't believe we ought to think in those terms," Schroeder said.

"How can you be so certain he will go no further?" Andrew said. "Surely the party must realize that Arthur is the weakest candidate we could nominate, and Blaine the most notorious."

"Never underestimate the power of entrenched jobbery," diGarmo said, waving smoke away from his face.

Someone laughed. Simon Dexter said, "I would rather underestimate the power of entrenched jobbery than the power of the party to regenerate itself!"

"Well, that is a fine motto," Alexander Ditson said. "But, Herman, how do we know that the Old Guard will not become so infuriated by our coup as to cut off all the reform legislation that we have under consideration?"

"I do not overestimate the tendencies of the Old Guard to work smoothly in its own interests."

Again there was laughter. Andrew breathed the fumes of tobacco, perspiration, and political concentration, and dreamed of the Tiepolo blue of the sky of the Bad Lands and the feel of the muscles of a cow pony at a lope, carrying him over his range.

"Well, then," diGarmo said, "do we go into the national convention as Edmunds' delegates, and chance the consequences?"

"The Massachusetts delegation will be for Edmunds also, remember," Andrew said.

"Or do we consolidate our position in Albany?" diGarmo continued. Cigar plugged into his mouth, he glanced from face to face. No one spoke. "Very well," he said. "It is regeneration over jobbery, then. Charley, let us examine the list of Arthurians and decide who is sweetly to reason with whom. For instance, does anyone have more than a nodding acquaintance with that antediluvian, cantankerous, purblind old sinner, Jeremiah Evans?"

He corked the cigar back into his lips and again gazed from face to face. Andrew stirred uneasily in his chair as the silence bore down. He felt soiled and sweat-stained. Finally he raised one finger.

"He's a friend of my wife's family. Her godparent, in fact."

"Friend of Kermit Darcy's?" diGarmo said.

He nodded.

"You will speak to him?"

He nodded again. He loosened his own cravat and collar button.

"It may be all that is necessary," Chester Bliss said.

"We had better leave Jennings alone until we discover how bloweth the Evans breeze," diGarmo said. "Who is next, Charley?"

"Rukeyser."

"I'll be pleased to sally forth to meet old Ben," Ditson said. "But I would also like to hold off until we hear Evans' reaction."

"I think that would be best," diGarmo said, knitting his fingers over his belly and blinking owlishly at Andrew. "Apparently it is your move, Andy."

So it was that he made an appointment the next morning with Jeremiah Evans, Elizabeth's godparent and Kermit Darcy's old friend, who, he knew, considered him an irresponsible politician, a socialist on many issues, and a "Prussian" in the matter of civil service reform. Probably he was listened to more carefully because of the power of the New York Republican Club, for all its dangerous tendencies, than because of "family connections," but Evans did seem to find his arguments worthy of consideration.

And so it was that the Independents of the state convention, or, as they came to be known," the Big Eight," playing on the distrust of Blaine, persuaded the Arthur men to support Senator Edmunds of Vermont, and thus carried the convention for him.

Andrew himself was selected a delegate-at-large for the national convention in Chicago in June, and it occurred to him that he had not been half so clever in convincing Jeremiah Evans as diGarmo had in inveigling him back into New York politics.

Book Two

1884

1

When she was a girl, Cora Benbow would tell the truth when asked how she had come to her profession. Later on she would give a man any story she thought would satisfy him. Now she did not sell anything of herself anymore and owed no man anything.

She was a woman of property. It had taken years, and a good deal of wear and tear, but she had got where she was before she was thirty. That had been a goal. Now she had the rest of her life planned so that in ten more years, before she was forty, she would retire. She had seen a town not far from Philadelphia, a friendly place of brick buildings and a square with grass and paths and curlicued iron benches where people sat in the sun. She would buy the general store there, and her transactions with men would be limited to selling them gum boots, chambray shirts, or perfume to take home to their wives on birthdays. Probably she would have a pug dog.

She came from a part of Missouri that was much fought over during the War Between the States. Her father was killed at Vicksburg. Their place was burnt twice, and each time she, her mother, and her brother returned to try to farm it again. A raiding party raped her and her mother, and broke her brother's arm when it was thought he might interfere—although all he had done was stand by with a silly grin. She was ten at the time and had always been pleased to think she had given those eight Yankees the smallpox, for she had broken out with it herself two days later.

When she was thirteen she was taking on flatboat crews on the riverboats, learning to speak with her mouth full of silver, for it was the only place she could keep the coins safe, and she managed to keep the family from starving in those terrible times. Then her mother died of consumption, and her brother left for Texas.

She went into a house in Memphis run by an old German couple who were the first people in her life who were kind to

97

her. She became Mrs. Schimmelpfennig's favorite and slept with her at first as the new girls always did. It was Mrs. Schimmelpfennig who dinned it into her to save her money. She was a very popular girl, for all her size or maybe because of it, and she kept a third of what she made but gave her money to Mrs. Schimmelpfennig to hold for her, and did not spend it on finery or buttonhook collections or throw it away on fancy men, whiskey, or cocaine. She was ambitious even then, although she had no idea what she was to do with her life, except that she knew she would not just drift downstream like the other parlorhouse girls. The Schimmelpfennigs kept her money for her because she didn't know where else to keep it safe, and they could have robbed her if they pleased. But they did not, and so she was lucky as well as ambitious.

When she was about eighteen she had a steady customer named Fred, a plump, pink-cheeked fellow of forty or so. He was a businessman in the river trade, and he wanted to set her up in a cottage on Aster Street. The Schimmelpfennigs said she could always come back if Fred did not marry her. Mrs. Schimmelpfennig was a romantic woman, always pleased and proud when her girls married well out of the house, and they made better wives than most whores, for she had taught them manners. Most of the girls, however, seemed unlucky in love or grew bored; they drifted back into a house or onto the street, which led to a crib in a big city and eventually the gutter and the potter's field. It was not a route Cora intended to follow.

Mrs. Schimmelpfennig warned her to keep herself dosed against constipation and not to take a drink waiting for Fred to come. Mrs. Schimmelpfennig disapproved of novels, but considered them better than whiskey.

She found that she did not have to pretend to be interested in Fred's business. When they were together, which was usually in the afternoons, she would ask him about his dealings. He was pleased to brag about them, and she learned the tricks of buying cheap and selling dear. Fred looked on his business as kind of great poker game, where he bluffed and tried to see the other fellow's cards and knew how to read all kinds of signs. She began spending time along the docks where it took the coldest eye she could muster to keep the men off, even though she dressed plainly and did not advertise herself. If she encountered Fred they would pretend not to know each other, which was exciting to him, and she enjoyed seeing the cargoes of bales of cotton, bags of cotton-seed, fancy iron stoves from Massachusetts, or gingerbread trim for houses.

It was a pleasant time in her life, for Fred was not a demanding lover and could easily be put off if she did not feel inclined. Sometimes his negotiations would take the head off his need of her, but if he had lost out to someone else's cleverness, then it would seem that he had to prove something by sawing her almost in half or taking her by the back door or nuzzling at her breast like some great pink-cheeked, bald-headed infant.

One day the biggest nigger she had ever seen came to the door and said he had a message from Mrs. Ketchel, who was Fred's wife. He pushed her back inside the kitchen and hit her in the face. She was a strong woman and put up a fight, but he gave her a bad beating. Her teeth were loose, both eyes swollen shut, and she was bathing her face when Fred came. It seemed his wife had set a detective on him, found out about the cottage, and hired the nigger to beat her up. Fred was so scared and so sorry that she went back to the Schimmelpfennigs with five thousand dollars. She put the money straightaway in the bank, because now she knew about banks.

The nearest she had ever had to a fancy man was a gambler named High Red, a skinny, very white-skinned fellow who was softspoken and gentle with her. One night he brought her a beautiful ruby ring he had won at a game of cards. She had never had a gift like that, for the money that Fred Ketchel had given her was a very different thing, and she found herself responding to Red's kisses as she had never responded to a man before.

But High Red got in trouble with another gambler, a fat fellow named Carolina Floyd, who carried a knife with which he was always paring his nails. High Red came to her, very shaky, his skin so milky pale it was as though you could see the blood running beneath it. His eyes were running too, like he had taken a bad chill. He said he owed Carolina Floyd money.

She asked him how much. It was six thousand dollars. She told him he had better leave town.

"That wouldn't do any good," High Red said. He took out his pocket handkerchief and mopped his eyes and blew his nose.

"You had better head for Mexico," she said.

He just shook his head and said again that that wouldn't do any good. "Corrie, will you lend me the money?"

"I don't have money like that," she said.

"Corrie, everybody knows you save your money."

"I mean I don't have any money for lending to high rollers," she said. She felt cold as an iceberg; she could feel the cold coming into her eyes.

"Corrie, he will cut me with his knife," High Red said. Then he began begging.

But she told him she knew that if she didn't lend him the money she would lose him, and if she lent him the money she would lose him and the money both. She took off the ruby ring and gave it back to him. He called her a cold-hearted woman and left, mopping at his eyes and blowing his nose. She wept for what she had done, and she never saw him after that. But she knew she would do the same thing again. She had seen too many girls lose their money to gambling men.

She left Memphis and headed for Leadville, where she had heard money could be made in a hurry. She had some of her savings in the Merchants' Bank in Memphis, and some of it still with the Schimmelpfennigs. Sometimes she would find herself worrying about that money in a way that was like her monthlies, that same dirty, nervous feeling, and almost a monthly thing too. She worried about it so much that she was afraid to ask them for it for fear she was going to find out she would never see it again. So she went to Leadville without it.

In Leadville the madam was a Mrs. Florian, a sickly woman who was unfair to the girls, having favorites that she would suddenly turn against, so that girls were always coming and going, and there were quarrels and hard feelings. Finally Mr. Middleton, who owned the house, asked Cora if she would take over, and she did. She threw Mrs. Florian out along with her mangy lap dog and put the place to rights in a hurry. Before the year was out she learned that Mr. Middleton was in trouble with mining stocks, and she made him an offer of money for the house and furnishings which he accepted.

So then she wrote Mrs. Schimmelpfennig for her money, and it came right back, along with three German girls, for she'd also asked if they had reliable girls to spare. Mrs. Schimmelpfennig wrote to congratulate her for moving up in the world, and said she had always known she was different since she first came to them in Memphis, big-eyed and rawboned and strapping, with an appetite she had never seen on a girl before. Mrs. S. was an honest woman; Cora had not met many men or women who were as good as that plump old German madam.

She had been in Leadville for two years when she had a chance to sell her house at a good profit. She had never liked that high, hard, cold town full of claim jumpers and contention. She traveled a bit before she settled in Pyramid Flat, which was only a railroad town then. She rented a place that burned down in the first month. So she decided to build her own house.

Little by little she provided the furnishings she had always wanted—teak, golden oak, and mahogany furniture; a five-octave little organ, cute as a button with mother-of-pearl inlays; Chinese vases; Venice glass lamp chimneys; chromos for the walls. She had a fine cook, a big Irisher woman with a face like a slab of corned beef; a housekeeper she could trust, a little humpbacked woman named Daisy who she thought would have died for her. Often Daisy went upstairs with men, so she made good money, and saved it, and would probably have her own house someday. Deformed girls were often popular, which was one of a number of things she accepted in men without understanding it. She herself had never suffered from the fact that she was almost six feet tall with a face corncob rough from smallpox. The most popular girl in the house in Leadville had a shriveled leg, though she had the face of an angel above it.

She also hired a spunky little fellow named Wax, who had a reputation with a six-shooter. He was polite and soft-spoken, though every month or two the liquor would get to him until he was screaming pink snakes. Pyramid Flat had been a hard place then, with cowboys target practicing at the windows, buffalo hunters who were a quarrelsome lot and the railroad construction crews of Swedes and Irishmen who loved to get drunk and bash each other. Wax had his hands full in those days.

She was proud of her house. She loved to wander through in the early mornings while the girls were still sleeping, the quiet and the cool, and the smells of body powder, Lysol, dead cigars, spilled liquor, full chamberpots, and soapy slop water, for Daisy would already be cleaning up. She loved the musky smell the house had.

There was nothing much else she loved at that time. Not any of the girls, fools every one and bound for the gutter, except Daisy. Not men, although sometimes she would remember High Red, especially the flesh of his fundament, soft and white as kid gloves, which would make her shudder in a queer way.

For a while Jake Boutelle camped in her parlor, giving her slidy glances and winks as though they had some fine secret together, and making mysterious remarks. Finally she told him that she was not interested in taking on a business partner, if that was what he was hinting at. Doc Micklejohn had hung around the same way, but she had realized that it was being with a bunch of women that fascinated him. He loved to dose the girls with Autumn Leaf Extract for Females or Cedron Bitters if they showed the slightest sign of being off color, and he would listen by the hour to them spin out their lies of how they had been wronged, or lost the only man who ever truly loved them.

Bill Driggs was the first man in Pyramid Flat she was interested in. He had enough height and force to him to make her know he was a man to be respected, and, though rough-spoken, was gentle as only a big man could be, and respectful of her. He had a queer pride to him, though, and would insist on paying her always, saying he would feel a pimper otherwise, and he would not come when he had no money, which was often.

But one day Daisy had called her to the window, where the other girls were looking out and giggling, and there, passing in the street, was the biggest man she had ever seen, bigger than Bill, bigger than the nigger who had beaten her up in Memphis. He was riding a black horse, and he wore a fawn-colored suit, a cravat with a diamond stickpin that looked as big as a muffin, and a black slouch hat that swept down on one side and up on the other. He rode by on the prancing horse waving a hand at them where they watched from the windows, and at the cowboys and the loungers along the street gaping at him with their mouths hanging open like fly-catchers. Behind him rode a clean-shaven, soldierly fellow, very straight-backed in a short jacket, with a queer-looking thing tucked under his arms with sticks poking out of it. The big man swung around to shoot a finger at the other, who lipped one of the sticks and high squealing music began. The two of them went on down the street with the dust drifting behind them, the big man waving this way and that even when he had run out of anyone to wave to, and the soldier one behind playing that music that seemed to penetrate to

102

somehwere behind her eyes. All the girls were clamoring—who is it, what could it be, they had never seen the likes of it—and that afternoon. they learned it was a Scotch lord named Machray. And perhaps all of them knew from that first glimpse that Pyramid Flat, and the Bad Lands, were never going to be the same again.

That night he came to the house alone. She didn't know what to make of him, although the girls all hung on him, with his lovely way of talking, as though he was the all-time nonesuch. He drank more whiskey than was good for him, and bawled out filthy poetry in a queer, Scotch way of talking, like glue in his mouth. She was considering calling Wax to put him out for the filthy talk when he got up, shook off the girls that had been clustering about him, and came over to her where she stood on the bottom stair.

"I crave a big woman, madam," he said, looking at her as though he had been sober all the time and only humbugging the drunkenness.

She said it was not her practice to go upstairs with the clients.

He bowed his head politely. "I am a big man, as you see, madam, and cannot be satisfied without a partner of large frame and expansive spirit."

She said that Annie was a good-sized girl, if that was his preference.

He kept looking at her, in that way he had, as though when he was speaking to a person he was thinking of nothing else in the world but her. "Madam," he said, "that is avoirdupois, not amplitude."

So she had taken him to her room. He had a terrible scar on his shoulder that made the backs of her legs crawl to look at. He had got it at Tel-el-Kebir, he said; in Egypt with Wolseley, fighting the pasha Arabi. She had never heard of any of those except Egypt.

He made love to her as though it was her pleasure that mattered and his own was of no importance. It was something she had never encountered before. Later he told her it made his ballocks churn in a most delightful manner to hear her groaning and squealing. It was not that he had such a length on him, for she had known men hung like stallions that all they knew to do was poke and brag. But because of the way he had made love to her she had opened in a way she never opened before, and deep in her he had touched some springs she had not even known were there. That first night she had realized that Lord Machray owned her if he wanted to take possession, and, after he had gone, she knew she was mooning for him worse than the most foolish young whore believing her own lies of lost loves. And Machray had claimed her, and had owned her for two years now.

He would speak of his wife back in Scotland sometimes, a wee bit of a thing, with red gold hair, beautiful as a Highland morning. Other times, though, he would sound as though he hated Lady Machray. Once he said she was such a lady she liked to pretend there wasn't anything of her below the waist. He said that she slept sitting up in bed because she had heard it was better for the organs. She didn't admit she had any of those, mind; and he himself didn't doubt that if she was opened up there would be inside her only something like the inside of a rosebud, with dew on it. That winter he announced that he must return to Scotland to perform his duty. His old father, the marquess, was ailing, and it was time a little laird was produced, although he did not know how the conception was to be accomplished, since the process would involve parts Lady Milly did not admit she possessed.

There was a song he had sung once when he was in her bathtub and she was scrubbing his back with the brush. He had a poor voice, loud and flat, with no music in it:

"Me gudewife's sa' modest,
    When she is at meat,
    A laverock's leg, or a tittlin's wing,
    Is mair than she can eat:
    But when she's in our bed at e'en,
    Betwixt me an' the wa',
    She is a glutton deevil,
    And swallows cods and a'!"

When he finished he swung around on her, very solemn, and said she must not think the first part of his song had referred to her, nor the last to his own saintly Lady Milly.

Although he knew so many things and had seen so much of the world, she came to realize that there were areas in which she was wiser than he. She would listen to him talking of his enterprises as once she had listened to Fred Ketchel, and realize that Machray was no businessman at all. He had a book, which he took great stock in, called *The Beef Bonanza, or How to Get Rich on the Plains*. The book was full of whoppers. The man who wrote it claimed, in one place or another, that there were profits of 11, 21, 33, and even 40 percent per annum to be made raising cattle on the Great Plains. Machray had managed to buy government land, as well as railroad land, and so he had private range, and fenced, where every other cattleman in the Bad Lands was trumpeting free grass and hallelujah. Machray was right and they were not, though they called him a foreign despoiler and made life miserable for him any way they could think of. If the range was public property there was just going to be more and more public on it, with their cows. Still, he had spent a ton of money and kept on spending more on what seemed to her pure foolishness, though she had seen him have a tantrum like a spoiled child when one of the clerks from that brick building brought him a stack of bills that had to be paid.

So though Machray's Ring-cross Ranch was as big, he said, as a dukedom in Scotland, it was not showing any profit at all, much less 11 or 21 or 33 or 40 percent per annum. Yet right away he had jumped in with both feet to build a meatpacking plant that was going to drive Phil Armour to the wall. Next thing, because he was having trouble working matters out with the railroad, he was full of starting a company that would own its own refrigerator cars, building icing stations to go with it; he would keep the cars busy in the off seasons transporting salmon from the west coast to the eastern markets.

He could mesmerize people, taking in such a grand fashion that in some way his listeners became a part of his dreams. But it was as though he mesmerized himself at the same time. He would make himself drunk spinning out the wonders he was going to accomplish in the Bad Lands, as though it were not just the acres he owned, it was the Bad Lands themselves, and the whole West.

She could not help thinking how much better she would be at running the Ring-cross than Machray. She knew how to write contracts, bank money for the best interest, buy cheap and sell dear, and watch the other fellows' eyes or fingers with the cards, things women were not supposed to be able to do well. She could do them well, and so she was a madam. Machray did not do them well. He considered it beneath him to engage in making money. In a way she agreed with him. He should be free to pursue his dreams without clerks with gartered-up sleeves and green eyeshades pushing stacks of due-bills in front of him. Sometimes she thought he considered it nobler to lose money than to make it.

The money he had brought to the Bad Lands was not his. It was not his father's either, for he had told her the old marquess hadn't a bean. The money had been lent by Lady Milly's father and some associates of his that Machray called "the jews," although she came to understand that they weren't really Jews, only Scotchmen from a different part of Scotland than Machray.

If Machray had married Lady Millicent to get the money to come out to the Bad Lands to play his great game, how was he better than a whore who went upstairs to turn a trick for two dollars? And, in another way, wasn't Machray just a high roller like High Red, only for bigger stakes? And wasn't he going to lose out to some pack of Carolina Floyds in the end, that he called "the jews"?

The summer that Lady Milly was pregnant the house on the bluff was only started and Machray was still living in his railway car on the siding. One day he decided that nothing would do but that she, Cora, go to Chicago with him.

They traveled to Chicago in *Aurora*, with Dickson to wait on them at mealtimes, and champagne on ice. She undressed and dressed so many times in those two days that she complained she would wear out her buttonholes, but Machray said those were not the ones he worried about. Besides, he would buy her lovely raiment in Chicago. She was to throw out her Pyramid Flat weeds and be a great Chicago lady.

He did just that, too, shopping with her in fancy stores, the like of which she had never seen before, and, at the couturier's sitting planted in a chair with his legs spread apart, wearing spats, a checked waistcoat, and a carnation in his lapel, conversing in French with the fat, mustached Frenchwoman who was overseeing the trying-on of costumes. He chose the gown she was to wear and then interested himself in the underclothing, fingering the silks and laces, and the gloves. She loved trying on gloves, her elbow braced on the kidskin pillow while the girl worked the glove down on her hand, finger by finger, and then down the palm, and the arm, and the buttons fastened with a buttonhook, while Machray nodded and smiled. He bought her some fine cologne too, to splash between her breasts and at the nape of her neck where it was his pleasure to nuzzle her, and then they strolled on to the milliner's, where she spent two hours seated before the triple mirror trying on hats with different arrangements of ribbons, feathers, and birds, with foot-long hatpins, veils, and, when Machray had finally settled on one, elaborate as a pearl-gray wedding cake, a great dustcover for riding in open carriages. All the while he sat behind her smoking his cigar and looking pleased with himself. He directed one of the girls to paint her face for her, liquid rouge for her cheeks brushed on with a tiny sponge, and lip pomade. All too clearly in the glass she could see her roughened cheeks and the darkening of hair on her upper lip. Though she knew her eyes were her best feature, it had never been a face she wished to examine for hours on end in a mirror as she had seen some girls do, and which she had been forced to today. But in the glass behind her was Machray, with his eyes fixed upon her and not the young Frenchie with the lovely bosom who had painted her face and affixed the tiny butterfly-shaped plaster beauty mark to her cheek. She realized finally that he admired *her* looks, and he was spending his time and money seeing her dressed so that others would admire her too.

At their hotel they had a fine meal in the high-domed dining room with painted cherubs holding bugle horns flying this way and that, and the biggest chandelier she had ever seen sending out electric glints. Afterwards they retired to their room for a rest, which did not take long, and then Machray changed into his own fine clothes and hired a hackney cab for a drive to see the sights—State Street, the parks, the vast gray lake extending away to the horizon, and a neighborhood of fine homes where nurses strolled with children dressed as she had never seen children dressed anywhere.

Machray had brought a bottle of champagne along and kept their glasses filled with it. Sometimes he kissed her, saying he craved the taste of the luscious lip pomade, and then he got a hand up her skirts, laughing when her breath got away from her. He was all for stopping and having the hackie put the top up, but she said there was to be no houghmagandie, which was his word, to tear up the beautiful clothes he had bought her; so he desisted.

He asked if she was ready to meet the swells, and she said she was dressed for it at least, which made him laugh. He was in a queer mood, though; he had been drinking all day, and his eyeballs were veined with red, swollen and shiny. He lit a cigar and sat quiet for a while gazing at the lake and the houses like palaces, and finally he said Pyramid Flat would look this way one day, and not too far off either.

He directed the hackie to a great pile of a house of rough reddish black stone with a gate and a flagged courtyard where other hacks were pulling up and fancy-dressed people getting out. Machray helped her down and tipped the driver, who said, "Thank you, sorr!" He took her arm climbing the curving stone stairs. Inside there was a crowd of men like shiny beetles in their black tailcoats and white shirtfronts, and women bustled and padded like puffed-out pigeons. Many of them were promenading up and down a high central space where there were paintings on the walls, men leaning forward to peer at the paintings through glasses perched on their noses, and the women reading to them from tan booklets.

Machray was loud and boisterous, hailing this one or that one across the room, shaking hands with an old gentleman with a white beard, pink bald head, and vague blue eyes behind eyeglasses. With him was a woman with bare powdered shoulders almost as broad as she was tall, and another couple not quite so old. Both the ladies curtseyed to Machray and to her, and the younger one said, "How do you do, Lady Machray?" When Machray introduced her as "Mrs. Benbow," both the women froze up like the river in January, but the little old man, who was a Mr. Parsons, took her hand and kissed it, and the other gentleman did the same.

Machray kept hold of her arm, which she gripped to her side so his hand was locked there as they passed on through the crowds of men and women, both of them nodding and smiling, and Machray making little bows and saying, "How d'ja do, Mrs. Penfield?" and "Good evening to you, Miss Wertembacher!" whispering to her that everyone was abuzz over who she was and jealous fit to go up in smoke, which made her giggle. They did look at her hard, and none of them friendly. And Machray said that there must be drink somewhere in this great pile if only one persevered.

They found a room with a fireplace where a butler in a striped vest was pouring champagne into little glass cups for the people lining up before him. It seemed to her that a great deal of champagne was drunk in Chicago, and she was already tipsy from the wine in the hackney. She was not used to strong drink.

As they stood there with their cups a man and his wife approached them. He had colorless hair brushed sideways over a balding head, glasses on his nose, and a white shirt stiff as a shingle, while she was tall and cold-looking with a prune of a mouth, although a fine figure of a woman otherwise.

They were Mr. and Mrs. Guffin. The fellow called Machray "George," and Machray called him "Harry." The woman looked at her as though she saw with one glance through her fine clothes to what she was inside, puffed out her prune, and looked away.

"And how is the Bad Lands empire progressing, George?" Guffin said, half as though he were making fun but half not quite. Machray said very well indeed, far beyond his fondest hopes, and Harry should make the little railroad journey to visit the wonders he had wrought; bringing Mrs. Guffin of course. To this Mrs. Guffin smiled a little, like February.

Guffin said he understood there might be a rather unfavorable change in the freight rates on the horizon. He raised his hand like an Indian spying into the distance.

"Must mean these fellows are properly frightened of me," Machray said, with a grin. He tipped his glass in a salute to Mrs. Guffin.

"Oh, I don't think they are frightened," Guffin said. He had a way of bouncing on his toes when he spoke.

"Not frightened, eh?" Machray said.

"They are merely careful men. Certainly there has been discussion of your schemes, and I must tell you that they are looked upon as fantastical."

"Fantastical, eh?" Machray said softly.

"Preposterous," Guffin said, bouncing on his toes.

"Well, I put it to you that your friends were looked upon as preposterous before their day came round."

Matters seemed a little tight between Machray and Guffin, so she asked Mrs. Guffin if she lived nearby.

Mrs. Guffin acted as though she was hearing only with great difficulty, having to squinch up her face to understand the question. Yes, she lived nearby.

She said this was a beautiful house, and both Mr. and Mrs. Guffin now looked at her in the squinch-faced way. Machray had his hands in his pockets. He had taken to bouncing on his toes copying Guffin, and saying, "Hem! Hem!" when there was a silence, as there was now.

"And how will it affect your plans if the freight rates on dressed beef are indeed changed, George?" Guffin asked.

"Why, not at all," Machray said. "Unless the change is to be west of Chicago only."

Guffin said that that didn't seem farfetched to him, given the feeling in certain quarters. She could see the little bloody veins showing in Machray's eyeballs as he stared at Guffin, but he sounded easy enough when he spoke.

"In point of fact," he said, "I have come to Chicago to discuss a new enterprise I have in mind, that I see may become a necessity. To capitalize a refrigerator car company which will operate between Pyramid Flat and the eastern markets, with some transport also in west coast vegetables and fish."

"Yes, I understand you have an appointment with the Kalb brothers, George."

Machray didn't say anything. Still gazing past her, Mrs. Guffin asked where she was from.

She said she had lived, at times, in Memphis and in Leadville, a mining camp, but that now her residence was Pyramid Flat. Mrs. Guffin began to blush like a red hand slipping up over her face from her throat. It appeared to make her angry to feel herself blushing.

Machray kept his grip on her arm while Guffin said that he was afraid Machray would find the Kalb brothers not much interested in such an enterprise. As a matter of fact he had had some conversation with Ed Kalb on the matter only yesterday.

"Ah, did you, now?" Machray said cheerfully. "And only think, I considered you a friend of mine!"

Guffin assured him that he entertained only the friendliest of feelings toward him, which was why he presumed to advise him to look for his capitalization further east. "I'm afraid you will find no capital available in Chicago. Capitalists have become careful here, if you understand me. They are very cautious about making investments, and very careful indeed about safeguarding those already made——" He paused to take a breath before he said, "Against the encroachments of gypsies and pirates."

Machray stood there staring at him like a stunned ox.

She said to Mrs. Guffin, "Do look me up whenever you come through Pyramid Flat, dearie. I expect you know where to look for me."

"Yes," Mrs. Guffin said sharply. "I do expect I do."

She saw that Guffin had turned red also, either from hearing her exchange with his wife, or something else; his voice rose louder:

"I would further advise you to cut your losses and return where you came from, George. Let me tell you this. There are forces here that are simply never going to allow such a company as you describe to be capitalized. Nor operate if it *is* capitalized. Nor will it ever transport dressed beef from that slaughterhouse of yours, for that is never going to operate either!" Then his teeth showed between stiff lips as he

110

said, quietly, "And may I ask what you *mean* bringing a woman like that here?"

Machray's hand dropped from her arm. *"Harry,"* he said, in a quiet voice too, "surely you wouldn't insult the woman I have brought here? If you *did*, there would be no course open to me but to send my seconds around, you know. Unpardonable conduct and all that."

Guffin stood frozen with his teeth bared. There was a queer silence. Then Mrs. Guffin gave a little squeal and jerked back.

She saw where Mrs. Guffin's eyes were fixed. Machray had opened his fly and was pissing on Guffin. The steaming yellow stream arched over onto Guffin's trousers and had wet them slick, and was spreading out on the floor around Guffin's foot. Mrs. Guffin whispered. *"Oh! Oh! Oh!"*

"You wouldn't like that, would you, Harry?" Machray said. Guffin just stood there with his face turning from red to white, not even looking down. Machray finished and buttoned up. Nobody seemed to be paying any attention but the butler with the striped vest, who was staring.

"Look what you've done to yourself!" Machray said, very easy. "Disgustin', I call it. Come away, my dear."

He took her arm again, steered her around, and away. He didn't look back once. They wandered on, not headed back the way they had come, but progressing on through other rooms, in one of which were two suits of armor. He paused to describe these to her, naming all the parts, although she was too rattled to take it in. She asked who Guffin was.

"Solicitor fellow for some of the meatpacking jews here."

She asked if he was important.

"No man is as important as he likes to think himself, as me auld Mither used to say." Then he squeezed her arm and told her he was proud of her, and finally they were outside and descending the stone steps into the courtyard where a hackney was waiting.

But Machray was silent and dour that evening, and not interested in her. The next day *Aurora* was coupled to the westbound. On the return journey Machray tried to teach her to play chess and was displeased that she was so miserable she could not make herself understand the queer little wooden pieces that each must do such very different things.

2

Sometimes Cora would lie awake at night wondering why Machray had taken her to Chicago, and to that house with his fancy friends. She could only settle it in her mind that was the way he was. He was a front-door man. Certain respectable townsmen and ranchers came to her house the back way, circling around through the alley after dark so they would not be seen. One of these had had a stroke in Annie's bed, gibbering with terror because one side of him was paralyzed and his whorehouse habits might be found out, wrenching at Doc Micklejohn's hand and rasping out, *"My wife mustn't know!"*

Most men, in fact, came in by the front door because no one bothered about what they did or didn't do, but Machray was a front-door man because he simply didn't concern himself with what others thought of him. Once she had asked him if he didn't worry that people saw his buggy tied before the house so much, or the two of them joy riding. He had replied that men of worth did not concern themselves with the gossip of storekeepers and livery stale hostlers.

As he was a front-door man so was he a loyal man. She thought his loyalty must come from his having been an officer in Her Majesty's Army. He had quit the army when he had almost died of a fever from the terrible wound in his shoulder. He said all wars now were fought in hot countries where there were fevers. He had almost died of fevers twice and knew the third time would do for him. Dickson had been his servant in Africa, and she thought he would have died for Dickson, or Dickson for him.

After they came back from Chicago that summer it was as though there was a hoodoo on the construction of the slaughterhouse. There were little fires, and quarrels, and men brought in from St. Paul to tend to the boilers quitting; everything seemed to go wrong. She was certain that Grogan, the nasty, feisty little Irishman who was superintendent at the slaughterhouse, was in the pay of Guffin and the Chicago meatpackers. She tried to get Machray to fire him, but he wouldn't. She thought she was going to have to persuade Wax

112

to do him in when Grogan was knifed by one of his own Swede carpenters, and that was the end of him.

It was after they returned from Chicago, too, that the pot-shooting began, shots fired at Machray out of gulches or from behind trees, so he could never see who was sniping at him. Once they were shot at when they were on a picnic.

Often he would bring along a gentle horse for her, and they would ride north of town beneath the buttes along the river, with a picnic hamper and a blanket. This time she was helping him spread the blanket in cottonwood shade along a little creek, when the shot came. Machray went down, and she thought he was killed. He had only ducked. Still bent over, he grabbed her arm and pulled her along with him toward the butte behind them. There was a cave there and, before it, a blade of a butte that had calved from the bigger one. She scrambled behind this, and in a minute Machray was with her, panting, with his rifle and the hamper. He had lost his hat and he looked wild, green eyes blazing like lanterns. She ducked back into the shallow cave, which had a mound of dried mud heaped in the entrance like a high sill. Machray knelt beside the calf butte with his rifle braced. Out under the cottonwoods she could see his hat, and the blue and green blanket spread, and the two horses grazing unconcerned.

Dust sprayed above his head and he cursed, ducked, and got off a shot of his own, muttering, "Missed the bugger!" He turned his face, bright with excitement, back to her, saying it looked like two of them. He slid the hamper back where she could reach it. "See if you can pull the cork on that Medoc, will you, my girl?"

He shot again, and cursed again, while she drew the cork and poured the blood red wine into the two glasses Daisy had packed in the hamper. Machray put his hand back for his, and drank a bit, and put the glass down to aim and fire. He announced that it was a good vintage. Crouched back of him in the cave, she could not keep from giggling.

She unfolded the napkins in which the venison was wrapped and handed him a slice, which he stuffed into his mouth, muttering, "Good! Good!" She saw a tiny flower of smoke down among the trees along the river; again there was a spray of powdered clay. Machray cursed as he dipped his finger into his wine to skim out bits of dirt.

She spooned potato salad onto a plate with another slice of venison and passed it to him. He ate the salad scooping it

113

into his mouth with a curled finger, reaching back for the napkin she was quick to give him and saying, with his mouth full, "You are to fill your own kyte, now, Cora—you are not just to feed your warrior!"

She stretched out holding her glass and he tapped his smartly against it; it seemed to her she could almost hear the excitement buzzing in him. He went back to firing after careful aim, and between times sipping wine until she had to fill his glass again.

She said it would not do for him to fuddle himself at a time like this. "At a time like this!" he mocked. "Ah, Cora, sometimes you *will* be a woman instead o' yourself!"

Then he crawled back into the cave with her, lying grinning beside her with his rifle braced on the mound of earth. "It is not just food and drink a bonny fighter needs!"

A fashionable woman on a picnic outing was considerably encumbered with skirts, petticoats, and drawers, and Machray had to do a great deal of digging, like paging through a book for a paragraph he knew must be there. She was not able to help him much, weak with stifling laughter, and from time to time he had to halt his efforts to squint down toward the river to see if anyone was sneaking up on them. Then whenever he fired she could feel the shock right through him, and her giggle swelled and spilled and changed to something else. When it was over she felt her soul floating out of her body to hang like a tiny puffy cloud in the hard blue of the Bad Lands sky, and her limbs felt scattered out and slowly returning to their proper places. Machray's sweating red face hung over her like a balloon, speaking words in a voice hoarse as a frog croaking. "Ah, love—love—love; was that not a lovely time, love?"

She said she had thought she'd been in heaven except that the ground was so hard.

After that Machray crawled out to see what he could see, while she tended to her clothing. There were no more shots. It appeared they had gone on their way, being polite fellows at heart, as he said. He squatted beside her and poured out the last of the wine, carefully measured between the two glasses, and he piled on her one more time before that picnic was done.

That night she asked Fanny, Jessie, and Carrie, girls she could trust who had steady clients, to find out who it was doing the pot-shotting at Machray. She did not think it was Jake Boutelle or Bill Driggs, who might hate Machray for their different reasons, because they were old hunters who would hit what they were shooting at and would not be inclined to play games. Nor did she think it was Guffin and the meatpackers conspiring this time. She thought it must be cowboys, and she was certain that, in time, her girls would find out what was behind it.

3

At the end of April, Andrew returned to a Bad Lands mired in mud. As Chally said, "A man with fair-sized feet can carry a good quarter section on his boots." Many animals were adorned with thick anklets of gray, dried gumbo.

The river, which he had last seen as little more than a chain of puddles connected by a sluggish trickle, was now in considerable flood. He was warned that it was safer to swim a horse across, the fords being no longer trustworthy because of shifting banks of quicksand. Now he understood another of Machray's sins, that of cutting off one of the best fords, for the lower one had become dangerous.

The ground around every alkali spring had melted into a trembling quagmire, and deep holes of tenacious muck had formed in the bottoms of gullies. Range cattle of many different brands, as well as his own, tramped into these pools to drink, soon became hopelessly mired, and would perish unless hauled out by straining cow ponies. Although work had begun on the "Big House," Chally, Joe, and Degan, the cook, having felled trees and dragged the stripped logs up to the site, construction had to cease while they went to the aid of endangered livestock.

On his third day he and Chally came on a longhorn bull feebly struggling, the old fellow having broken through a crust of dried mud near a waterhole. He managed to toss a loop over the animal's horns and spurred Blackie to drag him out. The bull floundered out, bellowing, with a flatulent suck of sound, and immediately charged Chally's horse.

He had not had the presence of mind to release his rope, and the bull's lurch knocked Blackie into a heap. His leg was pinned beneath the saddle. As he struggled to free it, the bull swung toward him, the astonishing spread of black horns still decorated with his rope. Before he realized his danger, the bull charged.

There was a shot and the animal collapsed. The horns were not eight feet from him. Beyond, twisted in his saddle, Chally still had his revolver braced over his left wrist, muzzle smoking. The face above it was very white.

After that he was never without a revolver himself.

Next there were horses to break, for, over the winter, many of the saddle band had become so wild they might never have been broken at all. This was Joe Reuter's specialty, and a new trade to be learned. He finally tried his seat on the big, dark horse he had named Cicero for his Roman nose.

With the lunging, bleating animal stretched out between the snubbing post and the fence by ropes on a front and hind leg, Joe flung on the saddle blanket and clapped the saddle on top of it. He reached for the latigo beneath the straining belly and cinched the saddle into place. Then he gripped Cicero's ear, twisted the long head to one side, and, with swift sleight-of-hand, made fast the lead rope, which Andrew had released, as a curb on the under jaw. "Get set, Andy!"

Andrew ducked back to loosen the rope that held the rear leg. The long, taut muscles beneath the brown hide trembled to his touch. He planted his boot in the stirrup and swung himself up. Joe slapped the rope into his hand and leaped back. Andrew had one glimpse of his worried face, and, beyond, Degan standing near the shack with a basin in his hands.

Cicero shot into the air so violently that the arched neck smashed into his face. He was blinded with pain as he clung to the rope with one hand and the saddlehorn with the other. The poles of the animal's forelegs pounded on the packed earth. A steady grunting in his ears must be his own. Then he was floating free of the saddle.

He sprawled on the ground so hard he thought he must have broken every bone in his body. He lay on his back trying to catch his breath.

"All right, Andy?" Joe called.

"All right," he said. Slowly he sat up, brushing the dust from his eyes. Cicero stood spread-legged, the curb made fast to the snubbing post. Joe helped him to his feet.

"Took a little crack on the nose there," Joe said.

He was astonished that all his limbs seemed to work. Daubing at his bleeding nose with his bandanna, he limped toward the horse.

"Where you going?" Joe said.

"I just got a bit off balance that time."

Joe wrenched Cicero's ear sideways again. "Don't have to prove to anybody here you are full of sand," he said casually.

"I know it," he said, swinging into the saddle. Joe slapped the rope into his hands.

The second time he lasted longer, but lay longer in the dust.

"That is one mean, sunfishing critter," Joe said. At the snubbing post the horse stood more easily, head hinged sideways to watch them. Degan had disappeared, no doubt in embarrassment. Chally was out on the range.

"Believe I'll take a rest," Joe said, and seated himself on a fence rail to construct a cigarette. Andrew sat beside him, massaging a shoulder.

"I'll try one more time," he said. "I think I can stay on next time."

Joe nodded, licking the paper to seal it. "Enjoyin this, you'll get a real whoop out of roundup. Too bad you can't stay the route, but maybe stirrin around with them politicians in Chicago is pleasurable too."

"Not necessarily."

"Who'll your man be at the convention there?"

"Senator Edmunds of Vermont."

"How's his chances?"

He laughed and said he didn't know. "With the Old Guard," he said, "you just have to keep going back and convincing them they are beaten."

"Sounds like bustin saddle stock," Joe said. "Sounds like some local stockmen I know. Well, the Montana Stockraisers big do is comin up pretty quick. You don't want to miss any of that!"

The Hardys overwhelmed him with the warmth of their welcome, although Mary Hardy seemed wan and thinner than he remembered, and rather mechanically bright in her manner. There was much talk of the suicide of the hired girl of a rancher named Lamey, who had blown her brains out with a shotgun in despair midway through the long winter. The Hardys, too, were excited about the spring meeting of the Montana Stockraisers Association in Miles City. There were many smaller, local associations, such as the Western

117

Dakota Stockraisers, which would be holding the Bad Lands roundup next month, but the Montana Association's domain covered all of Montana and great areas of the adjoining states and territories. The spring meeting was a not-to-be-missed social event, and all roads would be leading to Miles City.

May 17, 1884
'Miles City,

"*Dearest Cissie:*

"I've come to Miles City aboard *Aurora* with Machray, hearing in detail of the antics of the 'little laird' whom my host views as the eighth wonder of the world, and who, with his mother, will be taking up residence in the Bad Lands sometime this summer. Our route passed through mile after mile of prairie in full bloom, carpets of wildflowers of every hue imaginable. What a lovely sight!

"Miles City is a much larger 'cowtown' than Pyramid Flat, and I am very glad to have seen it in its full flood of the stockraisers' convention. There are true 'cattle kings' in attendance here, many of them English or European, such as the Freling brothers, James Osborne, and Pierre Bidault, with his handsome English wife. These are men of great personal style, who belong to the Cheyenne Club as a matter of course and have brought culture and civilization with them to the Great West. The Bad Lands' own Lord Machray is much more at home in this company than he is in Pyramid Flat. He is positively bursting with energy, enthusiasm, and new plans.

"The town is thronged with men and women from the surrounding districts. Its wooden sidewalks are so crowded it is often necessary to promenade in the street. Men of fifty different callings jostle each other or lounge before the straggle of cheap boardinghouses that extends to the edge of town, which, here as elsewhere, is demarcated by an enormous dump of rusting tin cans and mackerel boxes. There are hunters in buckskin shirts and fur hats, teamsters and stage drivers with faces seamed by the hardship and exposure of their trade, silent sheepherders, railroad men with their air of jovial cosmopolitanism, gamblers with string ties and box-back coats, Indians with dark, flat, rather ugly faces, cattle-

118

men with their calling's scars and disablements, and their entourages of cowboys. The cowboys predominate. In twos and threes they gallop their wiry little ponies down the streets, seeming to be standing in their stirrups—for they wear stirrups so long their knees are hardly bent. They bang in and out of the saloons and gambling halls, sometimes quarrelsome but more often simply merry. Their appearance is striking, revolvers stuck in their belts and bright handkerchiefs knotted at their throats, keen-eyed, bronzed faces beneath broad-brimmed hats.

"Nor must I forget the festive granger, present in this town in some numbers for the entertainments. They come in their wagons with wives, children, and dogs, by the roads one notices more and more these days, twin wheel-ruts winding off into distance across rolling country, many of them following the deep trails cut by vanished herds of buffalo. The grangers are the lowest of the social stratifications, and are often the butt of crude jokes on the part of the cowboys, who, I am certain, do not intend their casual cruelty.

"In addition to the meetings of the Association on a variety of subjects, there has been much frolic, horse races, contests in roping and bulldogging, gambling in every form, and even a Grand Ball! At this affair I participated in the Virginia reel, an exhilarating experience. I danced with young Miss Hardy, her mother, several of the Cheyenne Club ladies, including the gracious and glamorous Mme Bidault, and with a number of others neither gracious nor glamorous. As one often hears remarked, this is hard country on women. A local man named 'Hard Winter' Jones received his appellation because he is said to introduce his wife with the statement, 'She may look like a hard winter, but she's my wife.'

"Miss Hardy, closely chaperoned by her parents, along with a few other young women of her station, is much on display, no doubt in the hopes she will take the fancy of someone of higher station than a mere cowboy. The marriage market, however, seems a discouraging one, consisting of middle-aged, hard-faced widowers or confirmed bachelors, with a few eligible young men. The girl is poorly equipped to mingle with the Cheyenne Club set, for her dress, while neat, is not stylish, and, self-conscious of her situation and her crippled hand, her manner unfortunately combines the diffident and the assertive. What a pitiable position our young women are cramped into by the need for capturing a suitable spouse! I will never forget those well-bred girls in Newport, with their gay and coquettish manner, and desperate eyes. . . ."

4

He stood with Mary Hardy in Miles City's Cattlemen's Hall, beside a low railing that separated the dance floor from the raised circumference, where members of the Montana Stockraisers Association and their families sat on benches at plank tables, waiting for the music to begin again. On the far side of the floor the fiddlers, guitarists, and drummer were chatting among themselves.

Machray and James Freling strolled up, two big men, Machray resplendent in his kilts and decorations, Freling in formal dress with a massive gold watch chain stretched across his massive corporation. He was a cattleman from western Montana, an old friend of Machray's, whom Machray introduced as the man who had first shown him the Far West, to his abiding sorrow. Freling pulled at the ends of his black handlebar mustache and bowed over Mary Hardy's hand, as did Machray. Her face burned dark red.

She inquired if the slaughterhouse was completed yet.

"Fortunately not, my dear," Machray said.

"Fortunately?" she said.

"I visited a number of the most modern abattoirs in England and Germany this winter, and there are improvements I am fortunately still able to incorporate in the structure. But I have a new project which I must describe to you, Miss Hardy."

He began to tell her of his scheme for a stage line into the Black Hills, Pyramid Flat a much more logical depot for such a line than Mandan, where the stage coaches currently connected with the railroad. He described with enthusiasm the great Concords rolling out behind their fine teams, laden with miners and freight westbound, and returning with gold from the mines. The mail contract could be had for the

120

plucking, and freight, passenger, and mail lines would expand as new mining strikes were made.

Mary Hardy gaped at Machray as though she could not decide whether or not he was serious. She wore a complicated blue velvet dress, with her hand concealed in a lace-fringed pocket.

"But Lord Machray!" she burst out. "It would cost such a great deal of money!"

Machray halted as though punctured, which set Freling laughing. "Yes, my dear fellow, aren't you sufficiently occupied with your great hulking abbattoir?"

"Clearly not!" Andrew said. Machray gave him a suspicious glance. Light gleamed on his medals, and made ruddy highlights on the cliff of his face.

"Opportunities knock but once," he said, a little sulkily. "As Will Shakespeare put it, 'Things in motion sooner catch the eye, than what not moves.'"

"So, Geordie, you must always be in motion so as to catch the general eye!" Freling said. Mary Hardy laughed nervously with him.

"Well, I have been dead, you know," Machray said. "Perhaps I must keep in motion so as to be sure of my mortal state."

Freling opened his mouth, then closed it, frowning. Andrew cleared his throat and said, "What do you mean, Machray?"

Machray sighed. "Fearfully wounded in Egypt, you know. Great spear sticking out of me, fellow hanging on the end. Shipped me home about as lively as mutton. Lower and lower. Finally I died."

"You are joking." Freling said.

"Far from it. I *died*."

In the silence Andrew could hear the rustle of his breath over his lips. One of the fiddlers began to scrape his bow over strings, a faintly sour sound that traveled like electricity along his nerves. A second fiddler joined the first.

"I can see it as clear as clear," Machray continued. "My old dad there beside the bed, the sawbones chittering about like a field mouse, and meself in the bed. I had floated up above the scene, you see— Ah, you are not interested in such a queer tale."

"Please—" Mary Hardy said. Freling had folded his thick arms on his chest, frowning.

"Floating up above the room," Machray said. "How I

121

knew I was dead. Sawbones was calling for this and that, uncapping bottles and jamming them to my beak, chafing my wrists. Me lying there with my nose poking straight up and my mouth open. Gray as—gray as death! My old dad was praying powerfully. I could hear him. I must say it was peaceful up there. And the light—such a clarity of light! I was just getting used to it, thinking this is not bad at all, old boy, when the praying seemed to come through in some queer way. Then I was back, sneezing and gasping from the smelling salts, and my wrists chafed raw. A miracle! they were saying. A miracle! I was back, and not much pleased, either."

Machray laid a finger to the side of his nose and squinted at Andrew. "But then I have always been half in love with the old easeful," he said. "Have not we all?"

Andrew's eye was caught by a black-haired man, who, however, turning to his partner, proved to be a stranger and not Boutelle. "What did you—feel?" he asked Machray.

"No fear, if that is what you mean." Machray said. "Awesome moment, but not in that way."

"Sounds a bit morbid," Freling said.

Machray shrugged. "Miss Hardy, I wonder if you have been engaged for this polka?"

"Oh!" she said. "No—I haven't."

Machray led her to the floor, and they pranced away. Andrew stood beside Freling, watching their progress. Freling was frowning, jingling coins in his pocket. "It is a known fact," he said, "that a virgin will cause an otherwise sensible man to babble nonsense." He strode off to join other friends.

When the polka ended, Machray steered Mary Hardy among the retiring dancers to rejoin Andrew. He watched Machray bend his head to speak to her. She laughed, smiling and brushing a strand of hair back from her flushed forehead, but all at once he saw her expression turn wooden. Her father was approaching at his stooped, sidling walk.

"Lord Machray!" he said. "I will ask you not to seek to dance with my daughter again. Our standards are different from yours. Mary, you will join your mother at once!"

She wet her lips as though to speak. Her eyes slid sideways to meet Andrew's. Then she fled, hurrying across the floor with her dark hair bobbing on her shoulders, head down. Once she halted to glance back, and he was surprised, in his own embarrassment, at her expression, which was triumphant.

Machray had folded his arms to gaze down at the older man. "You seem determined to dislike me, Mr. Hardy. Why must that be so?"

"Surely you are aware that your conduct in Pyramid Flat has been notorious, Lord Machray!"

Hardy's eyes bulged. He jerked around away from Machray.

"This criticism comes from a curious source, sir!"

"One moment, if you please!" Machray said. "I would like to know if your dislike is due to the fact that I have purchased my land—as the cattlemen of this and every district will soon be impelled to do, Mr. Hardy. Or because you and I happen to have been born upon the same island, but of different social classes. The latter is scarcely my fault, sir!"

"The two matters are one and the same!" Hardy said in a stifled voice. "Your class has never recognized the necessity of cooperation between equals because it recognizes no equals." He glanced at Andrew as though they were strangers. "A class which buys when it cannot expropriate by force, and considers its privileges superior to other men's rights!"

"By God, sir, I am an admirer of bald-faced hypocrisy!" Machray said. "It happens that I am aware of wheels within wheels in the Western Dakota Association. Committees within committees, I should say. From which certain members are carefully excluded. Where matters of rights, privileges, and force are the subjects of lively discussion. Including, if I may go so far, sharpshooting in its various aspects!"

Hardy turned and limped away across the clearing floor. Grimacing with distaste, Andrew watched him join his son; Mary Hardy and her mother were not in sight. Machray was mopping his sweating face with his handkerchief.

"What have I done to so incense that poisonous fellow, Livingston?"

"I believe it is as you said. That, and his daughter."

"Protective of the girl, of course," Machray said with a shrug. "Exercised that I will besmirch her." He laughed angrily.

Freling joined them, and together they strolled outside into the darkness to light cigars. Other men stood in groups nearby, pale glow of cigars and cheroots on cheeks, flashes of matches, laughter, snatches of conversations. Freling and Machray were speaking of the Abyssinian campaign.

"Quite mad, you know, the Emperor Theodore," Machray

said. "Killed himself when it became evident he was defeated. I managed to lose myself in that great mud palace of his in Magdala, wandering about until I blundered into the women's quarters. Lasses rushing this way and that in their white robes, like water running. Came upon one of his daughters. She wasn't black exactly, blue-black rather. Face like a beautiful hawk. Noble blood running back to Ham himself!

"I will say I was a bit windy," Machray went on. "Those warriors of the Negus liked nothing better than parading about with the ballocks of their enemies slung from their spears, and there I was on thrice-forbidden ground. Difficult to concentrate upon the business at hand! Moreover, neither of us could understand a word the other spoke. Ah, but she understood that poetry was holy stuff! Got the *shamma* off her fraisin' poetry!" He laughed fatly.

"Talked the clothes off her without even speaking her language!" Machray crowed. "Long and narrow all over, she was; narrow feet like runners, in golden slippers. All blue black and quivering like jelly in a mold. By God, she was a lovely piece! That is something that comes a man's way once a lifetime! A virgin princess!"

Freling laughed appreciatively while Andrew reflected that Professor Rudolph Duarte must have had stories to tell of this nature also, improper for undergraduate ears.

"Disgusting!" a tight voice said behind them. In the shadows Hardy stood with his son. "Contemptible and disgusting!" Hardy hissed.

"Offended you, have I, my man?" Machray said loudly.

"And anyone else within hearing!" Hardy said. "Filth!" Jeff stood beside him, pale and round-eyed, looking from Machray, to Andrew, to Freling. Other groups of men nearby had fallen silent.

"In certain social classes it is customary to seek satisfaction for an offense given," Machray continued, in the bullying voice. "No doubt I must describe the punctilio. A friend of the offended is selected as second. He calls upon a friend of the offender. A meeting is arranged, and satisfaction obtained. Or not."

Hardy seemed visibly to shrink. When Machray's voice ceased there was a tension like wire cable pulled to a strain, and Andrew could feel an icy beading on his forehead. Jeff had taken his father's arm.

"Come away, Father," he said. Their feet shuffled, turning; they disappeared into the darkness. Machray stood straddle-

124

legged, gazing after them, orange glow of his cigar tip illuminating his hard face.

"Nasty-minded little eavesdropper," he said.

"I say, but don't you think that was a bit severe?" Freling said.

"It was unforgivable!" Andrew said.

"Believe he is one of the local poltroons who's set his cowboys to sharpshooting at yours truly." Machray said, still in the loud voice. "Face them down one by one, if I must." He turned toward Andrew. "Take his side, do you?"

"I'll take his side against that kind of bullying!"

"Well, then—" Machray began, but just then Jeff Hardy reappeared. He carried his head thrust forward like a cornered animal's, crouching facing Machray.

"If y-y-y-y-ou want to pick a fight with somebody, I am not escared of you!" Jeff whispered. "But you leave my father alone!"

"I've no quarrel with you, young Master Hardy," Machray said.

"Well, y-y-y-you just leave my father alone." Jeff halted; Andrew could hear him panting.

"I say I have no quarrel with you," Machray said in a sharper voice.

"My young friend," Freling said, sounding as though he had a cold in his nose, "please let me urge you not to pick a quarrel here where none exist."

"Just let it be now, Jeff," Andrew said.

"Well, he can apologize!"

"I will apologize for Lord Machray," Andrew said. In the darkness he could not make out whether the boy was armed or not.

Jeff straightened. He shook his head as though to clear it. Then he was gone.

"Love o' *God*!" Machray groaned. "What a monstrous *banality*! All this because I danced with a fellow's *daughter*?"

"I believe it is known that Troy fell," Freling said, "because someone danced with a fellow's wife."

Machray shouted with laughter and Andrew blew his breath out slowly, feeling as he had when the charging longhorn had turned to harmless carrion not eight feet from where he lay pinned by the fallen horse. As he had detested Machray for his bullying of Hardy, so now he found himself liking the man the better for his capitulation. But violence had seemed very near.

The next morning Andrew stood in a crowd packed along the boardwalks of the main street to watch the cow pony racing, four young cowboys abreast dashing by, bent low in the saddle with hat brims blown back, quirting and yelling, to be followed in five minutes or so by another quartet. He encountered Mary Hardy, in a blue bonnet; her mother was nearby, but out of earshot.

"You must tell me what happened last night," she whispered to him and, as he told her, nodded with an expression that seemed unsuited to his words. When he finished she said, "Yes, that is what Jeff told me. Father threatened to take us all straight home. So everyone would have been punished for my crime, you see. Lord Machray is not a suitable man for me to dance with."

She laughed and, glancing toward her mother, said, "Actually, there are not many men who are suitable. Mr. Yarborough, Major Cutter—" She listed other names that meant nothing to him.

"I must be included," he said.

"Quite too obviously, I'm afraid. On my mother's part, anyway." He felt his face burn and she laughed delightedly.

"I didn't see young Matty Gruby at the ball last night," he said. "But I suppose he is not considered suitable."

"He was there. No, he is not suitable. If those I might find suitable are subtracted from those they deem suitable, few remain. Who, I am afraid, do not find *me* suitable!"

"I'm sorry to hear you speak this way."

"Why so? It is the truth." She laughed as though she were making a fine joke. "I am beginning to realize that no young Lochinvar will come riding to bear me away from the Bad Lands! Oh, there's Matty!"

Another group whirled by, one forging ahead to yip tauntingly over his shoulder and rise in his stirrups as he crossed the finish line the winner. Riding back along the street among admiring friends, Matty waved and called out to Mary Hardy, but his face stiffened when his eyes caught Andrew's.

Later, after Andrew had separated from Mary Hardy and her mother, Matty Gruby, wearing chaps, a blue silk neckerchief, and a revolver tucked into his belt, confronted him on the boardwalk, standing with his boots apart and his hands on his hips, lower lip protruding beneath his sparse mustache.

"I just want to tell you something. You'll stay away from Mary Hardy if you know what's good for you!"

"I assure you that I am not interested in Miss Hardy in the way you seem to think."

"Well, I saw you just now. And dancin with her last night!"

"I also danced with her mother, and a number of other ladies. I am a friend of the Hardy family, not of Miss Hardy in particular."

"Old man won't even talk to me," Matty said, swiping the back of his hand across his mouth. "Pretends I'm not around. Old lady thinks you are the all-time trump for Mary. But you just leave be. She doesn't care for you!"

Before he could speak again, the boy turned his head to spit, gave him one more hot, resentful glance, stepped around him, and swaggered away down the boardwalk.

He had put off too long facing the fact that the Hardys considered him a well-qualified suitor for their daughter. Moreover, he had had the presumption to pity Mary Hardy in her role at Miles City, where now it seemed she was quite the belle of the occasion and the center of a variety of emotions.

5

"Dakota Bad Lands,
June 5, 1884

"*My dear son:*

"Last winter you and I had some talk about what it is your Papa is doing out here in the 'Far West,' 'Horseriding,' as you put it. I am writing to tell you what I am doing now, which is horseriding on a roundup. When your Aunty reads this to you you must ask her to explain anything you do not understand.

"During wintertime on a ranch there is not much work done with the cattle, which are left to shift for themselves. The big event of the spring is the roundup, when the 'outfits' in a district gather to herd together all the cattle on their range, and then separate them by brands. Thus it is to be seen how the animals have fared through the winter, and how many calves have been born.

"We have at the present tally (which means count in cowboy language) sixty-seven new calves, and no doubt more will be found as the roundup proceeds. In fact, my herd has done very well, and I am pleased.

"In April when I returned to the Bad Lands it was already time to begin getting our horses ready for the roundup. Each rider requires six to eight ponies for his work on the roundup, and so a great number of saddle horses must be available. These are called the saddle band, saddle bunch, cavy, or remuda.

"At the meeting of the great Montana Cattleraisers Association, roundup districts are mapped out for all the vast open pasture of this northern range. The districts and the dates when the roundup will cover each part of the country do not change much from year to year, so everyone knows where he is to go and when. Large outfits may employ a dozen cowboys, with a saddle band of over a hundred, while the largest, with herds numbering up to ten thousand, amy run a roundup all by themselves. Smaller ranches, like my own, require only four or five men, and we, who are newcomers, must be very 'humble and mild,' like new boys in school. The older and larger outfits think of us as 'horning in' on the range, and so we must not seem 'pushy' or forward until we have been accepted.

"My outfit, the Lazy-N, with its home ranch on Fire Creek, and a herd of some six hundred, has a stout wagon to carry bedding, food, gear, and a mess chest, which holds utensils and canned food. There is no space for much spare clothing, nor even for books! Behind each man's saddle is his roll of personal effects, wrapped in a stout jacket for night herding and including a 'slicker' to give protection from the rain. This bundle is called a man's 'plunder.'

"We gathered first at a place called 'East-of-the-Slope.' It was a brave sight to see the heavy, four-horse wagons jolting into the area through a pass among the buttes, the saddle bands driven along at a smart pace by the horse wranglers, who urge stragglers along with smart cracks from the knotted ends of their lariats, and rush up and down to keep their bands of horses from mingling together. The cowboys, meanwhile, who tend strictly to the cattle, jog along in a carefree manner.

"In the morning the cook is up preparing breakfast long before dawn, and probably about three o'clock he calls out, 'Chow! Chow!' The sleepers then spring from their bedrolls, rub their eyes and yawn, and draw on boots and trousers—if they have even bothered to remove the latter for the night. We all crowd around the smoldering fire to warm our hands, and then form a line to receive coffee, biscuits, fat pork, and beans. Nothing has ever tasted so delicious.

"After breakfast the foreman, or 'captain,' divides the men into two crews, which ride out in different directions. These crews ride in large circles, while individual cowboys ride in smaller circles within the larger ones. In this way all the terrain is covered, and each man drives before him the cattle he has found.

"These long, swift, morning lopes through green grasslands are wonderful times! The sweet air, still with its early morning touch of chill, and the rapid trot of the tough little horses make a man's blood teem with the pleasures of being alive. As we climb the steep sides of the buttes, out of the mists that still cling in the hollows, the sun flames in the east. Care does not sit heavily upon a rider whose pony's hoofs are dashing through carpets of flowers, and whose shadow is thrown level and long behind him!

"As soon as the circle riders have come in and snatched a few hasty bites of midday meal, we begin to 'work' the herd that has been gathered. The animals are held in a compact bunch by the cowboys ringed around them, while men from each outfit look through the herd for animals of their own brand, cutting out from the rest those so marked, to form a smaller herd.

"Attention is meanwhile turned to the cows and calves, which have also been formed into herds by brands, the calves following their mothers. Now the branding begins. A fire is built, the irons heated, and some of the men dismount to 'wrestle' the calves. A first-class roper invariably catches a calf by both hind feet and, having taken a twist of his lariat around the horn of his saddle, drags the bawling creature to the fire. There he is wrestled to earth and immobilized, and the proper brand burned upon his side.

"The ropers chase down their quarry with yipping cries and swinging loops of lariat; the men with the irons, blackened with soot, rush to and fro; the calf wrestlers, grimy with dust and sweat, work like beavers; and the tally man shouts the number and sex of each calf in a bellow. Dust rises in clouds, and the cheers and laughter of the cowboys and the lowing and bleating of the cows and calves make a perfect pandemonium of noise. This wild confusion goes on from dawn until dark, and it is not remarkable for a cowboy to be in the saddle for longer than that. Yesterday I was astride my pony for thirteen hours!

"At night you may hear night herders singing to their charges, and some play mouth organs. Music soothes! The herd may become nervous on nights when there is thunder and lightning, and when the animals are 'spooky,' anything may send them into a stampede. Then all are instantly in flight, and there is no more sleep to be had that night, every man running to his horse to go to the aid of the 'nighthawks.' Our task in a stampede is to bring the herd under control by gradually turning the lead animals until they are moving in a circle, and the best men race their horses for the 'point' of the stampede, where they can start the fleeing cattle in a long curve back toward the rear of the herd. It is dangerous work, and again the best-trained horses know exactly what is required of them with little instruction from their masters. We had one of these avalanches of animals in a thunderstorm two nights ago, and no one slept any more that night, for the herd remained spooky until dawn broke.

"Indeed, the only fault I find with this life is the hours of work and the lack of time to sleep. The food is rough, but tasty enough, the cowboys good-humored and expert in their work. It is superbly healthful, exciting, and adventuresome, and it brings forth the best in men in the way of pluck, self-reliance, and dashing horsemanship. I have made good friends here among the cowboys and wranglers, although the cattlemen themselves are standoffish, prey to their own responsibilities and worries, like all their class.

"I am writing this by lantern light, lulled by the lowing and movement of the herd nearby and the distant song of a night herder. It has been a long day, and the

130

sandman has scattered his wares heavily upon my eyelids. Goodnight, dear Son. I think about you every day. My regards to your Aunt Cissie and Uncle James, your cousins, Miss Connell, and Spanny. I will mail this from Chicago, for I must leave the roundup tomorrow and take the train to Chicago, in order to attend the national convention there. I will enclose some very rough sketches of the activities I have described, so you can 'see.'

"Your loving
"Papa"

*With the cheers for James G. Blaine ringing through Conven-*tion Hall behind them, the Utica Big Eight of the New York delegation, reduced in Chicago to an irreconcilable very small five, retreated to diGarmo's hotel room to smoke cigars, drink whiskey, and mutter threats of "bolting the ticket." They drifted off, first one, then two, until Andrew was left alone with diGarmo, who lounged on the bed in his shirtsleeves.

"There is a lesson here somewhere," diGarmo said philosophically. "We thought we had won a great victory over the Arthurians, only to find the portcullis had been left down for 'the Plumed Knight.' "

Andrew paced the room, worrying that it did not seem to matter enough to him that the machine forces had won again, as they always seemed to win in the end. Schroeder had been almost weeping when he left, and he knew that diGarmo was heartsick. He himself was thinking of sending Chally and Joe to purchase a second herd, despite their chilly reception by the other cattlemen on the roundup.

DiGarmo sighed and said. "Well, now to begin mending fences."

He said he would be taking the morning train back to the Bad Lands.

"Life of a Far West rancher appeals more than usual just now, I'm sure," diGarmo said, locking his hands behind his head. "Well, I have a bet that you won't be out of politics for long."

"I'm afraid I'm out of New York politics for good."

"We'll see, Andy," diGarmo said pleasantly.

6

When Andrew stepped off the westbound in Pyramid Flat, he left his luggage at the station and walked to the saloon. The place, dim as a cave, had a potbelly stove with a high, crooked stack in the center of the long room, tables along one side, and on the other a counter which the barkeep was polishing.

Leaning against the bar, sipping the raw whiskey, he had an amused vision of himself, the wound-be adventurer who had just cut his eastern ties and decided to commit his life to the Bad Lands, lounging here, a very self-conscious saloon habitué. Across the room he recognized Bill Driggs, stripes of sunlight from a louver shutter barring his wrinkled face and graying hair. The hunter was seated at a table with another man, hats stacked between them, whiskey bottle before Driggs, whose companion was leaning forward with his chin on his hands.

"Come on over here and sit with some fellows," Driggs called.

Andrew carried his glass to the table and shook hands with Driggs and the other, whose name was Conroy. Driggs, unshaven and shabby, appeared to have fallen on hard times. He indicated an empty chair with a flip of his hand and Andrew seated himself. They grinned at each other.

"Still in your city clothes, I see. Just come back to the Bad Lands?"

"Just in from Chicago," he said.

"Him and Chally's partners takin on range down between Hardy and the Duke of Puckered-Asshole," Driggs explained to Conroy. Outside, hoofs passed in the street, and wagon wheels creaked. The pattern of barred light changed on Driggs's face as the doors swung inward. The man named Cletus lurched in, to stand peering around him in the dimness of the saloon. He wore a cartridge belt and revolver. One pantleg was stuffed into the boot top while the other hung out.

"Afternoon, there, Bobby!" Driggs called. "Come and take

a seat. It's me and Connie, and you remember Andy Livingston from down on Fire Creek!"

Cletus set his bulldog jaw, bowed his head in a kind of nod of greeting, then shook it. He moved toward the bar, progressing as though on a pitching deck in a high wind. At the bar he swung around, to prop himself there on his elbows and stare at Andrew with one eye slitted as though aiming down a rifle barrel.

"Suppose it bites?" Driggs said in a low voice. "Seen any more of Jake?" he asked Andrew.

He said he had not, gazing back to Cletus, who at last turned away to engage the barkeep in argument.

"Why, I remember this fellow!" Conroy said suddenly. He had a thin, rather lop-sided face with mismatched eyes. "He is the one the lord knocked on his fundy up on roundup last fall. Box-fightin," he said to Driggs. "That's with those big piller gloves on." He said to Andrew, "Say, you was doin just fine there, too, till the lord bashed you that one."

"Knocked you down?" Driggs said. His ugly face was twisted in a kind of comic dismay. "Thought you said you and him was *friends!*"

"It was a friendly matter," he said. He was feeling some irritation that Cletus' presence should affect him.

"Huh!" Conroy said. "Somebody knocks me down it's not going to stay friendly long!"

"It is a sport, not warfare. If you lose your temper you have lost the point."

"Huh!" Conroy said. "I'd—"

"Hush, now!" Driggs said. "He is tellin you that box fightin is like a game him and the Duke of Green Eyeshades was playin." He squinted at Andrew. "Not every feller out here would understand that, you see. There's been a time if a man knocked you down out here you had better get up and knock *him* down, and harder, or plan on leavin the country."

"Why?" he said. His face was prickling with anger. Cletus had turned to gaze at him again with an expression of drunken disdain.

"Because of folks thinkin of you as the kind that got knocked down and didn't do nothin about it," Driggs said.

Conroy, with care, trickled liquor from the whiskey bottle into the three glasses, In a placating tone, he said, "Well, that is one big Scotchman. I expect he could knock down just about anybody he took a mind to."

"Course, it is different now," Driggs continued. "Folks

133

don't put so much stock in that kind of business. It was a harder time, back then. But that old hard time passin is a sad thing, too."

Cletus staggered outside, leaving the louver doors swinging behind him. Driggs shook his head. "Can't believe the old great days is gone, and they will try to whiskey it back. Me, too," he said with a sigh, brooding down on his whiskey glass. His face resembled something carved from hard, dark wood, grained with time and weather.

He asked what Driggs was doing this spring.

"Nothin much. Market for game's off something fierce. Just can't understand how come it jerks around so."

Conroy said he must be going, picked up his hat, and nodded to Andrew. "Pleased to met you." He left.

Driggs stretched mightily. "How about gettin us some grub, Andy? Then we might take a look-in at Big Cora's."

It was a moment before he connected Big Cora with Mrs. Benbow. "No, thanks," he said, and felt his cheeks burning again.

Driggs propped his cheek on the palm of a big hand and regarded him across the table. "Don't approve of whores?" he said mildly. "Oh, my! I had better tell you somethin if you are set on livin out here. Whores is all we have got in the Bad Lands. Cora's is the only women a feller can even *talk* to in Pyramid. It is a place for socializin any way that's wanted, you see."

Mrs. Benbow's house was a two-story frame structure half as large as the hotel and separated from it by a narrow alley. Horses and buggies stood at the hitching rail before it, and in the dusk, a blue light burned beside the door. Inside, a small, tough-looking man wearing a derby hat lounged on a low seat. He nodded silently as they entered.

They passed on into a lighted parlor where there was a hum of conversation. A girl in a white shift darted forward to attach herself to Driggs's arm.

"Come in to turn a trick, Billy?" She was coarse-faced, painted, very young, with a trim figure. Andrew noticed that her shift was none too clean.

He had visited a house in Boston with a friend his last year at Harvard, but he had been so embarrassed he could recall neither the parlor nor the girls. In this room were perhaps a dozen people, more than half of them girls in white shifts like the one clinging to Driggs's arm. Three other men in towns-

134

men's clothes were comparing cigars, a cowboy was seated in an easy chair with a boot propped on the arm, a whiskey bottle on a low table beside him. There did seem the sense of easy camaraderie Driggs had mentioned, and nothing blatant. His eyes caught those of a girl seated on a man's knee and teasing with his hair; she had been laughing, her painted lips like red ribbons, but now she quieted to smile at him almost demurely.

"Ouch, Billy, that hurts!" the first girl said; Drigss had clasped her buttock with a big hand. The color was high in his face.

Andrew stood with them uncertainly, examining the chromos on the walls, mainly hunting scenes and mountain peaks, certainly nothing chosen to inflame the senses. From an Ali Baba pot in the corner sprayed a cluster of bright-colored feathers. Light from lamps with colored glass shades gleamed on the pale faces and bared shoulders of the girls. Although he did not approve the taste of the place, he could see that there had been an effort toward taste. A gauze of smoke lay across the ceiling, and there was a complicated smell he tried to analyze: cigar smoke, whiskey, soapy water, powder, perfume—women and men.

"You wouldn't mind ante-ing up a couple dollars for Fanny here, would you?" Driggs said casually. It seemed that this was to be his treat, as supper had also been. He produced the greenbacks, which the girl appropriated in a businesslike way. She and Driggs climbed the stairs together, bumping hips and laughing. They reminded Andrew of children on a romp, for all the hunter's grizzled hair and wried face.

A humpbacked maid in a black and white uniform asked if he would like whiskey. She brought him a glass and collected fifty cents. One of the townsmen nodded to him in a friendly fashion. The girl with the bright lips came up to take his arm.

"Looking for company, mister?"

He responded in the negative, but she seemed not to understand, continuing to clutch his arm and smile up into his face. Her eyes were light blue and unblinking, one of them marred by a flaw in the pupil. What he wanted at this moment was his sketch pad, to catch the motion of Driggs hurrying upstairs with his Fanny, or his first glimpse of the girl now clinging to his arm, that quick eagerness of her face turning toward him in both expectancy and the lack of it, as she sat on the knee of one man while another, conversing with him, peered down at her breasts.

135

A big man lurched down the stairs, halting on the landing to sway against the banister as though to topple into the group below. One of the girls squealed.

It was Lord Machray in his shirt sleeves. Following him came Mrs. Benbow, to lay a restraining hand on his shoulder. Her head was piled high with dark hair, and jet earrings flashed in her ears. Her eyes encountered Andrew's, but she made no sign of recognition.

"Lads o' parts and sonsie lassies!" Machray called down, in thick Scots accent. His face was scarlet. He straightened, a head taller than the big woman beside him, and struck an oratorical pose.

"It has been said," he went on. "That the Scots fornicate gravely but without conviction. I will ask Mrs. Benbow to refute this canard!"

There was laughter. The woman flushed. Machray swung an arm toward her. "Identify the master plowman of the continent for the multitudes, my dear woman!"

"Why, you, Machray, who else?" she said in her rather coarse voice. He remembered her on the veranda at Widewings, her head on Machray's shoulder gazing at the shower of falling stars. Now she took Machray's arm as he lurched again.

Machray drew himself up comically and raised both his hands as though in benediction. "I will gae ye the words o' me auld mither, friends! 'If it does ye nae guid it'll dae ye nae harrrrm!' Now, there is wisdom encapsuled, the secret of potency in the male, and a specific against diseases of the liver!"

Andrew felt the girl's grip on his arm loosen, finger by finger, and her hand drop away. Looming on the stair, Machray and the big woman looked larger than life, electric in their vitality. Mrs. Benbow's black gown had some style to it, and she was handsome in a proud-headed, hard-featured way, her coarsened face illuminated by the dark eyes.

"Friends!" Machray said again. "The abattoir will soon be finished—" Someone cheered, and Machray beamed down at him. "But they are seeking to stab us in the back! The freight rates on dressed beef have been raised! Higher than the rate for live cattle! The meatpackers connive with their toadies of the railroad! But we will prevail! The Bad Lands will not be denied!"

He leaned forward to shake a big finger at the circle of faces gazing up at him, the madame grasping him by the back

136

of his shirt. "Friends! We have found kaolin. Up on Muddy Creek!"

"What is that, Machray?" one of the men called.

"The finest clay! From which the finest porcelain is made! Pyramid Flat will take its place with Copenhagen, with Sèvres, with Meissen!"

Applause, more cheers. "He *does* go on when he is tipsy!" the girl beside Andrew whispered. He could not tell whether the mood of the parlor was one of ridicule or honest enthusiasm. Machray held up his hands for silence again.

"And I give you the simple cabbage! Are you aware that we have the perfect climate for cabbages here? We can raise enough cabbages, beef, and mutton to supply the hunger of the world! The Bad Lands will come to be called the Food Lands! We will carve an empire from these old buttes and bottoms!"

It seemed to Andrew that Machray was using the royal "we." The madam tugged at his arm as he leaned over the rail. "That's enough now, Machray. In your condition—"

"Condition!" Machray roared. "Marvelous condition! Body of an athlete. Body of a lad of twenty! Douce or dour, the laird is always fit! Daisy, a cup of whiskey for the assembled, set down to the account of the Master of Ring-cross Ranch!"

Mrs. Benbow led him on down the stairs, where men crowded around to shake his hand and clap him on the shoulder, Machray a head taller than anyone else in the room. Machray's eyes met Andrew's across the room, and his face lighted up.

"Ah, Livingston! Another gentleman captured by the beauty of the place. We'll work together to make the Bad Lands the garden of the world, eh, Livingston?"

"Hush, now, Machray," Mrs. Benbow said, as the maid circulated, pouring whiskey into proffered glasses.

"Got a case on him," Andrew's companion whispered, giggling. "It is a stitch to watch her!"

"And you?" he said suddenly. "What do you think of him?"

She looked up at him with round, pale eyes. "Oh, he is a fine gentleman! It is always good times when Lord Machray is here!" Then her face jerked toward the stairs with an expression of worry.

Driggs was descending alone. Andrew saw his features twist sourly as he looked down on the scene below. He came on down, as tall as Machray; the girl clutched Andrew's arm again as the two tall heads appeared drawn together. There was a scuffle, a feminine shriek, ejaculations from the men; now only Machray's yellow head was to be seen.

"You need not drink my whiskey, my man!" Machray said in a thick voice. "But you will not call me that!"

The madam called out, "*Wax!*" Pressing closer, Andrew saw Driggs rising from the floor. Mrs. Benbow had placed herself between him and Machray. The little man with the derby hat appeared; there was a glint of a pistol. Wax moved with Driggs in lockstep toward the door with a placating mutter.

The twisted, gargoyle face turned back: "*Come and settle this outside, Much-a-muck!*"

Then Driggs and Wax were gone. Mrs. Benbow turned to face Machray, the girls and their clients retreating around them. Machray raised a hand to brush hair from his forehead.

"I will need to borrow a weapon," he said.

"No, you will not!" the madam said, others chiming in. Andrew heard his own voice among them. It seemed a nightmare, and it was he who had furnished the wherewithal for Driggs to come here. Machray was shaking his head, his whole body swaying with the effort.

"Never refused a fight in my life! Ancestors would spin in their graves like dynamos!"

"You are drunk, Machray!" Mrs. Benbow said.

"Drunk as a hoot owl!" another voice said. Andrew forced his way closer.

Machray lurched around. "Will no one lend me his weapon! Buckley, will you? You have had my custom."

"No!" Mrs. Benbow said. "I will not have it!"

Machray stood teetering, facing Buckley, his chin thrust out. Andrew clenched his fist, carefully arranging his thumb so he would not disolcate it, and dropped his shoulder. He swung from his knees. Pain shot up his arm. There was a chorus of screams and the house shook as Machray fell. His hand groped out, drew back under his body; he lay still, face down.

Two of the girls in their white shifts knelt beside him, one on either side like attendant angels. Everyone else stared at Andrew, the madam with her dark, comprehensive eyes.

"Bless you," she said. "Bill would have shot him."

A man with a graying beard was shaking his head. "I

would not want to be in your boots when Lord Machray comes around, young man."

"He will not remember a bit of it," Mrs. Benbow said. "If he does, there'll be thanks due."

"Someone should take him home," Andrew said. Massaging his fist he reflected that he had employed it in the Bad Lands more frequently than he approved. But if he had placed himself in deadly danger with his assault on Cletus, the blow that had felled Machray had at least been intended to remove the big man from it.

"His man has been sent for," the madam said. She placed a hand to either cheek, as though holding her head on. "Daisy!" she said. "We'll have another whiskey, on the house!"

Andrew refused this new glass the maid brought him; he needed no more stimulants. The girl with the bright lips was watching him with a worshipful expression. But his own satisfaction had already dissolved into anxiety for Machray. Hardy's challenger had himself been challenged, the bully called out, and murderous violence seemed to have swerved even closer in Pyramid Flat than it had in Miles City.

Before Machray came around, Dickson appeared, to squat beside his master, loosening his cravat, feeling his pulse, and clucking with disapproval.

"We can take him out the back if you'll bring the buggy around in the alley," Mrs. Benbow said.

"I believe he would prefer to go out the same way he came in, thank you, madam," Dickson said. "Could someone give us a lift here?"

Andrew and two others helped him carry Machray, the big man mumbling, protesting, and snoring. "Sixteen stone of him," Dickson panted. Mrs. Benbow held the door as they maneuvered the body out of the parlor.

Outside, in the blue glare of the lamp, Machray's face looked ghastly. Beyond was pit darkness, in which Driggs, if he was there, was invisible. They staggered with the limp bulk down the boardwalk, and managed to stuff Machray onto the seat of his buggy.

"Thank you, gentlemen," Dickson said. The two others started back toward the blue light, but Andrew gathered from Dickson's gesture that he was to remain. In a low voice, Dickson said, "It is because he misses Lady Machray and the bairn so much, you see, Mr. Livingston. He is apt to take a dram too much when he is lonely."

139

"Of course, Dickson."

Dickson climbed into the buggy and clucked to the horse. The buggy rolled away on its high, frail wheels, the occupants invisible now beneath its bonnet. He stood under the dimmed stars until his eyes were accustomed to the dark, looking for Driggs.

There was no sign of the hunter as he circled the block to the hotel, stepping carefully on the rough street in the darkness.

7

A week later a cowboy delivered a note from Machray:

"*My dear Livingston*:

"I am sure you are aware of the Western Dokota Stockraisers Association, and its particular powers and functions. This organization does not accept new members readily, and its rolls are in effect closed, which policy is due to what is considered to be overcrowding of the range, a condition that does not affect me, but certainly does you.

"For complicated reasons, I have taken it upon myself to persuade the organization's Powers to hold this month's meeting at Widewings, and I am inviting you to attend as my personal guest. You will not find the other members a hospitable lot. However I am confident that your charm, natural reticence, and quiet good breeding will recommend you to them. This affair convenes mid-afternoon tomorrow, and I trust I will see you there.

"*Machray*"

There was a postscript:

"I am advised that thanks are owed you for your actions of the other evening. My thanks, then."

When Andrew told Chally he would be attending the Stockraisers Association meeting tomorrow, Chally said, "Good! Maybe you can find out how we sit in those old bodgers' craws. Best see how the wind is blowing before you decide on bringin in a second herd."

"Machray says there is a policy against accepting new members."

"Well, if you have got a stand-in with him and Hardy it ought to help. It was surely unfriendly on roundup, and I believe we are goin to get tired of bein treated like nesters, Andy."

Ring-cross cowboys sat on a rail fence above the bunk-houses, which were ranged in an L in a shallow canyon just beyond Widewings, observing the Bad Lands stockmen arriving, on horseback and in buggies, buckboards, and spring wagons. Andrew, who had taken a room at the hotel for the night, turned over Blackie's reins to one of the cowboys, and clumped on up the wooden steps with his neighbors, none of whom took any notice of him.

In the great hall benches had been ranged in rows facing a wooden table before one of the fireplaces. Between the rows were the gleams of brass spittoons. The air was already thickened with cigar smoke, and Dickson approached to offer him a Havana from a cedar box. Beyond him, standing against the wall, was Jake Boutelle.

He halted, staring at the gunman, who met his eyes once, casually, and then glanced away, raising his cigar to his lips. His black hair was neatly brushed and parted in the exact center of his head. Staring at him, Andrew could feel poison pumping in his veins.

Machray loomed over the heads of the other men. "Glad you could come, Livingston!" he boomed. He raised a hand to his jaw, waggled it back and forth, and winked solemnly. "Ah, Pelke!" he called, catching the arm of a fattish man to introduce Andrew.

Pelke had a glazed patch of scar tissue over one eye, in which a pulse was visible. "Meetcha," he said, and moved away. Two others Machray introduced were no more friendly, although one shook Andrew's hand. He noticed Hardy sidling between the benches, and he left Machray to take a seat beside his other neighbor, who, however, also seemed distant.

The benches continued to fill, and it struck him that the faces of the members of the Western Dakota Stockraisers were all excessive in some way, grotesque, many of them— here a swollen nose bursting with blood vessels, there one knocked askew in some accident, a disfiguring roll of fat

141

around a sunburnt neck, a sharp configuration to a bald head, like the keel of a ship, Pelke's scar. Most were smoking Machray's cigars, but others chewed tobacco and spat copiously into the spittoons. He noticed one pointing out to another the Union Jack tacked to the wall beneath a set of royal elk horns, dirty and ragged, bright diagonals fretted with bullet holes. Boutelle stood with arms folded, looking from face to face with that curious absorption Andrew had noticed that day at Fire Creek.

Everyone seemed to ignore Machray, who, in kilts and sporran, captain's pips on the shoulder loops of his jacket, stood at military ease before the brick fireplace, legs spread and hands behind his back.

"What is Boutelle's position here?" Andrew asked Hardy.

"He is employed as a range inspector by the Association," Hardy said curtly.

He wondered if Hardy could be simply jealous that he had come here as Machray's guest. In any event he did not feel like employing his charm, natural reticence, and good breeding. "I was informed that Boutelle did not visit me in an official capacity," he said.

"He did not!" Hardy said, and turned aside as a young man squeezed past to take the space on Andrew's right.

This one wore a brown suit, and the bone-white margin of a new haircut gleamed. "Well, if it went the New York punkin-lily!" he said, grinning at Andrew, who remembered him as one of the "reps" at Machray's roundup last fall. "Fred Rademacher," the other said, as they shook hands. There was silence as Machray stepped to the table.

He apologized for the condition of his house; every available carpenter was at work on the abattoir, which he hoped would open within a month. "Believe we can proceed here. Mr. Hardy will preside in the place of Mr. Lamey, who is sailing."

Hardy scuttled to the table, to ignore Machray and tap lightly with his knuckles to establish his chairmanship. "Gentlemen: Last meeting we ended our discussions on the subject of thievery, and I believe we will begin with old business. Unless there is objection?"

Under a rising sibilance of conversations, Fred Rademacher said, "Hear you have brung in some head south of here."

He said it was true, and the other again proffered his hand.

142

It was the first friendly gesture here, apart from Machray's wink. Hardy tapped for order.

"The historical method of dealing with such problems," he said, glancing out over the tops of his spectacles, "is simple progress. County organization, statehood—all of which I have no doubt are in store for us eventually. Including that concomitant of progress, taxes." He smiled frostily. "I wonder if we are suffering that intensely."

There was a ripple of laughter. Behind Andrew a man said, "Might as well just go on payin our taxes to rustlers the way we have been doin."

"Had any stock stole yet?" Fred Rademacher said in his ear and, when he said he had not, "You will. It will be a good shock to you to find out just how mad you can get."

"Rustlers have been known to change their ways," Yule Hardy continued. "Governments, never! The question still remains— How are we to persuade rustlers and horse thieves to change *their* ways? Hazel?"

A lean man had risen, hands clasped self-consciously before him. "S-some of us that was out here before everybody and his brother started crowdin in'll remember when times got so bad up around Bannack and Virginia City. Well, Ash Tanner did change those fellows' ways! I remember the story of how the lady come up to Ash and said so he was the devil of a Regulator that had lynched thirty men? And Ash said, right back, 'Yes, ma'am, and I done it all alone!' "

There was loud laughter at this, and Andrew, who had felt a chill at the words 'crowdin in,' craned his neck to see where others around him were looking—at a stocky, grim-jawed elderly man with a short white beard and cropped hair like white moss.

Rademacher whispered, "Ash must've known this'd come up!"

"I s-sure hope Ash'll give us the benefit of his advice," the man called Hazel said hurriedly, and plumped down. The man with the bony bald head had risen.

"Pard Yarborough," Rademacher whispered. Hardy waited until the noise subsided. "Pard?"

Yarborough had an angry, hectoring voice. "I say let's get right on to the list, Yule!"

"Perhaps that is next in order, then," Hardy said. "Major Cutter? Your committee."

A short, black-haired man with a pouter-pigeon bearing replaced Hardy at the table. He carried several sheets of paper.

"Captain Machray," he said. "Mr. Hardy. Friends. As you know, with the help of the range inspectors, we have been compiling a list of known or suspected rustlers in the Bad Lands. It is our opinion that there are not many in it full-time, except for that fellow Jack Berry, who was shot last fall down by Clear Springs. But there are a lot that make a hobby, so to speak, of rustling and horse stealing—as we all know. Old buffalo hunters, smallholders, grangers, a few dishonest cowboys." He raised his hands expressively.

"Who've you got down on that list there?" Yarborough called. Boutelle stood with his arms folded, glancing from face to face.

Major Cutter took spectacles from his pocket and propped them on his nose. He read: "Tom Waggoner, Jack Long, Frank Roswell, Tim Smith—"

"Hold on, now!" Ash Tanner cried. "You be damned careful what you are doing there! If that is Tim R. Smith, it's a damned lie! Tim Smith has been out here fifteen years. He was one of them in the Crazy Horse fight in '68!"

In silence Major Cutter made a pencil mark on the sheet before him. "That is the whole trouble with a thing like this!" Tanner said. "You have got to be sure!"

Cutter read on, names that meant nothing to Andrew. Fred Rademacher jumped to his feet.

"That's wrong. It must be that other Teasdale from over by Hastings! Martin Teasdale is no horse thief!"

"Sit down, son, and hear this out!" an older man roared.

Rademacher reseated himself, muttering: "My old daddy. Thinks I'm still in diaper cloths."

"Harvey Conroy," Cutter read. "Emmett Maugher, Challis Reuter—"

Andrew found himself on his feet. "Challis Reuter is my partner!" He stood there, all eyes on him, Machray frowning, Hardy blank-faced, Major Cutter removing the eyeglasses from his nose to peer at him. He looked straight at Boutelle and said, "It is a lie!"

"Why, I will vouch for Chally Reuter, too!" Fred Rademacher said. "This is a poor kind of list you have got up, Major!"

"It is a bad list!" Tanner said, rising also. He shook a stubby finger at Cutter. "It is too long, for one thing! And it has got to be *right*!" He slammed his fist into the palm of his hand. "Hazel Cole asked me for the benefit of my experience.

Well, if it has got any benefit, that is it! You can't be too careful! And then you just have to be carefuller than that!"

Still staring at Boutelle, Andrew slowly reseated himself. He felt nauseated with anger. "What is the point of this, anyhow?" a man demanded.

"It is a dead list," another said.

Machray said, "I believe we should apply pressure where it can be felt to get the sheriff out of Mandan to perform his bounden duties!"

The man with the sunburnt ruff of flesh rose, hands on hips. "I'll tell you what Sheriff Cece Brown said to me. Said if you fellows want to stop horse-thievin out there you should get yourself a man with a rifle, not a *pencil!*"

There was an uproar at this. Andrew saw Machray frowning. His eyes encountered Boutelle's obsidian chips studying him.

"By God, that is dry-gulchin!" a man cried. "And that is plain murder!"

Cutter had put his eye glasses back in his pocket and folded his papers, tight-lipped. Machray stepped forward with hands held up for quiet.

"I for one would like very much to hear from Mr. Tanner in this matter. May we not have your counsel, sir?"

Cutter returned to his seat, and there was a clamor for Tanner, who finally shuffled up to the table.

"Squaw man," Fred whispered. "Married to a real pretty little Snake. He sure does keep a tight rein on *her*. Got a fair-sized spread over our way."

Tanner said in his harsh voice, "Well, fifteen years ago things had got pretty bad, as some of you know, and some of you don't. Worse than now. There was gangs around them mining camps that everybody was afraid of. So some folks got together to start a vigilance committee—Regulation Committee, as it was called. They wanted to elect me to run things, but I wouldn't do it that way."

He leaned on the table glancing around him while this was digested.

"Told them I'd do it or I wouldn't do it," he went on. "But I wasn't going to be *elected* to it. Because that was putting some kind of lawyer front on it that was the bunk. For it was plain murder, and that was all it ever was!"

He waited again before he said, "Things had better be pretty bad if you are thinking murder. And maybe they just never are that bad.

"Well, I will give you what counsel I have, which is what our host here has asked of me. If you think it has come time for a Regulation Committee, don't let on to many what is going on. Maybe only those that are doing the riding, and a few besides. One good man in charge, and four, five others he can trust. And access to all the saddle stock that's needed, good stock too, not just cast-offs from somebody's cavy. Two or three strikes—the worst ones, and a few scares. And *quit!*"

He gazed from face to face again with his jaw twisted queerly to one side. Andrew felt the old dangerous eyes brush past his. "If you have got to do it, do it. But be *sure*. For it has been like a curse on me since. I was sure, those times; thought I was. But I have never been sure of anything since.

"And *quit!*" he said again. "I quit. And we had a good name then still. But some thought there was still work to be done. So others took it up. And they made mistakes. And worse. There were some to put on white masks and run some fellow off range they had got to quarreling over. Or water rights. Or a girl. And where was the good name then?"

He was leaning over the table, and Andrew could see his hands, white-knuckled, gripping the edge. "Fellows! When you take the lid off the box it is mighty hard to get it back on again!"

There was a silence. Finally old Rademacher rose, and said, "Ash, won't you take on this task for us? I don't believe there is a man we could trust to get the lid back on again, excepting you."

Tanner shook his head. All at once he seemed smaller, old and tired, who had been the terror of the gangs of Bannack and Virginia City fifteen years ago.

"You would have our gratitude, Ash," Yarborough said, but the old Regulator only returned to his seat in silence. Hardy took his place at the table again and tapped with his knuckles.

"If we find it in our hearts that we must do this thing, I am sure we will ask for Ash's advice again. Roy?"

The man with the ruff of flesh had risen. "I say we should hire us a man with a rifle!"

"Count me out of that!" a man cried, and while others seconded the motion, another shouted, "I will never be part of such a thing!"

"You won't be part of this range before long, either! Stole blind by rustlers and grangers, and new outfits shoving in taking up our grass and water!"

146

Andrew could hardly absorb what he was hearing. The fact that a man like Chally could be accused of rustling had shaken him, even though he suspected that Boutelle had placed that name on the list. And he could not believe this talk of lynching and murder. He had had warning enough that the small ranchers were disliked by the larger, the newcomers by the older, and certainly Machray had cautioned him of the Association's policy against new members, but despite all that he had assumed, with Chally, that Machray's and Hardy's friendship would assure his acceptance. It occurred to him that Hardy's unfriendliness was due to embarrassment at the subjects under discussion here, and the violence of his colleagues.

The arguments now turned to other problems he must try to understand, of the need for a "brand book" of brands to be officially recognized at roundups, of the further need for "inspectors," and of the danger of "pool-outfit roundups." Next came the problem of the continuing incursions of grangers. Each man here, it seemed, had his story of granger confrontations and granger depredations, of grangers fencing their acreages, of granger dishonesty and granger poor-spiritedness, of granger women, children, and dogs. Hardy adjourned the meeting with nothing decided, and Machray announced whiskey in the library.

Andrew left the room with Fred Rademacher. Dickson poured them whiskeys and they stepped outside onto the veranda, where there was a breath-quickening view of the eastern sweep of prairie. Pyramid Flat huddled half in shadow beneath the bluffs, with the spidery strands of the railroad bridge spanning the river. A banner of black smoke rose from a train in the station. He asked if the Rademacher ranch was nearby.

"Over on the west slope," Rademacher said, with a wave of his hand. He tossed off half his whiskey and wiped his mustache. "Well, now, don't Machray serve easy-slidin whiskey? What's a Easterner make of talk like that in there?"

"I make it that everyone is angry and fearful."

"Well, that is the truth," Rademacher said. "Did you catch the drift with old Ash?"

He didn't know what Fred meant.

"Said he wouldn't allow the Association to elect him to ride, but he didn't say he wouldn't ride. What I thought he was sayin was he might do it just the same as he did before, on his own with some fellows he could trust."

Rademacher's father approached, a gaunt man with a cigar in one hand and a glass of whiskey in the other. He wore striped trousers stuffed into his boots, a rusty black jacket, and a shirt buttoned tieless at the throat. He jammed his cigar between his teeth to shake hands.

"Jim Rademacher," he said. "This squirt here's daddy. You're the fellow settled in between Yule Hardy and Machray down along Fire Creek, I understand; Chally Reuter runnin the spread for you. Range'll be shapin up a little dense down that way. Gettin along with Machray, are you?"

He said as far as he knew. The two stood looking at him, the father six inches taller than the son.

"He is the one that had the boxing-fight with Machray up on roundup last fall, Daddy. He's a Jim Dandy flingin his fists about!"

"That so?" Jim Rademacher said, squinted at him, and moved on.

"You'd think folks out here had nothing better to do than gossip about strangers," Fred said. "You are a mysterious gent from New York, very educated talkin, and so rich he can write out a check for any amount. Missed you on spring-roundup. I was reppin up on the Yellowstone. So you are friendly with Machray."

"No one else here seems to be."

"Well, that is a fact," Fred said.

"Why is it?"

"Comes in here all elbows, makin so much *noise*. Got everybody worryin they are goin to have to buy and fence the same as him. These old farts, they just hate to see range goin; the old days goin, that to hear them tell it it was so bad nobody but them could've survived it. Reason Daddy don't exactly fall over himself tellin you you are welcome out here."

"I understand that."

"And somebody's been tellin lies on Chally Reuter."

"I'm obliged to you for speaking up. Would it have been that man Boutelle?"

"Sure, it might've been Jake."

He told Rademacher of his experience with Jake Bountelle and Bob Cletus, and Fred whistled silently. "That'd sure give *me* the willies. But I don't believe that was Association work. Jake just naturally has his nose in everythin that goes on in the Bad Lands. Probably thought that shack ought to've been his just as soon as he saw you in it. Probably come to nothin if you offered to buy him out."

148

Machray came up to knead Andrew's shoulder with a big hand. "Hadn't realized what was coming up for discussion, Livingston," he said in a low voice. "I'm told I've made a mistake; good deal of criticism. Must apologize if I have let you in for unpleasantnesses." He tramped on down along the veranda.

"Some day I'm going to ask him how he keeps his privates warm in that getup," Rademacher said.

Andrew asked how one went about joining the Association.

The other looked painfully embarrassed. "Well, there is committees for just about everything. I guess I'd just wait till I was asked."

"But I won't be asked?"

Fred shrugged elaborately.

Andrew told himself he was not anxious to join an organization where the arguments over violence seemed merely of degree, but the Association controlled the general roundup, and the talk of a "brand book" and "inspectors" had been disturbing. We are going to get pretty tired of being treated like nesters, Chally had said.

Fred obviously found the subject painful, so he dropped it, and the two of them strolled on around the veranda, following a smell of broiling meat. On a spit over a cherry-glowing bed of coals the carcass of a steer revolved, dripping fat that spat viciously in the coals. A cook in a white chef's cap turned the crank and mopped at his face with a bandanna. On plank tables cutlery and glass glinted in the late sun.

Hay bales were stacked with small targets affixed, and cattlemen clustered at one of the tables. Andrew and Fred joined the group to find Machray arranging a pistol competition. A matched pair of dueling pistols rested in shaped depressions in blue velvet in a mahogany box. Five shots apiece were to be fired at one of the targets, which a cowboy replaced when they had been perforated. Andrew was humiliated by only hitting the target once in his set, Boutelle standing slightly apart from the other cattlemen to watch him. Others, however, were just as inept. Many used their own revolvers, although Machray pointed out that the dueling pistols were machine calibrated, and no more accurate weapons were to be found. Fred Rademacher did well, as did his father and several of the younger men; but the finalists were Machray and Boutelle.

Machray took aim carefully and slowly, perforating the bull's-eye of his target with each shot, while Boutelle fired much more casually, holding his revolver lower. His next to last shot was just out of the bull's-eye, and Machray was declared the winner. Andrew saw that no one was pleased by the contrived affair, as Machray bragged of practicing every day. "A chap who has been shot at from ambush eight times cannot afford to do any less!" he said loudly.

After the competition Boutelle disappeared, and Andrew did not see him at supper. He sat at a table with Hardy, the Rademachers, Hazel Cole, and the first man he had met here, Ollie Pelke. There was continuing complaint about the pistol competition.

"I have never seen such a sissified set of shooting irons," Pelke said. "Well, I know a shootin man or two could do as well with a pair of Colts."

"Like Boutelle didn't," Fred said.

"Did a bit better than you did, Sonny," his father said, "Anyway, Jake don't have to prove nothing about shootin to anybody." They all laughed, and Andrew glanced toward the center table, where Machray presided. Dickson came by with a wine bottle, pouring claret into the glasses.

"You are quiet, Andy," Hardy said in an aside, looking at him directly for the first time.

He said he was trying to understand the hostility directed at their host.

Hardy lowered his eyelids patiently, as though he had explained this many times, but would endeavor once more to make it clear. "These are uneducated, self-made men," he said. "If they do not seem cordial to you, it is because they are naturally wary of a stranger. In Lord Machray's case, they are objecting to privilege. It is what their ancestors came to this country to escape. They have only half-forgotten ancient wrongs—that their forebears starved when the feudal lords of England enclosed the common lands."

"It seems to me that that is exactly what they are trying to do here."

"Just what do you mean?" Hardy glared at him.

"Machray has fenced land he has purchased. This Association is seeking to enclose lands it has not purchased for its own use only. You want to keep out everyone who is not one of yourselves. By brand registration and stock inspection, and by violence. What is the difference?"

As he stared back into Hardy's eyes, magnified by the lenses of his eyeglasses, he thought that he had insured that he would not be asked to join the Western Dakota Stock-raisers Association.

The moment was broken by a tapping of metal against glass. Machray had risen, to stand looming against the red glow of the fire. "Gentlemen, I confess to being a bit ashamed of the demonstration that was held just now. As I say, I have been shot at from ambush on eight separate occasions. I have come into the knowledge, by devious routes, of the identity of the men who hired those shots fired, on a kind of bounty system, or cowboy's game." He glanced from face to face. "I see all but one of those men are here tonight.

"I am, of course, aware," he went on, "that the effort was not upon my life. They would have succeeded in that. They will not succeed in driving me hence. Surely they must be aware of *that* by now. However, I do apologize for my little game just now, with which, as you no doubt guessed, I sought to impress those of you I have mentioned with my own steady hand with a pistol.

"But gentlemen, my guile extends further. No doubt some of you wondered why I made such a matter of holding this meeting here. It was so that you should eat my meat and drink my wine, accept my hospitality, in other words. It is well known throughout the civilized world that those who partake of a man's hospitality cannot plot his harm on the pain of the disfavor of the gods!"

There was utter silence. Andrew glanced covertly at the stony faces around him. Machray stood facing them, grinning easily. "Therefore," he said at last, "I now give you a toast in which we can all join with a clear conscience. To American beef, gentlemen!"

Andrew raised his glass. He watched others raised around him, a grin or two break out. He could almost deduce the men Machray had mentioned, who had hired those shots from ambush, for they raised their glasses reluctantly; but raised them in the end, all but Hardy.

Machray continued, "It is said that in the time of the Crusades English soldiers in the Holy Land were discomfited because the French and Austrians had means of preserving meat whilst they had none. So it proved again in Egypt, hot country also, as I can attest. And who did the British turn to in their need but America—who has led the world in perfecting methods of canning beef. I give you some verses that were current in the Egyptian campaign."

He folded his arms on his chest and recited, in a big voice:

> "The roast beef of old England
> Is famed in song and story.
> Without it where was English brawn
> That won old England glory?
> But in these days of England's trial,
> When war's dread notes alarm her,
> What does she send to save the Nile?
> Beef canned by Philip Armour!"

Machray paused to tip his wineglass to his lips. Andrew watched the men leaning forward to listen as at first they had leaned back, and glanced sideways to see Hardy's white-knuckled hand gripping his glass. Then Machray continued:

> "When Gladstone first resolved on war,
> No lack of ammunition
> Delayed the march through Egypt's land,
> The problem was nutrition.
> 'Our cannonade,' the premier said,
> 'Must needs be sharp and brief.
> Our cannonade therefore shall be,
> Of England's own tinned beef!'"

There were shouts of laughter, mouths open to show half-chewed food, lips red with wine. Yarborough was slapping his hand on the table and shouting, "Hear! Hear!" Grinning, Machray made a gesture as of pulling up slipping trousers to illustrate the summoning up of memory.

> "At every mile along the line
> The warriors of Arabi
> Will soon be skirmishing to find
> A soul to fit the body.
> The Pasha had a host of Khans,
> And some were brave and able,
> But must have known they could not win,
> They lacked the Armour label!"

The whooping laughter and applause rose again. Machray held up a hand. "Seriously, my friends," he said, "I do not believe Pyramid Flat is ever going to compete with Chicago in the tinning of beef. But feeding armies is something I believe we can do, if Mr. Armour and Mr. Swift will only let us!"

Again Andrew joined the applause. The verses had been apt and clever, the invocation of Swift and Armour, greater villains to this company than Machray could ever be, inspired. He grinned back at Fred Rademacher. He turned to Hardy.

"Very well done, I thought."

Hardy wouldn't look at him. "I did not say he was not a clever man," he said.

Now another clamor rose. Some of the Ring-cross cowboys had assembled on the far side of the fire. They were calling for Machray to dance. "Do the handkerchief one, lord!" They kept it up until, after demurring, he gave in and called for Dickson to bring his pipes.

Machray stripped off his jacket, and, tugging a handkerchief between his hands, moved to one side of the fire. Dickson appeared. The first raw, sour notes sounded, became music; Dickson paced up and down, piping. Machray postured. With the handkerchief strained between his two hands, clumsy-seeming at first, he raised one leg, pointing the foot. He hopped, swung one way, back, the other and back, spun, leaped, shifted legs. Massively graceful, he swung his handkerchief-connected arms right and left, the cloth glowing like phosphorus in the firelight. The piper piped and the dancer danced, moving through intricate repetitions and changes.

The cattlemen watched, some open-mouthed, others merely puzzled, many blank-faced, a few openly contemptuous. Andrew saw old Jim Rademacher turn aside to spit. Others averted their heads. The haunting music shrilled, Machray postured and leaped. His face gleamed with sweat; his panting was audible. Andrew watched the faces of the cattlemen close against him. Despite his hospitality, or because of it, despite his cleverness or his guile, or because of his openness, maybe because he was foreign, or merely different, he would always offend these men who were so ready to be offended by him.

Late the next morning Andrew presented himself for the third time in his life at a bordello, this time with his sketchbook. He pressed the bell, heard its note within, and turned to watch a wagon passing in the street, a rusty piece of machinery in its bed. Neither of the overalled grangers on the seat of the wagon paid him any attention. The humpbacked maid opened the door.

She followed him into the parlor, where a lone girl sat engrossed in a brightly jacketed dream book. She put the book aside and rose, coquettishly smiling, but she was not the one he wished to see. Mrs. Benbow appeared on the landing, the jet earrings glittering in her ears, although today she seemed to him to resemble a schoolteacher, with her black skirt, white shirtwaist, and velvet ribbon at her throat. He said he had come to sketch one of her girls. He would pay.

She nodded, the dark discs of her eyes in her pock-marked face fastened on him. No doubt she had heard every possible kind of request.

"How long will you be needing her?"

"Not more than an hour."

She shrugged. "Two dollars, then. Mornings are slow. If you require anything else you should double it."

He felt himself flushing as he nodded. "There was a girl here last time— She had rather a wide mouth, and a mole just here." He touched his throat.

"Call Maizie," the madam said. The girl with the dream book disappeared, and the hunchback maid hovered close. He gave her two greenbacks. In a few moments the girl with the bright lips appeared, to take his arm and smile up into his face.

"Come to see Maizie, did you, mister?"

"He wants to draw some pictures of you, Maizie," Mrs. Benbow said from the stair. "He thinks he'll need you for about an hour."

In a cubicle with a shuttered window, there was a bed with a white coverlet, a bureau holding a large white crockery bowl and matching massive pitcher, and a single chair. Ev-

everything seemed cleaner than he would have expected. Maizie stood facing him with her forehead marred with wrinkles, and plump, childish hands folded at her waist.

"You just want me to stand here, or what? Take off my shift?"

"Let me show you how I'd like you first."

She bent pliantly under his hands as he posed her at the edge of the bed, one hand on the ornamental metal foot, smiling coyly at him, head bent forward from the seventh cervical. He removed his jacket, laid out pad and pencils, drew up the chair, and seated himself to make a series of swift sketches. Next he posed her with her head turned so that the muscles of her throat pulled with the strain. She stifled a yawn.

He said he supposed this seemed strange to her.

"Oh, no," she said. "Lots of times men just want to talk. Older men, mostly. It's very restful for a girl." She giggled.

He placed her on the bed with her hands behind her head and elbows jutting, a provocative pose, or anyway so she seemed to feel, for she appeared not quite so bored. "What'll you do with those?" she asked him, as he flipped pages making rapid drawings.

"Some I'll do over again with care, and a few I'll use to plan paintings." He asked her to take off her shift. Her flesh was chalky white beneath. Folding her arms over her breasts, she smiled at him broadly. He asked her to put the shift back on but with the top rolled down so that her breasts were bared. She was shy about exposing her breasts, however, managing to shield them with her forearms, with her hands touching her chin, or cupped to her throat. Once, when he asked her to hold still, she flushed prettily. Her smile never seemed to waver.

"Do you think I'm nice?" she asked.

"Very nice," he said, and now positioned her with her arms folded over her breasts and her torso slightly inclined, like Angelico's virgin; and again with one hand grasped in the other, in the same pose in which he intended to sketch Mary Hardy. He asked if she was getting tired.

"No, it's very restful, really," she said. One waxy nipple peeked out past her forearm. Her pale eyes watched him as he worked swiftly, sometimes abandoning a sketch after a few lines had gone wrong. "You're a funny one," she said. "You talk like Lord Machray, a little."

"Do I?"

"I don't expect *he'd* be satisfied just sitting there drawing pitchers of a girl."

He did not respond to this, but he was feeling some tension and he cut the session short, giving Maizie a dollar for herself. "Will you come again?" she asked pulling up her shift. He said he would.

In the parlor the hunchbacked maid said that Mrs. Benbow would be pleased if he would take a glass of wine with her. He was led back upstairs to a small office where the madam sat at a rolltop desk, its cubbyholes filled with papers. Muscles visibly tugged at the corners of her mouth, not quite producing a smile. She asked him to sit in the tapestry chair near her while she brought from her desk a bottle of sherry and poured two glasses. Female laughter sounded from the depths of the house. Seated at her desk, Big Cora might have been a ranch owner at her accounts rather than the madam of a frontier brothel. She smelled of rosewater.

She asked if he had got what he wanted.

He said he had, leaning down to prop the black sketchbook against his chair. He sipped good sherry.

"You did a good turn for Machray the other night," she said. He was fascinated by her face, at times quite ugly, at others almost beautiful. Her large, pale hands, devoid of rings, were folded before her. "They say Bill Driggs is sworn to kill him," she said.

He stared at her, astonished that he could receive this one more revelation of threatened murder so calmly. "But what can be done?" he said.

"I don't know. If I was *sure* I'd set somebody on him."

He absorbed that.

"I am fearful for Machray," she went on. "Not just because of Bill Driggs. He has enemies in Chicago he won't . . . take any stock in. And there is a bunch of cattlemen that have set their cowboys potshotting him."

"I think he has put a stop to that."

Her eyes met his without curiosity. "They hate him," she said calmly. "Those—men. If they didn't have a reason they would make a reason. Well, I will be glad if he has found a way to stop that."

They sat in silence. He finished his sherry and rose.

"I will have to think of something to do about Bill Driggs," Mrs. Benbow said.

"Dearest Cissie,

"Yesterday on my way home from town I had an experience that has shaken me a good deal. Because of Machray's fence, the ford accessible to us is, in this season, a treacherous one, with shifting banks of quicksand. I had guided Blackie safely across until, scarcely six feet from the west bank, he became mired. Immediately he went mad with fear, pitching and tossing and quickly exhausting his strength. Unable to calm him, I dismounted and, tossing my saddlebags ahead of me, scrambled to the bank, losing one of my boots to the sucking mud. When I tried to aid Blackie in his struggles from there, pulling on the reins and speaking calmly to him, I was horrified to see the unfortunate animal simply give up. Perhaps his heart burst from his exertions, but I think that he died of terror. Indeed, I believe he actually preferred death to the terror of dying. He threw himself over on his side, with the one eye that was visible gradually clouded over by the moiling brown water. That eye was filled with such despair that I will never forget it. Nor will I forget that while I had the presence of mind to save my saddlebags, I did not draw my revolver and put poor, doomed Blackie out of his terror. . . ."

9

He and Chally, *stripped to the waist and sweating,* wrestled the peeled logs into place. When they halted to rest, Chally took makings from the pocket of his shirt, which he had dropped over a bush. He was long-limbed and lean, with an impatience to him like a teakettle singing to a boil. Andrew had come to treasure him.

"So they didn't exactly knock you down with the welcome mat," Chally said, frowning as he tipped tobacco flakes into the paper.

"The welcome mat was not in evidence."

Chally shook his head. Yesterday he had been noncommit-

157

tal to Andrew's report of the meeting, but he seemed to have been thinking it over.

"Guess I thought we'd be all right with Yule Hardy in our camp."

"I believe he was offended that I had accepted Machray's invitation to the meeting."

"Hard to feature grown men actin in such a fashion," Chally said. "And talk of Regulators, too. Ash Tanner there?"

"He counseled against it."

"Did he now?" Muscles bunched in Chally's jaw like hard little fingers. "Well, thieves're becomin bold, no doubt about it. Some say it is Crees off the reservation, but it's not only Crees that's thieves."

He had not told Chally that he had been accused of rustling. "Tanner seemed to be an authority," he said. "He once led a band of Regulators in Montana, apparently."

"Don't I know that," Chally said, and snorted. He tended to licking and sealing his cigarette. Degan, in his threadbare overalls, was grubbing in the kitchen garden that had blossomed under his ministrations. "Saw those whitecaps once," Chally said.

"Whitecaps?"

"Wore a pillercase thing over their hat and down over their face, holes in it to see through. Enough to give a boy fits. Grown men too." With that sense of taut wires straining through sheaves, Chally leaned back against the stack of logs. He screwed the cigarette into the corner of his mouth. "They put a rope around Daddy's neck like they done with you."

He felt suddenly short of breath. Chally's hot eyes avoided his.

"Daddy'd been a hardrock miner up around Bannack, but he'd got hurt in a rock fall so he got him a little saloon and billiards place where folks could gather. Maybe there was some fellows from one of those gangs droppin in, but Daddy always said it was because whitecaps wanted land he was tryin to patent on. They put a rope around his neck. It was right in front of Momma and Joe and me. I was about eight then, Joe ten.

"Took a deal of care fittin the rope, I remember. Well, they was just trying to scare us, but we didn't know that. I told them I would kill them every one when I had my growth, and they laughed at me. Daddy was pretty scared. That was natural enough. He said he'd get out if they'd let
158

be. He went to beggin. Well, I can understand that, him a family man with Momma and us to care for. But it was poor to hear him. I have had a poor time of it squarin that up in my head."

He scraped a match, applied the flame to his cigarette, and puffed vigorously. "So we cleared out and come here. They was known to string up fellows that didn't run, too. They surely did. I guess I would like to get back at that bunch as much as anything I can think of."

"Was it Tanner? That time?"

"Don't think so. Tanner and his bunch wasn't so bad. Maybe they was just doin what had to be done. But then there was another bunch doin it that was the bad ones."

"Emotions were running high about that and other things at the meeting. What's a pool outfit?"

"Little outfits gettin together to run their own roundup. What we'll be doin, looks like."

"They don't like pool outfits. They don't like new outfits coming in, like us. Or grangers. Everyone I met seemed to mention that the range was overcrowded."

"Durn old bodgers," Chally said. "Run their stock on public land for a while and they get to thinking they own it fee simple. Well, so it's only Machray that's friendly now." He blew smoke from his nostrils and straightened. "Day's gettin away," he said.

That afternoon Mary Hardy came to call without her brother in attendance. He described for her the room arrangements in the Big House, while Chally, after a few shy words, disappeared. Her bonnet hung from her throat by its ribbon, her crippled hand lay concealed in the pocket of her dress, and her upper lip was beaded with perspiration. He remembered his mother admonishing him that horses sweated, men perspired, and women "glowed." Her face glowing with color, Mary Hardy stood inside the rectangle formed by the four courses of logs that had been laid up, self-consciously turning and exclaiming as he pointed out the location of the kitchen, his studio, and the stairs to the sleeping quarters. Then he offered her tea and led her up the beaten trail to the shack, where Degan promptly made himself scarce. He seated her at the pine table which gleamed silver from scouring, and she asked if he had any new sketches.

He was showing her his watercolors when he was called outside to settle a construction problem, Chally having recruited the cook to help him lift the logs into place. When he returned Mary Hardy had his portfolio of sketches open before her, and her face was bright pink.

She held up one of the drawings of Maizie and said in a small voice, "These are new, aren't they?"

He said that they were. She continued to leaf through them. "She's pretty," she said.

"I suppose she is." He sketched for her the design of Rubens' great "Descent from the Cross" to show the lines of force he had tried to copy in the drawing of Maizie, the bureau, and the crockery bowl. She seemed more interested in the depiction of Mazie with bared breasts, one in particular where she was bent over the washbasin, shift wadded at her waist and face turned to gaze out of the drawing as though surprised at her ablutions.

"That's very good, I think," she said. She put it down and closed the portfolio. On the stove the pot began to sing.

He made the tea, brought the teapot and cups to the table, seated himself opposite her, and invited her to pour.

"I've been there," she said suddenly.

"I beg your pardon?"

"I've been to that place." Her face flamed. "F-father had an attack there. Mrs. Benbow sent for me.

"Father didn't want Mother to know, and Jeff was too young. So I went in the spring wagon to bring him home. He is better now, but he still limps sometimes. You've seen him. Sometimes more than others."

She smiled brightly. "It was very interesting. I don't suppose many young women of my—*station* are allowed to see the inside of establishments like that one. Even to know that they exist! There is the dearest little organ there. Mrs. Benbow said I was welcome to come and play it any time I wanted!"

She laughed delightedly, maybe a little hysterically. "Often I think how *shocked* father would be if he knew I'd been asked to play the organ in a place like that!"

She raised her cup and smiled at him over the brim. Then she laughed again. This time he joined her.

Sobering, she said, "Mother has admonished me because I don't know enough about you. So I've come to ask you about your wife."

He leaned back in his chair. "Her name was Elizabeth. Elizabeth Darcy. Elizabeth Livingston."

160

Mary Hardy licked her lips with a pink tongue tip. "Was—was she ill a long time? Before she—"

"She died in a boating accident. The canoe turned over. She and my daughter drowned in quite shallow water. No one knows how it happened."

She cradled her hand to her breast, her face squeezed into a little knot. She said in a low voice, "Did you love her very much?"

His cup rattled in the saucer when he put it down. "Very much."

"Was she beautiful?"

He nodded. "She was quite slender. Almost—slight. On your arm she seemed as light as air. Sometimes she would seem to me a creature of air. I had a fancy that when she died she returned to air—" He stopped, feeling a satisfaction he did not understand to see tears on his guest's cheeks. *Now get you to my lady's chamber, and tell her, let her paint an inch thick, to this favor she must come.*

He took up the teapot and watched his steady hand refill their cups. A parallelogram of sunlight fell across a corner of the table. He could hear the buzzing of flies against the windowpane.

"She was full of life," he went on. "It seemed very cruel of fate. And the little girl. Alice was her name. For a long time I felt myself a victim singled out by a malevolent fortune. I am ashamed of that."

"Was it no one's fault?"

"Just an accident. God's fault. And so I choose not to believe in Him." His head felt hot, his face hot, as he stared down at a few tea leaves slowly spinning in the amber liquid of his cup.

With a crisp scrape of petticoats, Mary Hardy rose and glided past him to stand in the sunny rectangle of the doorway in her dark gray riding habit, hand pressed to the door frame, back to him.

"And your sister cares for your little boy?" she said.

He said that was correct.

"And will you bring him out here to live in your new house?" she asked.

He said that he hoped to. When she glanced at him over her shoulder he said, "Miss Hardy, you asked me once if I loved my son very much. I do love him, as a father must his child, but human affections have become very difficult for me. I am sure, for instance, that I will never marry again. I

161

cannot allow myself to embark upon relationships that exist only to be destroyed."

Her blue eyes stared at him steadily while his face burned with his own pomposity. She said in the small voice, "Am I to tell my mother that, Mr. Livingston?"

"I'm sorry," he said.

"There is no reason for you to be sorry."

"I'm sorry that I am not—Young Lochinvar."

She shook her head mutely. Then she burst out, "I am resolved that I will never spend another winter in the Bad Lands! *I will not!*"

He rose as she shook her head and continued to shake it, her mouth a pinched line, her face an ugly red. "But you would not have taken me away anyway, would you, Mr. Livingston?"

"I do plan to make my life here, Miss Hardy."

She turned. At a brisk walk she started down toward the Big House, where her horse was tethered. Her gray back was very straight, her bonnet bounced on her back; she looked determined, and very vulnerable. He almost called out to her, but he could think of nothing to say of comfort or of aid. Chally and Degan carefully ignored her as she mounted and, with one slight gesture of good-bye, rode away.

10

As Fred Rademacher had prophesied, when the horses were stolen Andrew was shocked at the quality of his anger, which however, was tempered by the violence of Chally Reuter's. Chally trotted his horse on an aimless course through the south meadow, where they had discovered the loss of about twelve head, sometimes snapping his fingers in a curious way. His color seemed to come and go, so that at one moment his face would be dead white, and the next dark with blood. They were able to follow the tracks a few miles to the southwest, only to lose them in broken terrain. When they returned Chally set off for town to see if he could learn anything.

"Well, there's a good market," Degan said, spitting tobacco. "Them traction companies back east is payin fifteen-twenty dollars a head unbroke. That kind of news gets around."

The next day he was sitting in the shade of the shack with his chair tipped back reading, when he saw four riders coming fast among the cottonwoods near the river, raising a trail of dust there, two in the lead and two following, hidden from time to time behind the trees and fringe of brush, but always either one pair or the other visible. Then they cut up through the grassy bottom, winding among the grazing cattle. He reached inside the shack for his rifle and leaned it against the wall beside him.

"Looks they are coming here," Degan said, rounding the corner of the shack with a pail full of clinkers.

The four galloped straight toward them, surging up over the terraces of land, each time larger and closer. The leader, white-bearded, he recognized as Ash Tanner; behind, raising a hand in greeting, was Fred Rademacher. The third man Andrew remembered seeing at the Association meeting; the fourth was Boutelle. He knew what this expedition was.

They drew up, and Rademacher came on alone. Andrew went out to meet him.

"New York, we need some ridin stock to trail along with us," Fred said. The three other grim-faced men sat their horses staring at him.

He said they had just had half their saddle stock stolen. "Where is Chally Reuter?" Boutelle called.

"Gone to town."

"Somebody is makin one big haul," Fred said, turning toward Tanner. The third man had a short black beard and a mouth like a trap.

"I'll furnish what I can but I want to ride along with you," Andrew said.

"Maybe we can get you your stole stock back," Fred said. The other three were conferring; Fred eased himself in the saddle to glance again at Tanner. Evidently some sign passed.

"Get a move on, then," Fred said.

Andrew called to Degan to take them to the corral to cut out whatever they wanted, and to saddle Ginger.

"Bring your artillery," Fred said.

"May be a piece yet," Tanner said. "They have got a day's start on us."

When he had packed his bedroll, heavy jacket, a change of clothes, and hurriedly selected some canned goods to store in the middle of the roll, he filled his cartridge belt and slid his

Winchester into its oiled scabbard. He hurried outside carrying the bedroll and rifle. Degan helped him lash these to Ginger's saddle while the others, each with a remount on a lead rope now, watched impatiently.

"Sam Staples," Fred said. "Andy Livingston." The black-bearded man nodded curtly. Boutelle leaned both hands on the saddlehorn gazing steadily at him.

The moment he had mounted, Tanner swung his horse around and, with a general wheeling and stamping, the little expedition was in motion again, to splash through Fire Creek and head south below the devil faces of the gray buttes along the river. They rode at a pounding trot, Tanner in the lead with Boutelle close behind, and Staples usually bringing up the rear. It was Staples' horse herd they were in pursuit of, Fred said; but probably Andrew's as well. He grinned at Andrew under the blown-back brim of his hat. "Well, did you get mad when they hit you?"

He said he had gotten mad. "How does Tanner know where he's going?"

"He's guessin they'll be headin for a ford downriver called Farragan's. That's what I'm *guessin* he's guessin; he don't just spout whatever it is he's thinkin. Expect we'll catch up with them there, if we catch up."

"Who are they?"

"Well, that's what we don't know," Fred said.

Near Palisades Ranch Tanner led them inland, pounding up a long, winding ravine with thickets of wild roses along either side of the trail, a few last dry pink blossoms nodding in the wind of their passage. A trickle of sluggish water wound down a muddy bed, and on either side of them towered the buttes in their tortured shapes and brick-red blushes, irregular strata of black lignite like messages in code. A jackrabbit bounded ahead of them for a hundred yards before veering off.

They rode on south through eroding ridges, through cedar brakes, clumps of wild plum, through fields of dry grasses and fields of bare earth like clay-colored cement. At dusk they watered at a pool surrounded by cottonwoods that murmured and twinkled overhead in the last of the light. Tanner sat alone, hunkered down. With a knife he spread jam from a pot onto bits of bread, which he poked into his mouth. Staples chewed on a strip of dried beef while Fred and Andrew shared tinned sardines. Fred opened a can of peaches, passing it around for fingers to fish out the golden slices.

Boutelle paced up and down. He had a way of throwing his knees out as he walked, hands resting on his cartridge belt, darkly handsome, a most delicate face pointing straight ahead while his eyes shifted left and right. He reminded Andrew of all the school bullies he had known. Boutelle halted, to stand over him and Rademacher. "Got some of your riding stock, too, did they, Livingston?"

"Twelve head." He gazed back into the blank, black chips of eyes, feeling a hateful sick faintness. But he gathered that his previous encounter with the gunman was to be ignored.

Boutelle continued to gaze at him as Staples muttered, "Got most of my saddle bunch. Thievin hounds!"

"Chally have any ideas?" Boutelle asked quietly.

Tanner sat impassively poking food into his mouth. Fred was scrubbing shiny peach juice from his chin with his shirt sleeve.

"At first he seemed to think it might've been Indians."

"Headin the wrong way for Crees," Staples said.

"Everybody yells Injun first crack," Boutelle said.

Watching him swagger away, Andrew was ashamed of the fear that had constricted his lungs so that it had been an effort to speak. Yet it occurred to him that Boutelle had been trying to show him he bore him no particular ill will—perhaps as Death itself bore no grudges.

They started on again at a slower rate under a pale moon. Andrew could no longer feel his buttocks, and his backbone seemed to have been compressed inches by the jarring of the saddle. At moonset they halted in a grove of cedars to sleep for what seemed no more than minutes.

The dawning landscape was magical in his smarting eyes. Long shadows from the incandescent globe in the east lay across the knife-edge ridges, and the leaves of cottonwoods caught the sun like silver coins. The dark blue of the sky lightened to a hue that might have come from the palette of a Flemish master. For breakfast they roasted two jackrabbits Boutelle had shot and washed down the chicken-tender meat with sweet coffee.

The second day they were twenty hours in the saddle, and his only comfort was that Staples was obviously more exhausted than he. Tanner, Boutelle, and Fred Rademacher seemed tireless.

The third day he began to doze in the saddle, jerking awake with frightened starts, to spur on after their grim leader. That morning, in a timbered bottom where the grass was deep, with a muddy creek twisting through, they encountered the trail of the horse herd.

Tanner dismounted to hunker down and prod at a horse turd with a forefinger. They followed the trail at a trot. Within an hour they saw dust rising ahead. When the dust cloud had blown away Tanner halted them in a swale and with Boutelle went forward to scout. Andrew dozed leaning on the saddle horn.

He awoke with the jolting start to see Tanner returning alone, hunched and short in the saddle, his face wizened as a walnut behind the scurf of white beard. His cold eyes glanced from face to face.

"They're at a camp just over the hill there." He rubbed at his eye with a curled forefinger, like a sleepy child. It was the first sign of weakness in him Andrew had observed. "Jake's gone around to head them if they start to move on. Fred, you and Andy come straight on when you hear a yip, or a shot, one. Sam with me."

They sat watching Tanner and Staples trotting off to the left. Fred said, "Well, how do you like this trackin down horse thieves, New York? Beats your huntin trips somethin fierce for pure pleasure, don't it?"

He tried to grin, clinging to the pommel with one hand and his Winchester with the other. He had already concluded that he would gladly sacrifice the half of his saddle band rather than submit to any more of this torture. He licked his cracked lips carefully so as not to split them more. Beneath him Ginger stood head down, unmoving. They waited. It should have been the most exciting moment of his life, he supposed, beyond the hunting of the buffalo, an ultimate moment of raw experience, for this quarry was well able to return fire for fire, and they were no doubt desperate men.

He only wanted to lie down and rest in the soft grass. He remembered his father telling him of the campaigns in Virginia. There had been little excitement, only fear, and more than fear the desire for a hot bath, and most of all the need to sleep.

There was a distant yip, followed by shots.

Fred cursed with surprise. They set spurs and urged the exhausted horses into a slow trot. From the crest of the hill they could see two stockade shacks, very much like the one on Fire Creek, set close together near a big corral where the heads of horses pitched and milled.

As they started down toward the place, Sam Staples, rifle

166

in hand, appeared from behind one of the shacks. Seemingly attached to the muzzle of the rifle was a cowboy with his hands raised so high he appeared to be reaching for something among the eaves.

A sound like a ferocious insect passed between them, and Fred cursed and ducked. Andrew's slow mind revolved to the fact that that must have been a shot. He ducked too, and urged Ginger faster. They joined Staples and the cowboy, who had retreated behind the shack again. Tanner was there also, tying the young thief's hands behind his back. Boutelle held the reins of the three horses.

The boy turned a face as white as paper toward Fred and Andrew. He had a smear of dirt on his cheek, a fuzz of fair mustache, and Andrew could make out the shape of his mouth organ in his shirt pocket.

"Well, if it ain't Mister Livingston!" he cried in a shrill voice.

"Who's with you, Matty?" Tanner said. Staples jammed the muzzle of the rifle into the boy's ribs.

"Nobody! Nobody but me!"

There was another shot that whined past the corner of the cabin; Andrew dodged with the others. The boy cackled with laughter, then gasped as Staples jammed the muzzle against him once more.

"Ain't nobody but me, I tell you!"

Boutelle had made the horses fast. He had a sheet of paper pressed against the log wall and was tracing figures on it that Andrew couldn't make out.

"Who's shootin, then?" Staples demanded.

"Must be a friend I didn't know I had," Matty said.

"Say your prayers or name him, Matty," Tanner said. He took the paper from Boutelle.

"What's that?" the boy said, craning his neck as Tanner fastened the paper to his shirt front with a safety pin. "What're you doin there, Mr. Tanner?"

"Durn thing," Tanner said, who had pricked his thumb.

"What you stickin on me, there?" Matty cried in a shrill voice. "Now wait a minute, now!" Andrew made out the figures on the paper: 7-11-77.

"What's that mean?" he asked Fred.

"Old Regulator sign. Dimensions of the grave, it's supposed to be." They had both dismounted, and Fred leaned against the side of the cabin watching the others.

"Wait a minute, now!" Matty Gruby cried, as Boutelle

took the coil of rope from his saddle. Andrew felt his breath come suddenly hard, as though he had been running a long way.

"Who's in it with you, Matty?" Fred said.

"Speak up, boy!" Tanner said.

The side of the building beside Staples exploded; he cursed and lurched away, holding his cheek. Matty giggled hysterically until Boutelle laid a coil of rope over his head. Suddenly he sobbed.

"Who's that with you?" Tanner said.

"Ain't nobody with me!" the boy screamed. "Told you and told you and told you—"

Tanner slapped him across the face with the rope end, and the squalling broke off. Another shot knocked splinters from the log wall beside them. The marksman had moved to a copse of trees on the hill not far from where he and Fred had come over. They all backed between the two shacks, where there was sudden chill shade, Boutelle pulling the boy along by the rope. Matty staggered and fell, and Fred and Staples boosted him to his feet again. There was another shot.

"Somebody's going to have to get him off us before he does some damage," Tanner said.

"You're a hunter, Andy," Fred said. "Go see what you can do."

"Up that ravine there and come around behind him," Tanner called, as he swung into Ginger's saddle. He spurred on beyond the cabins, keeping them between himself and the copse of trees on the hill.

He heard the boy shout, "*Watch out, one of 'em's—*" The sound broke off.

There was another shot as he urged Ginger on, bent close to her neck and, over his shoulder, saw the little bloom of smoke from among the trees. The ravine angled upward toward a shoulder of the hill. For a way the going was clear, then a tangle of brush and scrub pine forced him to dismount. He tried to lead Ginger through the brush, but it was impossible, so he tethered her and continued afoot, carrying his rifle. To his right and out of sight the shooting continued at intervals.

When he reached the hilltop his shirt was soaked with sweat, and he felt enervated, as though his body had been soaking in some warm, thick fluid. He sprinted across a patch of bare ground, and, in the thicket, dropped to his hands and knees to lie breathing in painful gasps with his cheek pressed into the soft grass and the rifle pinioned beneath his body. His eyes closed gratefully. Somewhere ahead the rustler's rifle crashed. He heard a voice cursing in a monotone, like sobbing.

On his hands and knees, dragging the rifle, he inched his way forward. He burrowed under a down timber that was propped a foot above the ground, and clambered over another, carefully parting the branches before him. In the tangled gloom ahead something moved. A ray of light struck along a gun barrel. Now he could make out the man's bare head bent over the sights, the jut of his elbow. The rifle cracked. The sobbing cursing began again.

He braced his own rifle barrel in a crook of branch. He centered the bead on the man's head, lowered it to the center of his back, raised it again. He couldn't shoot a man in the back. Finger crooked on the trigger, he moistened his lips to call out. No sound came. He kneeled straining for what seemed minutes, the bead of the front sight trembling, then steady. But he couldn't do it. He raised the muzzle higher and pulled the trigger.

The stock jammed against his shoulder; the bullet tore through the brush above the man's head. He had a glimpse of a white face with a smear of blood on the forehead as he levered another cartridge into the chamber. The face disappeared instantly. There was a yell: "Goddamn *stranglers!*" and a crashing through the brush. After a silence there came a pounding of hoofs, diminishing.

He retraced his steps, out of the thicket and back down to where he had tethered Ginger. When he came out of the ravine at first he could see no one, only the two shacks, one half-hidden behind the other, and the corralled horses beyond. There was a kind of ticking silence. "Oh, no," a voice said in his head.

The words were repeated as he approached. First he saw Tanner and Staples squatting in the shade, watching him come; then Fred, face averted. "Oh, no," the voice said.

They had braced a corral pole from the roofpeak of one shack to the other. The body hung from this, hands bound behind, head bent askew, the paper pinned to the shirt front. "Oh, no," the voice repeated, like a parrot.

Boutelle stood spread-legged, watching him come. He was stretching out the chain of a small, gold locket, dropping it into his hand, stretching it out again. He had seen that chain and locket the night Matty Gruby played the mouth organ in the hunting camp.

Ginger's steps slowed as though reluctant to approach, and, when he prodded her with his spurs, trotted skittishly on past, toward her fellows in the corral. He, too, averted his eyes from the drooping, motionless slump of death. His head throbbed with the reproach of Bill Driggs, who had considered men putting a rope around another's neck to be his put-in. Would he have so considered this treatment of a horse thief? And hadn't he himself known what the punishment of a horse thief must be, who stole not merely another man's property but his means of locomotion, and so endangered his life? *Hadn't he?*

That night, in silent camp on their way north with the recovered horse herd, he had his first asthma attack in almost a year. First there was the sensation of total exhaustion, which he did not question, for all of them were exhausted. Next came the burning in his chest he remembered all too well, followed by secretive gasping not so much for air as to empty his lungs, while he sat apart with his chin braced on his fists to hold his torso stretched upright and his lungs open, trying to conceal from his companions both his physical distress and his terror that this time the disease would strangle him.

11

When that terrible journey was over, he took to his bed for a day, and for a week treated himself as an invalid. The asthma attack had passed, to be replaced by a moral one. If horse thieves were punished by hanging, what was the punishment for the greater crime he and his companions had committed?

He was grateful that Chally expressed no surprise that the eleven Lazy-N horses had been recovered and asked no questions, although he was certain that, quite soon, both Chally and Degan either surmised or learned via the grapevine what had happened.

One morning, confusing dream with reality, he wakened

bursting with relief that he had only dreamed it all. But he had not dreamed it.

A week after his return, when he went to town for his mail, Bill Driggs hailed him in front of the hotel. "Come and buy me a whiskey. I would stand treat but I am flat broke."

He looked it, his lined face ill-shaven, and his eyes bloodshot. His holstered revolver slapped against his thigh as they crossed the street with dust spurting around their boots.

"I hear it was you kept Machray from comin outside that night," Driggs said in a neutral tone.

"Yes, it was!"

Driggs glanced sideways at him silently. They turned into the saloon. The barkeep was polishing the gleaming counter, and a group of railroad men lounged at one of the tables, the brass lettering on a conductor's cap catching shards of light. Cowboys sat at others. Driggs signaled for whiskey as they seated themselves. He did not pursue the subject of Machray.

"Heard about the lynchin?"

He said he had. He felt his lungs pump so that for a moment he thought another asthma attack was coming on. The hunter's face fell into bitter lines.

"Sorry times," he said. "Young Matty Gruby got himself in bad company. Wouldn't have thought it of him."

The barkeeper brought a brown bottle and two glasses. When he had gone, Driggs said, "Hear you was at that meetin at the lord's. And he was fulminatin to go out and dis*pose* of anybody that ever shot a steer for slow elk."

"That's not true." His hand slopped liquor as he picked up his glass.

Driggs observed him with a raised eyebrow. "No fulminatin?"

"There was fulminating, but not by Machray."

Driggs massaged his face with a big hand. "Well, it is a trial to figure," he said. "I just don't hold with ropes, but livin out here a hundred miles from law, what's there to do when some take to stealin? But I did like that boy. I just can't hardly believe that boy went bad."

He watched Driggs rearrange his long legs. "I can't hardly believe it was Ash Tanner did for him, either," Driggs said. "There was hard ridin done, I hear, and he is plain *old*."

"What would you have done?" Andrew asked.

"What would I have done which?" Driggs said. He tossed off a gulp of whiskey, and sighed. "Well, one, if I'd been Matty caught with the goods, they'd never took me alive to

171

strangle me." He frowned at Andrew apologetically. "For *you*, you didn't know what was comin. But Matty would've known."

"I meant if it had been your stock stolen."

"I'd just never have the stock to steal, Andy Livingston."

"That is no answer."

Driggs shrugged and sighed. "Hard questions," he said. "I have been thinkin on getting out of the Bad Lands. We are fell on poor times here. Stealin on the one hand and lynchin on the other. How's a man to keep decent? Man can't make a livin anymore, either, less he goes to work for some iron-bottom rancher that first thing tells him to take his rifle and blow down some poor granger for illegal calf-butcherin. Hard times," he said.

"We must have county organization and law out here," Andrew said. "We can't have lynch law. A human society that will not tax itself for what it knows is right is despicable."

Driggs's face twisted sourly. "You think that's the answer, do you? I tell you we got on just fine out here before *people* started comin in. And *cows*."

"Just Indians with torture stakes, and grizzlies."

"At least a man knew how to conduct himself!" Driggs leaned forward on his elbows. "This come hard, Andy, but I have run through my credit everywhere. Will you lend me five dollars to buy cartridges?"

It seemed to him that he no longer need consider Driggs morally superior in view of the hunter's threat to Machray's life for a schoolboy injury. "To shoot at Machray?" he said.

The legs of Driggs's chair jarred on the floor. For a moment he thought the hunter would strike him. But finally Driggs said softly, "No, not for that, Andy. Shoot some game for the cars. I have got to get off dead center somehow. Pay you back," he said, and scrubbed the back of his hand across his mouth.

"I'd heard you had sworn to kill him."

Driggs shrugged affirmatively.

"You have no case against him."

"No?"

"He struck you. I am in your debt. I knocked him down. I consider your injury to have been satisfied."

Driggs scowled at him. "Sound like a lawyer-feller," he said. He shook his head. "Tell you what I'm tryin to do. Tryin to fix it in my head he was the one that brought us ruin out

172

here." He produced a hack of a chuckle. "Somebody surely did."

"People and cows, you said just now."

"Or if I could just fix on it he was the one that sent to dis*pose* of Matty Gruby," Driggs continued. "For there is more kinds of ruin than comes from stringing fences and holdin land. If he was the one sent those whitecaps out . . ." he said, and fixed bloodshot eyes on Andrew's.

Andrew sat with his hand to his throat, feeling the pulse there. "I assure you that he did not."

Driggs shrugged. "Seemed more proper than shootin him just for knockin me down, though I could whiskey myself into *that*."

"His men would kill you for it. Or you would hang."

Driggs just stared at him uncomprehendingly. They finished their whiskey in a gloomy silence. He took a greenback from his billfold and extended it to the other, who gave a grunt of thanks.

When he had taken his leave and stood outside on the boardwalk, squinting in the sun's glare, he saw a hazy figure dismounting from a spotted pony, a fringed buckskin shirt, a black hat pushed back, a crusted scab on the forehead—

He stared at Driggs's friend Conroy, whose scratched face he had last seen contorted with terror and loathing in that stand of trees above the corrals at Farragan's Ford.

There was no sign of recognition on Conroy's part. He ticked the brim of his hat with a gloved finger, said, "Mornin," and passed on inside through the louver doors, while Andrew continued to stand paralyzed. A granger wagon, oxen-drawn, turned the corner and creaked slowly along toward him.

The second rustler had been Conroy. There was absolutely nothing he knew to do with the knowledge.

"Fire Creek Ranch,
July 16, 1884

"*My dear diGarmo*:

"Thank you for your letter. Yes, of course I wish to be kept informed of developments. I am glad to hear that 'fence-mending' is proceeding to your satisfaction, and that Jeremiah Evans, once the most tenacious of dragons, has been transformed into a man with whom compromises can sometimes be effected. Winds of change?

"Winds have been blowing pretty constantly here these last two weeks. There is a story of a tenderfoot who inquired if the wind blew this way all the time, and the native replied, 'No, mister, it'll blow this way for a week or ten days, and then it'll change and blow like blazes for a while!'

"You would find some of the strains of 'Far West' life to be familiar ones, although quarrels are not between 'Stalwarts' and 'Half-breeds' over how patronage is to be distributed, or Republicans and Democrats as to who will command the spoils. Here the contention is more elemental, between a small entrenched class and a growing deprived one. Our old guard is frightened of newcomers, of rustlers, and of grangers. As we both know, frightened men are dangerous men.

"The early settlers of a region such as this one, with their large herds, hold a considerable weapon against newcomers, whom they accuse of 'overcrowding' the range, and smallholders whom they suspect of 'mavericking' their calves. On the claim that the range is supporting as many cattle as it safely can, they will unite in refusing to cooperate with anyone who brings in another herd. In cow country a man is peculiarly dependent upon his neighbors, especially at roundup time, when his cattle, which have mingled with the other brands, must be identified and separated.

"On the other hand the victims of this kind of ostracization soon begin to organize against it, and the battle is joined! We 'independents' tend to regard ourselves as knights upon white chargers, carrying onward the cause of justice and humanity, but are regarded by others as Huns who would demolish the old decent standards, and open the gates to a ruthless canaille.

"Certainly grangers are on the march. White-topped wagons lumber into town, laden with domestic goods, the men slouching along beside the slow tread of their oxen, the women sallow and dispirited, always with a two-headed child or two. I am told that very few stick it out for very long. These northern pastures are too dry, the soil too poor, the winters too severe, and the quarter section they can claim too small for any hope of successful agriculture.

"Major Powell's surveys, and his conclusions as delineated in his *Report on the Lands of The Arid Region,* seem to me the only possible means of dealing with the problems of homesteading in this part of the country. Lands of sufficient acreage to the purpose for which they are suited, and with reasonable access to water, must be granted. However, it is discouraging to speculate that if these bills pass, this great pasture and the way of life we know here will be quickly destroyed by successful homesteaders. Meanwhile the grangers continue to push in. . . ."

Book Three

1884

1

Once the Bad Lands had been the greatest country for game anybody ever saw. Bill Driggs could remember the sky filled with birds in their Vs in the fall of the year, those great flocks at different heights and heading at different angles, but all heading south. Now there were still birds, but not like the old days. All that cow-stuff with their heads like haired-over skulls and brains about the size of a buckshot had tramped the waterholes to mud, and the birds in their multitudes had moved off to some other part of the country where men and cows coming in hadn't mudholed everything.

Sometimes he would get steaming mad thinking what they had done to the Bad Lands, and sometimes he would get drunk thinking about it, and sometimes he just told himself he had better sit down and figure out where he should move on to, but he never had yet.

It seemed to him that men just naturally ruined everything they came upon. But it was easier to get mad at the cows. More than once he had unshipped his rifle to shoot one of the critters down, just because he hated them so much. You would see them tramping in a line from one mudhole to the next when everything started drying up in late summer. They beat the grass into trails, and, when the long rains came, those trails washed into gullies, and of course with the beavers trapped out and their dams gone—*he* had done that, he and his kind—then the gullybusters banged straight down into the creeks, and the creeks flooded, and the river looked like one big roaring mudhole. You could see the Bad Lands washing straight down to the Missouri and the Mississippi and out to sea. You could see the Bad Lands washing away right before your eyes, that had been a fine place once.

Fellows like Conroy and Cletus and Boutelle would get together and talk about the old days hunting buffalo. He could remember the buffalo before there were buffalo hunters, before the buffalo were busted into the northern herd and the southern, and the northern herd banged away at like it was some kind of insult to the white race that had to be wiped out. He himself had killed many a beast just to cook the tongue and waste the rest, but he had never shot them by the hundred, by the thousand. Still, the buffalo killed off like that had put the Sioux on the reservations and starving. That seemed worth almost the loss of the buffalo, for it would grafity him to see those redskin devils starving until there was not a one of *them* left, either.

One time he had watched eight of them ride by where he was hiding in a bramble thicket, and still he would wake up all but screaming remembering their filthy painted faces and the stink of them, they had been that close, and wondering how many he could take with him before he gulped the strychnine down. For by then he had seen what they had done to Banty Howard up on the Yellowstone, and knew of others they had caught.

So it was not all to the bad, what had happened to the Bad Lands, the redskins starving on the reservations, and the grizzlies run out so you wouldn't find one east of the Big Horns. He hated grizzlies as much as the Sioux, but he thought he had come to hating cattle about the same. Though in the end cattle were only the men that had driven them into the Bad Lands for the grazing. There was some kind of principle waiting for him to understand it—where every kind of thing carried its own ruin along with it.

Maybe he was the same, and in his turn he would be cooped up in some way like the Indians, or driven off west into the mountains. Most likely he would only drink himself into a stinking sot, boring everybody with stories of the old days nobody would believe, and a liver like a poison pup.

Once he had been the stoutest-muscled man he knew. He had known what was right and what wrong in those days, too. He had never been one to set up with a brace of Sharps rifles and a team to pull the skins off, and slaughter buffalo all day. There was big money to be had that way, though it was murderer's work. He had never set himself to making more money than he needed to keep himself, with enough left over for liquor and women when he came to town. Now he had to borrow money to buy cartridges so he could shoot game for the dining cars that weren't even paying enough to be worth it.

It seemed to him that he, who had been here first, was being elbowed aside as of no account by the later-comers. He had taken the long chances, starving and freezing and baking, and so lonely he would catch himself talking to the prairie dogs, and seen his friends murdered, so full of arrows they looked like porcupines, or staked and hacked to something that wasn't even shaped like a man anymore. Then just about when you had a breathing spell, here came the railroad that you knew already was the end of something, and herds coming in to feed the railroad gangs, and more herds behind them, and people arriving on the railroad, one of them a fellow in the queerest clothes he had ever seen parading through town with another fellow behind him playing squealy music like souls in pain.

Next thing he knew there was a brick two-story building going up in town, and a house on the bluffs the size of a riverboat, and fences everywhere where once he had been able to travel for a week without seeing another man, much less a cow or wire, with deer and elk and buffalo grazing, and pronghorns so tame if you would just sit quiet one of them would sidle up to you out of curiosity so you could slit his throat with your Bowie for dinner.

So he had come to hate Machray about the way he hated redskins and grizzlies and cows. But more than that, there was Cora Benbow. It just showed you what a woman was made of, that she should give value to a fellow just because he was a lord in Scotland, with fancy uniforms and kilts to show his bare legs and a fancy way of talking. And it showed you what a man was made of that he would be crazy jealous that a big-assed whore should take a shine to anybody else but *him*.

When Machray first came to the Bad Lands people thought it was the finest thing that could happen. He himself had known that Machray and his plans were about as fine a thing as a stampede heading for a chicken house, or the grangers traipsing in the way they were starting to do now. For everybody's ruin came marching along with him, or right behind him, seeming at first peart and cheerful like that one-man band of music that Machray brought with him.

So Machray brought in a trainload of gear and people, surveyors and engineers and architects, a regiment of Swedish carpenters and masons, a herd of cowboys and foremen and supers. The dust flew that spring. There were crews of mules and scrapers brushing out roads and sites for buildings, masons laying up brick, and carpenters banging and jabbering in Swede, and fellows with rolls of blueprints, and a nasty

181

little cock of a fellow named Grogan rushing around in a buggy shouting at everybody.

Then some fancy longhair cattle from Scotland came in on the railroad. Nobody'd seen any *westbound* cattle before then, and they were so busy making jokes on those queer-looking cows that they didn't notice what else was on that train—wire, boxcars full of reels of it the size of beer barrels. Crews began carting it off, and right then everybody started to realize that Machray had not only bought land but he was going to fence it.

And then it was that people began to think twice about what a fine thing Machray was. Men took it as their bounden duty to buy a set of wirecutters and go out and cut wire. Then Machray hired Boutelle and a crew of hardcases to stop it, or it was rumored he had done that, and things began to settle down. Machray had his way, and his land fenced, and people used to it, some of them.

Then Machray knocked him down in that brawl at Cora's that made him ashamed of himself every time he thought of it, which was often, and steaming mad just a step behind ashamed. Sometimes at night he would groan in his bed from being so mad. He thought the only way out of that kind of pain was to shoot Machray down like a dog. He would shoot him down for ruining the Bad Lands.

When Matty Gruby was strangled there was talk Machray was behind it. He thought he would shoot Machray for *that*. But when he looked at it straight he had to see that it had not been Machray, it was the same old iron-bottom Association cattlemen that had put their cowboys to taking potshots at Much-a-muck out of gulches. If he was to shoot Machray it was going to have to be for his own sake. The urge to move along came on him more and more, north, or south, or west, with the Bad Lands spoilt. But he never seemed to get around to thinking out where he would head.

There was Bohannon's saloon not far from the depot where you went when you wanted a plain drink, and Evers' place up past the hotel where you could shoot billiards while you drank, although Evers' whiskey was poorer quality than Bohannon's, and whenever the billiard table was knocked there was a considerable business necessary to level it so the balls wouldn't all drift over into the northeast corner. He was in Evers' shooting a game with Conroy when Jake Boutelle came in, sauntering in that way he had with his hands braced on his cartridge belt, and his eyes sliding right and left.

Jake was not exactly a young fellow, since he had been in the Bad Lands a good ten years, but he had a smooth, handsome face without a line in it, so that he looked like a mustached boy except in certain lights. His reputation was sour from fellows that had been in business with him in a bone-gathering outfit, when that was profitable. They had found it was more profitable for Jake than the rest of the partners. And he had some reputation for a hardcase and a bully, too.

"Well, if it ain't Bill and Connie," Jake said, as the batwing doors flapped shut behind him.

"Last time I looked, anyway," he said, bending and squinting to shoot. He noticed the balls creeping toward the northeast corner. Probably Boutelle just walking in the door had done it. Connie was standing by, chalking his cue.

"How do, Jake?" Con said.

"Tolerable," Jake said, drifting to the counter, where Evers banged down a bottle and glass. "Took a good scrape on the head there, I see," Jake said.

Connie picked at the scabbed place and said he'd had a whack from a tree branch, riding back one night from seeing a pal over at the Double-eight.

Boutelle nodded as though he was pretty sure there was more to it than *that*. "You keeping well, Bill?"

"Tolerable," he said. He wondered what Boutelle wanted of them. Of *him*. He could feel it like a pushing in the air, but it was not likely he would be told straight out. When he pointed to the table, Evers came out from behind the bar with his level and cigar box full of shims. He squatted beside the table leg, grunting.

Boutelle drank whiskey and wiped his mustache. "Bad business," he said with a shake of his head, meaning Matty Gruby of course. It was as though every fellow in the Bad Lands had to mention it to every other fellow personally.

"Bad business," Connie said, shaking his head.

"Well, what can they do?" Jake said. "Stole blind by rustlers, what's there to do but make some examples?"

"The Association, you mean?" he said.

Boutelle ignored him as though he had cut a bad one in close quarters. "Hear they are thinking of laying on some stock inspectors," he went on. "Crew of them. Stock inspectors, range detectives, something like that."

"Something like Regulators?" he said.

Connie giggled nervously and Jake pursed up his mouth like a kitten's button. But now he knew what Jake was up to: recruiting.

"Heard talk Ash Tanner's back at the old stand," Connie said. He sounded as though he had taken a cold.

Jake was shaking his head. "Too old, for one thing. Disinclined, too, so he says," Connie stood by, grimacing in a queer way, and picking at his scab. Evers straightened up.

"Believe that'll do her," he said, and headed back behind the counter with his box and level. There was a sound of a wagon passing in the street, and dust filtered in the door mixed with sunlight. When Jake looked at him he could feel the pushing in the air.

"Ned," Boutelle said. "Why don't you step outside and see if that is another damn bunch of grangers coming through. Pour my friends here a drink before you go."

Evers set out two more glasses, filled them, and bustled outside. Boutelle leaned on the counter. "Know anybody'd be interested in some stock-inspecting work, Bill?"

"I guess it might depend on the pay, Jake."

"Pretty fair pay, I hear. I'd think you'd be interested, Bill." Jake looked him up and down as though checking to see that he was on his uppers a bit. "Expect they'd pay forty a month and found," Jake said.

"My, that *do* sound interesting!" he said. "But not to me." He didn't like that pushing of Jake's.

"Why not?" Boutelle snapped out.

"Too old," he said. "Like Ash. And disinclined, too. No, sir, I just believe I'd be a happier man counted out. Sounds complicated to me. I get mixed up easy." This outfit sounded like just the kind of business to make things going on in the Bad Lands worse than they were already. Too difficult to explain it to Jake, and probably just end up in a shouting match.

Jake's eyes flashed at him once, and then away as though no longer interested in him. "There is some it would pay to get off a list the Association has, and onto the payroll," Jake said.

His head heated up so it seemed he would blow steam if he sneezed. "Are you talking to *me?*" he said through his teeth.

Jake ignored him, looking at Connie, who had got a smear of blood started picking at his scab. "How about you, Con?"

"Might be interested," Connie said. "If the pay's that good."

"Maybe you can persuade Bill to come in with us."

"*Why*, Jake?" he said. "What do you want me so much for?"

The flat black discs stared straight into his eyes. "You are a good man, Bill," Jake said. "And you need the work."

"I have got enough trouble looking at my face in the mirror shaving as it is," he said.

Jake shrugged, finished his whiskey and shoved the glass away. "Hear you're gunning for Machray," he said after a time.

It was his turn to shrug.

"A man'd do well to have his friends by him, he pulled a stunt like shooting the big fellow," Jake said. He laughed. "Saw his buggy over at Cora's last night. That surely must be a houseshaker, when he climbs on. Like a 4-4-0 coupling onto a tender."

Jake had caught him on a narrow edge. If he spoke up to tell him to shut his filthy face he had lost something, and lost something too if he just let it go by. Which was what he was going to have to do.

Jake had brought out his poke and was counting out coins for Evers. "Be seeing you, boys," he said, sauntering out just as Evers bustled back inside, saying that it was grangers, all right.

Back at the billiard table with Connie, he took up his cue and banged the butt on the floor, still steaming over what Jake had said about Machray and Cora, and about his name on some list. His name did not belong on any man's list. Then he wondered if Jake had not meant Connie, for he suspected Connie had done a bit of rustling in his time.

"That's too good wages to turn down, Bill," Connie said. "You'd best think it over."

"I can remember those old-time Regulators when they was pure trash," he said, shaking his head. "That was one rotten outfit."

Con didn't say anything to that. They were still at the billiard table when Wax looked in the door. Cora wanted to see him. A perfect day all around.

She was at her desk in the office upstairs at the house. He leaned in the doorway looking at her, remembering her with her clothes off, the finest-built woman he had ever seen. "Hello, Bill," she said.

"Wanted to see me, Corrie? My, you do smell fine today!"

Her face looked paler than usual, and her mouth was set to one side. "What are you going to do?"

"About what?"

"You know."

He rubbed the side of his jaw where Machray had hit him like a kick from a mule. "You know," he said.

She rose and came half way around the desk in her black skirt and white shirtwaist, stopping to lean a hip against the desk. "You will be a dead man," she said. "Understand that. I can have you shot down for a hundred dollars."

He managed to grin at her. "My, that is *dear!* I bet I could hire it done for fifty. Less in winter."

"I'd pay what I had to."

"Corrie, did you think you could scare *me?* Bill *Driggs?*"

She shook her head silently. He thought she was going to cry, which first shook him and then made him mad. He had promised himself that he would not get mad here.

"Such a fuss for a big, yellow-belly Scotchman."

"He never knew what happened that night. He was drunk. You've been drunk like that. He doesn't even remember what happened."

"*I* remember. Corrie, I think I will have to kill him, and I don't believe he's a yellow belly—he'll come out if I call him out again. Corrie, I hate his guts so much it gnaws at me all the time. Not just because you are soft on him that used to be mine. I hate his guts because he thinks the earth was made for him. You can see it the way he drives around in that buggy, with that big cigar in his teeth. Women, and land, and cattle—whatever he takes into his mind he wants to own, he goes after it. Corrie. I used to feel for the Bad Lands what I used to feel about you, and he has took it all away."

"I don't know what you mean," she said, rubbing her arms as though she was cold.

He leaned against the doorjamb, staring at her, and thought he should not talk so much for it came out wrong.

"I will ask you a favor," she said.

"Shoot."

"Let him be."

Now he just felt tired. "What'll you give?"

"Five hundred dollars!"

"I don't take whores' money."

She lifted her two hands and let them drop. She whispered something.

"Let's have your duds off and see your stock in trade there. Maybe that'll do."

She dropped her skirt and stepped out of it. He felt so ugly he thought that if he looked into a mirror just now it would surely smash to smithereens. He cleared his throat. "Never mind," he said. She dropped her hands from where they'd been unbuttoning at the back of her neck, and stood facing him, pink showing in her cheeks.

"Never mind it," he said. "I am leaving the Bad Lands, Corrie. It has got too many for me here. Folks trying to hire me for filthy work. Whores offering me money. Having to borrow money from tenderfeet. Gone bad here and getting worse every day, that was a fine place once. I was leaving anyway. But you can tell him he *owes* you."

He turned away. "Bill," she said.

He kept going. Then he had to go back and borrow whores' money for trainfare to Indiana, where he had decided to go to his sister's place for a new start.

2

Andrew had been reluctant to call at Palisades until one day Jeff brought a note from Mrs. Hardy, inviting him to supper. He duly presented himself, to sit with a more than friendly Yule Hardy on the veranda in the creaking rawhide chairs, watching Hardy's prize herd grazing in the pastures along the river and the birds skimming the brownish-gray water. Mrs. Hardy sat with them, with a carpetbag of knitting, while Hardy, eyeglasses propped on the end of his nose and spread fingers tented over his belly, lectured:

"Those who practice the art of animal husbandry can never be satisfied, you see, Andy. Their triumphs can only be achieved through the most painstaking systems of selection and rejection. A good breeder will tolerate no animals but the best, on a basis of intrinsic worth. He must protect his females from inferior males, in order to mate them with bulls of equal or greater quality."

He laughed. "It appears that a great deal of attention must be given the private lives of one's cattle."

Mrs. Hardy's needles flashed. Her lips were set in a printed

187

smile. He glanced toward the open door of the house for some sign of Mary Hardy.

As Hardy droned on about cattle breeding, he found his mind drifting off to his drawings. In the best of his sketches of Maizie the girl's shoulder converged with the thick, white, almost organic shape of the pitcher behind her, and it had come to him that the *things* in the room, and not the girl herself, were the subjects of the painting he was planning. Since discerning this, he had brought out many of his old sketches to reexamine the details, remembering how Jan Steen, van Ostade, Teniers, and Ruysdaal had used detail in their Dutch and Flemish interiors. Now he considered the best of his own the one of Chally mounted, the gauntleted hand, the broad-brimmed hat, the high-heeled boot in the stirrup, and the revolver in its sweated-dark holster all meaningful in themselves, but also galvanizing lines of tension.

But the image haunting his mind's eye, which he knew he would never commit to paper, was of one man standing, two squatting, and the fourth half raised glancing up to the figure that accomplished the pyramidal form, the sad, sagging, sacklike shape, almost devoid of detail, of the hanged boy.

"Tell me, Mrs. Hardy," he said suddenly. "Can the wife of a rancher be happy out here in the Bad Lands?"

She smiled more genuinely. "It can be very lonely. When that wind blows over hundreds of miles—thousands of miles!"

"'Nuns fret not their convent's narrow room,'" Hardy said.

"Young people may fret theirs, Mr. Hardy!" Mrs. Hardy said sharply. "Not having taken vows of quietness, but having had quietness thrust upon them." To Andrew she continued, "Of couse I miss chatting with other women on the issues of the day. But one of these days, if Lord Machray has his way and Pyramid Flat becomes a metropolis, we will have an opera house, and an Arnoldian Society with Thursday meetings!"

"And the Browning Club on Tuesdays!"

"Heaven forbid!" Hardy said, while Mrs. Hardy laughed.

Jeff Hardy appeared, slapping dust from his chaps with his hat. He greeted everyone and plumped himself down in a chair, staring at his father with a stiff, furious face.

"They have done it again!" he announced.

"Done what, my boy?"

"They have lynched another one."

His chest constricted until he could hardly breathe. Mrs. Hardy held her knitting pressed to her bosom. Hardy was frowning over his spectacles.

"With that Regulators' sign on him," Jeff said.

"Who was it?" Hardy asked.

"Fellow named Roswell. From over by Orcas."

"I believe he was a well-known horse thief," Hardy said mildly.

"Well, I don't know about that!" Jeff said. "But I know Matty Gruby wasn't any horse thief!"

"It has been very difficult to believe that young Matty Gruby had turned to thievery, Andy," Hardy said. "Although he was young, impressionable, and foolish as the young can be."

He watched Jeff glare at his father, slumped in his chair with his fists lumped in his pockets.

"It was a savage, tragic thing," Mrs. Hardy said. "He had never been a bad boy."

Hardy removed his eyeglasses to polish them with his handkerchief. Without them his eye sockets looked pink and naked. "We can only assume that those who have suffered at the hands of thieves have banded together to take action."

"Dirty stranglers!" Jeff said. He looked ready to burst into tears. "Well, they made a mistake! Matty never——"

"I believe it is time you changed and washed," Hardy said, and Jeff excused himself. "Mary?" he could be heard calling inside.

"The Bad Lands will have to have laws and the legitimate means of enforcing them," Andrew said to Hardy. His voice sounded very tight.

"Laws are the beginning of the end of freedom," Hardy said. "And laws enforced by police officials are the end of it. I repeat my position. This range can only exist in natural co-operation of man and man, man and animal, man and the land. If that cooperation is systematically contravened . . ." He did not go on.

"I repeat my position also. When more and more people come to inhabit a place, then the laws governing their intercourse must be written and enforced. Or else there is only jungle law, which is the law of the strongest. I do not see the inherent evil of policemen. Or of opera houses and Browning Clubs."

Hardy stared at him tight-lipped, then smiled and said to

189

his wife, "I believe we would welcome a cup of tea, Mrs. Hardy."

She rose and disappeared, to return in a few minutes with a pot of tea. Following her was Mary Hardy, with a tray which she grasped with her sturdy hand and steadied with the other. Her face looked almost transparently pale, and she wore black, with a strip of black ribbon at her throat fastened with a gold, owl-headed pin. She greeted him, as he rose, with a ghost of her quick smile. He had looked forward to telling her of the shipment of books and magazines he had received from his sister, but she seemed remote and preoccupied as she passed the cups her mother had filled. Jeff reappeared in a clean blue shirt, combed hair shining with damp.

The subject of the lynchings was not absent from the conversation very long, Jeff telling his sister in an aside that he had seen someone in town who assured him of Matty Gruby's innocence.

Hardy sighed, and leaned forward to put down his cup. "I'm afraid the probability must be accepted that they did *not* catch the wrong fellow."

"Probability, Father?" Mary Hardy said, in a loud, clear voice. "Do you condone cruelly murdering someone on a *probability?*"

"My dear, I believe I have heard it reported that he was caught red-handed."

"No!" Mary said. "Red-handed is what murderers are!"

"We will not continue this argument before our guest, Mary," her mother said.

"Men must protect themselves from predators, my dear," Hardy said gently. "I think one must condone a little."

"*Predators!*" Mary cried. "That boy was not a predator, Father. I would call the men who killed him *predators!* I call them red-handed *murderers!* Whoever they are!"

"Mary, you must leave us if you cannot control yourself," Mrs. Hardy said, with an edge to her voice.

"Very well, Mother," Mary said. She carefully put down her cup, rose and swept inside, carrying her pale hand before her.

"She was so fond of the boy, you see," Mrs. Hardy said, turning to Andrew. Jeff leaned back stiffly in his chair, fists shoved into his pockets.

"May I be excused, Father?"

"You will sit with us and make amends for your sister's be-

190

havior. Mrs. Hardy, I believe our guest would accept a little more tea."

It seemed simpler to accept more tea than to refuse it. Hardy inquired how he was getting along with his neighbor to the north.

"Very well," he said. "Except for one little disagreement that has been forgotten."

Hardy nodded and smiled. "If you have not had a run-in with him yet, I prophesy that as his neighbor you will. You will find that Lord Machray considers that there are no rights in the Bad Lands but his own."

"I wonder that there seem to be no topics of conversation in this place but Lord Machray and poor Matty Gruby," Mrs. Hardy said.

She was right, there did not seem much else to talk about during that painfully long evening at the Hardys'. Mary Hardy did not join them at supper. After supper he played several pieces on the piano and listened to Mrs. Hardy play. He retired early, announcing that he must return to Fire Creek Ranch at dawn. He felt a liar, although he could not say specifically how he had lied, except by omission, and a coward for that omission. He felt stained with sin, who heretofore had thought it a word abstractly—and excessively—used in church. And he felt sick with pity for Mary Hardy in her brave argument that Matty Gruby had been innocent.

Sheriff Cecil M. Brown of Mandan, 120 miles from Pyramid Flat, sat at his rolltop desk in his adobe office next to the jail, listening politely to what Andrew had to say. He leaned back with his chair balanced on its back legs, fat fingers knitted over his belly.

"Heard there's been some lynchings out that way," he said. "Well, now, Mr. Livingston. I expect that will take care of your problems over there."

"You misunderstand me," he said. "The problem is the lynchings."

"Well, I dislike disagreeing with a bright young fellow," the sheriff said. "But I do believe the lynchings are the *end* of the problem. That is the way it has always been out here, anyhow."

"It is murder," he said. "That is your responsibility, Sheriff."

"No, sir, I do not see it as my responsibility. It is better than a hundred miles over there from here, and the fact is those fellows running cattle out that way just don't want any truck with me, and they have said so. The fact is, it is plain too far over there, and somebody traipsin back and forth on the railroad just costs the taxpayers good money. And for what?"

"Presumably to maintain law and order," he said tiredly.

The sheriff shook his big head, smiling. The front legs of his chair rapped down as he leaned forward to take a sharpened matchstick from a delicate china cup and prod between his teeth. A wagon passed in the street and fine dust filtered through the door. The sheriff spread his hands.

"Mr. Livingston, we could set us up another office over there, surely. Deputies coming and going, complaints and warrants and judgments and the like. But you know, and I know, that right away everything has to be just about twice as big as it started out to be. The tax assessor has got to get himself over there lookin close at things, and how do you think that is going to set with people like Lord Machray, and Yarborough, and Major Cutter, and old Ash Tanner. And Hardy! That is a hardshell bunch over there. We know that! I expect you will come to that way of thinkin yourself, pretty soon. Fact is, those fellows out there just want to be left alone, settle things by themself."

The sheriff worked his bottom around on his chair and flexed his shoulders. "And the fact is, I am willing to leave them be over there so long as things don't get out of hand and unruly. If they are catching their own horse thieves and dealing with them themself instead of bringing them over here to stand trial, why, you and I might think the punishment a bit severe, but the fact is it is not punishment exactly. What it is, is a warning to the next fellow to think twice before he goes to stealing. You had any stock stole, Mr. Livingston?"

He said that he had.

Brown smiled and nodded comfortably. He locked his hands behind his head. "I believe you will not see any more of your stock stole for a while," he said.

"Then you intend to do nothing in this matter?"

"Well, if you have come in here to file a complaint against some people, I will sure take down the facts."

Andrew got up and went to stand at the window, gazing through the dusty glass at horsemen passing in the street. He had not thought he would be able to accomplish anything by

192

this trip to Mandan, except to prove to himself what he knew to be true, that there was nothing to be done.

"Who must I see, then, who will inform you that you must do your duty? What kind of a court is there in Mandan?"

"Well, sir, we have JP. There's the governor, though I understand he is out of the territory just now."

He stood at the window, nodding. He felt as though he had a cold in his head.

"My advice to you is not to exercise yourself," the sheriff said. "I believe you will find that it is all over and done with. These things come up like this, like a thunderstorm looks like it will tear the place loose, and next thing you know it is blown on by. Gone like that." He snapped his fat fingers.

3

Chally Reuter came galloping in from a loop he had ridden north along the river, calling, "Andy, you had better come along! There is a herd and some riders up in Sloping Buttoms!"

He buckled on his cartridge belt and holstered revolver while Chally saddled Ginger. They set out north along the river, cutting through scrub juniper and scrambling up a butte in the noon sun. From the top they could look out over the broad tract of grassy meadows tilting down to the river's edge just south of the fence. The meadows were crowded with clumps of round, brown backs of grazing cattle, here and there a tossing white face. Three mounted cowboys moved among them.

"Look about two hundred head," Chally said. They rode twisting and sliding down the far side of the butte, and at a hard trot through the bottom land toward the nearest of the cattle. A steer raised his head and sidled ponderously. Andrew could see the circled cross of Machray's brand on the brown flank.

"Puckered-A, all right," Chally said, and rubbed his gauntleted wrist hard across his mouth. One of the cowboys approached, a mustachioed boy with his hat tipped back on his head.

193

"Who's in charge here?" Andrew demanded. Chally was clearly on the verge of explosion.

The cowboy rose in his stirrups to cup his hands to his mouth and yodel. A second cowboy trotted over to join them. Andrew recognized him from the roundup; the foreman named Goforth. He made a saluting gesture of recognition.

"Are these animals just passing through?" Andrew demanded. Sweat stung in his eyes.

"Lord Machray intends to hold this bottom for fattening beef cattle," Goforth said. "We'll be putting up a cabin here and some corrals."

"By God you won't!" Chally yelled.

"You will have these cattle out of here by tomorrow!" Andrew said.

Goforth glanced from one to the other of them with his cold eyes. He took makings from his vest pocket and tipped tobacco into a paper.

"If you think we can't move you fellows out of here you have another think coming, Johnny Goforth!"

Goforth's horse curvetted a half revolution while the foreman calmly finished putting his cigarette together and lit it. "Why, I believe we could handle you, Chally," he said. "If it come to it."

"I'll get an order to move those cattle from Lord Machray," Andrew said. He put out a restraining hand toward his partner.

"We can get twenty men here in half a day!" Chally said. "Glad to come and Winchester armed!"

Goforth just sat looking at him. He drew on his cigarette before he said, "So can we."

"Is Lord Machray in town or at Widewings?" Andrew asked.

"Believe you'd find him in town," Goforth said. He said to Chally, "You want to raise some hell, we will give you as much hell as you're lookin for." The cold eyes switched to Andrew. "There's maybe ways of workin this out, but one is not chucking out threats like birdseed. That is nothin to bother Lord Machray, and it sure don't bother me."

The other cowboy was pretending not to be hearing any of this. Goforth sat his horse, slightly slumped, only his eyes moving in his impassive face. Andrew headed Ginger north across the meadow, through the cattle there. Chally caught up with him, white with anger.

"Are you sure you can get twenty men?"

194

"I could surely get ten in a hurry."

"You mean Driggs and Conroy?"

"Them, and Daddy and Joe. And Bob Cletus. There is a bunch that'd just love to come out when I tell them the kind of play Machray is makin here."

"That would be war."

"Well, we can't let that land grabber buffalo us!"

"No," he said, remembering Yule Hardy's prophecy.

When they rode into Pyramid Flat the eastbound was in the station, a gray pall lying over the town. They inquired for Machray at the office building, where a clerk said he had been there only a half hour previously, he could not be far off. The gleaming red and varnished buggy was drawn up before Mrs. Benbow's house. They dismounted and tied their horses to the hitching rail alongside Machray's handsome bay. Chally followed him along the boardwalk.

In the parlor were two men and three girls, one of them Maizie. Before she could rise Andrew announced that they must see Machray on urgent business, and the hunchbacked maid hurried upstairs. While they waited, Chally pacing, he found himself staring at the little organ of which Mary Hardy had spoken. It was squat but graceful, shining with furniture polish, a cover with goldscrolled decoration closed down over its stops and keys. The maid returned to usher them upstairs to a sitting room with red drapes, where Machray lounged in an easy chair in his shirt sleeves. Mrs. Benbow stood at the window, one white hand gripping a fold of red velvet.

"What can I do for you, Livingston?" Machray asked. His long legs were stretched out, booted feet crossed, arms lying along the chair arms.

"You can write an order to Goforth to move those cattle off my range."

"And what if I do not, that being range I consider my own?"

Hat in hands, boots set apart, white-faced, Chally said, "Mr. Machray, we will stampede that herd right out of there!"

"If Goforth isn't told to move the herd, we will move it ourselves."

"And if it comes to shooting we are prepared for that, too!" Chally said.

"Be damned to you, then," Machray said.

"Will you move that herd or not?"

"I will not, sir!"

Andrew turned on his heel; he was shaking with anger. Outside, when Chally swung into the saddle he stood staring up at the other's furious face. "Where are you going?"

"Going looking for Bill Driggs and them, and then Joe and Daddy. You just tell me what's the choice but war, Andy!" Chally spat into the shiny buggy, jerked his gray to his haunches, and raced off down the street. Andrew untied his reins and mounted; he felt leaden.

The maid appeared in the doorway of the house; she came along the boardwalk, beckoning. Machray wanted more conversation with him.

The two in the second floor room appeared not to have moved. Mrs. Benbow at the window, Machray in the chair. Machray regarded him sourly.

"I will make you this offer, Livingston. I will pay you a thousand dollars for the use of that piece of bottom land this summer. What do you say to that?"

His first instinct was to accept the money and dissolve the contention, but it was too much money, too clearly a bribe, too clearly a sop imposed by Mrs. Benbow. He shook his head.

"I'd like those cattle removed tomorrow."

Machray shrugged and stretched. "I'll trouble you for some paper, and the wherewithal to write upon it, Mrs. Benbow."

The madam left the room with a scrape of taffeta. Machray squinted an eye at him.

"You are of a warlike nature, then, Livingston?"

"I don't like being bullied."

Machray studied him closely, apparently with amusement, so that he felt patronized. "You have powerful friends, my man," Machray said.

Mrs. Benbow reappeared with paper, pen, and ink. Machray wrote, scrawled a signature, folded the paper, and handed it to Andrew.

"I'm glad we could come to an agreement in this matter, Machray."

The other nodded as though no longer interested. The two of them, the one seated, the other standing, watched him silently as he left. He remembered Dickson saying to him, "It is because he misses Lady Machray and the wee bairn so much." It occurred to him that Lady Machray and the bairn must be due in the Bad Lands soon.

He found Chally in the saloon, with Conroy, Cletus, and two others he did not know, halting for an instant in the doorway to observe the grouping in its tension, Chally with his knees bent, body half turned and on the strain, one hand extended, and jaw thrust out as he spoke, the others surrounding him listening. Chally's face jerked toward him as the louvered doors swung to behind him.

He handed Chally the note. "We are all right," he said.

Chally hardly looked at it. His face twisted with contempt, or maybe it was disappointment. "Caved in, did he?"

He didn't reply to that, glancing at Conroy with the two-inch scimitar of scab on his forehead. Cletus stared back at him, wooden-faced, the pupils of his eyes darting from side to side.

"Ought to take on down there anyhow," one of the others said, a beefy-faced man with a drooping mustache. "Move things along a bit faster."

He shook his head. "It is all right," he said. He tried to understand the sense of blunted passion in the saloon. It seemed to him a will to violence. These men had been primed for a fight, and it had been snatched away. They resented him for that. It seemed to him that violence was always nagging and pushing these days in the Bad Lands, like insistent fingers plucking at a sleeve.

4

One morning in early August he himself discovered the second invasion of Sloping Bottoms.

The big, high-sided wagon with its rusty white cover stolidly occupied the exact center of the pastures from which Machray's cattle had been driven by Johnny Goforth and his cowboys on receipt of the note from Machray. Animals grazed near it, a cow, a horse, a mule, oxen. Strung between the wagon and a sapling was a line on which laundry hung in the windless air, three pair of overalls of varying sizes, different colored squares and rectangles. He heard a yipping cry, and a loud snapping. A yoke of oxen was dragging a log, a man striding alongside cracking a whip. Behind him trotted a half-grown boy.

He sat Cicero's saddle on the butte from which he and Chally had looked down upon Machray's herd, and examined his emotions. On the occasion of that previous invasion his own anger had been tempered by Chally's more violent anger. Now it was tempered by the knowledge that he was feeling what the old guard of ranchmen felt toward newcomers like himself.

As he waited he realized that the granger must have seen him. He clucked to Cicero, prodded his sides with his heels, and rode slowly down into Sloping Bottoms. The granger and the boy had halted to watch him approach, and a woman had appeared from behind the wagon, drying her hands in her apron. A white dog scampered toward him, barking furiously, and Cicero balked and shied.

"Rags!" the woman called, and the barking ceased, the small dog retreating.

He remembered Machray on his horse while he, on foot, had faced him resentfully, and he dismounted and, leading Cicero, went on to meet the granger. The man was painfully skinny, with a battered hat on his head and an Adam's apple like an elbow. His son was a smaller version with a mop of fair hair and oversized overalls. The two wore similar wooden expressions. The oxen slapped tails right and left in synchronized motion.

"My name is Livingston," he said.

"Feeney," the other said, accepted Andrew's hand, shook it limply, and dropped it. He brushed his forehead with a rag of a bandanna. The man was terrified.

"Just come to the Bad Lands?"

Feeney nodded jerkily. "From Pennsylvania." He made a gesture to include his family. "Things'd got wore out there." Then he set his jaw and said, "I have filed on a quarter section."

Andrew nodded. "I'm located about twelve miles downriver. Fire Creek Ranch. My cattle carry a brand that looks like a spread-out *N*. The Lazy-N."

"Them's the ones we been seein, Daddy," the boy whispered, and Feeney nodded with a kind of parody dignity.

"North of you is Lord Machray. The Ring-cross brand."

"Heard about him in town there," Feeney said. He mopped his forehead again, then folded his arms about him as though cold. The woman and the smaller boy, with the white dog seated at their feet, stood perfectly motionless beside the wagon tongue.

"He is very particular about his fence," Andrew continued. "He has men patrolling it. Fences aren't very popular out here, you see. But you will be obliged to fence any land you plant in crops."

The man seemed to be squinting at a point just above his right shoulder. He cleared his throat. "Now why would that be?"

"Otherwise you will be troubled by grazing cattle."

"I guess we can keep them off, me'n my boys."

"I advise you to fence. There is great resentment here on the part of settlers whose crops are trampled by cattle. There is greater resentment on the part of ranchmen whose cattle have been shot by settlers."

Feeney blew out his breath lengthily. "Well, I wouldn't mind fencin if I could get me some credit to buy wire."

"I can see that you get credit. Maybe we can help with some of the labor, too."

"Well—thanks!" Feeney said. He made an awkward gesture, half turning. "This here's my older boy, Buddy."

"How do you do?" Andrew said.

"There's skeeters!" Buddy said, motioning. His face flamed with embarrassment. "Down by the creek! They are somethin fierce!"

"They were worse earlier. They'll be gone soon."

"Mother!" Feeney called. "Come over and meet Mr. Livingston. He's our neighbor here!"

The woman moved promptly toward them, holding the smaller boy by the hand. She was almost as tall as her husband, broad-hipped and low-bosomed, with a sunburnt face and faded hair. The white dog trotted close to her feet, almost tripping her, and she whispered, "You! Rags!"

"How do you do, Mrs. Feeney."

"How-do, mister." She brushed a lock of hair back from her forehead. Her sleeves were rolled on her white arms, and her hands were large and red. When she saw him glance at them she tucked them into the pockets of her apron. The dirty-faced small boy had his thumb in his mouth, staring at Andrew with round eyes.

"You'll find this a pleasant place, Mrs. Feeney. Sloping Bottoms, we've always called it."

"Sloping Bottoms," she said. "That's nice!"

Feeney indicated where the cabin was to be erected, a number of stripped logs piled there already. Mrs. Feeney

199

asked if Andrew might be interested in buying vegetables when she had planted a garden.

He said he would. "What I would like is a supply of fresh milk. Is that a milk cow I see over there?"

The small boy took his thumb from his mouth and whispered something sibilant and unintelligible.

"Says that's Bossie," Buddy said.

"Buddy can bring you over milk whenever you want it," the woman said. "It will be good to have a cash crop right off!"

"Tomorrow, then," he said.

When he had ridden out of earshot of the Feeneys, he laughed out loud at life's ironies.

As Andrew had known he would be, Chally was furious when he was told that grangers had settled in Sloping Bottoms. He and Joe were sitting at the table in the Big House, drinking coffee.

"You ought to've run them right out of there!" Chally said. "That is your range!"

"They've filed on it."

Chally picked up his gauntlets and slammed them down on the table. "There's other bottoms with water that's not our range!"

Joe took his cup and retreated into the parlor, where he lounged in the chair by the door, one eyebrow arched in amusement. "Easy, Chally; easy!"

"Why don't they go back where they come from anyway! We don't need them out here. They just muck everything up!"

"You sound like a meeting of the Western Dakota Stockraisers Association."

"Hah!" Joe said.

Chally glared from one to the other of them. "Well, you are takin it very calm, I must say," he said to Andrew. "It is your range they have latched onto!"

"It seems best to be calm when faced with the inevitable."

"Well, I'll be gol-damned if I will just stand still! Those damned grangers are not running over me!"

"Chally, I remember your telling me about Regulators scaring your father off some land." He watched his factor's face, uncertain whether or not Chally could connect, whether or not he would be able to accept the changes coming. Chally sipped his coffee as though it was bitter brew.

"He has always been this way," Joe Reuter drawled. "I have seen him try to knock his head right through the wall when he didn't like where they had cut the door."

Chally glared at his brother. "Well, I have never run from a fight yet!"

"That is so, Chally, but you do get yourself a bad headache sometimes."

"There won't be any fight this time," Andrew said. "We will treat those people as we would like to have been treated here."

"Huh!" Chally said, and picked up his gauntlets.

"At least we will have fresh milk. Maybe eggs."

"Milk's for babies."

"Why, I believe I have seen you white your coffee, Chally," Joe said.

"That was Eagle Brand, not your fresh pap!" Chally said. He flung his gloves at his brother and stamped outside.

"Guess Machray'll be too busy to do anything about them grangers, either," Joe said.

"What do you mean?"

"Didn't you hear yet? His missus and baby's come to town." Joe grinned at him. "Reddest hair you ever saw. I will bet you she has got a temper on her. Speakin of!"

The next day when Andrew rode down to Palisades Ranch he found a crew fencing the pasture closest to the riverbank. He halted to observe the process. Posts had already been set and three rolls of wire were mounted on a wagon bed. The three strands were stapled to a post, and the wire unrolled as the wagon was pulled along by its team. After two hundred feet the wagon was halted and one rear wheel jacked up. The wire was then fastened to the hub and the wheel turned like a capstan to take up the slack of each strand in turn. The taut wire was then stapled to the intervening posts.

The foreman in charge, a Texan, came to stand by him and explain the process. Although there were a number of patent wirestretchers on the market, none was as effective as a wagon wheel, he said. It seemed that Hardy had filed on this pasture, where he would graze his prize herd.

Although he realized that he was witnessing another step in the end of the free range, he was amused by the evidence of Hardy's bow to changing times, and amused also not to comment upon it to Hardy. He told him of the grangers, to which Hardy gave no more response than a nod and a grunt.

From where they sat on the veranda, Hardy with his lips pouched out disagreeably and his fingers tented over his belly, the installation of the wire was hidden by the jut of the house.

"Are you aware of Mr. Emerson's dictum that photographs give more pleasure than paintings?" Hardy demanded.

He said that Mr. Emerson was welcome to rank his sources of pleasure as he saw fit.

"Photographs do not lie," Hardy said, tapping his fingertips together.

"On the contrary, they are the greatest liars, since they purport to be truthful, and are not. Photographs take all the color and life out of views of the Bad Lands, for instance."

Hardy sucked at his teeth, and said, "One might wish the drabbest photographs of the Bad Lands could be shown wherever it is these nesters originate. So a pack of them has descended upon you!"

"One family merely. Feeney is their name."

"Fenians!"

"Pennsylvanians."

"You take it lightheartedly," Hardy said.

"I don't see that it makes any difference how I take it. The fact exists."

"I will be interested in seeing you change your attitude when it becomes evident that your new friends are indulging in moonlight slaughtering."

"I had thought we might establish a barter system. Fresh vegetables and milk in exchange for beef. Yule, what is there we can do but accept a fact?"

"*Not* accept it!" Hardy said. "Must we accept evil just because it has always existed as fact?" He sulked for a time, then inquired if Andrew had made up his mind to vote for Blaine, or for Cleveland.

He said he would find it as difficult to support a man of questionable morality in the matter of women and marriage, as one he considered a common grafter.

Hardy smiled and tented his fingers. "And yet I have heard you speak in support of Lord Machray, whose morality in the matter of women and marriage is surely more questionable than Mr. Cleveland's!"

Having caught him so neatly seemed to put Hardy in a more expansive mood, and he sighed and said, "As you may imagine, I am not much pleased at having been driven to fencing land, Andy. How circumstances alter cases!"

When Hardy had strolled out to consult with his Texan, Andrew went inside the house to look for Mary. Mrs. Hardy was in the spotless, sun-flooded kitchen, rolling dough on a floured board. Mary had gone riding, she said. Mary spent much of her time riding alone these days.

"I am very much worried about her, to tell you the truth, Mr. Livingston. She is not herself at all."

"I've missed playing Schubert with her."

"Have you?" Mrs. Hardy said, turning from her work to look him straight in the eyes.

He felt his face burning. "Of course!"

"She misses it too, but I believe she is under the impression that you were no longer interested."

He did not know how to discuss with Mrs. Hardy the aspects of the word "interested."

"I know she has been disappointed that she has never been able to pose for you," Mrs. Hardy went on. "She had been looking forward to that. And we would very much like to have your sketch of her, you know."

"I do want her to pose. Indeed, we have discussed it several times."

"If she had some interest other than grieving over that poor boy it would be a great relief to us," Mrs. Hardy said.

5

*Dickson appeared one day, a Ring-cross cowboy in attend-*ance, to invite him to dinner at Widewings in celebration of Lady Machray's arrival. It seemed a summons rather than an invitation and, irritated and resentful, he hesitated while the cowboy squinted down at him from his horse and Dickson sat in his erect stance, slapping his gauntlets against his chaps.

But if Machray could forget past differences, so could he. "Of course I'll come," he said.

"We will ride along with you, if that is all right, sir. The Captain said he was certain you would not mind dressing for dinner."

"I'm afraid my wardrobe may be limited compared to Lord Machray's."

"We all make do as we must, sir, in the field," Dickson said, and the cowboy snorted.

While the two waited he packed his navy blue serge into a valise and rummaged through the tin box of his small effects until he found cuff links, collar button, and a stickpin for his cravat. He scowled at the wrinkles in his dress shirt. No doubt his host, whom he had last seen ensconced in a brothel, would be attired in full military fig. Riding north along the river with his escort, he asked Dickson how long he had been with Lord Machray.

"Seventeen years, sir. Since Annesley Bay."

"Where is that, Dickson?"

"Abyssinia, sir. The Captain—well, of course, he was but an ensign then—had come over from Bombay with the elephants. After Magdala we saw service in the Zulu War, and in Egypt. We have seen some hot countries, and some hot fighting, the Captain and I! He does enjoy listening to the pipes; and I know his ways. I have been taking care of him for a good many years!"

Dickson sounded wistful, and Andrew asked how Lady Machray liked the Bad Lands.

"Ah, well, that is difficult to say as yet, sir. She has been here but a week. Quite a surprise to the Captain her coming was, too! She only telegraphed from Chicago that she was en route, you see. Didn't wish the Captain to send *Aurora* for her and make a lot of pother for her arrival. Ladies have a very different way of looking at things than gentlemen, I believe, sir."

The cowboy, who had been listening, now pointed to one of the buttes and began a rambling tale of a bear hunt with Machray.

"Right over there!" he said. "We'd trailed that big griz must've been five miles! He was doin some travelin! Looked like a big hairy ball rollin down those coulees. Then he was gone like he'd fell down a hole. But Jim Hawkins spotted where he'd slipped into a cave there. Can't see it from here.

"Well, Lord Machray was bound to go into that cave after Mister Griz, no stoppin him. What'd he do but tie a lasso around his boot, and we was to jerk him out when he'd made his shot." He shouted with laughter. "Have you ever heard of a man loco enough to go in a cave with a *grizzly*? Well, he did, he crawled in there, and made his shot, and we all pulled like the devil, kind of scatterin like gettin out of the way of a express train. Lord Machray come out of there like a cork outen a bottle, but old griz *he* didn't come. Because he was shot straight through the mouth and dead as mackerel!" He laughed loudly again.

They rode on in silence. Finally Dickson said, "I wonder if you have heard that Bill Driggs has departed from the Bad Lands, sir."

"No, I had not heard that."

Dickson gave him a communicative look, as though they were allies in preserving Machray from the dangers that surrounded him. He added that Johnny Goforth and a crew had gone to survey a stage route to the Black Hills.

They came in sight of Widewings, crouched on the bluffs. As they approached the mansion Machray stamped down the steps to meet them.

"So glad you could come, Livingston! Wife's arrived at last! Tiptoed in when my back was turned, almost!"

Machray led him along the veranda. Beyond, the sun- and shadow-streaked prairie lay under a heat-curdled sky. Machray halted to point down at the yellow-brick chimney below the bluffs, a chalk line of smoke rising from it.

"Ochone, I'd hoped to have the place in operation for her arrival! Livingston, I believe there is a conspiracy. Sabotage! Niggling bits of things, mostly. But now there is a new man in the Land Office in Mandan. Seems I am accused of illegal enclosure! When I produce my deeds he mumbles priority rights, prior appropriation rights, something of the sort. He has been bought! Nor is this the doing of my neighbors. It is Chicago interests I have offended. Still, it is not altogether unpleasant to know the sods are afraid of me!"

He loped on. Any strain attendant upon their last meeting seemed forgotten. "Must see the wee chap," Machray went on. "Daddy's joy and pride! Grabs your finger like he will have to be prised loose. Juts out his little jaw! Ah, and when young Anthony grieves, how he makes the timbering ring!"

He laughed and clapped his hands together. "Some furnishings have arrived, and a carload still to come. Great hurlyburly these last few days. Terrific amount of chaos necessary to bring order, as no doubt the good Lord discovered in his week of labors."

They turned inside, past a curtsying maid in black and white. In the dining room a tiny woman in blue, with hair like spun gold, was sorting silver from a wooden chest into stacks. She had the pink cheeks of a China doll, and she looked no more than fifteen, tiny coral mouth pursed with her counting. Brilliant blue eyes glanced up as Machray introduced Andrew. Lady Machray smiled brilliantly and held out her hand. When he took it it was impelled to his lips.

"I apologize for the scent of silver polish, Mr. Livingston," Lady Machray murmured. "So glad to meet you. George has spoken of you often."

"Where's my Tony?" Machray demanded.

"Now, George, you are not to get him upset." She smiled the luminous and abstracted smile at Andrew again. "My husband insists upon coming at the child roaring like forty banshees, and wonders why the boy screams with terror."

"Fearfully spoilt by a regiment of women," Machray said, and led Andrew upstairs to view the wee laird in a large, many-windowed room. The child laboriously got to his feet and leaned in the corner of his crib like a boxer against the ropes, fat-faced and golden-haired, with an apprehensive expression. He wore a complex nightdress of silk and ribbons.

"Ought to see the greedy little bugger going after the tit," Machray said. "Like he is bound to turn it inside out. Just like his dad!" He shouted with laughter, upon which Anthony Ernest's face turned red and crinkled; he began to squall. A young nurse hurried in to snatch him up. Both of them looked at Machray reproachfully.

"Ah, goodness gracious, I have done it again," Machray said. "You must not tell Lady Milly of this, my dear."

"If you would only not be quite so noisy, sorr," the girl said, and Machray replied glumly, "Yes, yes—" turning to gaze out the window, hands on hips, as she comforted the child.

Watching young Tony Balater's tears subside and the trembling lower lip steady and suck in upon itself, Andrew was so reminded of his own son that his eyes burned.

"Never mind," Machray said, at the window. "It is a fine place to bring up a lad, out here, that women have not spoilt yet with their minching ways and mim-mou'd religions!"

As they descended the broad staircase together he announced that there would be another guest for dinner, a Mr. Beavey, "a kind of bookkeeper fellow of Old Minton's." Minton was Lady Machray's father, "the old jew," or, as Andrew came to understand, the financier who had organized a company for the purposes of backing Machray in his enterprises.

"Shameless great suck-up, the old Jew," Machray confided in a rather noisy whisper. "*Must* have a title for his daughter.

Still, one glance from those blue eyes and I was done for! I believe it was a standoff, however, neither he nor I knowing what we had let ourselves in for!" He laughed and slapped his leg.

Mr. Beavey was a gray-whiskered, gray-complected man of about sixty, with a few strands of gray hair combed over his bald pate, and a long, disapproving upper lip. The table gleamed with napery, silver, and crystal, and serving dishes decorated in gold with the Machray coat of arms. Dickson served the dishes and poured the wine; between his appearances they were attended by a uniformed girl who was stationed behind a folding screen. Machray and his lady wrangled, throughout dinner, in terms that Andrew found close to acrimony, although always Machray would turn the quarrel aside at the last moment with some joke or laughter, calling for a second and a third bottle of claret, while Mr. Beavey appeared to be slowly sinking, his head into his shoulders, his shoulders into his body, his body into his chair.

Lady Machray wore a blue gown that displayed her white, frail shoulders and throat, and a lavaliere gleaming with jewels. "Of course it is a new experience, Mr. Livingston," she said, "finding oneself the wife of a beef butcher."

Machray's convulsion of laughter caused her mouth to tuck into a tight line. "My dear, you will find yourself the wife of a teamster yet!" He cried.

"Very dubious, that," Mr. Beavey announced. "Very chancy, this stage-line enterprise. No faith in it."

"My dear man," Machray said to him. "If there is any way of taking high profits without chances *I* don't know of it, and neither do you!"

Lady Machray turned her radiant smile on Andrew. "As Father puts it, the Great West is naught but a faucet with a broken handle."

"These pawnshop chappies speak in splendid hyperbole," Machray said.

Andrew sat frozen with embarrassment. Mr. Beavey sank into himself the more, and Lady Machray glared at her husband, who was tossing off another glass of claret. He began to tap a spoon against his wineglass, singing in a tuneless voice, " 'The lady of the manor was a-dressin' for the ball—' "

He stopped, grinning, to lead forward with his chin supported on his hands and address Andrew drunkenly, but with something intelligent and appealing in his green eyes: "You were a married man, Livingston. Were you happy in the state, or was it a great humbug?"

"Perhaps some of both," he said.

Mr. Beavey stirred in his chair. "Can't remember who said it," he said. " 'To marry a second time is a triumph of hope over experience!" He cackled. Lady Machray looked at him coldly.

"You are no longer married, Mr. Livingston?" she said.

"I am a widower."

Machray declaimed:

> "King Davie, when he waxéd auld,
> An's bluid ran thin, an' a' that
> An fand his cods was growin' cauld
> Could not refrain from a' that.
>
> From a' that, an' a' that,
> To keep him warm, an' a' that
> The daughters of Jerusalem,
> They warmed him well, an' a' that!"

He closed his eyes and appeared to nap. Lady Machray's lips had turned white. She said to Andrew, "You see, Mr. Livingston, my husband loves anything that might embarrass me before my guests."

He had not managed to reply to this when the maid, summoned by mysterious means, appeared from behind her screen to clear the table. Machray sat with his arms folded on his chest like the stone representation of a dead knight on his bier.

Andrew asked Lady Machray's impressions of the Bad Lands.

"Seems to me the dreariest place imaginable, Mr. Livingston! The heat is stifling, the verdure dead or dying, and after one has drunk in a few splendid vistas . . ." She gestured negatively.

"We are having a very dry summer."

"Perfect Sahara, in fact," Beavey said.

Machray opened one eye to glare at him. "Sneaking in when my back was turned," he muttered. "Bringing along spies and catchpoles." He began to tap his glass with his spoon:

"The lady of the manor was a-dressin' for the ball—"

Lady Machray said, "You will continue in this way at your peril!"

Beavey excused himself, saying it had been an exhausting day, and stumped out. "Wha gars auld Meester Beavey look sae gash?" Machray muttered. "Lookin' at figures all day; exhaustin'! Dickson, more wine!" When Dickson had filled his glass, he rose unsteadily to make a toast:

"To the Bad Lands! Bounded on the east by the meatpackers of Chicago. To the north by hypocrisy and envy, the south by bloodsuckers, and the west by profit and loss. And all about by men of ill will!" He reseated himself with an off-balance thump and immediately began to sing, " 'Hangin' down, swingin' free—' "

"Yes, Mr. Livingston," Lady Machray said loudly. "I believe it to be quite fraying to the nerves out here, resulting in drunkenness and uncouth behavior. I would certainly not wish to bring up my son in such a place!"

"No, nor anything else!" Machray said, grinning savagely.

She thrust her pretty, contorted face at him like a snake striking. "I will not be any man's chattel, you drunken foulminded *confidence man!*"

Machray tapped his glass again:

"The lady of the manor was a-dressin' for the ball,
When she spied a Highland tinker lashin' piss against the
    wall—"

Lady Machray rose swiftly and dashed the contents of her wineglass in his face. Grinning, his face dripping claret, Machray continued to sing:

"With his great big kidney-cracker, and balls the size o'
    three,
An' half a yard o' foreskin hangin' well below the knee.
    Hangin' down! Swingin' free!
An' wi' half a yard o' foreskin hangin' well below the
    knee!"

Andrew rose as Machray sagged forward. "*O, felix culpa!*" he said, and lay his face on the table before him. He began to snore.

"I apologize for my husband," Lady Machray said. "As you see, life in the Bad Lands is too much for him."

"I think he must have missed you very much."

Her icy blue eyes gazed into his. "No, Mr. Livingston, he only wanted the son I have now given him."

He became aware of flickering light in the window behind him. He swung toward it, pushing the net curtains aside. The flames were tiny with distance, orange and golden, the chimney looming like a black spike in their midst.

"Lady Machray, the abattoir is burning," he said. Then he swung around. "Machray, the abattoir is afire!"

Machray strained upward; Andrew caught his arm and helped him to his feet, and to the window, where Machray stood gaping and swaying. "Milly!" he panted. "Call Dickson—"

Then he bellowed, "*Curse them!* A curse on their houses, on their byres and stables, on man and guest, wife and bairn—black, *black* be the curse upon them!"

Machray staggered awkwardly around, Andrew trying to support him. Lady Machray had disappeared.

"Curse them!" Machray shouted and fell then, dragging the tablecloth from the table with a crash of glassware.

Andrew and Dickson led a force of cowboys from the bunkhouse down the hill, where they joined the disorganized crew of clerks and carpenters fighting the flames. With the plentiful water from the overhead flume at last they managed to douse the fire in the smaller of the two buildings, but the larger was all but gutted, an echoing blackened shell stinking of char and dripping water when dawn came.

6

In a glade where there was thick grass along the margin of a tributary of Fire Creek, dense brush surrounding the place and changing patterns of sun and shade from the flickering of the cottonwood leaves above them, he posed Mary Hardy. He had not planned that this should be with bared bosom, but that seemed to have been her understanding of her role. She had immediately disrobed. Now she was seated upon the little folding stool in her skirt, her shirtwaist and collection of undergarments neatly folded at her feet, the sunlight knitting and purling on her marble flesh with the dark disc of her nipple framed in her crooked elbow, and her face with its bright set smile as dark with blood as the nipple. She held her hands, one clasped in the other, like some object she was proffering. Loose ends of her hair fluttered in the little breeze that filtered through the trees. In the silence the creek whispered through the grasses that lined its course. The wicker hamper rested in the shade.

He stood at his easel sketching her face with its distinctive shape, very broad across the eyes, tapering to her small chin, which was set in determination as well as embarrassment. He recalled Machray speaking of Lady Machray as having a whim of adamant, and he thought that Mary Hardy might have such a will also.

He sketched the breast half concealed, or revealed, by the V of her arm; the hands, twisted into a half spiral; the toes of her little boots showing primly beneath the hem of her skirt. He was perspiring in the sun as he measured, squinting, with his charcoal stick, then set to work on the long strokes. Always, now, he knew from these first encompassing lines if the sketch was to be successful. Stepping back to regard what he had done so far, he thought that it would be.

When he had finished the outlines of the figure, he told Mary that she could rest. He plucked up her stiff white shirt-waist and held it spread until she turned her back to it, and he could lay it over her shoulders. Holding the shirt closed with her good hand, she strolled along the edge of the brook while he filled in details, glancing up to watch her sometimes—a slender girl in a long black skirt that swept the grass, the coils of her dark hair gleaming in the sunlight as though varnished. Her figure was almost boyish with the astonishing bulk of her bosom concealed within her shirt. She circled around to watch over his shoulder, and he felt a catch of tension at her flower scent.

She asked in a low voice if he thought she was good-looking.

"Of course you are good-looking. But to an artist you are an interesting subject."

She withdrew along the course upon which she had approached him. "What do you think of the suffragettes, Andrew?" she asked.

He said he thought their cause was just but their antics sometimes embarrassing.

"I think if I lived in the East I would be one of them,"

Mary said. "I would march, chain myself to pillars, and be jerked about by policemen; all those things."

"What would your father think of that, do you suppose?"

"Oh, he would hate it," she said calmly.

He asked if she was ready to pose again, and she returned to seat herself on the stool, removing her shirt, folding it, and placing it on the grass at her feet. She settled into her pose again. This time her smile seemed easier. He began to limn her folded hands.

"So you are determined to leave the Bad Lands," he said. "To go east?"

"Or west. Or anywhere. The Bad Lands doesn't hold much for a young woman, except loneliness and disappointment and—seeing terrible things happen. I suppose in time one might become resigned to it, like my mother."

"You are speaking of your friend," he said, leaning close to his drawing.

"No, I promised myself I would not speak of him today. Maybe I am speaking of the burning of Lord Machray's slaughterhouse. The men who would do those things."

He brushed sweat from his eyes, squinting at his charcoal stick cross-hatching.

After a long time Mary Hardy said, "Now I think I would never become any man's *property*, unless he would take me away from the Bad Lands."

He rubbed out her mouth and began again.

"Father looks upon me as his property, you see. It is strange that he speaks so strongly *against* property. I think he came not to like you because Mother was so certain you were the ideal suitor." She laughed. "It is strange that a great war was fought to give Negroes their freedom, but suffragettes are looked upon as ridiculous!"

When he asked if she would like another rest, she went again to walk along the little creek, her shirt draped over her shoulders. "Shall we open our hamper and see what enticements Mother has heaped upon you?"

Seated across the red-and-white-checked cloth from him, she chatted about books, family conversations, and local gossip, while he held the plates for her to heap with cole slaw and sliced tongue. He was finding it difficult to keep his eyes from the free swing of her breasts inside her blouse, where they had such different implications from the same breasts bared for his charcoal stick.

212

"Could I make a living as a model, do you think?" she asked.

"It would be a very trying way to make a living. Artists being as they are."

"Certainly you cannot include yourself in that condemnation!" She laughed merrily, her nose crinkling; he was reminded of the girls of his young acquaintance humming tunes that seemed so meaningful, although he had never been able exactly to pin down the message.

He seemed to see her though a kind of haze, her laughing face, the pale hand in her lap, the movement of her breasts. He could see the moves ahead like those on a checkerboard.

There was a stamping from the direction of the invisible horses, a long whinny, a rush of retreating hoofs. He thought it was horse thieves, and he jumped to his feet. He ran toward the horses.

When Mary joined him he was squatting to regard the third set of hoofprints, which had arrived and departed, leaving their horses unmolested. She seemed much less disturbed than he, that they had been observed.

Book Four

1884

1

When Jeff Hardy leaned forward in Redboy's saddle to push some leaves aside and peer through at Andy Livingston and Mary, with her bare bosom gleaming like snow in the sun, his heart began to pump so hard he felt sick. He let the branch fall as though he had burned his hand on it. It seemed to him that he had got himself in bad trouble stopping by here, where he had seen Mary's dapple gray with another horse, and peeking through instead of riding on into the clearing. That was what he should have done. But what would he have said when he found them like that?

What he ought to do, still, was ride right on in as though he had not seen anything, be surprised to find them like that, and then like a man ask Andy what he *meant? What're you doing with my sister?* He had seen the easel where Andy must have been drawing her. Maybe it was all right then. But the sight of her bare bosom like that had made him feel sick.

Then one of the horses set up a racket, and first thing he knew he had lit out of there as though a grizzly was after him, panting, and sweat stinging in his eyes. Down creek a way he let Redboy slow to a walk. What was he going to do? He would say to Mary, *I saw you and Andy. What were you do-ing there like that?* She would call him a sneak. He couldn't even imagine telling Father what he had seen.

It began to seem to him that it was his duty to turn around and ride back there, and announce to Andy Livingston that he must fight him because of his sister's honor. *A meeting is arranged, and satisfaction obtained,* Machray had said. Fa-ther had talked a good deal, embarrassingly, about Mary's honor when Machray had danced with her at the Cattlemen's Ball in Miles City. He had thought it was his duty to shoot Machray then, because of Father. But Andy Livingston had eased him out of that, or Machray out of it; he had not been sure, after, which it was. Now it all made his head ache.

The word "hypocrisy" came to him. It was a word Mary was using a lot lately. He remembered those times with

217

Matty, he and Matty and Mary swimming stripped in the little pool with the rock hanging over it down on Pony Creek. Why hadn't that been wrong? Because it was Matty, not Andy Livingston, or because Mary was older now, and fatter in the bosom? Because there had been three of them, and not just two? Just because different times were different.

He remembered Mary and Father arguing about just that thing—why something was bad one time and not another. That had had to do with Matty too. Mary and Father had had terrible fights right after the lynching. He had been shocked at how strong Mary would go at Father, and he had felt sick to his stomach, as he had been to see Mary and Andy like that, but in a different way.

This time she had announced that lynching was evil, and anyone that condoned it no better. Right away his stomach had tightened up, he was so afraid of Father getting angry, but Father only removed his spectacles and polished them with his handkerchief, saying of course he did not believe in doing evil so that good might come of it, a man who tried to justify such a course only deceived himself. Then he aimed a finger at her:

"Are you certain that you mean evil, my dear? Many an act is right or wrong according to the time and place of its performance. According to its context. Beware of calling something evil on Monday because the same thing was evil on Sunday!"

Mary said that she understood morality to mean that evil was evil whatever the day of the week.

Mother said, "Mary dear, we know you and Jeff have lost a friend to a cruel incident—"

"Perpetrated and condoned by cruel men!" Mary said, very quick.

Father kept on polishing his eyeglasses. "Let us look at this example," he said. "On Sunday I visit my neighbor's house and I am made welcome. But on Monday he has put up a sign posting his property to trespassers, and I will be a law-breaker if I violate this restriction."

"That is not evil," Mary said. "That is only illegality."

Mother said, "Child!" for Father did not like to be interrupted when he had got under way like that, but Mary tossed her head and said, "Well, it is so!"

Father went on, mild enough still: "Now suppose I went over to my neighbor's on Tuesday, after the sign had been put up"—he pointed a finger at Mary again—"because I had

218

seen there was a fire! And my neighbor was sleeping and did not know it. So I violated his prohibition, and the law, to save his life and his property. To observe the letter of the law and allow the disaster would have been evil in this case, you see. I ask you to perceive, my dear, that the same act may have many aspects of right and wrong according to its *context*."

"That was not what I was taught in this household!" Mary said.

Mother said, "Nor were you taught to be impertinent in this household!"

Mary just sat there with her chin out and moved the knife and fork noisily on her plate, so it seemed to him that she hadn't even thought to be impertinent until Mother had mentioned it. And always when Mother spoke out strong to criticize Mary or him Father would turn easy and forgiving.

He said, "My dear, I must convince you that hanging horse thieves in the Bad Lands in private is a very different thing from lynching Negroes in Georgia in public."

"Well, you cannot!"

"You perceive no difference?"

"I believe that evil is evil in Georgia or Dakota Territory, and on every day of the week!"

Father only complimented her for concerning herself with philosophical questions, which was the sign of a maturing young mind, and Mary let it go at that.

Plodding on toward home, he wished that Andy Livingston would marry Mary. He knew his mother had her heart set on it, and although Andy was not young, he wasn't old. Most of the ranchers that had come courting Mary were *old*, like old Pard Yarborough, who farted even when he knew people could hear him, and had rotting teeth and a fearful breath. Mary could not abide men like Yarborough, and Father never liked the younger ones, especially Matty. Matty had never courted Mary, he was only their friend, although he did act like her servant sometimes, running to fetch something she had forgotten, and joking and playing his mouth organ for her.

But Andy had seemed like prayers answered, a widower and well enough off to stock a ranch without even thinking twice about it, and talking about doubling his herd. He was a queer fellow in some ways, quiet and watchful, and not much for jokes or easy talk, but he and Mary did have a fine time playing piano together, and he and Father had rousing arguments, which Father enjoyed, though Father was not as enthusiastic about him as a husband for Mary as Mother.

Without even thinking about it, he had been convinced that that was what would happen eventually, Mary would marry Andy Livingston and live in his new house up on Fire Creek with their own piano. But once lately, when they had talked about it, she had laughed and said it was never to be. Andy didn't think of her in that way, nor would she ever marry anyone in the Bad Lands, to turn into a lump of dried-up gumbo or blast her head off with a load of buckshot like Lamey's Annie Mooney.

Once he had known Mary better than he knew anyone else in the world, but lately it was as though he did not know her at all. He could never predict her attitude toward anything, except he could be sure she would go against Father on whatever it was. But it was not long ago that she had been just a girl reading books and reciting poetry and practicing the piano and dressing her dolls. She must have had three dozen dolls, each one more precious to her than the last one. She wrote stories, too, that always had in them a girl named Mary, or Marilynn, or Mary-Anne, who would be courted by fine fellows with "luxuriant mustaches." Sooner or later each of these fellows would go down on his knee to ask for the girl's hand but there would always be some trumped-up reason why she couldn't accept him.

He would never forget that pretty-gaited little horse of hers that was going blind. He had some disease in his eyes, and a film would come there. Father was going to have him put out of his misery but she would not stand for it. She had had a little curly dog that got distemper, Father had shot him, and she never got over it. So every day she would lick the film off that pony's eyes. He couldn't stand to watch her, but she would do it because she didn't know what else to do and Father was threatening to have him shot. She did it every day, and in the end it cured him.

Always it had been difficult for him to be together with Mary and Father. It was bad now, but it had always been bad, one way or another. When they lived in Spottswood Valley, where there were stores nearby where you could spend money, Father had never given them money. It was not that he was stingy, it was that he considered money a necessary evil, not to be indulged in more than it had to be. There was a competition at the school for declaiming poetry, and Mary won it. Father was so proud he gave her a ten-dollar gold piece. Later, when they were going home in the buckboard, Mary burst into tears; Father swung around to ask what was wrong, and Mary said her brother had pinched her because he was jealous. Father had punished him, and later on, Mary had apologized; she had burst out crying like that because Father had given her the gold piece, but when he had asked her what was wrong she couldn't say *that*.

Then there was the mysterious business of her hand. Father had used to punish them the way he had been punished as a boy at Ruthvens Hall in England. You would hold out your hand and he would smack it very hard with a ruler. Mary would never cry out when he did that, but just look straight back at him with her lips clamped together and her face blood red. He himself had always been a coward, begging and yelling because it seemed to him that was what Father wanted. But Mary would not make a sound. He believed that Mary's hand had been crippled in that way. He knew if he were Father he would suffer for what he had done to Mary's hand, but sometimes he thought that Mary had *helped* her hand go bad as her way of punishing Father for his way of punishing them.

There was a time, too, when Mary began getting her bosom, when Father would bear heavily on her, warning her of fearful things he did not name straight out, and calling women "frail vessels" as though they were ships on stormy seas. Once, though much later, Mary spoke up to say if there was an eighth deadly sin it ought to be hypocrisy, which caused Father to become angry enough to slap her, which he had not done for a long time. He thought he knew what Mary was talking about, though. Father had got himself into some pickle in Pyramid and Mary had had to go get him out of it, for Mother was not to know. Probably it was from drinking whiskey, for once or twice a year Father would do all his drinking at one time. Mary would never tell what had happened.

Last winter she had begun to change. He had thought she might be going crazy like that girl of Lamey's. She would say that living in the Bad Lands was prison and bondage, and everything was either barren and dried up, or frozen. She would rant that she was not prepared for anything in the world except to be a man's slave, and no one would ever marry her and take her away from the Bad Lands because she was imperfect, with her crippled hand.

When spring came, and the good time of the Montana

221

Stockraisers big meeting in Miles City, she was better for a while, but when Matty was killed she was absolutely crazy wild. She talked about Lamey's girl all the time, and once she told him Matty Gruby was the only man she would ever love, for all the rest were vile murderers and lustful beasts. And the way she went at Father at table sometimes would upset him so much that he would have to excuse himself and go out by the corral and throw up his supper.

Riding back to Palisades Ranch he knew he would not tell Father what he had seen, for one reason because Father would want to know why he had not been with Andy and Mary. He had not been with them because Mother had sent him to look for her Billy-horse instead, and that would get Mother in trouble along with Mary. But as soon as he got home he told his mother.

She just looked at him tight-lipped and said. "Why didn't you make yourself known, and stop them, Jefferson?"

"Well, they wasn't really doing anything, you see."

"*Weren't*," she said sharply, as though his grammar was more important than Mary with her shirt off.

When Mary came home the two of them disappeared into Mother's room, and after a long time there was yelling and bawling, and Mary's voice going on with a hoarse, insistent note to it. When he saw her later she swept by him red-eyed without a word.

Father came home just before suppertime. They had supper alone, without asking any of the hands in to the table, which Mother always arranged when there were family problems. Mary did not help with the table-setting at all, sitting in her place in her blue and white gingham poker-backed, with her shining brown hair hanging down, staring straight ahead of her. He could feel his stomach start to twist on itself and thought maybe if he claimed he was stomach-sick he might be excused. Right off Father asked what the trouble was.

"Mother believes Mr. Livingston should declare himself," Mary said.

"Ah!" Father said, and steepled his fingers together looking from Mary to Mother.

"It is time Andrew Livingston clarified his intentions."

"He has none," Mary said.

"Why, I would say that he has done so," Father said. "He has made it clear that he intends to make his home in the Bad Lands, and thus would never be acceptable to Mary." Father grinned in a way Jeff didn't like. "Although he may

222

find it uncomfortable here if he persists in his plan to acquire a second herd."

"What will they do?" Mary said. "Lynch him?"

There was a long, bad silence. He pushed the macaroni around on his plate with his fork. Father began to polish his eyeglasses.

"I believe I understand," Mary went on. "Young men are not lynched in the Bad Lands because they steal, but because they are out of favor."

"You will stop this impertinence!" Mother said. Father leaned forward with the bad smile.

"No, for stealing, my dear," he said.

"For myself, I prefer stealing to hypocrisy," Mary said. She gave Jeff a sharp, sideways glance. "And to sneaking and tattling."

"What does that mean, please?" Father said. His face had turned red and pale in unhealthy blotches.

He felt the bile mount in his throat, but recede again.

"You will go to your room, Mary," Mother said, and Mary rose without another word and left, carrying her hand.

But after a few minutes she reappeared in the doorway. She held up a gold locket on a chain, the locket she had given Matty last summer, with a curl of her hair in it. She stared at Father with her lips tight and pale.

Father's chair scraped as he pushed it back and stood up.

"My dear," he said. "I cannot believe that you would go through my private effects."

"I was looking for money so I could leave this place forever," Mary said. She kept holding up the locket, her eyes fixed on Father's face. "Why shouldn't I go through your private effects?" she said. "You go through mine. You read my diary."

Mother rose also, hand to throat. Jeff clamped his elbows to his belly to suppress the churning there. This must be something really *bad*, with Mary so quiet. She held out the locket.

"My dear—" Father started.

"You read my diary to see what I say about *men*," Mary said. "I will tell you what I will write of you, so that you will not have to go through my private effects this time. 'The men who killed Matty Gruby were sent by my father. They brought him the locket I had given Matty so that he would know it had been done.'" She thrust the locket toward Father as though she wanted him to take it from her.

223

"My dear," Father said in a rusty voice. "The boy was punished because he was a thief. As a warning to others. You must not think—"

"Who did it?" Mary broke in. "I know it was none of the cowboys on this place. I know it wasn't *you*. It must've been that secret committee of the Association. Never mind, I'll find out who they were. The murderers," she said, calmly. Jeff watched her lips stretch as though trying to smile. "Remember when they burned the cross in the yard? Do you remember, Father? Just before we left the Valley? The nightriders. Did you and your nightriders consider burning a cross to frighten poor Matty, Father? Before you decided to *kill* him."

"I will tell you what I had to go to your diary to ascertain," Father said. "That my daughter conspired to steal horses in order to leave this place. With a *horse thief!*"

Mary leaned against the door frame as though she would have fallen without support, her hand slowly dropping to her side. She said, "I believe it is better to steal to save your life than to murder to save your *property!*"

Father lunged at her, slapping her so hard her head banged against the door jamb. He slapped her again and again. She made no sound, but raised her hand to hold out the locket to him once more, until, shuffling, he turned away from her.

Mary left then. Jeff could hear her quick steps in the hall and the door of her room close. Father and Mother stood on opposite sides of the table, facing away from one another.

His head hurt so that he had to grit his teeth as he hurried down the hall to his sister's room. When he opened the door she was sitting on the bed. It was dim with the curtain drawn.

"Did you set Matty to stealing stock?" he said. Before she could reply he yelled at her, "*You did too!*"

She jumped off the bed, her face wild, snatched up the candlestick from the bureau and swung it over her head as though she meant to brain him. He backed out the door.

She slammed it behind him and threw the bolt. Inside the room he could hear her sobbing.

2

Hardy wore a dusty suit with a narrow-brimmed hat pulled forward over his eyes. He removed his spectacles and polished the lenses on a handkerchief, sitting a brown gelding just outside the corral fence where Chally was carrying a saddle, and Andrew waited to take it from him.

"Good day, Andy—Chally."

They greeted him. Chally set the saddle on the top rail of the fence.

"I see there's a herd come up from Texas, settling in over west of Box Creek," Hardy said.

"Looked in on them," Chally said, folding his arms.

"There may be more on the way," Hardy said.

"Why is that, Yule?" Andrew asked.

"There is considerable friction on some of the reservations where the southern cattlemen are used to leasing grazing rights."

Chally blew his breath out lengthily while Andrew wondered at the sense of urgency Hardy seemed to project. "Well, like my daddy said, there is always room for one more in the pew," Chally said.

"To a point, perhaps," Hardy said.

They exchanged opinions on the fire, and whether or not Machray would rebuild, Chally claiming he had heard in town that a large crew of carpenters had been imported. It was clear, however, that Hardy had personal business, and soon Chally excused himself, took up the saddle, and carried it toward the Big House.

"I wonder if you have seen Mary?" Hardy said in a curiously singsong voice.

He said he had seen her yesterday. He could feel the cool of perspiration break out on his forehead.

"She seems to have left home," Hardy said. "Her brother has gone into town to look for her. I decided to come here. I'm afraid her mother has got unfortunate ideas in her head."

"May I ask what those might be?"

Hardy's face was bland, pink, and expressionless. "Mrs.

Hardy has learned that you and Mary met alone. We had thought her brother accompanied her."

"I had asked her to pose for me. Mrs. Hardy knew that."

"I would be interested in seeing your drawings."

"They are only sketches. I'm afraid I have nothing ready to show."

Hardy swung the gelding away and clucked him into motion. He rode in a stiff, backward-leaning stance, stirrups thrust forward, headed back toward Palisades; he did not look behind him.

Returning from the Big House, Chally leaned on the corral fence beside Andrew. "Never seen *that* one screwed up so tight. He that tore up about that Texas herd?"

"His daughter has left home."

Chally whistled.

He didn't know where Mary Hardy could have gone except to Pyramid Flat, if she was making her attempt to flee the Bad Lands. He felt curiously breathless as he considered the warnings he had had of something like this. He did not wish to discuss her with Chally, but he knew her visits here must be on his factor's mind, combined with Hardy's visit. And now he knew that Yule Hardy was no friend.

"What will happen if we are barred from the Association's fall roundup?" he asked.

Chally shrugged. "There is that, and then there is their not recognizing the Lazy-N brand."

"Can they do that?"

Chally shrugged more elaborately.

He asked again what would happen.

"We'd lose some head. Have to see about getting a pool-outfit together. There's others in the same boat. That Texas outfit's a couple of brothers named Crowe. Fair-sized herd by the look of it. They have already got them a warning to clear out, all signed with those Regulator numbers. The one I talked to—his name is Davey—says they will stick, fight if they have to. Don't think Bad Lands hospitality is exactly trumps."

"I'm afraid that has been our experience also."

"Things gettin worse," Chally said.

The next morning he was seated alone at the table in the Big House enjoying a cup of hot, sweet coffee flavored with cream from the Feeneys' Bossie, when he heard hoofs approaching. He went outside to see Jeff Hardy swinging out of

226

the saddle. Jeff hurried toward him, pigeon-toed in his boots, slapping dust from his arms and legs with his hat.

"*Andy!* Mary's in that *house* in town!"

He felt as though he'd been kicked in the belly. Jeff's dusty jug-eared face was frantically twisted. "Andy! I don't know what Father'll *do!*"

He remembered Mary inquiring if she might be able to make her living as a model. There were not many accessible means of making a living open to a young woman like Mary Hardy. Schoolteaching. What else? Mrs. Benbow's.

"She is playing a little organ they have got there, is *all*— she says!" Jeff said. "For parties, like. But Father'll—"

"She is living there?"

Jeff nodded exaggeratedly. "I told her she had to come home but, Andy—she just laughed!"

It was late in the afternoon when he rode into Pyramid Flat, and the shadow of the bluffs lay across the town. With the powdery scent of town dust in his nostrils, he trotted down Main Street. He could already hear the notes of the little organ as he tied Brownie to the hitching rail among the other horses and hurried up the echoing planks of Mrs. Benbow's boardwalk. He halted before the door, listening. The song was "Go, Forget Me," but she must have a partner, for two hands were playing.

The hard-faced little man with the low-crowned derby let him in and took his hat. Down the dark entry the illumination of the parlor shone, furred at the edges by lace curtains. Now he found himself moving reluctantly. "Go, Forget Me" ended, to applause.

There were eight or ten men in the room, and as many girls, ranged in attitudes of listening on the chairs and couches, the girls in their white shifts seated on men's knees, or leaning against them as they stood behind the organ and the organist. Mrs. Benbow stood apart; she glanced toward him as he moved to where he could see Mary Hardy, alone at the keyboard. Feet pumping, she began to play "Hours That Were to Memory Dearer."

The lamplight gleamed in her brown hair. She wore a complicated white dress with a low collar. He could see her right hand; crumpled like a bird claw, it tapped and held down the keys of the little organ.

Maizie took his arm and smiled up into his face with her red lips. "Come to do a little more *drawing*, mister?" she

227

whispered, insinuating her body against him. Now one of the men standing behind the organ began singing in a deep voice; Mary Hardy's small, true one joined his. Doctor Micklejohn was nodding in time to the music.

He moved toward Mrs. Benbow. "I must talk to her," he said. He noticed that when Machray was absent the madam's face was colorless and uninteresting.

"Do not exercise yourself, Mr. Livingston," she said.

"You must not do this."

"Do what?"

He gestured. Her face twisted a little. "To whom?" she said.

"Her father, for one!"

"You mean because now he will have to go to Mandan to Mrs. Grindle's?"

He didn't know what she meant. He said again that he must speak to the girl.

"Go upstairs to my office," Mrs. Benbow said. "I'll send her up in a while."

As he mounted the stairs he paused to look down on the whores, and the men, none of whom he knew except the doctor, grouped at the organ with arms around each other's waists. Mary Hardy did not look up from her music, her soprano ringing through the heavier voices. He watched her crumpled hand pressing the keys.

He waited in the office, seated in a low chair before Mrs. Benbow's neat desk, rising when Mary entered. She closed the door behind her.

"Another visitor?" she said. He found her laugh intolerable. Her cheeks were stained dark with her natural color, but her lips had been artificially tinted.

"I can't believe you would do this to your father," he said, and felt as false as her laugh had been.

"No!" she said, facing him with her left hand running up and down her arm as though she was cold. "You are mistaken, then."

"I would like to give you money to go east and start a life there."

She shook her head. "I am very comfortable here."

"The offer will stand, however."

"Thank you, sir," she said, and curtsied. "But here I may make my living doing what I have been trained to do." It seemed to him that she was teasing. "Playing the organ," she added. "It is considerably easier for me than a piano. I am

228

given tips for entertaining these men in a manner that is acceptable to me. I appreciate your worrying about me, however. I did not believe you concerned yourself with my welfare."

"That is unfair."

She nodded, either in agreement or acknowledgment, he could not be sure which. "Have you seen what's come in on the freight cars?" she asked excitedly. "Such beautiful furniture! We've been watching the wagons go past. Beautiful unholstered chairs, and tables, and lamps. And statuary! And we've seen Lady Machray!"

He said he had met Lady Machray.

"Such a tiny woman! We saw the nursemaid with the baby, also. And Lord Machray riding alongside the buggy, so proud!" She looked at him expectantly. The silence extended until she laughed once more. "And now, if you will pardon me, I must return to my duties!"

She slipped out the door. When he departed the guests and the house girls were crowded around the organ singing "Days of Absence," with Mary Hardy's voice leading the rest.

Chally handed him a rolled sheet of coarse paper. "Look what got tacked up on the door when no one was around."

His hands clumsily unrolled the paper. Large numerals filled the top half of the sheet: 7-11-77.

Beneath the dimensions of the grave was crude printing:

GET OFF THIS RANGE OR
SUFFER THE CONSEQUENCES
REGULATION COMMITTEE

Sweat stung in his eyes. He didn't look into Chally's face. "Who is the Regulation Committee?"

"There is a lot of talk. Different names. I just don't know, Andy."

"This is the same warning the Crowes received?"

"Same. Degan's lit out. I expect he is just hittin the tops of the hills, headin west."

"What about you?"

"I don't run from whitecaps," Chally said.

3

Carrying his buckskin kit bag, Andrew stepped off the westbound in the hamlet of Waycross, rented a horse and tack at the livery stable, and set off south along the pale earth double track that wandered through brown grass toward the Rademacher place. The trail crossed and recrossed a dry creek bed. The ground was cement hard, and puffs of dust rose in the distance where cattle grazed. The range slanted away before him toward worn, grassed-over buttes like mired antediluvian beasts. A steady wind ruffled the spiky grass.

A horseman appeared on a converging course, finally halting on the trail to await him. It was Fred Rademacher, face shaded by a battered, greasy hat, in shirt sleeves with the flaps of his vest hanging open.

"Well, if it ain't New York come to call!" He crowded his black close to the livery stable nag to shake hands.

"Dry, ain't it? They'll be range fires this year!"

He took the folded paper from his pocket, unfolded it, and handed it to Fred, who whistled.

"Where'd this come from?"

"Tacked to the wall of my house. I came to see if it was you who put it up."

"Not me!" Fred said, handing back the warning.

"I thought you might have gone on other expeditions after—that one."

Fred was shaking his head. "I had a bellyful *that* time." His pale eyes in his sunburnt face gazed steadily into Andrew's. "Sure, if I was a Regulator I'd swear to you I wasn't. But I'm not."

"Who are they, then? Tanner?"

Fred shook his head again. Andrew took a deep breath. For the last two days he would suddenly find himself short of breath and his heart beating faster; it came and went like chills and fever, fear and whatever the opposite of fear was—anger.

Fred's black tossed his head and sidled, and Fred smacked his neck right and left with his hat. "Scary son of a bitch!"
230

He said to Andrew, "That's no *advice* to you on rustling stock, New York. That's get off the range."

"I understand that."

"So it is none of Ash Tanner's doin."

"But it is the Cattlemen's Association's?"

Fred grimaced painfully. "Andy, I just don't know for sure. There is sure fellows belong to the Association that believe the range is gettin overgrazed and overgrangered, and that somethin better be done before it's too late."

"I am going to talk to Tanner."

"I expect he is some upset about what's going on. He is a fellow that his old reputation is important to him." Fred removed his hat and scratched his fingers through his matted hair. The wind rustled in the dry grass, and clouds floated by like a fleet of pale longboats, dragging their shadows over the ground.

Finally Fred said, "I believe there is four or five hardshells behind this. Maybe more. Not everybody in the Association, though. And they have hired them a crew of hardcases to do the dirty work. It is no business for anybody decent, traipsin around in floursacks with eyeholes cut, issuin threats."

"Two men have been hanged," he said. His mouth was very dry.

"Andy," Fred said patiently, "that was the *other* bunch! I been *tellin* you!"

He took a deep breath. "How serious would you say they were?" he asked.

Fred's black bridled and circled again, while he cursed and beat it over the head with his hat. "You mean, what would *I* do?" he said. "Well, I guess no piece of *paper*'d scare me into a gallop. Have to see what else they had to lay on."

"There are two brothers named Crowe who've just come up from Texas with a herd. They got a warning also."

"Well, I'm not so surprised about *that*," Fred said. "Fellows pushin in new when folks's so tensy. Or *grangers*. But I am sure surprised about you and Chally. You talked to Yule Hardy?"

He had not.

"Come on over to our place and I'll give you a bite to eat."

"I want to see Tanner."

"Well, that's fine," Fred said. "But we are not much outen your way." He squinted at Andrew, unsmiling. "My daddy ain't home—up in Miles City on business."

231

Was Fred saying that his father was one of the group that had organized the Regulators? He accepted the invitation and they rode on along the wagon track, side by side.

"Hear about Hardy's daughter?" Fred said.

He said he had.

"If that ain't a *scandal*," Fred said. "Though some say she is just playin that little organ and singin there."

He said that that seemed to be the case. Fred was shaking his head and clucking. "Why, I will bet Yule Hardy is absolutely fit to be *tied*," he said.

"Fred, might Boutelle be running the Regulators now?" he asked.

"*I'd* sure guess he might," Fred said.

Tanner's house was a clapboard affair of weathered, unpainted boards clinging to a hillside, where it appeared to be leaning into the wind. Higher on the hill was a blackened stone chimney standing alone and propped against the sky by four poles, where another house must have burned. Tanner, hobbling and grimacing with rheumatism, led him around to the side of the house out of the wind, where a veranda overlooked limitless acres. He clapped his hands loudly together.

A slim young Indian woman appeared as though she had been stationed just inside the door. "Bring us wine," Tanner said in his rasping voice.

She nodded once and retreated, dark but fine-featured, with doe eyes and two braids of thick black hair. Tanner indicated a chair and sat down in another, grasping one of his legs to straighten it out before him. His cropped white beard grew dense as nappy fabric.

"My wife," he said. "Name's Pretty Bear. I was going to change it to Clara, but she didn't want to."

"She's very pretty," Andrew said.

"Get a lot of Snakes pretty like that," Tanner said. "She is learning her letters. She is eager enough, but it is slow."

Pretty Bear reappeared with two glasses and a bottle. She put them down and stood facing Tanner, brown hands caught together at her waist. "That'll do," he said, and she vanished once more.

"Fellow makes this up by Blairsville," Tanner said, pouring pale pink liquid into the two glasses. "You'll be surprised."

The wine had almost no taste, a kind of pale sweetness, very cloying. Andrew sipped, nodded to Tanner to express the appropriate surprise, put down his glass, and took the folded warning from his pocket.

Tanner leaned over it. Andrew saw a vein in his temple stand out like twisted cord. He said nothing as Andrew explained, finally straightening and shoving the paper away from him.

"I assume you are not responsible for this," Andrew said.

Tanner's eyes with their yellowed whites slanted sideways to meet his, and the old man shook his head.

"I've come to ask if you know who is responsible."

Still Tanner said nothing. The dark thin mouth tightened in the nap of white beard.

"I do not condone what we did that day," Andrew continued. "Nor can I claim I didn't know, at the back of my mind, what the culmination of our chase was to be. But this is something very different. This has nothing to do with righting wrongs, or frightening criminals, or regaining stolen property. This is only an arrogant, bullying outrage."

Tanner tossed his half glass of wine off at one gulp and rubbed the back of his hand over his mouth.

"I don't know how many of these have been posted," Andrew said. "More than one. The Regulation Committee once had a better name than this."

"When you have been alive as long as I have you will know that everything turns into shit and corruption in the end," Tanner said.

"I do not believe you are resigned to that," he said.

"Believe what you want!"

"I prefer to believe you are a man of honorable intentions."

The furious old eyes blazed at him savagely. "Maybe I don't like what you are saying!"

"I don't like it either."

Tanner sat in a kind of complete stillness, glass held before his face, his other hand clenched upon the chair arm. Slowly his booted foot slid further out. "Honorable intentions turns into shit and corruption the same."

"I believe certain members of the Stockraisers Association have hired a crew of ruthless men with Jake Boutelle in charge."

"Well, you are young yet," Tanner said. His face was twisted in a sneer. "To think you know something for certain sure." With a jerk of his hand he flung away the remaining pink liquid in his glass. "Makes you want to puke, don't it?"

Tanner clapped his hands and Pretty Bear immediately reappeared. "Whiskey!" he said in a rough voice.

"Mr. Tanner!" she whispered.

"I said *whiskey!*" He banged his glass down on the table.

She brought a bottle of whiskey. Tanner said, "Now you bring paper and something to mark with—show Mr. Livingston how you can make your letters."

The girl's eyes rolled once toward Andrew. She ducked her head in assent and disappeared to return with paper and a pencil. Tanner tented his gnarled fingers. "Man," he said.

She put the paper on the table and, holding the pencil between her thumb and forefinger, traced the letters. Tanner nodded.

"Woman," he said, and, when she hesitated, barked, "Woe-man! Woe-man!"

She wrote it correctly. "Cow," he said.

This time she did not hesitate. When she had written COW, she said, "I write my name!" Laboriously she traced it out, the letters slanting across the page.

"Horse," Tanner said.

She wrote HORS.

"You forgot the *E*," Tanner said, his voice roughening until he sounded hysterical. "Stupid Injun bitch! H-O-R-S-*E!* Go write it till you can do it right. Get out of here!"

With her head bowed she took the paper and left. Andrew watched her go with anger stuck like a knob in his throat. He said, "I ask you again what you are going to do about this!"

"Nothing," Tanner said. He sliced his hand flatly across in front of him. "No-thing! For I am not like you, I am not certain sure of everything I come across. *Anything!*"

"I don't know what you mean!"

"What I mean is I was a young buck myself to think I knew what was right and what wrong and that it was the fellow with the purple mouth'd been in the jam jar. But I know now I don't know a blessed thing, whether God made little green apples or my wife's a filthy Snake *hoor*. Or anything!"

He cleared his dry throat. "Surely—"

"You would think a man could be sure catching Matty Gruby with those horses. But I am not sure. I am *never* sure! It will come and sit in my mind like a buzzard. It is the trouble with Regulators. Honorable intentions," he said, and wiped his mouth with the back of his hand.

Andrew watched him pour whiskey. He tossed out the pink

234

liquid in Andrew's glass, and filled that too. His mouth slanted down savagely at the corners.

"Well, I did what I had to do," Tanner said. "And fool enough that had sworn never to do it another time. But it is a curse laid on me. Never to be certain of anything—any *thing*—again. Whether my wife goes down to the bunkhouse and spreads out for the hands there when I am gone." His voice thickened. "And how many she had before I took her in." He slashed his hand out again. "Whether we got the wrong boy there at Farragan's, even if I know we didn't, and whether it is Jake Boutelle running a bunch of whitecaps around to the ruination of anything decent I ever did once. That is the difference between us, son, that you think you know something and I know I don't know nothing!"

"Mr. Tanner—" he started.

"Drink your whiskey and get out of here," Tanner said. He was sitting stiffly erect. "For I have got an ache in my gut that is going to have me whooping and bellowing in a minute. Go on your way. There's nothing I can do for you."

That evening in Pyramid Flat he walked up and down in the dusty street outside Mrs. Benbow's house, listening to the organ playing and the voices raised in sentimental song. He was trying to make up his mind whether or not to leave the Bad Lands in the face of the Regulators' threat.

He remembered the game of war they had played as boys in Van Buskirk Park. The game had begun in the distant past as a contest between the West Side and the East Side boys, but in his time it had been the students of Mr. de Bakey's Grammar School against all comers. Whenever there was a half-holiday and the weather was mild enough to soften the snow, the Park would be the scene of a great snowball fight.

These would begin with the School boys out in force, but their numbers would gradually dwindle until by nightfall the young roughs would hold the field. As long as snowballs were the only weapons no one was much hurt, but as their opponents had begun the practice of putting rocks in the snowballs, they followed suit.

One afternoon the fight was especially violent. He remembered Ben Bowes, struck over the eye by a stone, being led from the field bleeding in a ghastly manner. As the shadows grew longer the School boys were steadily forced back until retreat was impossible without disbanding and *sauve qui peut*. By that time only a small band of them was left, headed by the school heroes, Bully Farrington and Charley Higgins. A dark mass of the enemy could be seen, making ready for the final rush, and it was rumored that a swarm of toughs had collected from the farthest, blackest slums, sworn to put an end forever to the "rich boys."

As they surged forward he flung his last snowball with its stone core full in the face of an overgrown blackguard. There was a moment in which Andrew was frozen while the boy swore and clasped his hands to his features. Then the other looked him full in the eye, as though never to forget him, and snarled from a bleeding mouth, "I'll get you for that!" Andrew fled with the rest.

He had fully believed that boy would make good his threat. He ran to and from school. He crossed the street to avoid blind corners. He wakened crying out from nightmares whose cause he could not describe to his parents. Often these were of terrible weights on his chest, as though his pursuer had him pinned to the ground preparatory to working some horrible savagery.

He had that same sense now of hostile eyes watching his every movement and calculating the moment to strike, but the remembered fear was stronger than the present one. When he summoned it up he could feel its sensations still, that weakness in his legs, the thickening at the back of his throat. He found himself ashamed to be considering fleeing the Bad Lands, like Degan hitting the tops of the higher hills, and he wandered on down Main Street past a few late lights burning here and there, toward the lights of Machray's office building. The door was open; in the dark corridor he rapped on the door of Machray's office. "Come!" Machray called.

He was seated at his desk beneath the tiger's yellow gaze, heaped papers, a whiskey bottle and a glass before him. "Livingston!" he cried, rising. "You are late abroad, man!

"What art thou that usurp'st this time of night
Together with that fair and warlike form
In which the majesty of buried Denmark
Did sometimes march?"

He told Machray of receiving the Regulators' warning. Machray scowled, shook his head, and poured him a glass of whiskey.

"Scum!" he said. "I would ignore it, Livingston. Ah, the cowardly sods! Hire some men with rifles! My advice."

236

"Yes," he said. He sipped his whiskey.

"Are you fearful, man?"

"Yes," he said, and grinned.

"Thou'rt human, then," Machray said. He stood spread-legged beneath the tiger's head. He raised his glass. "To all the cowering little forked beasties on the blasted heath!"

They drank. Machray flipped his big hand over the papers on his desk. "Damned meeching due bills. Quarterly payments overdue. Glad you stopped by. Been sitting here so fashed. So vexed! By God, I would rather face that mad lot of the pasha's, bellowing and flourishing spears, than Marston with a bundle of due bills.

"Livingston, that cursed conflagration you well remember does not slow my stride. I have put on more carpenters, and men with rifles to see it does not happen again. A trifle. What weighs me down is the chip and lash of bills! Contracts and rate schedules and solicitors whining and boards and advises and percentages and carefulnesses to turn me into a bleeding, bleerie accountant. They will not do it! But they hedge me round with their damned interest and damnable profits. Surely the planets will falter in their courses if they do not receive their profits! Livingston, such a city I could build me here, such a state, such a nation! If they would only leave me be!"

Machray glared at him with the corners of his mouth slashing down like a shark's. "I am not by nature a fearful man, you know," he went on in a lower voice. "But what a state these devils can put me into! Cold sweat on my brow, mind a turmoil!" He clapped a hand to his forehead.

"Thou'rt human, then," Andrew said, grinning. He felt a good deal better, in Machray's company, with Machray's whiskey in his belly. "I was a banker formerly, and I know the symptoms well. I have seen strong men faint over money. Hearts have stopped because of quarterly payments."

"Mad!" Machray said, grinning back at him. "Each to his own devils, then, is it?" He raised an arm, tipped back on his heels, and sang, operatically, in a voice that shook the windows, *"Corrrraaaagggggiiiiooo!"*

Running footsteps approached; a clerk looked worriedly in the door.

"It is nothing, Deems," Machray said, frowning. "Bit of song merely, to illustrate a point. More whiskey, Livingston?"

4

As August wore on the sun became an enemy, sullen and fierce in a metallic sky. Temperatures ranged up to 120 in the shade, Fire Creek and Box Creek dried up, and the river was reduced to a trickle running through banks of baked mud. The range stock were continually on the move in search of water.

One morning smoke rose beyond the buttes to the west, and Andrew and Chally set off in a hurry with a can of kerosene for backfiring, and shovels and slickers for beating out the flames. It was the first range fire Andrew had seen.

The smoke leaned forward over two low wedges of flame driving down a miles-wide slope. They tethered their nervous horses to a tree and rushed forward to slap at the advancing flames that nibbled at the dry grass in little flashes of ignition and spurts of smoke. Sweating and coughing, they managed to stop one of the points, but the other continued its advance and a third could be seen coming up behind. Chally swung his slicker in a kind of fury while Andrew tried to keep up. Soon he saw that others had arrived, the granger Feeney with Buddy, and others as well, until there were seven men working on the fire line, Chally with a kerosene torch setting back-fires, which he and the others—who all seemed to be grangers—beat back toward the advancing points of flame.

Two horsemen arrived, driving a steer before them. These were the Crowe brothers, the newcomers from Texas. They slaughtered the steer and split the carcass lengthwise with an ax. One lashed his lariat to the forelegs, the other to the back, and they mounted and spurred their horses along the fire line, dragging the bloody carcass at an oblique angle. They dashed around the fire to the left, then retraced their course, the dragging, bouncing carcass effectively snuffing out the edge of fire. Andrew and his crew of grangers continued to slap at isolated patches of flame with shovels and slickers in the acrid air. Saliva had turned to thick brown tar in his mouth. Chally had gone for more kerosene.

The Crowe brothers continued to drag the carcass along the blackened fire edge until the wind died and there were no new spits of smoke rising. Andrew went over to thank them where they squatted at a remove from the grangers, in the shade of a scrub cedar, tipping a brown water bottle to their mouths. They were twins, with flat, brown, wind-gnawed faces and black mustaches, one named Davey, the other Ben.

"Think it got set on us?" one of them asked, squinting up at him.

The possibility staggered him. "We have seen it done," the other said, rinsing water through his mouth and spitting it out. "Back in Texas."

"It would seem foolish practice if the complaint is that the range is overcrowded."

Squatting on their heels in the shade, one shrugged and then the other. "Where's all these grangers come from?" the first one asked.

"The tall one's claimed a quarter north of me on the river. I don't know the others, though I've seen some of them in town."

"Known nesters to fire range too," the second one said.

"I don't believe they would then come out and help fight the fire."

Both shrugged again. "Where'd Chally go?"

"He went for more kerosene. I don't know why he's not back yet."

He returned to the other group. Conversation with the grangers was difficult, for it was clear he was classed with the Crowes, and the common effort that had brought their interests together was already disintegrating. He led his crew on one more tour through the acreage of blackened grass looking for signs of flame or smoke, but the fire seemed effectively out. Buddy Feeney kept close by him, shovel on his shoulder like a soldier with a rifle.

He asked where the other grangers were located.

"Over beyond the river, mostly," Buddy said. "My daddy an em's been helpin each other with the buildin. That one with the wry neck ain't worth a durn."

"At least he came out to help."

"Oh, they'll come out to help. It is just that some is better than others."

There was still no sign of Chally when he returned to Fire Creek Ranch. He rode through a few Lazy-N cattle grazing in the brown grass, a doe springing up to vault zigzagging away. Finally there were winks of light which were the win-

239

dows of the Big House catching the late sun. Brownie kept lagging so that he had to prod the wise little horse to a faster pace. "Chally?" he called.

There was no answer. He saw Chally's saddled horse tied to a corral post. Then he saw Chally. He was lying against the lowest corral rail, a square of white on his chest, and blood.

Brownie would go no closer, and he dismounted. Chally had been flung against the lowest rail as though by some gigantic force, one arm draped over it and the other pinned beneath his body. On his face was an expression of animal ferocity, lips drawn back from his teeth, eyes glaring. Beneath the paper his shirt was blood-soaked, and his revolver glinted dustily where it had fallen from his hand. I'll never run from whitecaps, Chally had said.

He heard someone's breathing wheezing in his ears; it was his own. He could feel that alive pressure of the rope Jake Boutelle had tossed over his head. He found himself astride Brownie again, heading for the river crossing at a dead run, heading for Pyramid Flat and the train east. But presently he let the panting, steaming horse settle into a walk, and turned west for the Reuters' place.

He returned with Joe and the old man that night. They brought Chally's body inside the house and covered it with a blanket. He offered whiskey.

The old man leaned the sharp angle of a buttock against the table, drank, wiped the back of his hand across his mouth, and then across his eyes. Joe sat slumped in the chair in the corner by the door.

"Well, he was a good boy," the old man said. "Though I will not say he wasn't a bunch of trouble sometimes. He had a temper on him."

Joe was nodding down at his glass. "Set a fire and then waited by till they caught somebody alone," he said.

"I suppose it could as easily have been me," he said. Both of them nodded. Maybe Chally had forced the issue, as once he had forced it; but he had not understood the issue he was forcing.

"Sheriff ought to know," Joe said bleakly.

"Nothin he can do about it," the old man said. "Nothin anybody can do till morning. We'll take him back to our place. Expect that's where he'd want to be."

"I believe it was Jake Boutelle," Andrew said.

The old man's bloodshot eyes slid toward him. "Hard to say," he said.

It was late in the morning before they had loaded the blanket-wrapped, heavy body onto the pack saddle of a mule, blindfolding the animal finally to steady him. The old man pushed the two of them out of the way in order to accomplish the lashing himself. "If this ain't one hell of a way to come home," he muttered.

Joe had squatted by a confused tangle of hoofprints in the gray earth near the corral, and Andrew leaned over him. His eyes kept running as though he had taken a chill. Joe pointed a finger.

"That shod one's got a nail tore halfway out. See how it is scratched there?"

"Let's go after them," Andrew said.

"Trail's pretty cold by now," Joe said, rising quickly.

"Just what would you do if you was to catch up with them?" the old man asked.

"I would know who they are."

"They'll have scattered by now, for sure," Joe said.

"We may not have been the only call on their list," Andrew said.

"Well, if you have any choice in it, you will gut-shoot them for me," the old man said. "That boy may have mavericked some calves in his time, but there was no call for shooting him down like a dog."

They followed the tracks of the five or six horses for several miles due east. Once when they had both dismounted to peer at the scraped dirt in a coulee bottom, he said to Joe, "What did your father mean, Chally had mavericked calves?"

Joe looked up quickly, his face turning wooden. "Well, Chally had done that."

"More than that?"

Joe shrugged. Then he nodded.

He felt a lacy chill on his forehead. Before he could speak, Joe said, "Well, he was bound he would be a stockman, you see. And he was a good one! But he didn't have checks he could write on some bank. So he went about it just the same way everybody else had went about it. Mavericked a few, and rustled a few, and doctored some brands until he had got a start. Then you come along, you see. But I guess they had not forgot."

"I see," he said, squatting in the dust staring at the tracks of the men who had murdered Chally Reuter.

He was convinced that if the Regulators had made a second call it would have been on the Crowe brothers, and so they abandoned the slow process of tracking to ride straight to where the Texans had set up, in an old line-camp near the headwaters of Box Creek.

On the high plateau where a line of cottonwoods marked the creek, there was a corral and a shack of weathered timbers, a wisp of smoke uncoiling from a chimney stack. A man lounged against the side of the shack. Sun glinted on a rifle barrel.

"Hold up there!"

Andrew identified himself, and the brother waved them on. The other Crowe emerged from the shack, his left arm in a sling.

"Regulators killed Chally Reuter," Andrew said, dismounting. "This is his brother. We thought they might have come this way."

"They came this way," the first brother said. The two wore identical checked shirts and filthy jeans pants. "They nicked Davey here." Hands were shaken. Ben had cold, pale eyes, very sharp; his brother seemed more easy-going.

"Chally was the only feller we ever heard a pleasant word from in the Bad Lands," Davey said to Joe. His wound was not serious, he said, just a chink out of the muscle that hurt like the dickens when he moved it.

"We was ready for them," Ben said. "Winged one, I believe. *Thought* they might be droppin by about the time we come in from fightin range fire."

The Crowes had taken the Regulators' warning more seriously than he, for all his promenading through the Bad Lands trying to find who his friends were. "I had thought it was all a bluff," he said.

"Well, we've been through the same thing in Texas, you see," Davey said. Ben asked where they were headed.

"Doin some trackin," Joe said. A little cool breeze swept up, to riffle the dead weeds on the clay roof of the shack. The sun was low. Joe shivered and gripped his crossed arms to his chest.

"Welcome to take grub with us," Davey said. "I have got a stew goin, and hot bread too."

Inside the shack it was dim and smoky and hot, with a delicious damp odor of stew boiling. On the earthen floor were a squat black stove, two shuck beds with rolled bedrolls on them, a chair, and a stool. Andrew was urged to the chair and Joe to the stool, while Ben seated himself on one of the beds and Davey stood straddle-legged at the low stove, stirring a long spoon in the stewpot. The shack stank of smoke, cooking food, and unwashed bodies.

"Had them floursacks over their heads when they come by here," Davey said over his shoulder. "Know who is doin it?"

"We have got some ideas, nothin certain," Joe said.

"They are hirelings," Andrew said.

Davey turned; both brothers looked at him, frowning. "Hirelings," Ben said.

"You fellers had better put up here," Davey said.

"We'll ride a bit with you tomorrow," Ben said. "And we will sleep better with you all here. Wouldn't surprise me if we got another visit right quick."

"We will take shifts sleepin," Joe said, sitting on his stool with his knees together and his arms folded close. Then he said, "Well, they shot Chally I expect because he pressed them to it. But I keep wonderin if they meant to string him up. That is a hard way to go."

"Down where we come from they will burn a man," Ben said. "It was big fellers doin it down there and I expect it is the same up here. Shoot one of these people—what'd you call them? hirelings—and you are just shooting somebody's hand."

"Never mind," Davey said. "It would surely pleased me to've knocked somebody's hand out of his saddle, with his damned floursack on."

"Things got pretty bad down home," Ben said, and he told of the Texas range wars, big men against little, in his flat, emotionless voice.

"There is a thing we learned back home," Davey said. "It is that small fish had better herd together."

"We run once," Ben said grimly. "But we will not do it again. Charge hell with a bucket of water if we have to."

Andrew did not protest when he was given the early watch. He did not sleep after it, trying not to rattle the shucks of the bed in his wakefulness. He thought that there was an extension here of his reasons for quitting Republican politics after the national convention, the big against the little, the more ruthless against the less, the entrenched against all comers,

Chally Reuter dead deduced from the nomination of James G. Blaine.

It seemed the narrowest of chances that Chally had been surprised by the Regulators instead of him. Would he have died as Chally had died, or begged for life with a rope around his neck? Cruel images paraded in his mind's eye, those old horrors of his father's death and the poor sodden drowned girls laid out on the grass fading now, Chally's face with its defiant snarl more prominent, the familiar grouping from his nightmares of the hanged boy and the company of men, like a photograph of a hunting party with their quarry, and the terrible eye of the horse Blackie giving himself to death in the face of terror of death.

Joe Reuter, whispering, was replaced on guard by Davey Crawe. He must have dozed, then, for he waked with a start to another whispered exchange, and waked again to a shot and a shout. In the block of solid dark he fumbled for his rifle, which he had kept beside him through the night, and lurched toward the oblong of gray that marked the door, banging against another moving body in the process. Outside there was a flurry of shots, the long whine of a ricochet, a voice cursing.

In the graying darkness Ben Crowe lay behind a log. He levered and fired, cursing in an almost happy tone. At a distance flames flickered red and yellow from some unidentifiable source.

"Keep hid!" Ben whispered. "They'll be thinkin there is only two of us here!"

Ducking low, he hurried to sprawl beside Ben. Beyond the flames were mounted shapes. He fitted his rifle to his cheek and shoulder, drew a deep breath, and squeezed the trigger. The butt thumped against his shoulder. The mounted figures faded away.

"What's burning?"

"Son of bitches rid in tryin to fire the shack. I surely ventilated one, to hear him yellin."

There was a shot from behind them, where either Joe or Davey crouched in the doorway. Another form separated itself from the shack and dashed toward the horse corral, rifle in hand—Davey, by his slinged arm. The burning object flamed and subsided. A bullet sang past to whack into the log wall behind them. He had marked the muzzle flash in the deep gray, and fired on it an instant behind Ben's shot.

"Can you make out where they are?" he whispered.

"That one's up in a stand of trees on high ground. I expect they'll keep one bird there pluggin away while the others try comin in again."

"Could I get around behind him?"

"You want to try that?" Ben said. "The crick runs just past the corral. If you could get over there before it lightens any more, you could make time up behind the cutbank. Go about a quarter mile, then take on back toward where you hear him firin from. Maybe Joe could work his way around the other side the same."

"Just tell me where to go," Joe said behind them.

"Tell you what, you stay right here and I'll go—I know where to find me some cover. Andy, you tell Davey what we are up to."

Crouching, sweating in the cool dawn air, he hurried around behind the shack and toward where he remembered the corral to be.

"Who's that?" Davey whispered.

"Andy." He located the other in the dark; a hand gripped his arm tightly. He explained the plan, and Davey directed him toward the creek. Another shot struck the shack. Davey said he hadn't seen anything to shoot at yet.

He came upon the creek before he expected it, and slid down a slope to a sandy bottom. Drenched with sweat, rifle cocked, he moved close along the bank, which was about three feet high here. The night was lightening. He was panting so that it must be audible, and he halted to get his breath, leaning against the bank to scrub the sweat from his face with his bandanna. There was an irritating pebble in one of his boots. Just as he started on again he heard the quick padding of hoofs. He froze against the bank again.

The hoofs came closer. He thought this was probably one he could get—rise up, rifle at the ready, aim, and fire—but it was still too dark to aim well, and he would give away his position. The sound of the hoofs diminished to silence. He hurried on. Now he could make out the ghostly shapes of the clump of trees on its rise. He went on past until they faded into the gloom again, then climbed out of the creek bed to work his way back. His heart leaped when he heard a shot close ahead.

Now there was a light mist around him, the trees rising out of it; the same mist that cocooned over Fire Creek in the early mornings. The low-branching cedars loomed closer. A

245

dark shape moved; there was a snort and stamp. One horse. A flurry of shots, one from just ahead of him.

It was lighter. He could see the tangled tree trunks and branches, a white-faced horse standing head down. He was moving toward the nearest tree when from off to the right came a long whistle, like a bird call. He halted half crouching as ahead of him there was rustling.

A man appeared, pushing branches aside. He carried a rifle. "Jake?" he said, halting. It was Conroy, his face opening in an expression of recognition; he jerked his rifle up. Andrew stared into the face of the man he had had in his sights once before. His hands with the rifle seemed to be moving against some dense resistance. The explosion knocked him back on his heels and with a yell Conroy slumped to his knees, dropping his rifle and clasping his arms over his belly.

He levered another cartridge into the chamber. Conroy stared up at him. *"Don't!"*

He fired again. Conroy was jerked around, to fall on his face with his hat rolling free.

Instantly there was firing from all around. Just as swiftly it ceased. Two horsemen came toward him out of the grayness at a fast trot. He rushed into the thicket, limbs slashing at his face, to fling himself behind a down timber, bracing his rifle barrel awkwardly to aim back the way he had come.

"Conny!" a voice called. "Let's get out—there is a *bunch* of them."

He fired as they came into his range. With a shout they spurred on past. He fired again, too fast. Silence. Brightness was spreading in the east.

He moved back to where Conroy lay and prodded the body over onto its back. At the sight of the face he lurched backward to lean against a tree, puking weakly. He circled the body with its shattered face to where the white-faced horse grazed unconcerned. Taking the reins he led it down the slope toward the line shack. He could see Joe and Davey standing there and, off to the right, Ben Crowe. Ben hailed him with a yell, holding up a hand with one finger extended. Then he beckoned.

It was another dead Regulator, this one Bob Cletus. Ben lashed his feet with the lariat from Conroy's saddle, and the horse dragged the corpse back to the shack where the others waited. Then Joe went back up to the clump of trees to bring Conroy down. Two for Chally. And he had been right about

246

Boutelle. "Jake?" Conroy had said, mistaking him for the other.

"Well, now we will see if they will back off," Ben said grimly as they drank their coffee.

5

On his way into town he practiced firing his revolver at Machray's fence posts, halting Brownie to brace the barrel over his left wrist and squint along it. He did not hit them very often. Adrenaline chills like alternations of exaltation and despair chased through him. There seemed now an iron pattern in his coming to the Bad Lands, from the hunting of animals to Conroy's destroyed face, to Boutelle. It had been a curse on him, Tanner had said; never to be sure. But he was sure.

When he reached Pyramid Flat he went first to Mrs. Benbow's. He was directed upstairs to Mary's room, a tiny, stifling low-ceilinged cubicle beneath the eaves. There was a pallet of a bed, a bureau with a mirror over it, and a low rocker. Several books and a sewing basket were on the bureau, and Mary stood before it, her back to him and her face visible in the mirror.

He told her that the Regulators had murdered Chally. It struck him that she did not seem shocked.

"What will you do?" she asked, turning toward him.

"We have killed two of them." He told her of the fight at the Crowes.

"Good!" she said. "Oh, good!" Then she said, "Won't you sit down? My mother came to see me. She wouldn't sit down either, as though she were afraid of getting soiled."

"There is something I must tell you. I was among the men who lynched Matty Gruby."

She stared at him with a curious half smile, her expression unchanging as he tried to explain. When he had finished she said in a stilted, schoolteacherish voice, "I believe that you are truly regretful, Andrew. I believe you have been punished, in your own mind, but it is good that you have finally told me. It explains certain matters of conduct— But I al-

247

ready knew, you see. The girls here know everything like that, that men think are secrets."

He breathed her rather cloying flower scent. His face was damp with sweat in the hot room. She turned back to the bureau and fished in the sewing basket with her good hand. "Watch!" she said.

She held her right hand over a thimble resting on the bureau as though manipulating a mechanical device, lowering it over the bit of silver. He found himself holding his breath as the waxy thumb and forefinger slowly came together. Then she withdrew the support of her left hand and the pincered fingers rose with the thimble. Moisture glistened on her short, curled upper lip. She smiled in triumph.

"Isn't that marvelous?"

"It is marvelous."

She continued to hold her right hand out. He saw that it was an effort. Assisting it with her left again, she lowered it to the bureau top to relinquish the thimble, which rolled eccentrically and dropped to the floor. She bent to pluck it up. Then she swung around to face him again, leaning back against the dresser with her breasts pressing against the material of her blouse.

"They want me to clear out," she said. "F-father wants me to clear out. Now that I'm soiled." She giggled. " 'Soiled' was the word Mother used. They'll give me money to go. If I'd only known sooner what a young woman had to do to be free of this terrible place!"

"I told you I'd give you the money to go."

She tossed her head. "I could make a great deal of money here, if I wished. Crippled girls are very popular, if they are young and pretty. But especially if they are crippled. Isn't that *strange?*"

He said it appeared that she would not be crippled much longer, and she laughed.

"Do you know that there is a girl in this house who thinks you a *most* mysterious and fascinating gentleman? You sketched her once and did not require anything else of her. She is both titillated and insulted! I haven't told her you did the same with me.

"Mother had told me a girl always knew how to make a man declare himself," she went on. "So I thought if I let you sketch me as you had Maizie, then naturally you would seduce me. Being a gentleman, you would have to marry me.

248

Once I had you in my clutches I would make you take me away from the Bad Lands! But—"

He didn't let her finish, stammering that it had been an awkward situation for him even if he had had such designs. Her father was a friend, who trusted him, and her mother—

"Oh, no he doesn't," Mary said.

"What do you mean?"

"He thinks you *did* seduce me. He blames you for my being here. So my mother says."

He stared at her with an awareness of hatred that made him feel boneless and weak.

"I told her it was not you," Mary said. "I told her it was Lord Machray I was meeting when I went riding alone all those days."

"But that's not true."

"No," she said smiling. "But it will cause a great deal of suffering."

He asked if the girls in the house had learned who the leader of the Regulators was.

"It is Jake Boutelle," Mary said. "But I thought everyone knew that."

A few men were bellied up at the bar in the saloon, one of them Ash Tanner, bent forward over a whiskey glass. With a peremptory gesture Tanner beckoned Andrew to an empty table, tacking drunkenly with a whiskey bottle in one hand and his glass in the other, and plumping himself down with a jarring of chair legs. The barkeeper handed Andrew a glass, and Tanner filled it with an unsteady hand.

"Didn't like for me to take whiskey," Tanner said, intent on the pouring, his jaw jutting with its moss of white beard. "Hated it when the whiskey got at my guts so bad."

Andrew watched the horizontal lines of sunlight in the saloon doors. His revolver in its holster thumped against the side of his chair.

"My wife," Tanner said, as though he hadn't understood. And then he said, "She's dead."

His eyes jerked back to the grim old face. "How—"

"Took a little knife she had and opened herself up." Tanner's gnarled thumb flicked at the inside of his wrist.

"That's terrible!"

The other's face twisted as though he were chewing on a sore tooth. His eyes were scarlet-rimmed. "She was a *hoor*," he said. "Should've known nobody'd've married an old man but a *hoor*. Sneak down to the bunkhouse and lay herself out for all comers when I was away. Oh, there is no doubt of that! They are all *hoors*."

"I'm sorry to hear you talk like this," he said.

Tanner glowered at him. "The pretty ones the worst!" A spasm dissolved his face, a twinge of pain so violent that Andrew almost gasped to see it, but so brief that, after it had passed, he could not be sure he had seen anything at all. "Drink your whiskey," Tanner said.

He drank. It tasted very bitter. He watched the doors. Behind Tanner four railroad men sat at one table, and at another two ranchmen he remembered seeing at the meeting at Machray's.

"She was a very pretty young woman," he said to Tanner.

"She was working hard at her spelling, but she wasn't getting nowheres." Tanner poured himself more whiskey, slopping liquor and cursing beneath his breath. The doors swung open.

Boutelle entered. He passed slowly along the bar with his distinctive swagger, hands resting on his cartridge belt as his sharp, dark face turned to glance and nod at each man in turn.

As Andrew rose his heart swelled in his throat to stifle him. Tanner had also risen.

"Jake!"

"Why, evening, Ash," Boutelle said, halting to teeter on his boot heels. "Evening, Livingston."

Before Andrew could speak, Tanner said in a gently reproving voice, "Damn you, Jake Boutelle. You have turned everything I have ever done into shit and corruption."

"I guess I don't take your meaning, Ash," Boutelle said.

A moment of silence ached with intensity as the two men faced each other, Tanner swaying where he stood. Then, so swiftly Andrew was not even aware of the movement until it was complete, Tanner had drawn his revolver. The saloon exploded. Boutelle in motion seemed much more deliberate. He fired twice. Tanner staggered back, knocking the table aside. He crashed to the floor. Boutelle stepped forward to fire twice more. The room rocked with sound.

Andrew stood paralyzed as Boutelle halted not three feet from him, staring down at the dead man sprawled on his back. His revolver felt like a lump of lead on his hip, and he discovered that he was holding his hands protectively before his chest.

Boutelle's eyes blazed at him. *"Was there something you wanted?"* Boutelle whispered.

He did not answer. Tanner's blood looked black in the dim light.

"What got into you, old fellow?" Boutelle said, standing over the body. He flicked out the cylinder of his revolver on its crane, and punched out the empty shells, which rattled on the floor. Then he filled the cylinder from his cartridge belt. He didn't look at Andrew again.

The railroad men stood against the far wall, the row of their heads neatly graded by height. The ranchmen bracketed their table stiffly. The barkeep, who had ducked behind the bar, rose. Andrew had to force his hands down to his sides.

His features cramped in a delicate frown, Boutelle turned to the barkeep. "You saw it, Jens. He went to shooting when I had done nothing to him."

"I sure did see it, Jake."

Boutelle swung the other way. "Matt? Chuck?"

The ranchers chimed in together that they had witnessed it, and there was a chorus of agreement from the railroad men. Boutelle nodded.

Men began pushing inside through the louver doors, quietly at first, whispering to inquire what had happened, but more and more of them entering until the place was crowded and noisy.

Andrew had not moved from where he stood, but at last he thrust his way outside. Boutelle, leaning against the bar, glanced at him as he passed, not even contemptuously. Behind there was a jam of men congregated around old Ash Tanner, dead on the saloon floor.

Maizie stood before him, slowly raising her shift to reveal pale, plump thighs with a V of brown fleece between them. Bright lips smiling possessively, she seated herself naked on the bed with arms folded over her breasts, watching him as he stripped off his clothing. He had not come to sketch her this time, and she seemed to understand very well his need, which was some proof of himself he had almost lost in his resolution and his failure. She patted the small of his back with her two hands and, warm-breathed in his ear, whispered praise of his labors, and told him he was something rare and strange to her, but precious, and it had been long waiting for him.

251

6

The mud banks along the river were golden tan, cracked into curling lozenges. The cottonwoods rustled dispiritedly. Thorny's steps lagged. All vitality in the Bad Lands was low in the afternoon heat.

He came in sight of Yule Hardy's fenced pasture, the prize herd grazing in the brown grass. Beyond was the ranch house, and the cluster of corrals and barns. He loosened his rifle in its scabbard as he came upon the beaten road where he had first encountered Hardy in the buggy. There was no sign of life around the buildings, and a stillness that made the back of his neck prickle.

Mrs. Hardy appeared on the veranda with a rifle, squinting in the sun's glare. She wore black, with a strip of black velvet around her throat, and her hair in tight ringlets that appeared glued to her skull. She raised the rifle and set the stock against her cheek.

He reined up, Thorny dancing sideways. The rifle muzzle tracked him.

"Put that down, Mrs. Hardy."

She lowered the rifle slightly.

"I must speak with your husband."

"It is fortunate for you that he is not here, Mr. Livingston."

"Why do you say that?"

She dropped the rifle butt with a thump beside her booted foot. "You pretend not to know, sir. We trusted you!"

"I did not betray that trust, Mrs. Hardy!"

"You were seen!"

"I wished to sketch your daughter, as you know, and she was eager to be sketched. For some of my sketches she posed in dishabille. I assure you that everything was conducted in a professional manner."

She raised a hand to shade her eyes from the sun. "Yes, one knows of the professional manners of artists and models."

"Mrs. Hardy, I assure you that the wrong interpretation has been put upon this!"

252

She leaned against the wall of the house as though faint. "Are you well?" he asked.

She nodded, continuing to nod in a senseless manner, still holding the rifle at her side. "I have supposed it might not be as it seemed. That you . . . She has been—headstrong, lately.

"We pretend that she is dead," she went on, straightening. "Once I was foolish enough to dream that you and she might marry. But of course you had something very different in mind for a simple ranch girl with a crippled hand, who trusted you. Whose parents fed you—"

He could hardly trust his voice. "Mrs. Hardy, am I to understand that my partner was murdered because I failed to fulfill your plans? Or seemed to fulfill your suspicions? Where is your husband, madam?"

She brushed a hand in front of her face as though dislodging a cobweb. Her face was gray and exhausted. "I don't know where he is. He is always—somewhere."

"Planning to run off the range everyone they feel does not belong here?"

"They are certain that everyone will be ruined if more herds continue to come in, and more grangers—" She stopped. "I do not wish to answer any more questions," she said.

"Then they are organizing some larger force of Regulators?"

She only shook her head. She lifted the rifle again.

"Please tell me what is happening, Mrs. Hardy. It could save lives."

"I will say no more—I've said too much already. But if you would save your own life, Mr. Livingston, I suggest that you leave the Bad Lands immediately!"

He reined Thorny away. When he looked back she was still standing on the veranda with the rifle, the black figure shimmering in the heat waves.

Joe Reuter and Davey Crowe were sitting on the top rail of the corral smoking. Several dozen head of cattle were raising dust milling in the big new corral, a quarter of a mile further up along the creek, that had been Chally's last project. He reined up and told the two of them what he had learned.

"Sounds like interestin times ahead," Davey said, hitching up his slinged arm.

"Interestin times for movin on somewhere else, I'd say," Joe said.

"I thought we had bust up that bunch pretty good."

"Maybe we only galvanized them into more action."

"Galvanized, huh?" Davey said. "Maybe so, though I take it downright insultin bein lumped in with grangers."

"What're we goin to do, Andy?" Joe said morosely.

He said he didn't know what to do except hire a couple of more hands, whom they would be needing at roundup time anyway, with rifles.

"Looks like company comin," Davey Crowe said.

Two horsemen had separated from the cottonwood trees along the river and rode up through the brown grass terraces, one seated on his horse in a peculiar way. This proved to be Lady Machray on a sidesaddle; with her was a tall cowboy.

He rode out to meet them. Lady Machray wore a plum-colored riding habit with a pert, matching hat, one side pinned up to reveal an expanse of copper hair. She greeted him with a salute of her riding crop.

"May I have a word in private with you, Mr. Livingston?" she asked. There was a bright swath of freckles across her little nose.

Helping her to dismount, he showed her into the Big House, where she paced the room with short, quick steps, like a little pony, glancing around her and tapping her leg with her riding crop.

"A charming, rustic little house," she pronounced it, returning from her circuit to stand facing him. "Mr. Livingston, I have come to you for help. My husband has left me. He has taken up residence in the local brothel. He has absolutely abandoned his business enterprises."

"Please tell me what I can do, Lady Machray."

She turned her face away, a strong cord standing out in the gardenia flesh of her throat. "I'm afraid Mr. Beavey carried back a report that could have had only one result. Restrictions have been put upon my husband, which he declares he cannot countenance. Therefore—to spite *me*—he ha taken up this new residence."

He had a sense that she had rehearsed her speech and tha her actions were also contrived as she began pacing befor him with her short steps. She swung toward him again with flashing eyes, gripping her riding crop in both hands.

"So I find myself in charge of affairs I know nothing about! And care nothing!" she continued. "It is an outrage

254

All that has sustained him thus far has been my father's continued support. That is now terminated. Done!" she said, pivoted, paced, and again returned.

"Meanwhile I have invited a great many people for a hunting expedition my husband promised to lead. Very important people, whose time is valuable and whose plans must be laid far in advance. Lord and Lady Glazebrook. Count Fitz-James. Sir Edward Usher. Mr. and Mrs. Terence Dunne. Telegrams must be sent to cancel the affair. It is, simply, an outrage!

"Mr. Livingston, I believe he looks upon you as his only friend in the Bad Lands." She paraded around the room once more, alternately slapping her leg with her stick and gesticulating with a tiny, black-gloved hand. "It may be that he would listen to counsel in the matter of his health. Drunken, disgraceful living, the danger of disease. I believe Africa ruined him, Mr. Livingston. He loves to regale me with tales of the *harem* he kept there. *Black* women, Mr. Livingston. He has become a glutton of vice. He chooses to inhabit vile stews—"

She stopped. "I simply do not understand," she went on. "Mr. Livingston, perhaps you will advise me as a friend. *Why* is he like this?"

"I don't know, Lady Machray."

"I believe I can say that I have *never* had what I consider an impure thought. It seems to me that he has nothing else. Are all men like that, Mr. Livingston, or does he just enjoy bedeviling me?" Her face was clenched like a tight little fist, and a tear spurted almost comically from either eye. "Mr. Livingston, I believe he hates me simply because my father has lent him money and induced others to do so. Who will lose their investments!"

"Are you so certain of that, Lady Machray?"

"Quite certain. Oh, those bright dreams of his, that he can weave like magnificent tapestries. But he is not interested in his empire building anymore. He is simply bored, like a spoilt child tired of his toys. In his heart he believes commercial enterprise to be beneath the Machrays, although he will recognize the necessity for money. He will that! But I simply do not know what will become of him. The financial structure is crumbling, there *must* be reorganization. What can I report to my father but that he leaves the operation of his ranch in the hands of subordinates, as well as the rebuilding of the abattoir after that terrible fire which he is con*vinced* was sabotage, while he hares off after new projects—his precious stage line to the Black Hills! Not even that anymore, now that he has immured himself in that *place!*

"I certainly do not intend to remain here as an object of ridicule, to supervise his affairs and be despised for my pains as a shopkeeper by nature and by heritage. And I do not intend that my son have any contact with a drunken, vicious, *diseased* frequenter of prostitutes! No, Mr. Livingston, we will be leaving here as soon as I can *responsibly* do so!"

Her rosebud mouth was pinched into a tight little round of pain. She gazed into his eyes.

"Tell me what you want of me, Lady Machray."

"Could you bring yourself to go to that place and reason with George?"

He promised that he would.

7

*It was a month of trouble. First Bill Driggs's departure, al*though it was a relief, left Cora with a kind of heaviness of incompletion. Then there was a spate of killings. Chall Reuter was shot by Regulators in a fight, and Cletus and Conroy in another. The story the girls got was that those two had been hired by Boutelle as range inspectors for the Association—which, Wax said, was hiring horse thieves against cow thieves—and were shot in a scrape with a gang of rustlers. Then Ash Tanner's wife killed herself, Ash went on the prod and Boutelle shot him in a saloon quarrel, Boutelle making himself scarce afterwards, no doubt because of Ash's friends. All in all it was the worst time she could remember in Pyramid.

She had contributed her own part by taking Mary Hard into the house, and some of her old customers turned against her for it. Several told her she had done a terrible thing to poor Yule Hardy, having his girl in her place where everyone would know his shame. The girl should be run out of town. She did not mind saying right out that Yule Hardy was a hypocrite, and she pitied his daughter. She knew Yule Hardy's kind from long experience with mayors, police chiefs, city councilmen, aldermen, and preachers, who would

256

tub-thump against the evils of prostitution by day and sneak in the back door demanding free tricks by night. Though there was nothing much that could shock her anymore about where or in whom men had chosen to stick that precious knob of theirs, she had come close to it that night Mary Hardy had poured out her story, sobbing as though she would break to pieces. She did not entirely believe Mary, though how a girl brought up like that one could know of such things unless they had been done to her was a puzzle. She had been tricked by clever liars enough times so that she held certain information, and certain people, in a kind of suspension of both belief and disbelief.

She would have sent Mary Hardy packing if she had thought the girl would be a source of trouble in the house. She did not put up with quarreling girls, for when a house got into such a state men would begin staying home where there were bad-tempered females already. But Mary had the good sense to cultivate the other girls, and everyone did enjoy her playing the organ and singing in the parlor. They had some good times, all singing, although Mary did put her teeth on edge a bit playacting at being a younger girl than she really was, almost a child. She could have made them both a ton of money if she chose to go upstairs with customers. Mary hadn't done that yet, but the girl did make good tips, men chinking coins into the little blue velvet cap she kept on top of the organ while she played. She was saving her money to leave the Bad Lands.

She should have known that Machray would begin thinking goat thoughts about Mary Hardy sooner or later.

At first when he moved in he holed up in her room and seemed to have set himself to drink up all the whiskey in the place. He was on a fine rant against his wife, calling her "the jewess," and "the Judas-bitch," and against his backers, "the filthy pack of Shylocks." Great fine friends they had been, he said, when all was to be the profits of the Great Beef Bonanza, free grass and natural increase, and the cattle-slaughtering capital of the world, but one hint of a reverse and they hounded him like bailiffs. But he was bitterest against his wife, who he said had betrayed him.

Next he began worrying about his health. He would call for Doc Micklejohn two or three times a day, to look at his little toe that was hurting something fierce, or to listen to how his heart was beating down in his belly instead of in his chest where it ought to, or look at his piss in the pot that had a

257

queer color. Doc would prod and peer through his little, round, steel-rimmed eyeglasses, scratching at his nose that looked like an overripe fig the worms had got into, and say that nothing seemed out of the way to him, though he kept Machray dosed with Old Sachem Stomach Bitters. Doc was busier than he used to be, called out of town often to tend to granger women birthing, or feverish brats. Machray would be furious when Doc was called away, as though Doc were his personal attendant, like Dickson, who spent his days in the kitchen talking to Daisy and drinking coffee.

Machray would lie on the divan in her room with his big, white feet sticking out below the blanket, not shaved and his cheeks brown stubbled, stinking of whiskey, snoozing, reading, reciting poetry, or singing Scotch songs that were usually filthy. He would send Dickson to Widewings for books, but she noticed he never read very far into anything, tossing the book aside and calling for more.

She did enjoy his stories of the wars in South Africa, Abyssinia, and Egypt, and of his boyhood in Scotland. A good many of his stories had a girl in them that he would have on her back by the end, sometimes fierce native women he had tamed in bed. One had been an Abyssinian princess, that he came back to over and over.

He would spin out stories at supper, with Daisy bringing him heaping plates of food and wine, and she would sit by him in a kind of numbness somewhere between impatience and pleasure, disgust and happiness, for stinking, half-drunk, and unshaven, he was still the most man she was ever going to have in her life.

Best of all she loved it when he recited poetry. He could roll it out by the hour and never repeat himself, his voice deep and low, or fast and bright, the English sound of the words making plain American sound barren. She loved some of those poems so much she memorized them herself, thinking she might come to speak them along with him, though she never did. The darkling plain one she loved the best:

> Ah love, let us be true
> To one another! For the world, which seems
> To lie before us like a land of dreams,
> So various, so beautiful, so new,
> Hath really neither joy, nor love, nor light,
> Nor certitude, nor peace, nor help for pain;
> And we are here as on a darkling plain

Swept with confused alarms of struggle and flight,
Where ignorant armies clash by night.

That poem, and others, made her feel that she was better than she had always considered herself. Those words made her feel as no man ever had, touching her. It seemed that there was something good in her down inside, that had never had much of a chance but was there all the same. Other times she would realize she was no different from her girls, who sighed over their lost loves that they had made up in the first place, and wept when they sang sentimental songs standing around the organ with Mary Hardy playing.

At first he did not need her much in bed. She thought it was the whiskey, for she had known whiskey to do that to a man. She knew how to make herself attractive to him, and though sometimes pride would keep her from it, other times she would catch herself standing with her bosom turned a certain way, or, bending over him to straighten his blanket, letting her hair touch his cheek. Or she would do her hair up high to expose the back of her neck, which she knew he admired. Once he had said he wished he could devise a way to fuck her there.

She was very pleased when he began to call her to bed, often four or five times a day, stretching, or fondling himself, and saying, "I crave me a big woman, Mrs. Benbow."

But he began to crave other girls too, and she had to furnish a harem for his royal highness. "Send me Birdie, ma'am," he would say, or "I do crave Maizie, if you please, Mrs. B." Sometimes he called for two at a time. She did not allow herself to disapprove of a man's preferences, which was what she made her living catering to, within reason anyhow, and she knew that a man low in his mind must try to get his stock back up between a woman's legs.

Perhaps she would not have minded so much if Machray had simply gone through every girl in the house in turn. But Mary Hardy was a different case from the rest, not a whore but a kind of guest, young and pretty and educated. Once Machray had spouted some poetry in front of her, and the girl spouted some right back at him. It was as though they had a language only the two of them could speak. That was when she should have had the sense to send Mary Hardy packing.

Because one morning Machray woke up beside her with his

pecker swollen like a club, and said in a slimy voice, "Mrs. Benbow, I do crave a virgin this morning."

She said she would not have a virgin in the house, and knew she did not if the girl's stories were to be believed. She was able to joke Machray out of it that time, or else he was ashamed of himself, and got rid of his club taking his morning piss. But the next day he was back on the subject again: "It is such a lovely thought to a man, to deflower a virgin, Mrs. B."

That day what got Machray's mind on other things was Livingston coming to him.

8

Before Andrew had set out on his mission to Pyramid Flat in behalf of Lady Machray, he received another delegation with demands. This was four men riding in single file down out of the buttes to the north. He called to Chub Sawyer, one of the new hands he had hired, and they posted themselves with rifles on the veranda, but as the four came closer he recognized Feeney, with his battered hat, and other grangers who had helped at the range fire. He racked his rifle on the elk-horns fastened to the wall, and Chub propped his inside the door.

The four halted their horses in a semicircle, lean-faced men in worn work clothing, none of them armed with six-shooters, but each with a rifle butt protruding from a scabbard or a saddle blanket. He nodded to them, having forgotten their names.

"We have heard about your partner," Feeney said. There was an uncomfortable silence. He nodded silently.

"There was a fellow over by Black Tail Creek that had a set-in with Regulators, too," one of the others said, the wry-necked fellow Buddy Feeney had commented upon unfavorably.

"What happened?"

"He has left the country."

He apologized for asking their names again. Wry-neck was Bert Kettle, ginger-mustache Charley Strake, and a hot-eyed, skeletally thin man Willis Eigen. They dismounted and there was a general handshaking. Chub, Andrew noticed, did not conceal his cowboy's disdain for grangers.

They had all had warnings except Strake, Feeney said, some by riders with floursacks over their heads—whitecaps.

"Oh, I expect my turn is comin," Strake said, and grinned to show bad teeth.

"Not all the nesters hereabouts have got them," Eigen said. "We have been talking among ourselves, you see. But those of us that run a few cattle, we all got them except Charley."

Chub disappeared inside the house, where Andrew could hear him talking to the cook. The grangers stood with their hats in their hands until Andrew brought out some chairs; then they sat formally in a half circle, like a class facing him, hats on their knees.

"Those whitecap warnings is making our women pretty jumpy," Kettle said. "We have thought it was only nesters gettin warned, but we guess you did too since they kilt your partner."

"We were warned," he said. "We believed it was bluff."

The cook came out to fling away the dishpan full of water, and Andrew asked if his callers would like coffee. This was well received.

"We was wondering if there was others like you gettin the notices too," Feeney said.

He said the Crowes had, that he knew of. "The brothers that dragged the steer carcass at the fire. They are just up from Texas with a herd."

All of them nodded in concert. "The fellow on Black Tail run considerable stock," Kettle said. "And there is a fellow over on Fat Man that holds a hundred head. I will bet you he has got one, though he don't say so."

"First we thought it was just little fellows like us," Strake said, with his swift grin.

"We thought it was just little fellows like us," Andrew said. They all laughed. There was a general rising, jarring of chair legs, and milling as the cook brought out the steaming blue enamel pot and cups.

When they were all seated again, Feeney, his sharp Adam's apple working, said, "It is plumb hard to get any news out here, less a man spends his days hangin around town."

There was another silence. Strake said, "We hear there was a blowout and some of them whitecaps got shot up. Two of them were killed," he said.

"Well, hallelujah!" Kettle said. "Somebody has fit back! It was them Crowe fellows, was it?"

He nodded, holding his hot cup between his two hands.

"Well, hallelujah!" Kettle said.

"We thought we would ask you if you are a member of the Stockraisers Association," Eigen said.

He said he had not been allowed to join.

"So it is just the big fellows that's doin it?" Feeney said.

He continued to nod.

"Well," Strake said, "I can't say I wouldn't think the same way. Been here first and then a lot of johnny-come-latelies jammin in."

"Mr. Livingston," Eigen said, leaning forward. "I will tell you what we have come for. We have come for advice. The Association has announced their roundup for next month, and we expect they will take a poor view of us hanging around it. We are wondering if you are in that same position."

"I am in exactly the same position."

"They'd let you send a rep, surely?" Eigen said.

"They might have earlier, but I'm afraid this fight with the Crowes has established a state of war."

Eigen leaned back, whistling softly.

Strake said, "We hear they have got them a brand book, and they ain't goin to accept any brands not in their book. They will be takin our cow-stuff away just snatch-outen-the-box, if they do that!"

"Maybe if we got together a pool outfit and had our own roundup," Eigen said. "Wouldn't they have to send their reps to our roundup? And then wouldn't they have to accept our reps at theirs?"

"What *you* think they have to do and what *they* think they have to do is two different things, Willis," Kettle said.

"I believe if they take our cow-stuff like that it is plain rustlin!" Strake complained.

"That'd bother 'em a good deal," Feeney said. "Seein they are so sensitive about rustlin."

He remembered Davey Crowe saying that they had learned in Texas that small fish had better herd together. "We could establish another association," he said. "For those who have been excluded from the existing one."

Eigen said, "Mr. Livingston, we have been thinking of that, but we don't know how to go about it."

"We heard you have had some experience in politics back east," Feeney said.

The four tense faces stared into his. "I know how to go about it," he said. "We will name ourselves a committee to call a meeting for the purpose of forming a new association for Bad Lands cattle raisers. I will chair the meeting until proper officers have been elected. Is that what you have come here for?"

Strake and Feeney grinned at him. Kettle said, "But how do we go about callin this meeting?"

"We thought if we put up notices in town they would just get torn down," Eigen said.

"Then we will put up others."

"You had better get us one damned big *space*," Strake said in an excited voice. "For you will be surprised how many fellows will turn out!"

Machray lay on a divan in Mrs. Benbow's room, with the heavy red draperies drawn and a lamp burning. A comforter was drawn to his chin, which was rusty with beard. Machray glowered at him as he tried to speak to his charge from Lady Machray—that she was not responsible for the restrictions his backers had placed upon him.

When he had finished, Machray said, "Ask you to mind your own business, my friend."

"I had hoped, if there is misunderstanding—"

"There's no misunderstanding," Machray said. "I do not misunderstand a pack of canting bloodsuckers."

The blind rage Machray seemed so often to inflict gripped him by the throat, and he turned to go. But then he turned back to meet the Scot's green glare.

"Are you aware of what is going on on the range?" he asked.

"What is going on on the range, my man?" Machray said, yawning noisily.

He told him of the Regulators' warnings, Chally Reuter's death, the attack on the Crowes, and Ash Tanner's death. Machray might have been dozing, his eyes closed, face settled into heavy lines. Once he belched. Mrs. Benbow reappeared, to stand just inside the door listening, one pale hand plucking at the jet beads that lay in three strands around her throat. At some point in his narrative she vanished again.

"Have you been privy to any of this, Machray?"

Machray yawned again and shook his head. "Those fellows detest my entrails. Put a bounty on me. Secret meetings."

"Hardy is one of the ringleaders, at least."

"No doubt of it."

"Can we count you on our side?"

"And what side might that be?"

"The side of those who are on their dead list!"

Machray laughed arrogantly. "Giving yourselves airs! I am a list all by myself! Head every list they've ever made! Unseen guest at every table, subject of their innermost thoughts and cunningest contrivances. Plotting with my Chicago enemies, I believe!"

"I repeat my question."

"Answer is no," Machray said. "Can't advise you to count on me. Have it from a lady of my acquaintance that I am a fraud, a failure, a hog, a goat, and a son of Belial. As soon see a leper touch her son as myself. Disgrace known from Edinburgh to Cochin China. No, no, can't be counted upon for anything!"

Machray looked suddenly more cheerful. "O' course," he said, "I could put a stop to the whole miserable business in a wink of the eye. Commence buying their stock at six dollars a hundredweight. Quality of profit is not strained. Yes, yes, I could halt all this arming and girding in a fine Christian manner simply by buying up their stock for slaughter in my abattoir. Beaming friends standing arm in arm, feuds healed, enemies shaking hands and begging pardon, sweetness and light on every hand, forbearance and sweet reason. I am told the fire damage is not so great as was first thought, though of course I have not my pens finished. But there are no insurmountable problems. Except money. I ha' nae money, Livingston! No *monnnnnnneeeeee!* I say, do you want to lend me the money so I can placate the gory-minded old bastards by buying up their herds?"

"I would see them in hell first," he said.

"Ah!" Machray said. "Perhaps you are not quite the Christian gentleman I took you for."

"They are mad dogs!"

"Na', na', Livingston!" Machray said, keeping his eyes determinedly closed. "Merely poor, frightened little chaps! And I, a man whose all-embracing mind can ken the situation, powerless to act! I am become a rusted monument! I should be leading armies against the Paynim hordes. Favoring the houris of the east in their multitudes instead of buggering

264

railroad-town strumpets. I should be settling the fates of realms and empires, and here I am reduced to fretting over the slaughtering of cattle!"

"I will ask a favor of you," he said.

"Ask away."

"There is to be a meeting of the small cattle raisers who are excluded from the present Association, and so from the roundup, and others who feel themselves threatened by the Regulators. No hall is big enough for such a meeting except your slaughtering room."

"You force me to your side then!" Machray said. He laughed. "Very well. You have your meeting hall."

So the Bad Lands Livestock Association was born, in the cavernous, echoing slaughtering room of Marchray's abattoir, where there were wry jokes as to the location and the hint of hell in the charry stench from the fire. Andrew stood on a chair to address more than three hundred brown, weathered faces staring back at him, some of the men standing, some squatting or seated upon the plank floor. A dozen women in bonnets were seated on two benches, and men extended back into the vast darkness out of the light of the lanterns. Machray, clean-shaven and elegantly dressed, stood by the chair of his podium, arms folded on his chest, and an unlit cigar tilted from his teeth.

Andrew Livingston was elected president of the new organization. An aggressive small rancher named Cheyenne Davis, whose name he remembered from the same dead list on which he had been shocked to hear Chally Reuter's name, was elected vice-president, and the granger Eigen, who had been a schoolmaster, secretary. Dues of fifty cents a head of stock were to be collected at the new association's roundup, which was scheduled for two weeks prior to the old association's, with Ben Crowe as roundup foreman. Andrew managed to keep the discussions free of idle speculation as to the names of their persecutors, and of threats of counterviolence. He had never attended a meeting where, after an early recital of grievances, there was so little rancor or faction. When it was over he stood in line with Machray to sign the roster, among the grangers and their wives, the small ranchers and interested townsmen, who grinned at him and put out hands to shake his or touch his shoulder and call him by name. They greeted Machray in much the same way, and he saw by Machray's swaggering that the Scot was not displeased.

At the table where there was the roster, pen, and ink, Machray wrote his signature, large and flowing as John Hancock's: "George Eustace Balater, Widewings." Andrew signed his own name beneath, in smaller scale. Taking his arm, Machray escorted him through the crowded, echoing hall where the lanterns made deep shadows and white highlights.

"Well, Livingston, you have done it now. It is daggers drawn, you know." He halted to declaim:

"Then should the warlike Harry, like himself,
    Assume the port of Mars, and at his heels,
    Leashed in like hounds, should famine, sword, and fire
    Crouch for employment!"

"Why must that be?" he asked.

"Oh, man—they cannot accept an earlier roundup. They simply can't afford it!"

"Fire Creek Ranch,
August 23, 1884

"Dearest Cissie:

"The newspaper clippings you sent of the Rudolph Duarte scandal pained me a great deal, for I admired the man inordinately. I wonder if you realized that I came out to the Bad Lands in large part because of his tales of adventure and 'pursuit' in the Far West. Now he has been caught bribing employees of the Department of the Interior for information one would have assumed it would have been child's play for him to deduce. I suppose his position with his wealthy backers had become precarious with the lack of success of the New Mexico silver mines. And charges of even more serious venality to come! Yet I will never forget him as he was at Cambridge, bright small face aglow with excitement, eyes flashing, and hands grasping and jerking at the lapels of his jacket as though to tear the constricting garment from his body as the words tumbled from his lips. He preached that glistening dream of the Far West as the regeneration of the nation, and the proper pursuit of its youth. Now that vision of the West has become obscured by the same jobbery and vicious speculation that was the ruin of the Founders' dream, and of Rudolph Duarte himself.

"And Kermit Darcy is gone. Certainly it was not unexpected, poor old fellow. I am grateful that you insisted that I make my peace with him before he passed on, and I know that seeing the boy gave him comfort. I cannot help wondering who will now care for the profusion of flora in the hothouse in which he lived out his last years.

"Death has also visited us here. My 'factor' has been murdered. I can hardly bring myself to write of it, and I know it would be inexplicable to you. Indeed, it is not explicable in any terms but those of current Bad Lands passions and the whirlwind which we must now reap. Nor has his been the only murder. I myself witnessed the cold-blooded shooting, in a saloon quarrel, of an old cattleman named Ashley Tanner. I have just returned from his funeral.

"Tanner was as irascible, unreasonable, and unforgiving a man as Kermit Darcy, and yet of such a crotchety honor that I am honored to have known him. I find myself writing an epitaph.

"Twice in his life Tanner was called to lead a troop of volunteers against thieves and rascals preying upon honest men in lawless places, and each time he saw the righteousness of his efforts corrupted by the actions of others. In my time in the Bad Lands I saw the second of these 'Regulation Committees' formed. It hunted down at least two local horse thieves, catching them redhanded in both cases, and, I think, would have dispersed, its task accomplished, had its leader had his way—perhaps to be reconvened at some future time, to combat some future failure of the might of the law out here. I do not excuse the actions of this gang of lynchers, and yet I cannot think what else is to be done in a place a hundred miles from the nearest sheriff, and he one who resolutely shuns us.

"Yet there is an inherent evil in such extralegal police forces. It seems an implacable process that the good in anything be corrupted, in time, to the lowest common denominator of human meanness present. It is a process that Tanner liked to sum up in an earthy phrase. It is also the Second Law of Thermodynamics.

"So the function of the Regulators has changed from the pursuit of horse thieves and rustlers to the harassing of newcomers to the range. And so Chally Reuter is dead, and Ash Tanner also, in a futile and suicidal protest at what his 'Regulators' had become—the tools of the dragon Holdfast. I know these blackguards. The leader is one who threatened me when I first moved into this cabin, his name, Jake Boutelle. Behind him, among others, is my neighbor and erstwhile friend, Hardy.

"Surely no villain save Iago ever considered himself such, and every man has the best of reasons for his actions. The range must be preserved from overstocking, which would ruin all the cattlemen here, big and little, old and new. Moreover, I have already heard what must be the opposite view of the situation from the one I see: that the Regulators are, in fact, range inspectors of the Stockraisers Association, that they have, also in fact, been deputized so that they have legal status, their function the policing of range stock, and their enemies—rustlers and horse thieves!

"And as such, by this reasoning, I must be classed!

"Yesterday was, I think, the most satisfying day I have ever experienced in public life. I am back in politics with a vengeance. . . ."

9

Bill Drigg's luck had been bad ever since he let a man walk away from knocking him down. First crack out of the box on his Hoosier brother-in-law's farm he fell off the tailgate of the wagon and broke his arm. So there he was with his left arm in a splint and a sling, and no good to anybody, least of all himself. He got his exercise lifting whiskey glasses.

He took up shooting grackles. They would settle on one of the pear trees in the orchard like every grackle in the county had lit on that one tree to cuss and confab with a racket that went right up his backbone like a windowshade snapping free. They were as filthy a bird as could be found, all of them squalling at once out in the orchard of Ollie Prout's pig farm.

He had bought a little nickel-plated revolver and he would go out in the orchard and shoot grackles out of the pear tree. His sister had a gray, half-grown cat that had taken a shine to him, and when he reached the revolver out of his bureau

268

drawer with the grackles racketing, Puss would be right on his heel when he went outside, making sounds halfway between a yip and a purr, just prancing along with the tip of his tail floating high behind.

He would bring down a grackle with just about every shot, at which all the other grackles would give a little jump, so the whole tree appeared to jump, and break off their racket for about half a minute. Then they would go back to cussing each other again.

Puss always lit out with the shot, and when the dead grackle hit the ground, he would pounce on it and drag it back to lay it at his feet just like a bird dog, strutting around and leaning against his boots, and yip-purring. He would have a good row of grackles there at his feet before the flock of them would remember business somewhere else, and take off in a close-packed cloud, leaving the pear tree and the ground beneath it gray with grackle turds.

Shooting grackles kept his hand in with a pistol, and he would squint his eyes when he aimed and pretend those grackles were different fellows he was blowing straight to hell.

One time, though, he looked down to see that the grackle Puss had dragged back wasn't a grackle but a robin, with an orange belly and toes curled up dead. So then he gave up shooting grackles.

He would help his sister with her chores, or Prout with the pigs as best he could. His sister worried that he would overdo, with his bad arm, and Prout had got one up on him when he fell off the tailgate and considered him good for nothing. He could have tied that pig-stinking, fat-bottomed Hoosier into a square knot with his one good hand, and he was tempted to do it every time they worked together.

It was no great pleasure sitting in Moonan's saloon in town knocking back whiskey bought with money borrowed from his sister, for he would just get to thinking about Machray, and Cora. He was a bad drinker, too, who had always had a quarrelsome nature, and he was warned more than once to make no more fusses or he would be posted out of Moonan's.

Moonan's was where Jake Boutelle found him. Boutelle looked prosperous in a fine suit, new boots, and some kind of jewel in a stickpin in his cravat, very handsome strutting in and nodding to him casual as though they were both still in the Bad Lands and had seen each other only yesterday.

"Broke your arm there," Jake said.

He said it was so.

They sat at a table in the back of the saloon, and Jake leaned over it with his hands folded, looked him straight in the eye, and said, "Bill, Connie's dead. Killed by rustlers."

That jolted him. Connie had been a good enough fellow once, though he suspected he'd done a bit of rustling on the side himself. You overlooked things a bit in fellows who'd been around in the old days, not many of them left.

"Bob Cletus, too," Jake said. "The two of them."

He asked what those two had been up to, shooting it out with rustlers.

"Range inspecting for the Association," Jake said. "You remember."

"Looks like dangerous work for the pay." He had been so pleased to see Jake, just because he was a Bad Lands face, that he'd forgot about dealing with him. What had Jake come all this way for?

"Texians," Jake said solemnly. "Desperate hard men. A gang of them." He went on to say that southern herds had been moving into the Bad Lands, grangers were packing in too, with mavericking a scandal, and Texas hardcases on the shoot. Everybody was on edge, and the Association fit to be tied.

"Bill, the Association just can't afford to let two of its best men get dead like that."

He could understand that. "Guess I was lucky to leave when I did," he said. "Everything going to pot."

Jake leaned over the table like that, gazing straight at him, and said, "I shot Ash Tanner, Bill."

That jarred him again, not that Ash had been a particular friend, for Ash had been as crotchety and hard to get on with as he himself was. But he and Ash had been the last of the old-timers. Now he had left the Bad Lands and Ash was dead. He had a feeling of everything spinning faster and faster while he'd been gone.

"Bill, he come after me like a crazy man! Throwing lead all over the place. Drunk! That little squaw of his had did away with herself, and all anybody can make out was he was clean out of his mind grieving for her. There was nothing for it but shoot or get shot. Anybody'll tell you that."

"Whew!" he said. "Sounds like everybody's shot but Lord Much-a-muck."

Boutelle gave his head a shake, straightened, and poured himself some whiskey.

270

"What did you want of me, Jake?" he asked.

Boutelle looked thoughtful, sipping from his glass. "They are getting some good men together to run those hardcase Texans out of the Bad Lands. The ones that did for Connie and Bob."

"Who's 'they'?"

"Well, it's the Association, but me and Yule Hardy and Ted Cutter's in charge. There's a committee behind us, Yule Hardy and Pard and Jim Rademacher and some others. I told them the first man we had to get hold of was Bill Driggs."

"I don't see that a broke-arm fellow is going to be much use to you." He shifted his arm around in the bandanna sling. It ached something fierce sometimes, but whiskey did keep it quiet. Boutelle grinned at him.

"Almost turned around and walked out when I saw that," he said. "I guess one-armed you'd be only about twice as much as the next fellow."

That was not hard to take when he'd been low in his mind. He thought about how much he hated Ollie Prout and hated asking his sister for money to buy whiskey with. But he didn't understand.

"What's a puzzle to me," he said slowly, "is why you would come all this way to get *me*. The way you wanted me in the range inspectin thing. Why *is* that, Jake?"

"If you'd come in, Connie and Bob'd be alive today. I do believe that, Bill." Boutelle looked him straight in the eye again. "You know me," he said. "I am not a sentimental fellow, but there are just not many of us old Bad Lands people left. New ones horning in, and the old ones dying off the way they have been doing. Bill, the new fellows just aren't much good."

Watch out! he thought. "How's the money?" he said.

"Five hundred dollars and found. A hundred on your say you'll come along."

He said he'd come along.

Book Five

1884

1

Years later, when Jeff Hardy heard the Battalion referred to
as the "invaders," he would protest that they had not been
the invaders, it was the other way around. The Battalion
had been trying to protect the Bad Lands from invaders.
Time turned everything inside out, what had once been bad
turned into good, and good bad. Even he, who had been one
of the "invaders," finally quit protesting the name, and accepted it. It was better than "whitecaps," or "John Does,"
which were other names for them.

He was sixteen then. He had gone to some of the Association meetings, and he was with the Battalion when the men
had assembled and trained, and he had been along at the CK.

Later he found out some things he had not understood at
the time. What he had known then was just what all his
friends knew, that there had been a shoot-out between the
range inspectors and a gang of rustlers, and two inspectors
had been killed. Everybody knew that the rustler element was
becoming stronger and more daring. There were no two sides
about it. The range inspectors had been hired to protect the
stock and range rights of the Association members, and the
forces of order had been defeated by the forces of anarchy.
Such a defeat could simply no tbe allowed to stand, Father
said.

After their victory the rustler element felt themselves
strong enough to form their own association, and to announce roundup dates *before* the legitimate roundup. He had
attended a meeting of the Stockraisers at Lamey's Eight-bar
with Father. He remembered the jarring sounds of chair legs
scraping on the wood floor, and men's jarring voices, and the
sweat-sour stink of anger. Men had got up to shout that it
was bald-faced stealing, the early roundup. That they might
as well give the Bad Lands to the damned thieves. One of the
rustlers known to have been in the fight in which Conroy and
Cletus was killed had been elected roundup foreman, and
Andy Livingston president of the rustlers' association. The

275

rustlers' meeting had been held in Machray's slaughterhouse, and he heard Roy Huggins say he would bet that building would burn a good deal better the second time than it had the first.

There was a good deal of cussing of Andy Livingston for a traitor, and a cheap politician looking for votes when the Territory became a state. Fred Rademacher got up to say Andy Livingston would not be president of the new association if he had been let join the old one, but old Jim shouted his son down.

Later on, when he became concerned with how "history" looked upon the "invasion," he found out some facts as to why everybody in the Bad Lands was so exercised. Texas cattlemen were having a hard time negotiating new grazing contracts with the Tribal Councils. One of the tribes had hired a fancy lawyer to do its dealing, and others were taking up the practice. In the Cherokee Strip, and on the Arapaho-Cheyenne lands, they were demanding two cents an acre, which added up ruinously on enormous acreages. Some cattlemen were refusing to sign such contracts, while others quietly signed and began fencing land they did not own. Meanwhile boomers were pushing in to claim Indian lands, thinking to open the reservations to settlement. It was not happening in the Bad Lands, but it was coming closer, trouble between the cattlemen, the Indians, the grangers, and the government, with the President threatening to send cavalry to chase out the boomers and to cancel all the grazing contracts on reservation lands if the cattlemen couldn't settle with the Tribal Councils. And if the President did such a crazy thing, there'd be nowhere for those huge southern herds to go but north.

So those were fretful times for the northern stockmen. Then rustlers killed the two range inspectors.

Petey Lamey's father being president of the Stockraisers Association, Petey knew a good deal more inside stuff than Jeff did, for his own father did not talk much about Association business. Petey told him that the old Regulators, who had killed Matty, had been bossed by Ash Tanner. When they changed to range inspectors, with Jake Boutelle as captain, old Ash was crazy jealous. Which was why he had gone after Boutelle, who had to shoot him down in self-defense.

Petey also knew about the "Committee of Five." On that Committee were Father; Major Cutter, who had served with
276

General Sherman, and had more decorations, Father said, than Lord Machray; Jim Rademacher; Pard Yarborough; and somebody else who quit the committee and Roy Huggins took his place. The Committee of Five was in charge of the Regulators, and later the range inspectors, and when it was decided to recruit the Battalion to run the rustlers out of the Bad Lands for good, the Committee was in charge of that, too. Father was chairman, and Major Cutter chief of the Battalion.

At that meeting, Lamey had turned things over to Father, and he had been proud of his father standing up there, quiet-spoken and holding everything dead quiet while he looked from face to face. He said that everyone knew he was a peace-loving and a moderate man, they all were that, but now strong measures were called for. It was the Committee of Five's proposal that a "Battalion of Regulators" be recruited promptly, so as to be put into the field before the illegal roundup. Fifty men were to be hand-picked, Major Cutter was to train and lead them, and Association members would be taxed on the basis of stock head-count to pay the expenses. It would not be cheap, Father said grimly, but the Committee could guarantee that it would be effective. Time was of the essence, since there was less than six weeks left before the "rustlers' roundup."

The vote was unanimous, and the secretary was called upon to note that fact in the minutes of the meeting. But Petey Lamey told him later that some of the members, who might not have made it unanimous, had not been notified of the meeting, men like Machray and Blaikie, and Ash Tanner dead of course.

Major Cutter and Roy Huggins went to Texas, recruiting, and Park Yarborough to Denver, where he had friends. Father took him along to a place called Presle, just west of the Red River in Dakota Territory. The Battalion was there, more men coming in day by day. They were a hard lot, but some were pleasant to him. A fellow named Big George Roberts, who was a famous hand with a six-gun, promised to teach him to shoot, but never got around to it, being more interested in whiskey drinking.

Major Cutter conducted drills in a field on the outskirts of town, and lectured on tactics, against whiskey, and for discipline, though there was not much he could do to those Texas and Colorado men when they got out of line, except threaten to cut off their pay. Father lectured too, evenings after supper

277

when everyone was crowded in the hotel dining room, which smelled of boiled cabbage, boiled potatoes, and rank sweat. The men of the Battalion were great grumblers. They grumbled about the food and the work and Major Cutter's demands on them. They were great ones for spitting, too, hawking up gobs to spit into the spittoons, and belching and farting as they pleased. He was proud that they fell silent just like the Association members when Father spoke to them. He knew that his father should have been a statesman, instead of a cattleman in troubled times.

They stared at him in silence, slowly chewing food like a cow her cud, while he told them that the expansion of harmonious perfection had to be a *general* expansion, and that it was the good man's duty to see that it was. The good man was always responsible for his acts, he said, which were never ill-calculated. But neither would he fall into the sin of inaction, when action was called for.

"Contravention of the natural order has produced envy of position or possession, as well as the fear of losing position or possession to the envy of anarchic men," Father said. "We must seek a return to the old order and authority. We must return to the rule of natural instincts!"

He was on pins and needles those evenings that someone would belch or fart, and then others would begin to laugh, and Father would be ridiculed. But nothing of that kind ever happened, although he could see that Major Cutter was impatient, pulling out his watch to look at it as though to signal to Father that he was going on too long, and Roy Huggins scratching his fingers over the sunburnt bulge of flesh at his throat, scowling.

Always, when Father went on like that, a strain would come between his shoulder blades, as though he had been trying to stand unnaturally straight too long.

One day he heard Father and Pard Yarborough discussing Bill Driggs, word having come that Jake Boutelle was bringing him to join the Battalion.

"What's the jubilation about?" Pard said. "When's Bill ever been a friend of the cattleman? Distempered, drunken old coot as far as I've ever seen."

"I for one will feel a good deal comforted if Bill is on our side and not the other," Father said.

"How come is that, Yule?" Pard said. He was a little deaf, and he had a habit of palming one ear out when he did not understand something.

"Oh, perhaps because he was here first."

"Here? You mean in the Bad Lands? I expect you could find you some Sioux to dispute that."

"White men," Father said, very short.

"What about them Frenchies?"

"Decent men," Father said, and turned to walk away.

There was contention between Father and Pard Yarborough, and between everyone and Major Cutter. For his own part he was sorry to be on the same side with Roy Huggins. When Bill Driggs showed up, he had a broken arm in a sling, was scratchy and sour, and did not associate with the others, but drank whiskey with a Colorado fellow he had known long ago.

Jeff and his father returned to the Bad Lands to help get things ready at the other end, and the Battalion left Presle in a darkened car, with a freight car carrying supplies and ammunition. They were to be met at a place called Big Fork Station, about forty miles west of Pyramid, at sunup. He and Petey Lamey were there, with three wagons and teamsters bundled up in buffalo jackets against the cold, and other fellows coming in throughout the night bringing in riding stock, Fred Rademacher and a cowboy with a considerable herd.

In the green dawn the train came along, right on time, first the singing on the rails they had been taking turns listening for, and then the hard, solid-looking puffs of white smoke while they waited with their gloved hands in their armpits, stamping their feet and breathing out smoke. The 4-4-0 rolled toward them and stopped with a squealing and clanking and steam hissing. The men of the Battalion began swinging off the passenger car with their saddles and plunder, grouching about the cold and shaking their hands to keep the circulation going. They were slung over with cartridge belts and pistols, with rifles in scabbards, and the Major and Boutelle moved among them, trying to get them hooked up with the horses from the cavy.

Major Cutter was pigeon-chested and wore a white hat that looked half again as tall as he was. He was trying to direct everything, irritating everyone barking orders; so Jeff and Petey moved themselves out of his range. They were standing by the fire with Fred Rademacher when Bill Driggs came elbowing by, half a head taller than anyone else, his bad arm in a sling made out of a red bandanna, and an expression on his face as though everything was just about as bad as could be, but he would bet it could get worse.

"Jeff," he said. "Will you tell me what you are doing with this outfit, and your daddy, and *me?*"

He said he didn't know. Fellows near them looked around and scowled, for Bill had spoken loudly and he was not popular anyway. Bill asked him if he would help him saddle up a horse, which he did. Father and Jim Rademacher and Yarborough had come in, and they were walking along the tracks with Huggins and the Major, arguing about something, old Jim waving his arms and Huggins banging his fist on his chest.

"They have got themself a bobcat by the tail," Bill commented. "And not much tail to hold onto, either."

Pretty soon, by full light, the train pulled away heading west with smoke trailing back. Another bunch of men rode in, Lamey, Mogle, Pelke, and Hazel Cole, and some others, all decked out with rifles and cartridge belts, Mogle with earflaps on against the chill. They had a wagonload of supplies with them, mainly food, and there was a long wrangle as to whether the Battalion should be on the move or eating breakfast, with the men wanting food and the cattlemen motion.

The Major ranted and threatened, but in the end the cook had to fry up some bacon and boil more coffee before anybody would start out. He watched Bill Driggs seated on a rock with steam from his coffee rising in front of his face as though he was a devil, Jake Boutelle swaggering among the Texas men, and Father, who looked very small this morning, bundled up in his greatcoat like a sausage. Fred Rademacher squatted with him and Petey in the frozen grass that glinted like crystal spikes in the sun. Petey asked if Fred knew where they were headed first. They were going after the Crowe brothers, Fred said, who were the ones that had shot Conroy and Cletus. They were holed up in an old line shack not far south of here. The Crowes were first on the "dead list," Fred said.

It was the first time he had heard those words, and his heart swelled up in his throat like a toad. He knew of somebody who had been on the dead list before the Crowe brothers, and it was Matty Gruby. That was the first look he had at the puzzle that was to bother him the rest of his life, how one day Regulators lynching a fellow could seem about the worst thing there was, and the next you found yourself and everybody you knew and trusted on the same business, that was necessary and had to be done.

When they set out all the Texas men rode together, the

Coloradans a bit apart, and the Bad Lands men all in a bunch behind, except for Boutelle and the Major, who rode ahead. Sometimes he rode with Petey, and sometimes with Father, and for a while with Bill Driggs, who was nipping from a flask of what he called "painkiller" that he kept in his saddlebag for his bad arm. His Colorado sidekick, Eddie Park, told stories about the old-time cattle drives as though that was a hundred years ago and in another country.

As soon as the sun was well up it was hot, everybody stripping out of coats and jackets. The Texans groused about a place where first you froze and then you fried. The wagons had fallen behind, and there was no water. He and Petey were sent to bring some up.

They were on their way back, each with a jug, when they heard the firing. The Battalion had come up to the Crowe brothers' shack, and Texas men were shooting at Texas men.

One of the brothers had been shot first crack, and the other had dragged him inside. It was a log shack, very low to the ground, with a door on one side and a window on the other, but holes on the two ends where a rifle could be poked through. The men in there were throwing a lot of lead.

Most of the Battalion was in a clump of woods looking down on the line camp, but others were riding this way and that in a disorganized manner. The Association people were mostly back behind the woods out of range, where there was some shade. Pard Yarborough was pacing up and down in an excited way saying it sounded like Chancellorsville, but others were just slumped on the ground smoking or chatting together.

He crawled up through the trees bringing his water jug to the men firing there. He could see the spurts of dust flying up from the sod roof, and the smoke from the door where the Crowes were firing back. Off away from the shack was a corral, where first of all sharpshooters had shot all the horses. Out beyond, cattle were grazing. It was strange how quickly he began to feel bored with the shooting, and sleepy; he had not slept last night, when the waiting had been more exciting than the real thing today.

But when he crawled on back to where the Association men were standing around the wagons that had finally come up, he was feeling a hollow anxiety. There were sixty men and more here, firing on two, and one of those bad hurt. Books he had read kept coming to his mind, and poems like "Horatio at the Bridge," where the big bunch was the cowards and villains, and those standing against them heroes. And he was not the only one sick, for he knew Petey Lamey felt the same, and Fred Rademacher, and Bill Driggs, too, who was sitting under one of the wagons with his back turned, drinking whiskey. He understood then what whiskey was for, a way of hitting yourself over the head when you didn't like what was going on but there was nothing you could do about it.

He took a walk around with Father to see the layout of the "battle." Men of the Battalion were firing from among the trees, and out of a creek bed lower down. Two had got behind the corral, close to the shack, and, out in the meadows where the stock was grazing, were four saddled horses; so men were sneaking in on the shack through the high grass. Gazing out on the smoke of firing, Father looked ill; his face was yellowish and streaked with sweat, and he kept taking off his spectacles to polish them.

When they were back by the wagons, taking their ease on the ground while the firing continued, Father began talking about somebody named Bishop Wilson. Mogle and Yarborough stopped by to listen, and Major Cutter too, although soon he pulled out his watch, scowled at it, and hurried away. Driggs had crawled out from under the wagon, to sit with his long legs stretched out and his good arm crossed over his chest to knead at the shoulder of his bad one. The cook sprawled on the wagon seat, face shadowed by a dusty black hat.

Bishop Wilson had said it was essential that good men make reason and the Sublime Will prevail. Father took out his handkerchief and mopped his face. The danger, he went on, was that people tended to allow their routine to pass for reason. He had read in *The Nation* that it was of no use to attempt to force your neighbors to your own beliefs, you must accept things as they were. He did not agree with this, he said, if your beliefs constituted reason and the will of Nature's God. He went to scrubbing his face with his soaked handkerchief.

"Well, that is why we are all here, I guess, Yule," Mogle said.

"Action is always dangerous," Father said. "But failure to act, which is easier, can be even more dangerous."

"That is right, for certain," Pard Yarborough said, squatting on his heels. There was a new burst of firing. Jake Boutelle strolled up.

"Of course no action can be salutary which is not based on reason," Father went on. "Firstly, one must never go against the best light—by which is meant the light of reason. And, secondly, take every care that that light is not darkness instead."

Jeff was feeling the ache between his shoulder blades again, and fearful that Father was taken badly sick. He did look sickly, mopping at his face like that.

"I would worry that darkness one, Yule," Bill Driggs spoke up suddenly to say.

"Going to be dark before we are through here, that looks certain," Boutelle said.

"I do wish Cutter'd get a move on those fellows," Mogle grumbled.

Father stuck his chin out at Bill Driggs. "It is false pride to refuse to lend a hand to what may seem excessive action, when that action has been taken in the best light."

"Well, maybe that is all the pride a man has got anymore," Bill said. "You have done a bad thing, here, Yule."

"No—" Father started.

Bill leaned his lined, ugly, strained face toward him. "I believe the only thing to do is quit and get out."

"No!" Father said, upon which Bill hunkered around to sit with his back to him. Father leaned against the wagon wheel, and he did look sick, sweating, his face doughy. But when Jim Rademacher asked if he was taken poorly he just shook his head.

Then somebody was hit. There was squawling and fellows running toward the dry creek, and yelling back and forth. They carried the wounded man, who was a Texan named Dudley, up from the cottonwoods to lay him in the shade under the wagon, a dozen men milling and getting in each other's way. Dudley was hit in the arm, which was broken and bleeding bad, and his face was smeared with blood where he had tracked it from his arm. They got the arm set and the bleeding stopped while Dudley groaned and carried on.

Right away there was another hubbub, the firing picking up again. Word passed around that more rustlers had shown up and were shooting at the Battalion from over by the buttes. Major Cutter pranced up and down yelling names until he had ten men mounted and a Texan named Johnson in charge. They rode off in a sweep toward the buttes.

Meanwhile Father had settled himself down with his greatcoat thrown over him. Squatting beside Father, Jim

283

Rademacher squinted up at him: "Jeff, you had better take one of the wagons and get your daddy and Jack Dudley to a doctor."

He nodded, and said, "Doc Micklejohn?" although he knew Doc Micklejohn was always to be found at Mrs. Benbow's place in Pyramid Flat, and Father would not want to go there.

Jim Rademacher just looked at him for a while. Finally he said, "I expect you could flag down the westbound for Miles City."

"I will not leave the expedition," Father said.

"You are just going to be a drag on it, Yule. You go on along with Dudley."

Father shook his head, looking squashed there on the ground with the coat over him. Then Father gazed straight at him, and he knew what to say and do.

"I will stay here, Father. One of us ought to stay with the Battalion."

He knew that was right, though he had felt light with relief at the thought of taking Father and Dudley back to the railroad. He sat in the dirt beside Father while Bill Driggs squatted in the shade of the farthest wagon, facing away from them. There was a silence, in which he could hear the thin popping from over by the buttes. Major Cutter, Pard Yarborough, and Roy Huggins came out of the woods, arguing, the Major slapping a black riding crop against his leg.

They gathered around Father, saying the day was wearing away and it looked as though the Crowes might hold out until nightfall. Something had to be done. Father just lay there with his eyes closed and didn't seem to be listening.

The others decided that the only thing to do was to announce that a hundred-dollar bonus would be given any man who could set the shack afire. He and Petey were sent around to spread the news.

It seemed there would be no takers until a fellow called Smitty strolled up from the creek to say if they would raise the ante to a hundred dollars apiece, he and his partner would take it on.

The Committee people argued, but in the end agreed. Meanwhile it was quiet over by the buttes, though there would be occasional shots. He kept worrying about Father, who just lay there in the dirt waiting with a terrible patience for someone to take him to a doctor.

Smitty and his partner stacked up some dry brush and tied

284

it into a big ball. They slung this from the ends of their ropes, mounted, and dragged the brush ball as close to the line shack as they dared. In shelter they set the brush afire, and lit out toward the shack dragging the blazing ball, each one of them ducking down on the side of his horse like an Indian. They passed on either side of the shack so that the ball of fire smashed into the door and stuck there. Then they let go of the ropes and rode out of range.

He squatted behind a log watching. He almost yelled with relief when he saw a stick poking from inside the shack until the ball of fire rolled away. All around him men were cursing and firing until he could see the splinters fly. He squinted at the sun getting lower in the west as the fireball blazed out into a smoky heap. Then he went back up to the wagons again. The attempt to fire the rustlers' shack had left him shaky and lightheaded.

His father was standing by one of the wagons, his hands stuffed each into the opposite sleeve of his greatcoat. A Coloradan with a bad case of the runs had been found to drive the team, and supplies were being hefted out of one wagon into the others. Dudley already lay groaning in the bed.

Father glanced at Bill Driggs, then back at him. "Even when an action has been taken in the best light," Father said, "it is always possible to find a hundred reasons why it cannot be seen through."

"Yes, sir," he said.

"You have been raised to see things through," Father said. His face gleamed with sweat. "You have been raised always to look for the best illumination, haven't you, my boy?"

"Yes, sir," he said.

"Some things cannot be forgiven with honor," Father said. "Cannot be tolerated."

"Yes, sir," he said. He thought Father must be speaking of Mary. A hand came out of the sleeve of the greatcoat to pat his. He could not remember another time Father had touched him like that. It occurred to him that his father was dying.

"Always seek the best light, son," Father said. "And do not fail the action that must be taken in that light."

"Father, what was it Mary used to talk about, when we had to leave the valley? Somebody burning a cross. 'Nightriders' she said they were. In the yard there."

"You wouldn't remember," Father said, his upper lip stretching down tight over his teeth. "You were just a baby."

"But why did they do that?"

285

"They were a pack of stupid bumpkins, and we were educated people. Gentry."

"You mean gentry like Lord *Machray?*"

His father stared at him with his naked eyes in their sweaty sockets, and shook his head. "No, of course not like Lord Machray," he said gently. The hand patted his once more, and his father shuffled away to where men were waiting to help him onto the wagon seat. He was dragging his bad leg the worst he had ever done.

Jeff watched the wagon roll back along the route they had followed from the railroad. Father, on the seat with the Coloradan, never looked back.

What with the failure of Smitty and his partner to fire the shack, and the sun lower still, everybody was very edgy, and the firing had picked up in volume until it sounded like a real battle again. Men were calling for water and cartridges, and Jeff crawled through the woods with his water jug and a gunnysack of cartridges. Off to the north the dust of the wagon was still visible.

Smitty and his partner were packing together another ball of dry brush. They set it blazing and ripped out toward the shack again, the same as before. He had a glimpse of one of the Crowes in the doorway firing as the two horsemen raced past. This time, instead of releasing the ropes, they flung themselves to the ground, while their ponies held the ropes taut, pinning the fireball against the side of the shack. And this time it took. All around him fellows with rifles cocked and aimed were waiting for the Crowes to make a run for it. Because it was clear they would have to run or burn.

A man sprinted out carrying his rifle. Everybody began firing at once, and Major Cutter's voice shouted over the racket, "Kill him! Kill him!"

Then the rustler was stretched out on the ground like an animal shot down, his shirt bloody. The Battalion cocked rifles again waiting for the other to run for it, but soon it was clear by the smell that he was burnt up inside the shack, which was streaming up flames and greasy smoke.

Jeff walked down the hill with the others to look at the one who had been shot. He was on his back, and his face was not marked but his lips were pulled back away from yellow teeth so that he looked like a cougar snarling. Bill Driggs had come along with him, still holding his shoulder like that, and gazing down at the dead rustler.

"This is one of the ones that did for Connie Conroy and

286

Bob Cletus?" he said, with his ugly face twisted up like everybody else's, from the smell, but worse.

"These are the ones," Boutelle said. "And we have served our turn on them."

"And took a durned long time about it," Yarborough muttered.

Boutelle had squatted down to take a folded paper from the dead man's pocket, wiping the bloody paper on the man's shirt sleeve. Men crowded around to read what was written on it over his shoulder. Driggs took it from him and read it aloud:

"Well, boys, I expect they will get me this time. Davey died a while back. He would not like the burning. I expect some of these birds out there is Texas fellows that have done this before. We left Texas because of birds like them, but there is birds like them everywhere. I wish I could get me one or a couple before they do for me. Well, here they come again."

Huggins took the paper from Driggs, and with a stub of pencil lettered on the back of it: "7-11-77," and "DEATH TO RUSTLERS," and tucked the note back into Crowe's pocket. Driggs stood watching him do it, his face longer and uglier. After a bit he just turned and walked away from the bunch standing around the dead rustler.

The line shack was blazing up like a pine knot, and the stink from it was bad. He thought he might be going to throw up, and he moved on away from the others, where they stood in their three groups, the Texans, the Coloradans, and the Association men. Driggs came riding back down from behind the trees on a little black and white pony. He made to pass them on the right. Boutelle called to him to ask where he was going.

"Headin for town," Driggs said.

"No, you are not!" Major Cutter yelled, and everybody swung around to stare at Bill Driggs where he rode on between them and the blazing shack.

"Bill! Hold on, now!" Boutelle said, taking a couple of quick steps after the pony. "Bill!" Boutelle said, with his face twisting up like the shot rustler's.

Driggs reined up the spotted pony he looked too big for, and turned to face back. He said to Boutelle, "I don't know

287

whether it was you or whiskey that sold me out, but this i
not my trade, what has been done here."

"You have signed on, Bill," Boutelle said, very soft.

"No, I have signed off."

"You will not sign off," Boutelle said, softer still.

Jeff stood with his shoulders aching with strain watchin
Driggs sitting half-turned in the saddle with his bad arm
bound up like a chicken wing in the dirty bandanna. Bil
glanced from face to face among the groups of men standin
around the dead man in the sweetish stink of burning mea
Bill's eyes, cold as bits of glass, met his for an instant.

"I don't believe this outfit's got itself so low yet as to back
shoot a man," Bill said, and turned back square in the saddle
and spurred the pony on. Boutelle drew his revolver.

"Shoot him!" Major Cutter said in his high-pitched voice
Driggs rode on without looking back.

His throat had swelled to cut off his breath again. When h
tried to think what Father would consider the best light, h
thought that Father, too, would order Boutelle to shoot. Bu
Boutelle did not shoot.

"Bill is not a man to peach on anybody," someone sai
shakily, and it was as though a tight knot came unraveled
When Driggs was fifty yards away, Boutelle stuck his revolve
back in his belt.

One of the Coloradans said the day was about gone, an
nothing to do but make camp.

Smitty said, "We are not making camp here in this damne
stink." Another man said it would be warmer here than i
would elsewhere, and still another that he'd heard it was won
derful warm in the place the two rustlers had gone to. Ther
were a few laughs at that.

Watching Bill Driggs on the pony growing smaller heade
for Pyramid, he could not understand why he felt so angry
If he had been Boutelle he would have shot Bill Driggs dow
for a deserter.

There was wrangling as the sun sank lower whether th
Battalion should make camp here or move on along. Finall
it was decided that they would ride on to the next shelter
which was Mogle's CK, and they had started when they sav
the bunch coming back from the buttes. It looked as thoug
there were not so many of them. He counted only nin
horses, and one of them had an empty saddle.

2

Cora Benbow did not feel it was proper to go buggy riding with Machray while Lady Machray was at Widewings, but he was queer in insisting upon it, very hard-eyed and jaw-stuck-out supervising what she was to wear, deciding upon the pearl gray he had bought for her in Chicago, and her Chicago French hat. They drove through town in the yellow and red varnished buggy, with the big roan with his cropped mane and tail dancing between the shafts. Machray was very jaunty, nutcracker grin and cigar between his teeth, as he drove them down Main Street toward the depot. The eastbound was in the station, panting a black coal smoke cloud over town.

They passed a wagon bulked up with valises and round-topped leather trunks, and caught up with the carriage ahead of it. Machray guided the buggy close alongside. Lady Machray was in the carriage. Blue eyes under a perky little blue hat fastened on hers for an instant and then did not look her way again. A servant girl holding a fair-haired baby jerked him around so that she couldn't see him as though against the evil eye.

Machray laughed out loud and whipped up the roan. She had never been so angry at him. In her room, pulling off her gloves while he paced and smoked, she said, "That was a mean trick."

"But one the Judas-bitch will understand, my dear."

"I am not talking about her, I am talking about me."

He halted to face her, glowering like a bulldog. Faintly through the curtained window came the "Aaaaaaalll aboooooorrrrd!" and the chiming of couplings.

"There are ways you can use me, Machray, and you know it. But there are ways I will not be used."

He hitched his shoulders in such a way that she thought he would hit her. The chuffing of steam quickened, and the singing of steel on steel ran along her nerves. Tears started in her eyes when he said he was sorry.

"Oh, Machray, what's to become of you!"

He stepped to the window and pulled the curtain aside to

289

gaze out. When he let the curtain fall closed his slab of a face was blotched with color, and he grinned like it hurt him.

"Come, Mrs. Benbow," he said. "Let us tear our pleasure with rough strife, through the iron gates of life. Let us lie down and take our pleasure," he said.

She aid she would be surprised if this day was to hold any pleasure for anyone.

His eyes glittered at her. "Why, madam, when I have one of your fine hams in either hand, a tit in my mouth, and steam rising amidships, is that not pleasure enow?"

But she shook her head. "You will not use me anymore today, Machray."

"Why, what is this damned silly coyness, Cora?" he said softly.

They were still facing each other in a standoff when Wax knocked on the door and said there was a bunch of fellows from the new Livestock Association calling on Lord Machray, a matter of life and death.

There were five of them, grangers, three coming inside and the others bunched in the doorway, all with hats in hand, like schoolboys haled before the headmaster. Machary scowled at them with his hands behind his back.

One spoke for the rest, a skinny fellow with a wry neck. He said that fifty Texas badmen had been brought into the Bad Lands, armed to the teeth and enough ammunition to start a war.

Machray asked how they knew this. They had had it from the night telegrapher at the depot. A train had come through in the dead of night, and he had checked it back to where it had loaded, a place called Presle.

Machray paced and rubbed his jaw. "This is in response to the new association's roundup dates, is it?"

They all nodded and, talking at once, said that was it, that must be it. Every once in a while one of them would glance at her with a slidey-eyed look. Whitecaps, they called the Texas badmen. They wanted Machray to take charge of defending them against the whitecaps on that train.

"Hem! Hem!" he said, bouncing on his toes, and scowling and grinning at the same time, pleased as punch. He asked if Andy Livingston had been consulted, who was president of the association.

Livingston had been sent for, but they understood Machray was a military man, with medals for it.

Machray said "Hem!" some more while she felt anxiety and amusement rubbing together.

"We saw you signed on with the new association, Lord Machray," the first one said, and one of the two squeezed in the doorway said, "Expect those fellows from the old one don't like you much better'n they do us."

"They have not been liking me for a fairish time longer than they have not been liking you, my man," Machray said. He asked if they had discovered the destination of the mysterious train.

"It has not got to Miles City, so it has stopped somewhere between."

"Ah!" Machray said, and paced and rubbed his chin some more. "A couple of you had better ride out along the tracks, then."

They had fellows doing that.

Machray slapped his hands together with a crack that made them jump. "Very well!" he said. "Very well, then! The Rubicon it is. Gentlemen, I will meet you in my offices in twenty minutes!"

When the delegation had gone, bumping and bumbling and pardoning each other, Machray gave her a slap on the bottom. "That's what's to become of me!" he crowed. "Captain Machray at your service! A fine thing to be needed in one's chosen profession, eh, my girl?"

She had not always found it so in hers. She did not think he should take up with a bunch of frightened grangers, need him or not, but she did not say so. He sent her to bring Mary Hardy to him.

Mary appeared, in her young girl's dress, with her crippled hand held to her breast, wearing a secret smile. Machray paced before her, frowning.

"Mrs. Benbow has told me of some rumors about the house," he said. "That you have urged the girls to inquire into certain matters. For instance, a committee of the Stockraisers Association that is dedicated to violence. What do you know of this, my dear?"

Mary said there was such a committee.

"And what progress has it made?"

"I—don't know that."

"Might a band of mercenaries have been brought into the Bad Lands on devil's work?"

Mary nodded. "Mr. Huggins bragged of something like

291

that to Florrie—but she didn't know what he meant. Gunmen hired in Texas. Major Cutter to be the officer."

"Yes, he would be," Machray said dryly, pacing again.

"My father is chairman of that committee!" Mary said.

She thought she had never known a woman so filled with hatred as this girl standing before Machray, in her child's dress, smiling, her face bright with color. Her father had mistreated her, even to arranging the murder of her lover, if the girl was to be believed, and she was as tireless and determined on his track as a hunting dog. Cora had only contempt for dissemblers of Yule Hardy's stamp, but she was beginning to feel some pity for him.

"I believe men are to be murdered," Mary said.

"Who, my dear?"

"Some Texans who have come here with a herd. I don't know if there are others also."

"Did Florrie hear that from Huggins?" she asked, and Mary nodded.

"To what end, my dear, this investigation of yours?" Machray asked.

"To discover the truth!"

"Ochone, I must say that I do not find the truth very often palatable," Machray said, rubbing his chin.

"I was raised to seek the truth!" the girl said. She asked why Machray wanted this information.

"It is my intent to assist the fellows who are threatened by this army. It does appear that they need help."

"I would like to accompany you, Lord Machray!"

She vowed that Mary Hardy would not spend another week under her roof. Machray was smiling and shaking his head.

"Not today, my dear. Johnny and Dickson and I will take a bit of a ride to observe the activity about the countryside, after which decisions must be made. Later on, perhaps, you may help us spread consternation in the ranks of the Midianites."

"I will consider that a promise," Mary said, and went out with her bright, set face.

"Heart full of vengeance, like a true Highland lassie," Machray said, while she sat on the bed, in her pearl gray gown, to remove the pins from her Chicago hat.

He seemed to know what she was feeling, for he said, "A virgin is more honored in the breech than otherwise." He laughed then, squaring his shoulders. "Will you wish me well, my dear?"

She wished him well in this his latest enterprise, and he set off, whistling.

3

Andrew was riding west along the dry coils of Signal Creek with Joe Reuter, looking for strays from the saddle band, when they heard the dry popping sound, like Chinese firecrackers. They drew up to listen.

Joe's eyes regarded him worriedly from a mask of dust. "Sounds like over at Crowes'."

They rode on, hurrying now past the eroded walls of a chain of buttes, to halt again overlooking the grassy basin where the Crowes had settled. A tuft of trees surmounted a rise of ground beyond the old line camp, and cottonwoods marked the creek. His heart beat hard and slow as he squinted toward the tiny spurts of smoke, leaning both hands on the pommel. There was no doubt that it was gunfire, men among the trees firing on the shack, and the fire returned.

"There is a bunch of them, Andy," Joe said.

His throat felt parched. "What are we going to do to help?"

Joe scraped his gauntlet over his mouth, leaving a muddy streak on his cheek. "Andy, I don't think there is anything *to* do."

He stared at the little gray flowers, with the accompaniment of brittle crackling.

"I remember when they come after Daddy," Joe said. "I was just a little feller then, but I won't forget that day. And then Chally."

Cicero kept turning his head away so that he had to jerk on the reins. Joe's spotted horse had backed up too.

He took a deep breath and said, "Get Feeney and his boy to ride for help. And ride on and tell Machray."

Joe's hot eyes stared into his. "What're you going to do?"

He unshipped his rifle. "Try to get closer. Maybe I can make them nervous." Small fish had better herd together, Davey Crowe had said; now it seemed a kind of pact.

293

"Don't you go out there!"

"They would give us a hand if we were in trouble."

"Andy, I am just not going out there. I would ruther ride through hell in a celluloid suit!"

"I just want you to ride to Feeney's. And to find Machray."

With a curse Joe slashed his crop down, and his horse reared, lunged, and swung back the way they had come. Andrew urged Cicero forward and down a shallow ravine, where ducking, he felt that his approach could not be seen. Joe had asked what he meant to do. He had no idea what he could do, except that he might, by firing and moving, give the impression that there was more than one of him, even if it was hopeless.

He dismounted and braced his rifle on the saddle. He estimated the range as about eight hundred yards, and fired two shots, aimed well about the puffs of smoke in the clump of trees. Leading Cicero, he trotted back twenty yards to fire again. He did this several times, haranguing himself to approach closer to the line shack. Now he heard the whine of bullets overhead, and one snapped past so close that he ducked. Gritting his teeth, he led Cicero closer again, and braced the rifle barrel on the saddle.

The air went out of his lungs in a gasp as he saw the riders, fast-moving star shapes headed on a course that would intersect his retreat to the buttes, eight, nine, ten of them.

Cicero circled nervously away as he tried to mount, but when he was up, needed no urging to break into an ears-back run. He could not believe he had come so far from the safety of the buttes.

The pale cliffs loomed before him finally, one with a high blush of scoria and brush straggling from the top like unkempt hair. Shots snicked past him like furious bees, and he bent his face closer to Cicero's heaving neck. Suddenly he was in the shade of the buttes. Cicero was grunting now with every stride, hoofs kicking clay dust from the steepening incline, stumbling once. Then they were over the rise and into the first defile. "Good Cicero!" he said. "Good boy!" The sweating horse stumbled again. Groaning, he began to hobble; then he halted, panting and heaving.

Andrew's legs almost buckled as he swung out of the saddle, jerking his rifle from its scabbard again. He sprinted for a fissure between two eroded crags, wedging himself

294

through into a kind of room long and narrow, open to the shade of higher buttes, with a runneled wall on one side and a narrow, crumbling blade of clay on the other. Panting as though his lungs would burst, he jerked loose the strap that secured his revolver in its holster and, leaning against the earth wall, laid his rifle stock against his cheek and aimed past Cicero, who stood with one foreleg raised to balance on a hoof tip, head down and reins dragging.

Three of them came through the slot between the buttes in a bunch. When he fired one instantly disappeared from his saddle, while the others drew up savagely, horses rearing to their haunches. He fired again, cursing himself for his haste. The first horse sped on past his field of vision, the rider's boot visible but the man clinging to the off side like a circus rider. Then he was gone. Cicero hobbled a few steps in his wake, to halt again. The other riders surged back out of range just as others came up, all retreating in disorder while he fired into the pack of them.

The silence was enormous, though after a moment the distant crackling began again. With quick jerks of his head he examined his fortress, a corridor of clay walls with a crook in it so that he had to lean far sideways to see from end to end. The cruciform of a hawk floated over, very high. At least he was in shadow, and not full sun; already his throat was dusty with thirst. He counted the cartridges in his belt, fingering their smooth brass rims like coins. Twenty-five remained, and four rounds in his revolver.

He withdrew from his slot to run, crouching, to the rear entrance of his room, where there was a heap of tumbled clay clods. He would have to take care that the rider who had sped past did not sneak in behind him. Back at the other end he wedged himself into his crevice again with his rifle aimed toward the cleft in the buttes where the main bunch had disappeared, but glancing frequently behind him. Minutes crawled by.

Dust kicked into his eyes an instant before the report. He fired—at nothing, and cursed. But presently he spied the crown of a hat behind a low ridge, fired, and saw the hat spin away. A voice in his ear said, "Twenty-three."

He trotted to the rear entrance for a survey, then back again. Cicero had moved out of his field of vision. He could not seem to stop panting.

The sun in its course rose until his refuge was bathed in heat and light. Sweat dripped into his eyes, and he twisted a button from his shirt to suck upon. He trotted continually back and forth. He had spotted three of them now, one behind the low ridge, whose hat he had knocked off, another further back, the third up a gully and placed behind a clay crag. He had heard them calling to each other, Texans by their accents. There was no sign of the circus rider.

The ones he had located were so well concealed he knew he was only firing to keep them from advancing—but fire he did. "Twelve," the voice said in his ear. He tried to moisten his mouth sucking on the button with its bit of thread attached. Far off there would be frequent pauses in firing at the Crowes' camp, but always it resumed. The farthest Texan rolled sprawling down to gully slope to cover lower down, and he fired and saw dust fly, an instant too late. There was another one still farther up, he noted. On leaden legs he trotted back for a look out the rear entrance, this time to glimpse a boot tip protruding from behind the edge of a clay bank. He fired and the boot was jerked from sight. "Nine." He lurched back along the familiar track to wedge himself in his crevice again, rifle stock braced against his cheek. Abruptly the sun was gone.

There was a rapid firecracker popping from beyond the buttes that ceased in a terrible silence. Despair cramped his bowels. *Maybe if he surrendered, if he had not wounded any of them, they might—* A triangle of blue shirt showed, the man farthest up the ravine. He brought the blade of his front sight up carefully beneath that triangle, gritted his teeth, held steady, and fired. The bit of blue disappeared with a howl. "Eight," a voice whispered in his ear. "Got you, you son of a bitch!" he yelled.

A bullet snapped past his hat, and he stumbled back against the clay wall. There was a man on top of one of the buttes now. He must keep close to the inner face. Another bullet whacked into the clay close by him as he reloaded. Now there were three more cartridges left in his belt, four in his revolver.

Someone called his name.

He jerked his rifle barrel around as a man came into sight from the left, the circus rider, limping, hands stretched high above his head. He was hatless, balding, with a beard-stubbled face. Behind him rode Machray on a tall sorrel, his over-and-under gun trained over the horse's head on the man's back. They marched slowly forward, the circus rider once casting a careful glance over his shoulder.

"Livingston!" Machray bellowed.

"Here!" No sound came from his caked lips. *"Here!"*

Machray's face flashed toward him beneath the hat brim, "Lay in on this laddie," Machray said. "If anybody takes a shot at me, blast his liver out. Where're the others?"

The circus rider gazed at him with a perfectly blank face as he aimed at the fellow's belt buckle. "There's one on top of the butte there," he said. "Two up the gully, and one behind the ridge—the rest straight ahead, I think."

"Here's the drill," Machray said. "We are coming over your way very easy, with my friend here always sticking out straight ahead of me just like I had him on a line to my muzzle—yes, that's right, my man," he said, as the Texan limped forward. "Then when I am between you and the other sods out there, Livingston, you will come out to join our little procession. Whereupon we will swing about, my friend still leading the way, very slow and easy. And you will shoot the backbone out of him if any of these other lads so much as threaten my health. Understood, Livingston?"

"Understood."

"Understood, my man?"

The circus rider muttered something, hands still stretched high.

"Understood, out there?" Machray roared.

There was no answer. "Move," Machray said.

The sorrel sidled, turning, the circus rider sidestepping to stay in front. The toe of his boot had been shot away, Andrew noticed with satisfaction. Bloody stocking showed in the hole. Machray snapped his fingers, and, rifle trained, Andrew squeezed out of his crevice to take up a position close beside Machray's stirrup.

"Forrrrrrrrrwarrrrrrrrd!" Machray bawled. "Slow and easy," he said more quietly. The circus rider, with another cautious glance over his shoulder, limped forward. The sorrel followed close behind, with Andrew at Machray's stirrup, rifle trained on the leader's back. They paraded on along the winding trail through the buttes. He did not look behind them.

The Texan's horse was tethered to a bush, and Machray untied the reins and pulled the animal into line. After about a half mile Andrew mounted, and he and Machray rode on together, leaving the Texan limping back in the direction of his fellows.

Machray spurred his sorrel to a pounding trot. "Stroke of

luck I happened on Reuter," he called. "Quite by chance! Now we must do something for those other poor devils."

He said he thought that it was too late.

Machray rose in his stirrups to wave his hat as Goforth appeared out of the shadow of a butte, riding hard. The foreman reined up, pulling his mare to her haunches. His face was a mask of dust, pale eyes blazing from it.

"They have done their work there and comin on," he said. "Looks like about seventy of them. Fight or run, I'd say."

"Well, let us run for now," Machray said. "And fight with better odds."

4

Revived by a whiskey in the saloon and supper bolted down at the hotel, Andrew made his way back to Machray's offices through a Main Street crowded with men in heavy jackets carrying rifles. A fan of them was gathered before the building whose facade flickered with the light of torches propped upright in empty kerosene cans. Above the doorway were the letters set in brick: MACHRAY.

Faces turned to him as he passed, and men called out: "Here's Livingston! Here's Andy Livingston!" Hands were stretched out to shake his. "What do you make of it, Andy?" someone called, and another: "Heard they almost got you!"

His neighbor Feeney caught his arm, and when he halted he was instantly the center of a clot of men demanding to know what had happened.

Inside the building men were jammed still more closely together in a bitter stench of sweating bodies. "Here's Andy Livingston!" someone called, and Machray's voice boomed out, "Welcome to the war room!"

He stood behind a desk covered with maps, wearing his short woolen jacket with captain's pips on the shoulders, kilts and sporran, a cartridge belt and holstered revolver. A khaki-covered pith helmet rested on the desk with the maps.

"Quiet out there, gents, if you please!" he bawled. "The president and the captain are conferrin'!" He said to Andrew, "Come around here and we'll take a look at what is known."

Machray's finger jabbed at the map. "Engine, coach, and one boxcar came through about three A.M. One of the telegrapher laddies was curious enough to pursue the matter. Ffty armed men left the town of Presle, and unloaded roundabout Big Fork Station." His finger jabbed down twice more.

"We know they headed due south for the Crowes' line camp, where you encountered them." He traced the route on the map, then straightened. "And where would they be headed next?"

"Fire Creek Ranch?" he said.

He and Machray gazed at each other, Machray scowling and scratching his chin. He asked what Machray planned to do.

"Summoned some chaps for a council-of-war. I say, have you noticed the numbers of the fellows waiting outside there? 'Thick as the autumnal leaves that strow the brooks in Vallambrosa,' eh?"

There was a rising disturbance outside, yelling, some message repeated. They began to call inside the building: "They are at the CK! They have holed up at the CK!" A man poked his head in the door to relay this to Machray.

Machray was tracing the route on the map. "Gone to earth at Mogle's, then. Well, that is convenient. Dickson?"

"Right here, Captain!"

"Trot over to Mrs. Benbow's and inform the lady that she and her girls are in charge of feeding these men. Cannot lead them out of town without food in their bellies. Tinned meat, sandwiches, coffee—whatever she is able to provide. Where's that storekeeper? Parkinson?"

"I'm here, Lord Machray!" a man called from the corridor.

"You are to open your establishment to Mrs. Benbow and keep tabs on her acquisitions!"

"Never mind the tabs, Lord Machray! It is on me!"

There were cheers for Parkinson. Someone called in the door, "What about Mrs. Benbow's girls, Machray? No tabs there either?"

Machray glowered; he looked like Punch. "We have an old saying in the Scots regiments, lads. 'A tot o' rum before the guns, but nae bit o' gash till after!' "

Laughter exploded. Machray winked broadly at Andrew, who looked around at the laughing, admiring, worshipful faces of the men Machray knew well how to win to his com-

299

mand. These same men had unanimously elected Andrew Livingston president of their association, but they would follow Machray into battle.

Men began to push their way into the office for the council-of-war: Cheyenne Davis with his dark, big-nosed face; Johnny Goforth, taut and mettlesome as a thoroughbred horse, with his bleak grin; the granger Strake, hat in hands. Machray produced cigars, and soon the room was blue with smoke. Pointing a pencil at the CK ranch, Machray explained the situation.

"If they have got Cutter for captain we are in luck," Goforth said.

"He may not be such a military fool as he is in other matters, Johnny," Machray said. "Now: We know their numbers. Fifty of them, and some local laddies besides. Johnny counted about seventy in all. The fifty Texans riffraff for the most part, one would imagine. No very strong commitment to anything but their own continuing good health. Still, one must not underestimate the adversary."

"The ones I had to do with seemed committed enough," Andrew said. Goforth's grin flashed.

"Pack of killers!" Cheyenne Davis growled. "I say we had better find us a gulch and wait for them there!"

Strake seconded that, nodding and chewing on Machray's good Havana.

"Hold on a bit," Machray said. "Best define our purpose here. Livingston?"

"We are defending ourselves," he said.

"Their purpose bein to kill some others like they killed Ben and Davey Crowe," Davis said.

"We know their numbers, and something of their purpose, and can make a guess at their quality," Machray said. "What we don't know is where they are heading next. If we could be sure they were headed *here*, we need only find Mr. Davis' gulch and await them. *Or* we could ride out to meet them. How far to Mogle's?"

"Three hours' ride," Goforth said.

"That is the thing to do," Strake said.

"Best allow four hours with this great lot," Machray said. "Now: The foe should be up at dawn and on his way—whatever way that is." He consulted his gold watch. "So we had better be on ours by three—say two thirty. Then we will be on hand when they rise for their morning piss."

300

"What is it you have in mind we are going to *do*, Machray?" Davis demanded.

"We are going to arrest them," Andrew said. "They have murdered two men."

"That is correct," Machray said to Davis. "Moreover, I expect there is some law against the importation of private armies even within the woeful legal code of this territory. We will arrest the lot, and take them into Mandan to be bound over for trial. I believe it is our only course."

"We have got no more claim on legality than those bastards," Davis said.

"I believe we have," Andrew said. "We did not come here secretly, by dead of night. We have armed only to defend ourselves. We have only convened against what has been criminally convened against us. We have murdered no one, nor is that our intention."

"Hear! Hear!" Strake said.

"Speak for yourself!" Davis growled. "For I will give you more of a bill of indictment than that. Some of these may be a ragtag of Texans, but some is plain whitecaps. Do you know how those fellows outside here feel about what's been goin on in the Bad Lands? I expect they feel strong enough to do murder on somebody fixin to do murder on them. They will plain chew up the gang at the CK and spit out the buttons! Just how is it you propose to stop them?"

Machray had drawn himself up a head taller than anyone else. "*I* will tell you how, my man! I have been appointed to lead those fellows outside, and lead them I will. They will chew when I say chew, and spit when I say expectorate, or stay behind!"

"Well, if we are only going out to *arrest* somebody, I would just as soon *stay* behind," Davis said. "Get shot at without doin any shootin."

"And so you will, if I so order it," Machray said. "And certainly you may stay behind!"

"Hell I will!" Davis grumbled. "But I have got a itchy trigger finger, Machray, and it is not the only one about!"

"You will submit your finger to my direction, Mr. Davis," Machray said. Arms folded, Goforth was gazing coldly at Davis.

"Done," Davis said, and grimaced.

"Well, I believe it is time to make an announcement to the assembled," Machray said. He donned his khaki topee, gave

301

it a tap, and led them outside through the men jammed into the corridor. Before the building, by torchlight, there was prolonged cheering. Machray caught Andrew's arm and thrust him forward: "This is your job, Livingston."

Afterward he could not remember exactly what he told that silent mass of men. He began by saying that they were in good hands. Machray, who had consented to take command, had, as no doubt they all knew, been a captain in the British Army, decorated for bravery, and wounded in Egypt. They had an experienced and an honorable leader, and it was their responsibility to conduct themselves with honor also. The gunmen who were their enemy had been hired by the same frightened and arrogant men responsible for the band of Regulators, the whitecaps, that had spread terror through the Bad Lands until the Crowe brothers had taken their measure. Who had been murdered by these gunmen.

Those assembled here, for the most part members of the Bad Lands Livestock Association, would show themselves more temperate men than their persecutors, who were members of the old association. They would not themselves become "Regulators." They would harry this enemy force if it endeavored to come further into the Bad Lands, they would pursue it if it fled, they would capture it and transport it to Mandan, where these men would be tried and their guilt established by law before they were punished. In every way they would show that they were more lawful men than their enemies, who had proved themselves outlaws.

When he finished and stepped back between Cheyenne Davis and Johnny Goforth, there was a short silence. Then Machray waved his topee and shouted, "Bravo, Livingston!" and they cheered to the echo.

Afterwards they adjourned to the saloon where they bellied up to the bar, the other patrons making room for them. In the warm saloon, he remembered the warmth that night he had spent with Joe Reuter and the Crowes in the line shack, the warmth of men dependent upon each other in the face of an enemy. There was backslapping, hailing, threats, bravado, and anxiety, but he was proud to feel that same general pride he recalled from the night the new association had been organized.

Soon enough, however, there was a metallic beating outside, and they crowded into the street again. Men were mounting and gathering by torchlight, Machray, brass-voiced, dividing them into three groups, his own in the vanguard, Cheyenne Davis in the center, and Andrew to bring up the rear. Andrew watched Machray ride out in the lead, taller than anyone else and capped by the round helmet of his topee. Mary Hardy materialized, all in black, with a black hat and long, nodding feather, to ride at Machray's side. It did not surprise him to see her there.

His own company fell into line, and they rode out of Pyramid Flat under high, diamond stars. Frigid moonlight fell across the wagon tracks gouged into the gray clay. From time to time he glanced back at the shrouded double line of men following him, glint of rifle barrels, collars turned up against the cold. Now, riding through the sharp-cut hues of moonlight and pitchy black, his speech of a few hours past seemed to him much too simple, like the shadows that would lose their sharp edges when daylight came at the CK, blurring into the ambiguities he dreaded.

Somewhere up ahead the pipes began to play, sending shivers crawling up the backs of his legs.

By first light they looked down upon the CK buildings from a saddlebacked knoll, a long log house with three chimneys regularly spaced and a roofed veranda running its length. Facing it was the bunkhouse, a structure of the same size but lacking a veranda. A hundred yards farther on was a log stable, and a corral in which the heads of horses angled and tossed. Smoke drifted from two of the chimneys to form a low-lying gauze over the ranch buildings.

There were three wagons roughly aligned, and a figure sluggishly climbed from beneath one of them to prod a fire into flame, grunting in the still gray air. Others appeared, breath smoking. All at once the area between the buildings and around the wagons had thickened with moving men. Abruptly the motion halted, as though the scene had frozen, pale blobs of faces turned up toward them on their knoll.

With Mary Hardy's help, Machray fastened a large white handkerchief to a stick. Holding this aloft he trotted his bay down a slope toward the Regulators gathered around the fire and moving forward between the wagons. Andrew had already counted more than fifty there.

Machray was a splendid figure in his topee and jacket of military cut. He had removed his chaps and wore his kilts, plaid stockings, and gaiters. A man on a black and white horse rode to meet him; they halted facing each other, Machray holding up his flag of truce, the two horses nervously wheeling until they had completed a half circle. Presently Machray trotted back up the hill, the other back to the CK. The hoofs made a dark trail through the frozen grass.

Halting beside Cheyenne Davis and Andrew, Machray said, "I've given them half an hour." Mary Hardy sat her sidesaddle twenty yards away, gazing down upon the CK buildings. Machray consulted his gold watch. The east grew lighter. Someone dropped his rifle with a metallic clatter shocking in the silence. Machray instructed Davis where to take his men, parading them in full view to the right, while Andrew proceeded with his to the left; to situate each other so that, if it came to firing, they would not be shooting at each other across the ranch buildings.

As he led his sixty men parallel to Davis' movement, he saw that Machray had brought his own company up on top of the twin knolls so that the Regulators could see the size of the force arrayed against them.

It was clear, however, that they did not intend to surrender. The CK bustled with activity. The wagons were manhandled into a row between the two buildings, and timbers stacked before them. The man on the black and white horse, who must be Major Cutter, was very much in charge, trotting here and there to direct matters, shrill snatches of his commands audible. The CK had begun to resemble a fort.

He dismounted his men behind high ground, with the horses secured in a rope corral, and deployed them along the ridge. Davis' men were visible similarly arrayed, and Machray's had retreated behind the twin knolls. The sun, fat and orange, appeared in the east, misty along the bottom, visibly separating from the jagged sweep of the land. He could see more riders coming from the direction of Pyramid Flat. There was a squeal of bagpipes. Rifle fire crackled, and he saw the little gray bursts of smoke all around the CK. "Fire!" he yelled.

Rifles cracked around him. He lay in the damp grass with his rifle stock against his cheek, squinting down the barrel to catch a crouching figure in his sights. Carefully he raised the blade of the front sight; they had computed the range as two hundred yards. The butt jammed against his shoulder. The figure dived for cover, patch of face turned toward him, dust drifting where the bullet had struck. He levered and aimed again, but this time found nothing to aim at. Gradually the clatter of gunfire settled to occasional exchanges. Bullets whipped overhead.

During the morning a crew came by twice with a five-gallon tin of water and dippers. Another appeared with bread and sardines. About noon there was a commotion; a wagon had arrived bearing the bodies of the Crowes. He went to view them, the charred trunk of Davey Crowe, head and limbs gone, Ben Crowe's body with its thirteen wounds and terrible face. The note found in Ben's pocket was passed around, Ben's last words on one side and the Regulators' on the other. Men stood around the wagon with their hats off while Dickson marched behind the knolls playing sad music. "Manburning sons of bitches," the men said when they came back from seeing the corpses.

Riders continued to appear from the direction of Pyramid Flat, seeming more whiskered and tattered than the original force, as though these latecomers had come from farther away, from poorer claims. If he had been astonished at the first meeting of the new association at how many grangers and small ranchers lived hidden among the buttes and breaks of the Bad Lands, he was more astonished now.

Wagons arrived throughout the day with supplies, ammunition, and water; Strake's work as quarter-master. Machray rode over to inspect his line, and drew him off beyond the corralled horses.

"Livingston, the mood is very bad since the men have seen those poor cadavers. I believe we have been ill-served by their being brought here. I have given orders for the construction of a movable fortress. An armored wagon. This will take some time to complete, and one hopes murderous ardors will have cooled by that time. Can you control your men?"

He said that he didn't know.

Machray stared at him coldly. "You *must*, sir! Livingston, you and I have been chosen for the positions we hold because of certain intellectual and moral qualities, with which others may not have been so fortunate as to be endowed. We must put these qualities to effect. I have sent several messages to the sheriff in Mandan that he must come here and take command of us as a *posse comitatus*, but I am certain he will delay as long as possible. Meanwhile these fellows in their present mood would slaughter those down there to the last man."

"Those down there have brought it on themselves."

Machray gave him one more look and began to pace, hands clasped behind his back. Andrew sighed and said, "I think I could control my men if I had time to get acquainted with them."

"It will take some time to get our go-devil into operation," Machray said.

That afternoon Andrew sent his men in groups of four over to watch the construction of the "Ark of Justice," which served to allay their impatience. Saplings were wired in crossed layers upon the running gear of a wagon, six feet tall and with baled hay backing the logs. Meanwhile dynamite bombs were being constructed. Machray rode up and down with his ever-present cigar, and Mary Hardy always by him in her black riding habit and sweeping feather. She gave Andrew a regal smile when they encountered each other.

Men practiced pushing the Ark's enormous weight behind the knoll, out of range of the CK. There was no way to determine if the concentrated fire from three directions was having any effect upon the invaders, although through Machray's binoculars the logs around the barricaded windows were so thickly perforated they resembled pepper boxes. Andrew himself, after his first shot, no longer tried to find an exposed Regulator to aim at, but only occasionally pulled the trigger in order to swell the volume of fire. Dickson continued his piping, which sound must have been unnerving to the besieged men.

Toward nightfall Andrew was summoned by Machray to witness the first sortie of the Ark of Justice. There was a lull as it appeared on the top of the hill, then all the fire from the CK was concentrated upon it as it lurched forward, propelled by twelve straining men. It halted while one of the men limped back with a bullet-creased ankle. The only casualty so far was instantly loaded into the hospital wagon, with Mary Hardy and Doc Micklejohn in attendance. The doctor had brought the message that one of the invaders had been captured—none other than Bill Driggs.

Presently the Ark broke down, and apparently could move no more until repairs had been effected under cover of darkness. "Postponed!" Machray cried theatrically, striking his brow with his hand. "The very word is like a knell! We'll have to extend our lines tonight to insure that they don't make a break for it!" He ordered the shooting of the Regulators' horses. They began to go down in the corral, kicking, to sharpshooters' bullets.

The killing of the horses, and the news that Bill Driggs had been one of the Regulators, depressed Andrew, and he returned to direct the extending of his lines before the sun set.

Machray appeared at nightfall, to declaim to astonished grangers:

> "Poor naked wretches, whereso'er you are
> That bide the pelting of this pitiless storm,
> How shall your houseless heads and unfed sides,
> Your loop'd and window'd raggedness, defend you
> From seasons such as these?"

He instructed Andrew in the keeping of the watches, and confided that he thought the invaders would surrender in the morning. "It will be a long and dreary night for those laddies," he said, and spurred away.

That night, sitting at the campfire behind the ridge, Andrew got to know some of his men. All were strangers but Buddy Feeney, who stuck close by him, wearing worn overalls and a battered hat, but with a rifle that appeared in good repair and always his ready rabbit-toothed grin. The others, also, were grangers, except for one older, hard-bitten small rancher. Two of them spoke no English, Germans from Prussia who had come to the Bad Lands because of the railroad's advertisements for cheap land of marvelous fertility. Questioned in his schoolboy German they did not seem to regret their immigration. Others were Southerners, Nebraskans, Pennsylvanians; some raised cattle, the older man thirty head; most did not. All, however, had been terrified by the white-caps' reputation, even if they had seen one only today for the first time, running for cover behind the wagons at the CK, and hated them with a vengeance. They called them "Man-burners." Some had never been through a Bad Lands winter, more had been through one, a few two or three. He found himself arguing with them the suitability of the Bad Lands for farming as against grazing.

"Well, we would all like to be livestock raisers like yourself, Andy Livingston," one said. "But it do require something most of us have not got."

When he asked what this was, the man just scratched his palm with his thumb, grinning, and all who heard the exchange laughed.

He asked if they hated the big cattlemen, or just those responsible for the whitecaps. This time the older man answered, scraping a thumb over his stubbled cheek. "Maybe not so much. Maybe we would all like to be like that. Then we would act the way they do. Though a fellow would like to believe he would not go to manburning."

"I guess I will remember that one they burnt," Buddy Feeney said. "The time I seen him before he was helpin us fight range fire. And this time burnt like that."

Someone swore. Andrew could feel the bright warmth of the fire on his face. The older man hunkered closer, his eyes black pits in his face.

"You will notice you can tell how long a man has been in this country," he said to Andrew. "Those Krauties there—" He indicated one of the Germans with a jerk of his thumb. "They just naturally hate any man who is over them because in the old country they could not get past him. One man is up, and another down, and that is the way it stays. But in this country you do not hate like that, for with a little luck, maybe just hard work and time, you can be there yourself." He grinned, a third dark pit in his face, this one decorated by an incomplete set of teeth. "Well, it is too late for this old bastard, but I have got two boys. There is a good chance for them. So I don't hate so much as I uster."

There was agreement and disagreement with this. A man spoke up in a southern voice. "They are trina do the same thing in this country as in the old countries, old man. Those manburners we are going to flush out of there in the morning. They got in early and they will bust a gut to see nobody else gets in. I have seen it in Texas, and I have seen it happenin here the same. I hate their guts so I can taste it like spoilt bacon, and my people are so long in this country I never even knew who come over from where."

At dawn the repaired Ark of Justice resumed its jolting progress down the hill, stalled for long minutes by one obstruction or another, its progress cheered, and its halts met with groans. The Regulators continued to focus their fire upon it, though less and less heavily as though conserving ammunition for the final rush. The besiegers held their own fire, fascinated watching the Ark's halting, lurching progress. Finally the Ark gained the level ground at the foot of the hill and halted once more, men crouching behind it resting.

Machray on his bay appeared on top of the knoll, waving

the white flag for a parley. Immediately a similar flag appeared behind the barricade. Machray rode on down the hill, and Major Cutter climbed over the barricade to meet him. Negotiations began.

With Buddy Feeney's help, he placed his men at intervals along one side of the rutted wagon track, while Cheyenne Davis did the same on the other. Machray's larger company was arrayed upon the knoll behind them, Machray seated on his horse with a cigar slanting from his chin, the brim of his topee shadowing his eyes. Mary Hardy sat sidesaddle beside him, her feather twisting and bending in a little breeze that had come up.

Led by Major Cutter, the Regulators filed out between the wagons of their barricade. One man had a slinged arm, another a bandaged leg, a third was carried on a stretcher covered with a gray blanket. The arrangement had been that they leave their arms in one of the wagons at the CK, and now they trudged unarmed up the hill between the files of men. Andrew counted sixty-eight of them. First came the major, proud-jawed and erect, and staring straight ahead, then a ragged double line of mercenaries. After a space came the cattlemen, Yarborough, Mogle, Huggins—he did not see Yule Hardy. Jake Boutelle's eyes flashed blackly at him as he passed. Fred Rademacher walked beside his father, who had a bandaged arm. Jeff Hardy was accompanied by another half-grown boy. The tiredly swaggering men trudged on up the wagon track between the lines of their captors. Several were limping, and two fat-bellied men trailed behind. Andrew studied that old cattleman's shape of melon belly, narrow hips, and slack buttocks. The last man caught his eye and spat tobacco juice.

Mary Hardy's black mare danced sidling down the hill to ride along behind Davis' men on a parallel course with her brother. "Where is F-father?" she called, in a clear voice.

Jeff's reply was inaudible. His eyes showed scared white as he glanced at his sister.

"Hoor!" a voice said from the ranks of the cattlemen, and Jeff lurched around, fists clenched, pale dirty triangle of face twisting.

"Manburner!" one of the grangers called, and Jeff jerked toward him, panting open-mouthed.

"Quiet there!" Andrew said to the granger. He waved a peremptory arm at Mary Hardy, and the black mare retreated. Above, Machray sat his bay staring down with a set face.

"Whore," another cattleman said conversationally, and Jeff Hardy was jerked around again, as though by a string.

"Get along *quiet,* you sons of bitches, if you know what's good for you!" Cheyenne Davis called out, and that was the end of it.

Wagons were drawn up just beyond the knoll, and the invaders were loaded into them. Eigen, the secretary of the Livestock Association, wrote down their names as they queued up to climb into the wagons and sit slumped in the hot sun. Finally the five wagons began to creak into line, following Machray and Mary Hardy, companies of men riding along on either side, and behind, with more wagons following.

Crowded into the wagons, hip to hip and shoulder to shoulder, hands between knees, the cattlemen watched Andrew as he rode alongside. He could feel the hatred like an oppression in the air, and he wondered if it was ever possible to recover from such hate, like a cancerous disease. From each wagon a pair of eyes or two stared at him fixedly, out of dirty impassive faces, Jeff Hardy's slack-jawed and sweating. He met Boutelle's hard, black eyes; Boutelle made a curt, commanding gesture with his head, and he rode closer.

"When this is over I will come looking for you," Boutelle said.

"I will be watching for you."

Several others in the wagon glanced up. Others glanced studiedly away. "Won't do any good," Boutelle said.

"Maybe you had better be watching for me, then."

Boutelle's eyes slitted in his dark face; his mouth slitted into a thin grin. "Huh!" he said.

Andrew reined away from the wagon, and now rode at some distance from the slow train as it wound through the hills on creaking wheels, surrounded by the Great Posse.

5

Three nesters with rifles and slung all over with cartridge belts threw down on Bill Driggs coming around a bend, calling him a whitecap, and, when he disdained to speak to them and rode on by, shot him out of the saddle.

So there he was on the ground half dead with one broken arm and the other gunshot, bleeding like a hog while the nesters stood over him arguing whether they should kill him or just let him bleed to death. In the end they bound him up, though a wall-eyed tobacco chewer was of the opinion it was a deal of trouble for nothing. He was hurting so that he was on hand only about half the time, and then cursing helpless to scratch his nose when a fly got at him, and his right arm throbbing like red-hot pokers.

First they stowed him in a soddy that stunk of slop water and cooked cabbage. Whenever he came to one or another of them was sitting by him with a rifle muzzle stuck in his eye. They had strung about fifty feet of hemp rope around him and he asked them what did they think he could do, *kick* the soddy down, or *gnaw* their balls off, though he promised to do that in time. At first it was hard to figure which arm hurt worse, the right one hot and tight, and the left like cold slivers rubbing together, but as the night passed it was clear the shot one was going to take the prize. When he slept he could hear himself snoring, and when he felt like groaning he just groaned, though they yelled at him to shut his noise. Those nesters made the hardcases of the Battalion seem first-class gentlemen, though one of them that had the makings of a human being did loosen the rope and look at his arm pretty worried.

Next day they hauled him into Pyramid in a buckboard that shook him so he couldn't brace himself against the shaking and just lay there jarring, feeling that he would crack soon and all his guts leak out like broken eggs, and not caring much either, though he did try to lie over on his broken arm because the other was swollen like a pumpkin. He could hear himself snoring like a buzz saw sometimes. He had never been this low.

311

Town looked like it had been captured by grangers, bunches of scrawny, overalled, broken-hatted fellows gathering around the buckboard to joke at him, and some loose talk of stringing him up. When he told them he was *Bill Driggs,* they had never heard of him. In the end they locked him up in the storeroom of Parkinson's store where he snored on a stack of gunnybags, and Doc Micklejohn came to see him, gave him a jolt of whiskey, and then some sweet-tasting stuff that gagged him going down and took him swooping off in great descending spirals until he could not hear himself snore anymore.

When he came to he was in a bed with yellow light bright through a window shade. He lay there bellowing like a bull when he found what they had done to him. Though the arm was gone he could still feel it burning, red-hot nerves all the way down it, elbow, forearm, wrist, and fingers. When Doc Micklejohn came back to see him, bringing whiskey, he told the Doc he would kill him and put him out of his misery after he had torn off all his arms and legs. Doc left him the quart of whiskey, and he drank it down like hitting himself over the head with a maul. Sometimes he was awake and sometimes knocked out all in a hot blur of pain, with different faces jabbering at him, and once, it seemed, Cora sitting by him washing his face with lukewarm water and a cloth, though he could have dreamed her. Somehow he got from there to jail in Mandan.

He had a cell to himself. In another cell was a half breed who'd broken a leg jumping off the jail roof trying to escape. The half-breed would yell out sometimes, "They have hurt my boddddeeee!" carrying on wailing until the jailer came and banged on the bars with stick. The breed would be quiet for a while, but then he would take it up again. "They have broke my laiiigggg!" The jailer would come stamping back banging on the bars with his stick, and sometimes he would go in the cell and bang on the breed, who, when he was gone, would whisper, "They have hurt my boddddeeee!"

He thought before he went back to Pyramid Flat to tear Doc Micklejohn's arms off he would strangle that half-breed.

The Mandan doctor came a couple of times to look at his stump and say it had been necessary and well done, though how he could tell it was necessary without seeing the rest of it was hard to feature. The doctor did fix a better sling for his other arm so he could use the hand to eat with, and he would sit staring at that gray hand that didn't even seem to belong to him, except when he thought to move the fingers they would move.

The jailer would come and sit with him sometimes, a little monkey-faced Irisher who was not busy just now with only three prisoners. The rest of the Battalion, which had surrendered, was put up in hotels. It was a puzzle that he was the only one in jail, but the jailer explained that the place wasn't big enough to hold the whole bunch, and so it had been decided to put them in hotels. The sheriff was nervous about offending anybody. It was bad luck that he had come in separate. It was bad luck, all right.

He noticed that the jailer called it "the invasion," and he asked how the invasion had looked from Mandan.

"Well, first we heard there was a big gang of rustlers raising dust over in the Bad Lands," the jailer said. "And the cattlemen over there had to hire some hardcases to quieten them down."

"That's what I heard, too."

The jailer had a way of making a clucking sound at the back of his mouth. "Then it looked just the other way round. Bunch up from Texas raising the devil, and Bad Lands folks had to get together to round them up, bring them in here. Hard to know anything for sure, these days."

"I had a friend that used to say just when you was sure of something, that was the time you was due to get *sold*."

"That so?" the jailer said. The half-breed began wailing, and he grumbled and went off.

Once he waked up from snoozing, looking first very quick for his right arm on the chance he had only dreamed it all, and then glanced up to see Jake Boutelle standing inside his cell. Jake had on a good, town suit, a fresh haircut, and his mustache waxed to points, but it was queer to see him without a cartridge belt and defensive iron.

Boutelle sat down on the stool facing him. "Bill, if we all stick together there won't be trouble for nobody."

"That so?" he said.

Boutelle brought out a fancy cigar case and offered him one. He shook his head.

"Bill, we could get you out of here if we thought there was no bad feelings. We have got to all hang together in this."

He said he didn't care much how he hung, if it came to that.

Boutelle laughed. "There'll be no hanging or anything else. These fellows have got the best lawyers to be had, and friends in high places." He stuck his cigar between his teeth and lit it, going a bit cross-eyed in the process.

"You mean they are going to get off?"

A couple of Texas fellows might have to spend a month or two in the penitentiary for exceeding orders, Jake said, but that would be the extent of it.

"Ought to see the goings-on over at the hotel, Bill. There's girls in every night, and whiskey, and champagne and fine cigars. The cook over there's a plain marvel. Now, Bill, there is some that have took against you for quitting us like you did. I will not lie to you about that."

"Well, I believe you, Jake." He half lay, half sat on his cot, looking down at his gray fingers wiggling.

"I have told them you have reason to be the hottest against Machray for what has happened to you."

He didn't understand that. He stared at Boutelle's eyes, that blinked like turtle's eyes. "Just how do you mean, Jake?"

Boutelle jerked a thumb at his off arm. "Got those grangers incited against us, is what I mean. His doing and Andy Livingston's. I know you have got accounts to settle with Machray. And others have got them with Livingston."

Boutelle kept blinking his eyes in that way, like he was very tired, no doubt too many doings at the hotel with women and champagne. But it came to him that it was more than that. Boutelle looked *old*.

Boutelle asked him if he'd heard that Yule Hardy was dead.

He hadn't, and it hit him hard.

"Dead of stroke," Boutelle said. "Just keeled right over, they said."

"Well, I saw he looked sick out there at the shooting, but I thought it was just the same kind of sick I was."

"What do you mean by that?" Jake said, very quick.

"Same kind of sick you are, too. I will tell you the account *I* have got with Machray, Jake. Don't know about you, but I do hate a fellow that has got the right on me."

He yawned like it was of no matter to him, while Boutelle puffed blue smoke. "Man is known by the company he keeps—remember the old saying, Jake? I remember I shot a robin once, that got in the wrong company. And Matty Gruby got in wrong company. And I remember old Ash Tan-

314

ner, rantin drunk, goin on about *certain*. Like hell was going to be a place where there was not one measly thing you could be *certain* on. You certain about anything anymore, Jake?"

Boutelle just looked embarrassed at him raving. He hitched his arm into his lap and worked the fingers. Sometimes they would go to sleep on him too, so he would worry about that arm off like the other, leaving him all stump.

"Funny thing," he said. "Once Cora said to me she could get me killed for a hundred dollars. You bought me *live* for a hundred. That must be about what I am worth. Of course that was when I had a arm on both sides."

Boutelle leaned toward him. "Our arrangement was a hundred in advance, Bill. You forfeited the rest when you quit us. You know that."

He shrugged.

"That money could be had, though."

He sighed. "Are you trying to tell me that you, or the Committee, or the Association, or whoever it is, will pay me the rest of my five hundred dollars if I go out and shoot Machray for them?"

"I was thinking you might be doing it for *you*, Bill." Boutelle leaned back with his hands locked around one knee and his cigar between his teeth. "There is some to think a one-arm fellow couldn't handle it."

"I thought you knew me pretty well," he said gently. "You ought to know you can't pay me to kill a man, Jake. There is things you might trick me to, but I am not a murderer. That was why I quit you out there—didn't you understand that? And Jake, *he* isn't the one that did for my arm. *You* did, getting me in wrong company; you and your bunch. I did myself, for a measly hundred dollars. My, I do come cheap!"

Boutelle just gazed at him with eyes slitted against the smoke, while he lounged on his cot trying not to pant with pain.

"I will tell you why Ash went gunnin for you, too, Jake. He was a proud man. You turned his Regulators into whitecaps on him. *Bad* company. You ruined him, and ruined me too; but you are just *pure* ruin, yourself."

He shook his head at his stupidity. "I was fretful about the ruin of the Bad Lands. Machray fencin, and others land grabbin, and the game gone, and *cows* come, and *nesters*. I should have been fretful about people ruint. That is what has been happening, and it is not Machray and Livingston, it is

315

you and your bunch. It is people's souls you are buying up, Jake, when you give money for what you are offering money for. You will be damned for it, Jake Boutelle."

Boutelle got up tiredly. His face was a bad color. "Well, if you won't do it there's others that will."

"Jake, what am I going to do about *you?* That just won't *understand?*"

Boutelle dropped his cigar, and trod on it; he took a coin from his pocket and tapped on a bar for the jailer. "You are the ruin, Bill," he said. "That's who's the ruin. I give you your chance to come back for Yule Hardy's sake, but you are not man enough anymore."

He came off his cot to catch Boutelle by the throat with his left hand, jerking Boutelle's face close to his, panting, trying to get some purchase with his body that felt off balance. Boutelle didn't even look surprised, gazing back at him with popping eyes and his mouth coming open. He got out a kind of yell.

He stood there with his legs straddled and his stump twitching like a flipper while he gripped Boutelle's throat with his gray hand. Jake's face turned purple. He thought if his arm was going to fall off it might as well come off in one last decent business, but it seemed to hold together. He could hear the jailer running, keys jangling. Then the jailer was on his back, hitting him with the stick. He kept on squeezing until Boutelle's face turned black. The jailer hit him one on the stump that almost made him faint, and the three of them toppled and went over, with Boutelle underneath and his left hand still locked on Boutelle's throat.

6

When Machray came back to her after he had led the Great Posse with Mary Hardy riding beside him, he acted as though everything was the same between them as it had always been. She would wake up at first light with him snoring beside her, the sheer bulk of him and the warmth of his body, remembering High Red so that her eyes stung and the back of her throat felt raw. Where was Red? Dead, probably. Probably dead. If she had lent him the money, and lost it, and him, he

316

would still probably be dead by now. She knew Machray must ask her for money.

She had practiced answering him in her mind. There were three different answers that she gave. Finally she thought she might say yes if he would promise to send Mary Hardy away.

So when he did ask her she said yes, she would lend it to him, but at 25 percent interest per year, which was what she knew he paid on other money he had borrowed. He nodded and said that was fine. Nothing was said of Mary Hardy.

Ever since he had been called to lead the Great Posse, he had been very chipper, no more drinking a half bottle of whiskey a day and asking for girls two at a time. He had dressed very fine for the occasion of asking her to lend him money, which she considered proper, his plaid suit and white shirt with a high collar, and cravat thick-knotted. He was very much a lord standing at his ease with one knee bent, one hand behind his back, and the other holding the cigar he had not lit yet.

"I must get off dead center, my dear," he said. If he felt any shame taking money from a woman, and a madam at that, he did not show it. "I have asked Livingston for a loan as well. His people are moneyed."

"Then he has not worked so hard for his money as some others," she said.

Machray stuck out his ball of a chin and squinted at her down his nose. "Have no fear. I have put the screws to old Minton, and he and his fellow jews must come through even if it is kicking their heels and squealing like gelded hogs. I have wired them that if they will not advance the money for the abattoir to open this fall, then it must stand idle until spring. It is a cleft stick for them. You shall have your money back within a month. I am certain of it."

"Once another man asked me for money," she said. "I told him I would not, for one way it was lose him and the money, and the other only lose him."

Machray bowed his head politely.

"It was to save his life," she said.

"You will have my personal note for ten thousand dollars, my dear."

Anyone but a fool would ask for more consideration than that, but one of the things she had thought, lying there next to him by first light, was that if a person was not a fool at least once on her life maybe that life had not been worth the living.

"I believe with a bit of luck and money that abattoir could begin operation in a fortnight," he went on, striding up and down with the cigar between his teeth and both hands behind his back. "Then what a grand opening we will have! Ribbons, and fireworks, and games upon the green, and liquor flowing, and roast beef. I will slaughter the first animal, of course! What a day we will make of it, my dear. The Bad Lands will never forget the occasion!"

"Machray, there are more important matters to spend good money on than liquor and fireworks!"

"Not so," he said, halting to squint down his nose at her again. "My dear," he said, "I believe I am in deadly danger. I do not worry for myself so much, but ill winds are blowing. There is great hate all about. Those fellows have all just been released on their own recognizance, as you know. I believe they will never be brought to trial, my dear; and perhaps it is better so. But what plottings of revenge! I do not intend to let them hunt me down to satisfy their furies, but how will we bury these dark clouds that lour about the Bad Lands?

"Fireworks and liquor, and games upon the green!" he said. "And, of course, profits. The price of beef is very bad just now, four dollars a hundredweight. I will pay higher rates than can be had elsewhere, and ship direct to the eastern markets."

"The Cattlemen's Association will not sell to you, Machray. You'll have only the scrubs from the grangers' roundup."

"Will they not sell to me? Wait until they see what I am paying. Then those bitter, bloody-minded old bastards will fall into queue. Ah, it will be marvelous to see them thank'eein' and touching forelocks when the checks are passed out. Then all the old enmities will blow away—in the deep bosom of the ocean buried! And you will have had your good part in it!"

If she said she did not care much for her part in it, and that his views on forgiveness, human nature, and gratitude did not coincide with hers, he would say yes, but then he had not spent his life in a whorehouse. So she only said that she thought her money, and Livingston's, would not go very far with such a grand plan.

"Ah, that is the lovely part!" he cried. "For with these herds lining up for slaughter and money to be made for the plucking, so to speak, then the telegrams will fly like autumn

318

leaves! Ah, the running to and fro from boardrooms to telegraph offices! The groans! The shower of sterling! For the thought of a profit lost is a torment to the jews of Glasgow!"

There had never been such a one for self-delusion, though still he could almost persuade her. But he sobered to say that demands would be made, which he would have to meet.

"I shall have to give over to a new manager."

"I believe you could not stand for that, Machray."

"I will not remain to see it, my dear."

"You will go back to Scotland?"

"To Mexico!" he said. "There is this great lost silver mine, you see. The Tayopa Mine, once the richest in all Mexico! That mine kept old Spain afloat for centuries. High in the mountains! When the revolution went against the Hidalgos, they concealed it! The poor devils who worked in the mine, entire village of them, murdered to a man. Fifty years have passed, and no one has ever found it. But now there are modern, scientific methods that can be employed by determined men, to find the Tayopa! What an adventure!" he cried, and crowed like a rooster. "Great friend of mind wants me to pitch in with him. We will make our fortunes!"

So off he would go, one way or another. A heaviness came over her. You were a jew if you scraped for profits, but seeking a fortune was proper for a lord. And it was as though he knew her thoughts.

"A fortune is necessary to a gentleman of my station, my dear," he said, with a wry smile. "I cannot go on thinking merely of adventure. A man has to settle down in his middle years."

She thought that he would never get to his middle years, for one reason or another, feeling the house creak as he stamped down the stairs with that tread she knew one day she must hear for the last time. She watched him from the window as he headed for his offices, with his silk hat on and his cigar jutting, pleased with himself and the world. He was not a man who carried hate or old wrongs around with him like a load on his back.

That same day Mary Hardy came to see her. She had moved into the hotel and would be leaving town as soon as some matters had been arranged with her mother.

"Only think! I will never have to spend another winter of my life in the Bad Lands!" Mary said, with her bright smile, and said she would not forget the kindnesses done her when she was desperate and estrayed. "I will always be grateful to you, Mrs. Benbow."

She said it was a miracle the girl's hand was so much better.

Mary colored, holding her hand in that habit she had still, as though it were a procelain hand, which it did resemble. "I believe I have you and your little organ to thank for that also, Mrs. Benbow."

Mary wore the black gown she had worn to the funeral, and black ribbons in her hair. She did not look the child with braided hair whose dress she had affected playing the organ. Perhaps with Yule Hardy buried she could forget all her wrongs. She was a smart girl who would do well with her life, now that she was no longer "estrayed." She would never end up in the cribs and the gutter, and she would never even consider lending a man like Machray money.

"Do you have plenty of money for your trip, and getting settled in California?"

"Thanks to you, Mrs. Benbow!"

"You are popular with men and can always make more."

The girl colored prettily. She seemed to do this as though she pressed a button somewhere, and the blood came up in her face. No doubt it was in her mind to marry a wealthy man. She was surprised Mary had not set her cap for Livingston. He was a regular now with Maizie, who said he had become quite ardent, having got over merely wanting to draw her bare bosom.

She asked if Mary would be sending for Mrs. Hardy to come and live with her once she was settled in her life.

"Oh, dear, no!" Mary said, and laughed at such a ridiculous thought, clutching her pale hand to her breast. "She and Jeff will be running Palisades Ranch, you see," she said. "And I do intend to travel!"

She went on to speak of the places she meant to visit once she was free of the Bad Lands. San Francisco and New York, Europe and Mexico.

When Mary had kissed her and thanked her some more and had gone, she began to think with a pain like a stab to her heart, of those places Mary Hardy had mentioned: Mary waiting in San Francisco until Machray joined her there, then going with him to Mexico to make his fortune, afterwards New York, and Europe; Mary thanking her over and over for making it possible for her to leave the Bad Lands, who had also made it possible for Machray to leave, and to join the girl in San Francisco.

She pried the top from the jar of smelling salts and sat with her eyes closed breathing the pungent scent that went through her head like cold fire.

Just then Wax came upstairs with a message that Bill Driggs had strangled Jake Boutelle in Mandan jail and needed money for a lawyer so as not to hang for it.

7

At the grand opening of the slaughterhouse, three days before the new Livestock Association's roundup was due to begin, Andrew was not displeased to see that his loan to Machray had been spent upon frivolity: fireworks, the stack of the slaughterhouse chimney draped with red-white-and-blue bunting, a band of music, a baseball game between imported teams in the meadow beyond the abattoir. The cattle to be slaughtered were penned in corrals, tossing horns and lowing, and cowboys sat on the rails watching them. The beating of drums echoed raggedly.

Men and women promenaded among the buildings, the great shed that had been burned and rebuilt still with stacks of lumber along the sides. Two workmen stripped to the waist stoked the furnace. Farther along was the mainstream of traffic, buggies and buckboards crowded together, men in derby hats, a few silk hats, many sugarloafs or worn work hats, granger women in gingham and sunbonnets. He saw cattlemen who must have backed the invasion at least tacitly, in their white hats and rusty black coats, a few with wives, old Pet Jarvis on the seat of a buckboard, his ancient spouse beside him with her black hat sporting a single motheaten feather and her face thrust forward like a hatchet.

Perhaps Machray had been right, and the festivities and the buying of cattle were the road to reconciliation in the Bad Lands. Members of the old Association who had not actually been involved in the invasion might feel free to mingle with their erstwhile enemies, but those irreconcilables of Regulation he had watched filing up the hill from the CK to the wagons had radiated hatred like a magnetic field.

Certainly none were in evidence as he made his way through the press of men, who smiled and nodded or hailed him in greeting, as many "Andy"s now as "Mister Livingston"s. Women called to him from wagon seats and he passed three of Mrs. Benbow's girls in their Sunday finery, one of them Maizie, flipping a Chinese fan aside to reveal her bright lips and wink at him. Other instruments now joined the beating drum, the tuba oompahing, shriller tones rising and swelling. On a platform flanking the long ramp to the slaughtering room the Miles City band sat with sweating faces and unbuttoned frogged tunics, horn bells gleaming in the sun. Fireworks exploded against the sky, choruses of female squeals and ooohs and aaahs following the rocket's high ejaculation and shower of gold.

Fred Rademacher stood against the corner of the building, hat brim tipped down over his eyes, one foot braced behind him. He was twisting a ready-made between his fingers.

"Hello, Fred."

Fred tucked the cigarette into the corner of his mouth and gazed at him woodenly. "Well, if it isn't the president of the Bad Lands Livestockers," he said. "Got a roundup startin soon, I understand."

"That's so. And you one soon thereafter."

"Kee-rect," Fred said. "Say, I understand those pool-outfit roundups get pretty scratchy sometimes."

"How scratchy are the legal proceedings in Mandan?"

"Not scratchy a bit," Fred said, grinning thinly. "Expect you've heard," he said.

A Mandan grand jury had brought in a true bill indicting twenty-seven John Does for murder. Meanwhile the local men had been released on their own recognizance, and the Texans and Coloradans on bail. It did not appear hopeful that justice would be served.

Men and women flowed past, jostling and chatting. Many greeted him, none Fred. "Great favorite with the nesters, I see," Fred said.

"But not with you?"

Fred cocked his head to one side and shut an eye in a parody of deep thought. "Oh, I wouldn't put it just like that," he said finally.

"How is your father?"

"Mendin. Cusses a lot. He has got a good bit of bile runnin still."

322

He felt a flicker of fear even though Boutelle was dead. Anger crowded close behind the fear; others also had bile running still. "You were along on that outing, I noticed," he said.

"Yep," Fred said. There was another rocket burst, and Andrew watched Fred Rademacher's casual eye track it.

"Approved what was done, then."

"Nope," Fred said, and turned aside to spit. "Howsomever," he said. "There's some things thicker'n water. Like your own kitchen kind."

The band ceased with a blare. Fred watched another rocket climb. "Was I on the list, Fred?" he asked. It irritated him that he could not say it easily.

"Don't know," Fred said. "Never saw it, myself." He looked at Andrew with eyes like two hot holes in his face. "Probably," he said. "There was people down on you."

"Hardy?"

Fred shrugged. "Poor feller," he said. "Just up and died. I will tell you how my daddy is, New York. He is even so wrought up against Yule Hardy for *dyin* he can hardly speak of it. About the same as Bill Driggs quittin, I believe he looks at it. Some notches off you and Machray, howsomever."

He felt again the edge of fear, with its metallic taste. "You and I reacted the same way that other time," he said. He cleared his throat. "I assumed you felt the same way I did. You said you had quit too."

"I did," Fred said. "Did!" he said more loudly as the band swung into a march. "Then this came up. Sheep or goats. Easier for you, New York." He cocked an eye at the fireworks. Andrew saw Mrs. Benbow, in shiny black, big busted, bustled, taller than anyone around her, with a set, white face; she was borne past as though unconnected with the ground.

"You know what's thicker'n water?" Fred drawled. "Bad Lands water. Too thick to drink and too thin to plow. Don't lean on me, Andy," he said. "I am here, ain't I?"

"I appreciate that."

"What's the big fellow payin?"

"Four twenty."

"Not bad, the market being what she is."

He started to turn away. "Andy," Fred said, "you be careful, hear?"

"All right," he said. Fear washed over him in a surge. "Thanks, Fred."

"Tell the big fellow he is to be careful the same."

"I'll tell him, but I don't believe that's his style."

"Well, you just let it be your style," Fred said, and gazed off in the opposite direction as though the conversation was over.

As he joined the crowd moving on along toward the cattle pens and the foot of the ramp, he found himself walking as though he were very fragile. The band continued to play. In the meadow beyond he heard the crack of a bat, saw the ball arching high, men running, a voice shrilling faintly: *"I got it, I got it!"*

"Livingston!"

Machray, hand cupped to mouth, was calling to him from the ramp. "You must come up, old fellow!"

He managed to push his way through the clot of grangers and townspeople watching the fireworks from the ramp. The band played enthusiastically. Machray's hand engulfed his.

"A great day, Livingston! Thanks to you, thanks to you." Machray wore his kilts, high stockings, gleaming white gaiters, his military jacket and decorations. He was bareheaded, and for the first time Andrew noticed that the yellow hair was shot with silver. Machray jutted his big, round chin, grinning. "Everything blythe and braulies. Music, fireworks, rustic games, some loud-frasin'—there'll be dancin' later on!" He led Andrew on up the ramp and into the cavernous cool shed, which echoed with workmen calling back and forth. He took a sledgehammer from a red-faced man in a spotless white apron and brandished it aloft.

"I'm to slay the first of the run, instructed in the niceties by an expert here, eh, Mr. Lumpkin? Come sample a spot of whiskey to restore the confidence, Livingston."

They sampled whiskey from a flat brown bottle stashed in a leather case along with a loaded revolver. The little weakening floods of fear continued to wash over him at intervals, but the warmth of the whiskey was fortifying. He told Machray of Fred Rademacher's warning.

"Ah, well, Livingston, we each of us owe our little debt which must be paid sooner or later. Not worth fretting about, I don't believe."

The band struck up another march, and Mary Hardy appeared in the shed in a black dress padded front and rear, a black hat decorated with wax grapes, and a short veil. She stood peering into the gloom nearsightedly. "Ah, there you are!" Machray called, consulting his watch.

Machray strode past her to the top of the ramp, where he could be heard bawling instructions over the music. Mary Hardy approached Andrew at an angle, smiling, supporting her hand with the other, a parasol hooked over her wrist.

"I was sorry to hear of your father's death," he said.

"Were you?" she said. "He would have killed you if he could."

She stood at a light distance from him, smiling but not facing him directly. "I am leaving here on the evening train," she said.

"Westbound, then."

"Westbound." She moved away from him to promenade a small circle in the vast room, gazing around her as she swung her parasol.

He went to join Machray, who was greeting people coming up the ramp, Pet Jarvis and his wife, Blaikie in a gleaming new hat, the officers of the Bad Lands Livestock Association and their wives, grangers and small ranchers who had been a part of the Great Posse, townsmen and women. There were Ring-cross cowboys in their best clothes, a group of clerks from the offices, Dickson in uniform, bagpipes under his arm like a leather goose. Machray bellowed down to hail Mrs. Benbow, who was accompanied by the little gunman in his low-crowned derby. She demurred, but he continued to beckon and call until the two of them made their way to the foot of the ramp and started up amongst the others, to a rustling of disapproval from the wives. The band had ceased its playing, and Dickson began to march up and down with his bag pressed beneath his arm, fingering the chanter. The thin martial skirling began.

Machray made his speech from the top of the ramp, his accent, Andrew noticed, more gummed with porridge than usual, on this blythe and braulies day. Andrew watched Mrs. Benbow watching him, stiff-faced but with a hint of pink in her cheeks, Mary Hardy watching him gripping her parasol against her breast. More people had crowded up the ramp and into the shed as Machray spoke, Fred Rademacher among them. Finished, Machray held up his arms to the assembled, shouting, "Bring them along, Johnny!"

A line of white-faced cattle surged forward from one of the pens, Johnny Goforth in the lead, the crowd separating before them.

"Make way, please, ladies and gents!" Machray bawled.

The steers wound through the crowd to the foot of the ramp, and began to mount. Machray retreated into the dimness of the shed, picking up a sledge to lean on it in imitation of Millet's "Man with a Hoe," awaiting the first steer. Men and women had packed around him in close ranks, leaving little space before him. Mary Hardy was there, and Mrs. Benbow with her man Wax, cattlemen and grangers. Machray raised the sledge.

Andrew saw Jeff Hardy crouched beside Pet Jarvis, pale-faced, ginger slash of mustache like a smudge upon his upper lip. The boy's eyes were fixed upon him, as was the third eye of the muzzle of a shiny little revolver.

He looked at death, eyes squinting at him over a shiny metal tube. The eyes met his for an interminable instant. They wavered then, and the revolver barrel slanted toward Machray, who had let the sledge drop. There were shouts. Jeff's mouth had drooped open as though shouting warnings with the rest. The gun barked with a single sharp crack that reverberated through the cavernous space.

A cowboy smashed a fist into Jeff's face, and the boy collapsed to the floor, arms and legs drawn up. The little gun was kicked clattering away. Goforth, his face bleak as old bone, took two quick steps to aim his revolver. Wax was crouching with a hand inside his coat.

"*No!*" Machray said in a stifled voice.

He held a hand to his belly, grimacing, Mrs. Benbow at his side with her face paper white. Mary Hardy, hand to her mouth, stared at her brother huddled on the floor. There was silence inside the slaughterhouse, a rising clamor outside.

"*Damn* you!" Machray gritted. "You have shot me!"

He removed his hand from his jacket, where blood blossomed like another decoration. He examined his bloody hand with distaste and pressed it to his side again.

"You ruined my sister!" Jeff said, almost inaudibly.

"Love o' Jesus!" Machray groaned. "I have been murdered for a banality!"

Goforth thrust Mrs. Benbow aside to put an arm around Machray, while Dickson moved to support him from the other side, saying, "Captain—Captain—" Machray lurched around toward the brightness of the sunlight through the doors and the halted line of steers with their ghostly faces in the shadows. Andrew heard the suck of his breath. They could not hold him when he pitched forward, falling like a felled tree.

326

They took him to Mrs. Benbow's and Goforth rode for Doctor Micklejohn, who was out of town attending a granger childbirth.

"The time he has spent in this place when he was not needed!" Mrs. Benbow said through her teeth.

Andrew stood helplessly by as the madam and Dickson undressed Machray and tried to stanch the flow of blood from the nasty little hole which looked so much less fatal than the red and white scar on his shoulder. But each time they managed to fasten down a dressing they watched it turn pink.

Andrew leaned upon the brass curlicues of Mrs. Benbow's bed while she sat on a low chair beside it and Dickson went to gaze out the window, grimacing and jerking his fist up and down, as though to materialize the doctor with that pumping action. Machray roused himself to ask for whiskey.

He tossed off the glass and swiped at his lips with the back of his hand. He glared at Andrew and the madam. "Love o' God, must I lie on my deathbed surrounded by my creditors?" He squinted at Dickson at the window. "Dickson, play me a pibroch, will you, lad?"

"Aye, Captain," Dickson said and went to parade in the corridor, playing airs and variations. Whenever he stopped Machray would rouse himself to call out, "Dickson! Play on!" Once Mrs. Benbow was called to the door and Andrew saw her conferring with her man Wax.

Machray winked at him.

"The doctor will be along soon, Machray," he said stiffly.

"And what will he do here?" Machray said. "Illuminate the room with that gleaming proboscis of his? I wish no false solace, my friend. I am a damned blood pudding inside. Cora!"

Swiftly she was at his side, bending there, outside the door Dickson's tread and the squealing music, louder, passing diminishing.

"What have you done with Mary Hardy, love?"

"I believe she is leaving on the westbound, Machray."

Machray laughed. "And is she going on the westbound of her own free will, ducks? Or because Wax has her by the arm?"

Mrs. Benbow was so long answering that Andrew thought she did not intend to reply. But at last she said, "He has gone to see that she does not change her mind."

"Ah, you have never lied to me," Machray said, and closed his eyes. He held her hand. "Do not leave me now, love."

"No," she said, one hand in Machray's, the other touching her throat. She looked at Andrew coldly.

He turned from the bed to stretch the curtain away from the window. Outside, in the late sun, a group of men fanned out into the street from the boardwalk before the house, faces turned up toward him. All were men of the Great Posse. He stared down the street for some sign of the doctor, feeling his hand clenched like Dickson's.

"Livingston, where is your pencil and pad?" Machray said. "You must sketch this. A man dying! It is something to capture, surely! Find Mr. Livingston paper and pencil, will you, my dear?"

She found a pencil, and he tore from a volume of Shelley's poetry the blank frontispiece. With the book as backing, he drew quick lines. Machray closed his eyes and Mrs. Benbow seated herself again. Dickson paraded in the hall.

"Teach the rustic moralist to die," Machray muttered. Then he said, " '*Dulce et decorum est—pro patria mori!* Do you know Latin, Livingston?"

"I know Horace."

" '*O lente, lente, currite noctis equi.*' "

"And Ovid."

"That was a lover speaking to his lady," Machray said to Mrs. Benbow. He clung to her hand. "Wants his time with her to pass ever so slow."

The music had ceased. Dickson's frantic face appeared in the doorway, eyebrows raised at Andrew in question, chin jerked toward the window. He looked out and shook his head.

" '*Timor mortis conturbat me,*' " Machray said.

"I don't know who wrote that."

"Old Dunbar. When he was sick and fearful. Dickson!"

"I can only repeat myself, Captain!"

"Repeat thyself, then!"

"Sir!" Dickson said, and withdrew. Mrs. Benbow was bending over Machray to strip off the soaked bandages. Andrew stared out the window. *Timor mortis:* the breath to cease, and the functions, the flow of the blood to stop, the heart to fail in its beating, the lungs stilled, the warmth to desert the body, leaving it as chill and pale as marble, and of that hardness. His hand aching on the pencil he drew lines without thought, the dark-haired woman bent over the dying man like a cowled nun, the man himself with his bare white torso,

328

hands and feet crossed like the effigy of a crusader. It was as though the stage scenery of his senses was stripped away, leaving his mind acute and tender as a nerve, the marble nun grieving over her marble Lord, the marble piper in the hall, and only his eye and hand alive to capture this scene.

Was it possible to learn enough of the meaning of life not to fear death? And could that meaning be simply that there was no meaning? Once, at another deathbed, his father screaming behind that terrible rictus grinning, he had decided that a deity who would contrive such a torture was beyond any comprehensible reasoning, unless He was of the fiendish nature of the very worst of mankind. God might be, as certain churches had it, a Substance, but He was not a Person one could reverence, much less love. Later, seeing his wife and daughter laid out livid and composed upon the grassy bank, not dead of torture but only meaninglessly extinguished, he had decided that there was no reason for anything. It had terrified him so that his whole condition of life had become one of terror, like a turtle deprived of his shell or Blackie in the quicksand, with every other emotion he felt relative only to that.

Now he had seen a revolver, aimed at him with full intent, unaccountably change its direction. It was the other side of an equation he had not realized had two sides, even when it had been the sheerest of chances that it was Chally, and not himself, who had been surprised by Regulators at Fire Creek Ranch.

As he turned over his sheet of paper to sketch the detail of the head thrown back on the pillow, Machray said loudly:

> "In Edinburgh town they've made a law,
> In Edinburgh at the court o' session;
> That standin pricks are faultors all,
> An' guilty o' a high transgression!

"Give me more whiskey, and I'll give ye a toast to beat all!" Machray said. Mrs. Benbow poured whiskey, and he held up the glass:

"Here's to the Bad Lands! Bounded on the east by Primeval Chaos. On the west by Divine Harmony. On the north by the Music of the Spheres, and on the south by the Day of Judgment!

"Leave us alone for a wee bit, love," he said. "Whilst I talk to Livingston man to man."

329

She left the room, skirts rustling. When she had pulled the door closed behind her the piping ceased. "Dickson!" Machray bawled, and it began again.

Andrew put down his sketch, book, and pencil, to seat himself beside the bed. The chair still held Mrs. Benbow's warmth. "Smell the stench o' blood?" Machray asked. "It is the smell of mortality, Livingston."

"I know it is."

"Think of that demented little sod killin' me when a pack of dervishes couldn't! Well, it is a lesson—no good can come of temptin' a lass half one's age with visions of paradise. Only the one royal virgin to a customer!" His laugh turned into a sigh. "See here, Livingston, you have lent me money and I canna' pay it back. The truth is, my conscience does not pain me so much owin' you money as owin' that woman. For there will be nothing left. They will send out to run the ranch and the abattoir and everything else, and hope to pick up some pieces, but I think they will pay no attention to a brothel madam's claims."

"Shall I make it up to her?"

"I would not hesitate to ask you, you know, for you have had some favor of me, but I believe she is too proud. Livingston, I am afraid, being a woman, that she will treasure her loss. But I will ask you to do anything you can to aid her. And of course there are telegrams that must be sent. Milly, the jews. Marston will know."

"I will do all I can."

Machray lay silent for a time. "And what will you do after that?"

"I'm not certain."

"Pessimistic about the future here," Machray said. "Too much bad cess running deep. I had thought a fellow of good will might cut past it, but there are too many good haters out here. I am not advising you to abandon the place, mind, only—"

"I think I should not abandon those who placed their faith in you and me."

"Aye," Machray said. "Good man." His voice was blurred. He seemed to doze. A clanging bell and single whistle blast announced the arrival of the westbound in Pyramid Flat. He heard Machray chuckle.

"Comings and goings, eh?" Machray said.

"Are you afraid?" he asked suddenly.

"Not so much, you know. Told you I had been there before, for a brief bit. Some regrets at not having achieved immortality, but of course *that* is shameful vanity."

He was silent before he continued: "I do believe there is no need of fear if a man has lived his life out, you see. Livingston, I have plowed so many women I cannot even remember them anymore. Fine black women with that marvelous redolence they have. Respectable women too. And fought brave men. And lost a fortune. Loved poetry. Built a house. Planted trees. Fathered a son. No, there is no need for fear at the end of it if ye have nae shirked the livin'. Dislike goin' before my Maker to tell him I had not properly lived the life he had given me. I would that!"

"I believe I cannot forgive my Maker death," he said.

"Ah, He has made some mistakes, no doubt of it!" Machray said. "It is commonly believed that the inclination from the ecliptic is such an error. But not death, man! *Think* of the overcrowding without it! And look! He has given us the differentiation of the sexes! And poetry!"

"As for immortality," Andrew said, "think of the mark you have left upon others."

"Thank'ee," Machray said, and closed his eyes again. "Maybe you would call that woman back to change this clammy, stinkin' affair on my belly."

He summoned Mrs. Benbow back inside and stood at the window again. He could see the orange glow of cigars and cigarettes among the crowd of men in the street and the smoke cloud from the train in the station, which Mary Hardy, with Wax standing by, would have boarded by now. Machray remained silent while Mrs. Benbow changed his dressing. Andrew could hardly make out his face now in the dimness of the room.

"I can't see," Machray said, in a matter-of-fact voice.

"It is getting dark, Machray," Mrs. Benbow said.

Andrew took up the page and the pencil, and began to sketch in more details, but he himself could hardly see and his hand was unsteady. There was a disturbance outside, and he glanced out to see men running. Over beyond the low rooflines, in the direction of the slaughterhouse, there was light. He could see the flames leaping. They had fired the abattoir. He pushed the curtain closed and held it there.

So Machray was right, and he could not remain in the Bad Lands. It was not a matter of courage, it was a matter of too much bad cess running deep, too much bile running, too

331

much hatred, which, if nothing else, must infect the object of the hatred along with the haters.

"Listen, my dear," Machray said, in a voice as soft as pigeons in the eaves. "I have a poem for you. I canna' say it is original, but it is all for you—

"Yestreen I had a pint o' wine
 In place where body saw na';
Yestreen lay on this breast o' mine,
 The raven locks o' Cora."

Mrs. Benbow, face pushed triangularly toward Machray's breast, murmured a protest. At the same moment Andrew heard the clink of couplings, the bell and long whistle, the beginning of the slow, up-grade chuffing of the westbound. He watched Machray's hand rise to stroke the woman's shoulder, and ventured another glance past the drapery to see red light glaring beyond the roofs.

Machray's voice continued:

"Ye monarchs tak the east an' west
 Frae Indus to Savannah;
Gie me within my strainin' grasp
 The meltin' form o' Cora.

"For I'll despise Imperial charms
 An Empress or Sultana;
While dyin' raptures in her arms
 I gie an' tak wi' Cora!"

"Machray!" Mrs. Benbow whispered, bending closer to him. "*Stop!*"

In the corridor the music had changed, become a dirge. "Hark!" Machray said. "Hear what he is playin' now? I knew he would come to it when he had run through the rest!" Andrew could hear him panting, and he said in a whisper, "Livingston, I am afraid Milly will spoil the lad into a perfect little prick!"

He thought Machray laughed then. He watched the dying man's head thrown back on the pillow, strong white throat extended. He listened to the rustle of breath.

"*Machray!*" Mrs. Benbow whispered. "Shouldn't you *pray?*"

332

"Pray?" Machray said weakly. "Why, o' course I should pray!" He paused, panting, before he began:

"*Ante, apud, ad, adversus*—" The second time through, Andrew joined him in the familiar Latin class mnemonic. Machray's voice trailed off. He could no longer hear the thin thread of breath.

"Machray!" he cried.

"Why, man," Machray whispered. "I was almost there. It is like before. Fellow all made of light. It is all right, Livingston!"

Afterword

1885-1911

He often wondered who had been proven right, Yule Hardy and the violent hardshells of the old Stockraisers Association, or what came to be known as the Grangers Association, which he and Machray had helped to birth that turbulent summer. Progress had won out over the Dragon Holdfast, or the Mob over the Aristocrats; but victory did not prove right. Perhaps, in the end, only history was right. For 1885 was another drought year, but despite the theories of Adam Smith, the price of beef dropped and continued to drop. The Beef Bonanza was over.

That fall a slight young man in a black frock coat that looked a size too large rode down to Fire Creek to call on Andrew. His name was Adams, and he had just been appointed prosecuting attorney in Mandan. His intense black eyes were so close together that he resembled an angry cyclops.

"You have a reputation for a game fellow, Livingston!" Adams said, jutting a pugnacious chin.

Andrew's heart sank. He knew what this was even before Adams told him. No one had been brought to trial for the murder of the Crowe Brothers, and, of the twenty-seven "John Does," only John L. Boutelle, deceased, had even been identified. But now the invaders were finally to be prosecuted.

Warrants for conspiracy had been drawn up for the fifteen men of the Stockraisers Association who had accompanied the invasion, and who were still alive and residing in Dakota Territory. Andrew was to be one of the chief witnesses against them. Would he cooperate?

He asked for time to think it over and went outside to stand looking down at the fringe of cottonwoods along the dull mud banks of the river. He had come to think that the whole matter was over and done with, a sleeping dog left to lie, and he knew Machray would have wanted it that way. They would murder him if he did this and did not flee the Bad Lands. But there were men he could not disappoint. He went back inside to tell Adams he was prepared to cooperate.

"Didn't doubt you for a minute, Livingston," Adams said and grinned wolfishly. "We will nail their scalps to the wall!"

Preparations for the nailing moved slowly. There were many delays, during which he became appalled by Adams' ignorant righteousness. The case was scheduled for trial in Mandan in June, 1886, but a change of venue was asked by the defense because of the violent emotions in regard to the invasion in the western portions of the Territory. The change was granted, to Jamestown, in the east. At the same time Adams was relieved and a new prosecutor appointed. Andrew knew that the whitecaps were never going to be punished.

Jury selection in Jamestown dragged through September. For each defendant the defense was allowed twelve peremptory challenges and the prosecution six, in addition to the normal exemptions. Over five hundred veniremen were examined, and a jury was still not empaneled. The new prosecutor moved to dismiss the case, but the defense objected on the grounds that a *nolle prosequi* would leave the defendants open to further prosecution. If there was no trial, the doctrine of double jeopardy could not prevent some new Adams appearing in the prosecutor's office and reopening the case.

Opposing counsel conferred, the requisite additional jurors were quickly found, and the trial proceeded. The defense asked for a directed acquittal, which the bench denied. Again the prosecutor moved for dismissal, and the defense objected as before. The objection was overruled. After the dismissal it was realized that the case could never be brought to trial again anyway, for under law a case tried under a change of venue, even if dismissed, could never be retried. The whitecaps were free. In the end the only invaders who were to serve time in the penitentiary were Bill Driggs and Jeff Hardy, who was eventually removed to the Asylum for the Insane in St. Paul.

Andrew did not attend the trial, which he had known would be a farce. His relief was considerable, and he thought it might also be general, for that fall the Bad Lands had other concerns.

The turmoil to the south, in Indian Territory, had increased. Boomers squatted on land, were evicted by cavalry, and returned; the southern cattlemen quarreled with the Tribal Councils; the boomers and the cattlemen also quarreled. There were range fires set, and murders. And President Cleveland carried out his threat, canceling all the tribal leases and ordering the herds removed from the reservations, including the Cheyenne-Arapaho, nearest the Bad Lands.

There was nowhere for those huge southern outfits to turn

their livestock but north, where free grass still abounded. And no one could stop them. The old Western Dakota Stockraisers Association was in disarray and disrepute, and the new Bad Lands Association was ideologically handicapped in making a stand against those herds driving north.

Through the fall of 1886 the herds came on, five thousand head here, another six thousand close behind, with the dust rising and blowing for miles. One herd of thirty thousand was dumped on the range late in the year, that worst forage year in memory. With the dead grass trampled to dust, cowboys took to wearing bandannas as masks, with holes cut for eyes. There were jokes about whitecaps and John Does come again, but fewer and fewer jokes as the fall wore on. Prairie fires were very bad that year.

There were signs of a heavy winter to come. The woolly bear caterpillars were thick-coated, yellow jackets aggressive, and the few beaver left in the Bad Lands were piling up saplings in great supply. The bark of the young cottonwoods was especially thick and tough, and wild fowl were making their migrations early.

That terrible winter completed the ruin of the range cattle industry.

In February, when it was already clear that there was disaster in the Far West, Andrew returned to a Bad Lands frozen solid. He would never forget the cattle coming into Pyramid Flat to eat the tarpaper off the shacks, and clanking in the tin-can dump trying to get a tongue into anything that might contain a trace of nourishment. The thermometer hung at forty below for weeks on end, and livestock froze to death standing up. When thaws did come, the temperature would quickly drop again, freezing the melted snow so hard they had to break through it with crowbars to uncover a little grass for the desperate animals. The blizzards came down out of the north like wolf packs.

When he went into Miles City on the train to a stockmen's meeting, at every railroad cut they would have to pile out of the cars to run off the animals sheltering on the tracks and the roadbed was lined with bloody carcasses where the big rotaries had ground into the herds.

Cowboys looked almost as gaunt as the cattle, faces like skulls with eye sockets lamp-blacked against snow blindness. They did their best, knocking holes in the ice to grass and water, and trying to turn the animals against the blizzards to closer shelter, for, left to themselves, cattle would drift before

339

the wind until they stacked in a ravine and smothered. Andrew swore along with many another cattleman that he would never again run livestock he could not shelter in winter.

When the chinook blew, in March, and the water began to gush out of the coulees, they could see the extent of the disaster. The streams were thick with dead animals. When the river ice broke up and the jam moved downriver, tree-high, knocking down everything in its path, in the muddy torrent behind the ice front the carcasses bobbed and revolved, stick-legged, as they were borne downriver. Afterward Andrew heard a rancher say he had seen range where you could walk ten miles stepping from corpse to corpse. He thought it an exaggeration.

Most of the Lazy-N dead was piled up in draws. The blowflies were a nightmare. A carcass would be one swollen black cocoon of them, the whole mass twitching as though with life from the flies feeding.

The big, latecoming herds of southerners, unused to cold and weakened from their drives, lost upwards of 90 percent. His own herd, although more inured to severe winters, had been so weakened by lack of forage that dry summer that it survived little better. The spring tally showed that he had lost more than half of his steers, and 80 percent of his cows. Everybody was similarly wiped out.

It was nature's vengeance, not man's, that made the Bad Lands untenable for him. And when Widewings, empty and boarded up, burned to the ground several years later, it was due to lightning, not the bitter enmity that had consumed Machray's slaughterhouse.

He tried ranching for one more year, but there was no more pleasure for him in the Bad Lands. The land was so scarred it seemed it could never heal, and the old, thick Bad Lands grass was fighting a losing battle with weeds. Almost all the game animals were gone, although prairie dogs and coyotes flourished. Many varieties of migratory birds came no more.

There was still a place for small, close-herding cattle ranches. Wire began to be shipped in by the trainload, and windmills for irrigation. Horse ranches prospered for a time, until the street railway systems of the cities began to mechanize. But all the big, old cattle outfits were bankrupt. Homesteaders took over. So Andrew sold out, left the Bad Lands, and did not look back for many years.

340

But he continued to ask himself who had been right. Yule Hardy and those violent and selfish men had been right, for that country was best suited for open range. But they were wrong also, for there was no way, with justice, that newcomers could be kept out. The waves of newcomers ruined it, that beautiful place and the life that was there, the Indians, the buffalo, the game animals and wild fowl, and the grass, loomed by the western swarm of settlers. It was those restless people in their wagons, the "bone and sinew" of the nation, with their packs of dirty-faced kids, some stock, an ax, and a rifle, who destroyed the country.

He returned to New York and assumed his duties as a father, completed the "house on the hill" and sold it, and was elected to the Assembly from the Twenty-first District. He served on the New York Harbor Commission, and on the Civil Service Commission. During the war with Spain he was appointed Assistant Secretary of the Army, and soon after the turn of the century, in a Republican landslide, he found himself in Washington as junior senator from New York. He married a plump, pretty Virginia widow, with two pretty daughters, and purchased a house on H Street with a clear view of the White House, which view, however, was obscured year by year by traffic, by the erection of newer and taller buildings, by an equestrian statue, and finally by simple self-acceptance.

He interested himself in the complexities of the western lands. He knew from personal experience, and through tragedy, that the West was being ruined by the Homestead Law, which gave a settler 160 acres. That figure had been arrived at during the antislavery jockeyings, when it was felt that slavery could exist only on extensive plantations; 160 acres would make for a nation of free, sturdy yeomen. Instead the Homestead Law had made failures of homesteaders and criminals of the cattlemen, who were forced to every kind of illegality to obtain sufficient pasturage for their herds.

Congress had not been able to accept John Wesley Powell's recommendations of homesteads of 2560 acres on unirrigated land. That figure seemed to eastern legislators to represent a baronial estate, while to a cattleman it was hardly enough to graze a hundred head. Laws governing the West were being written by Easterners with no grasp of western problems.

So Andrew sought and found his niche in the Senate, hoping to do what he could not only for the grangers who

had trusted him, but for the cattlemen who had not. He wa
instrumental in the passage of the Kinkaid Act of 1904
which in certain cases allowed for filing on 640 acres instea
of 160. This was followed by the Three-Year Homestead Ac
Little by little he was able to convince his colleagues of th
similarity of the positions of miner and cattleman. The gov
ernment had long recognized the prior rights of miners nc
only to the minerals they mined, but to the water necessar
to the process, while it had never recognized the rights of ca
tlemen to grass and water.

He became known as a friend of the West, and h
maintained friendships in the Bad Lands, although he re
turned to Pyramid Flat only once, to campaign on behalf c
his friend Senator Byrum. He carried on a correspondenc
with Jeff Hardy in his St. Paul asylum, and was instrument
in his release. Bill Driggs, after his parole, visited him i
Washington on a number of occasions, twice in compan
with his wife, Cora. He had also had considerable correspor
dence with Lady Machray when Machray's remains were re
moved from Pyramid Flat to Scotland, five years after h
death.

And one day in the spring of 1911, a red-faced bounc
young man appeared in his office in Washington to introdu
himself as Tim Scarff, mayor of Pyramid Flat, and to extra
agantly admire the painting on his wall—a roundup scen
men wrestling a calf, another wielding a branding iron, ride
wreathed in dust in the background. Mayor Scarff brougl
greetings from Bill Driggs, who had recommended that h
seek advice about a certain problem from Senator Livingston

It seemed that Pyramid Flat had quadrupled in size fro
the old days, a reservoir was desperately needed, and fun
were lacking.

"I was out in Frisco on a trip so I stopped in to see Mr
Gilligan, thinking she might help us out," the mayor sai
hunching forward in his chair. "But they said she was in E
rope. Very snooty butler fellow she has there." He grinned.

"I don't expect Mrs. Gilligan feels much allegiance to tł
Bad Lands," Andrew said. Mary Hardy had married the so
of a Comstock baron, a man some twenty years older tha
herself. She had not remarried when he drank himself
death, but spent most of her time in Italy, although she st
maintained a mansion in San Francisco. He asked how tł
mayor would feel about changing the name of Pyramid Flat.

"Well now, change it to what, Senator?"

"To Machray."

"Well—now!" Scarff said, nodding thoughtfully. There would be no resistance to such an idea in the town, he was certain. Residents considered "Flat" undignified and were tired of explaining the significance of "Pyramid"—the shapes of the eroded buttes behind the town. "Some of those old buzzards out in the slope country won't like it *for sure,* but they don't like anything new anyway. What've you got in mind, Senator?"

He had Lady Machray in mind, and so he began another correspondence with that lady, in the course of which she offered not only to finance the reservoir, but to see that the old slaughterhouse site was presented as a park to the town of Machray, complete with a statue of her late husband, which she would commission.

With his son, a clerk in the Supreme Court and free that month with the Court not in session, Andrew returned to Pyramid Flat, now Machray, on a bake-oven day in July, 1911. The noon train was met by a delegation headed by Mayor Scarff, which included a middle-aged rancher with a familiar, grinning face, tabs of "makings" dangling from the breast pocket of a crisp, blue-and-white-checked shirt, a hard little lump of belly, broad-brimmed hat in hand.

"Well, if it ain't the New York punkin-lily!"

"Fred Rademacher!"

A hand with a missing index finger pumped his. "Well, it is sure fine to see you back out here, famous feller like you!" Fred shook Lee's hand enthusiastically. "Good-looking young chap you have got here, Andy. A bit taller than his daddy!"

He gave way to Bill Driggs with his elaborately wrinkled, ugly, grinning face, pink scalp showing through thinning white hair, and his pinned-up sleeve. Bill was black formal suited, as befitted one of the town's elders, and beside him was Mrs. Driggs, also in her best black. After Bill had embraced him with his strong arm, Andrew took Cora's two hands in his and told her she looked fine. Color swarmed in her softly scarred plump cheeks, and the dark eyes he had seen soften to beauty when she gazed upon Machray stared into his as though to whisper, "Remember— Remember—"

Lee was less reserved with the Driggses than he had been with Fred Rademacher, for he had met them in Washington. In fact, one of the few occasions on which his son's cool mask had slipped to reveal admiration of him was his discov-

ery that two of Andrew's oldest and clearly dearest friends
were an ex-convict and a genuine western madam.

"Town of Machray, eh, Andy?" Driggs said, kneading his
arm. "Don't know that that was exactly what I had in mind
when I sent Tim to see you." He winked. Stiffly corseted and
smiling, Cora Benbow stood silently beside her man.

There were other hands to shake, faces to remember, and
names to grope for. Then Mayor Scarff had his arm, and in
the tonneau of a touring car, Andrew and his son were
rushed off to view the paved streets of the center of town, the
new roller-skating rink, the baseball diamond and the school,
and the fine, brick-fronted saloon, restaurant, and general-
store block, which had been built by the Driggses. Then the
automobile rolled up into a coulee so that the reservoir site
could be viewed. Nothing was visible of Widewings on its
butte.

He excused himself from a preview of the statue, which
had already arrived and been set up on its site.

In the narrow lobby of the hotel, with its fly-blown window
and a spectacled clerk poring over the Bismarck newspaper
while he guarded the luggage that had been brought up from
the station, a middle-aged man waited on an oak bench. He
rose as Andrew and his son entered, smiling and nodding; he
had protruding ears, a weathered, bland face, and washed-out
blue eyes.

Once those eyes had stared crazily at Andrew down the
barrel of a six-shooter, and, just before the white finger had
tightened on the trigger, the muzzle had slanted away—Jeff
Hardy had known he was required to kill the man who had
debauched his sister, but had been uncertain whether to
blame Andrew Livingston or Lord Machray. And death, like
a roulette ball, had bounced out of one slot and stuck in another.

"Hello, Andy," he said shyly. He was sweating in a shiny
blue wool suit, white shirt buttoned tieless at the throat. He
gave Andrew's hand a brisk, single shake, and repeated this
when introduced to Lee. "Just thought I'd stop in town to say
hello."

He asked what Jeff was doing these days.

"Ranchin out at the old place. Things have got a bit better,
lately. Course, we could always use some rain."

Suddenly he addressed Lee: "Your daddy has been pretty
good to me! He got me out of a bad place I was in, and
wrote me letters that did a lot of good there, the doc said.

344

Because I had to write back some things I had to dig around inside my head for. That was good for me to do, you see. I had got a bit *loopy* there!" He tapped his forehead, grinning bonily.

Lee looked paralyzed at this outburst, standing at red-faced attention in his stylish dark suit, high collar, and cravat. But he managed to murmur something graceful enough, and Jeff looked satisfied.

"Do you hear anything from your sister?" Andrew asked, as the washed-out eyes turned toward him.

"Well, I don't hear from her so often. She sent some money when Mother broke her hip. I thought she might've sent more, but it is hard to say."

His voice was very low, and his expression blurred and vague; it was as though he was becoming disembodied, dissolving like a ghost.

"Well, I guess you will understand that I won't be comin in to the festivities tomorrow, Andy," he said. "But it has been fine chattin with you. You and your boy, there." Even his parting handshake seemed less substantial than the first.

He had requested a room at the rear of the hotel, and while Lee stripped the packing from the painting he had brought to present to the mayor, he stood at the window gazing across the alley at the big, square frame house there. Shades were drawn to different heights in small windows, cords and braided rings dangling, and bits of room and furnishings visible. There was no hint as to what was the present use of Mrs. Benbow's house.

"Would you like a glass of whiskey, Father?"

He said that he would and found pleasure in his son's pouring the liquor and bringing it to him.

"Do you remember that painting of mine of a man in a bed? That's the room." He pointed, and added, "I think that's the one."

Lee was nodding. "The man was Machray, and the woman Mrs. Driggs. And that fellow just now was the man who murdered Machray."

It was his turn to nod, turning to regard his son, the neat features, the careful composure, the almost prissy attention to haberdashery. He had never understood what went on behind the cool facade of the grown child whose mother had died when he was three, and whose father had deserted him for a life of Duartean adventure in the Bad Lands. What kind of mark had all that made?

"To tell the truth, I've never liked that painting," Lee said, pouring whiskey into a second glass. It was not the kind of remark he often ventured. "It gives me the willies. A good many of your Bad Lands paintings do, but that one the most."

"But why?"

"Such a mood of bleakness. Loneliness. As though the whole of man's estate is hopeless. Fear, too—in the one with the dying man. I suppose fear of death. Or that's what it makes me feel."

It was not what he had intended to convey; it must be what he had conveyed despite himself. He tossed down his whiskey. Flies buzzed and butted at the windowglass.

"I don't remember loneliness particularly," he said. "Though of course I was lonely after your mother died. But I remember fear. I always frightened in the Bad Lands."

"But why did you stay, Father? I don't understand that."

"I suppose to prove something to myself. That I wasn't frightened." He laughed. "All I proved was that I could remain frightened, and still—remain."

Lee's face was shocked. Theirs was not a relationship in which one admitted to emotions such as fear. "What were you frightened of, Father?"

"That someone was going to kill me."

"Good God!" Lee said. "What a terrible place!"

He had engaged an automobile and driver for the afternoon, and they drove south on a rutted track that skirted the east bank of the river. He wrongly identified a number of coves containing dilapidated farm buildings before what had once been Fire Creek headquarters camp came unmistakably into view. He asked the driver to halt, and he and his son disembarked to gaze across the muddy river at the buildings beyond a fringe of cottonwoods. They looked partially sunken in the ground and tilted as though afloat on an ocean wave, the "Big House," its logs turned white with age, not big at all, and the other no more than a shed. Even the buttes beyond were smaller than he had remembered. Beside the house was rusted machinery of mysterious function. There was no sign of life.

The buzzing of insects was irritating. Grasses bent in the wind, and a few long clouds drifted overhead like gunboats.

"I'd think that wind would be difficult to live with," Lee said.

"It would blow like this for a while," he said. "And then it would change and blow like blazes for a while."

Lee gave him a quick, surprised grin. "But you loved it," he said.

"I used to think it was very beautiful. It's not what it was. It was a very fragile place. Too many people crowded in, and too many cattle, there was too much contention. It has never recovered." What he had thought was insects buzzing was a distant engine.

He did not think he need ever come here again. He said he thought they had better turn back in order to wash up before the banquet that night. Lady Machray and her son, the Marquess, would not arrive until tomorrow.

For the dedication ceremony next day, stands had been erected, and a speakers' platform, decorated with bunting, in the shadow of the old, tall yellow-brick chimney stack of the vanished abattoir. The statue bulked nearby, shrouded in muslin. Townspeople were filling the stands as he and Lee arrived, shrill-voiced boys played catch; a baby wailed, dogs chased each other. The sun burned down until he could feel his shirt soaking to his back and his feet awash in his shoes. Lee appeared irritatingly cool and self-contained.

No sooner were they seated on the speakers' platform than the touring car they had engaged yesterday jolted down the road. A woman and a young man got out, the Marquess lean and graceful in a fawn suit, spats, a jaunty hat, yellow gloves in hand. He cast bored glances right and left, very much a young lordling. His mother was a trim figure in bottle green, a fringe of veil covering the forehead of an aging, discontented face. Her carriage was remarkable. Her son took her arm as they mounted the crudely built steps, his arrogant green glance taking them all in as Mayor Scarff bounced and jiggled nervously.

Panting from her climb, Lady Machray said, "Senator!" and swept Scarff aside. She proffered her hand, and he remembered well that lift, part physical and part will that brought her freckled knuckles to his lips. She introduced her son, and the two young men were introduced, whom Machray had once said would be friends, growing up in the Bad Lands with space around them. They shook hands with no apparent interest in one another.

"Bloody hot out here on the steppes!" Machray's son said, with a grin.

"Isn't it?" said his.

The ceremonies began. Andrew was fulsomely introduced. He spoke of the Old Days, to applause; the Old Days always elicited applause. He said that he and Lord and Lady Machray had been neighbors in the old days. He and Lord Machray had quarreled over land, like everyone else in the Bad Lands. Fortunately this quarrel had been settled amicably, for Lord Machray was a dead shot. There was laughter. He saw that the lordling was regarding him with more interest. So were Bill and Cora Driggs, two black-clad figures beneath her parasol.

In another situation, he said—a war, in fact—he had been rescued by Lord Machray from dangerous men intent upon killing him. There was a silence as his audience realized to what war he was referring, and this time his own son regarded him with interest.

He went on to say that Lord Machray had been elected captain of the Great Posse, the citizen-army organized to halt the invasion of the Bad Lands. Certainly Lord Machray had been decorated for courage in Her Majesty's Abyssinian and Egyptian campaigns, but he had also deserved decoration for his part in the Bad Lands Campaign. There he had exhibited courage, wisdom, and compassion. Healing wounds must be viewed as more noble than causing them, and Lord Machray had died trying to heal the wounds of the Bad Lands.

He addressed himself to Lady Machray. He said that he had held her husband's hand when he died. Lord Machray had spoken, then, of his love for his ancestral home in the Highlands, and his sorrow that he would never again see his wife, whom he loved, and the son he loved above all. He was not an uneffective speaker, if, upon rare occasions, a liar, and he concluded to great applause.

Reseating himself, he was pleased to hear his son clearing his throat. He could see the shine of tears on the cheeks of Lady Machray, and the Marquess was glancing away and slapping his thigh with the yellow gloves. The applause continued as Lady Machray stepped to the podium, assisted by the mayor's hand on her elbow. She daubed at her cheeks with a handkerchief taken from her sleeve and blew her nose with a dowager's honk.

She announced in a rather shrill voice that she was presenting this site, the site of her husband's grand dream, to the town of Machray. A park was to be established here, and a fund had been set up for its maintenance. The centerpiece of the park was to be a statue of Lord Machray.

With that she jerked on a string that ran through metal loops along the platform railing. The muslin cover fell away. Revealed was a startling likeness of Machray in gray marble, bareheaded, with that nose and tugboat jaw thrust forward, cartridge belt and holstered revolver at his waist, high boots, broad-brimmed hat in hand.

He leaned forward to peer across the river, larger than life, who, in life, had been larger than life. The shaft upon which he stood bore the words:

IN MEMORIAM
GEORGE EUSTACE BALATER
LORD MACHRAY
1843-1884

BELOVED OF THE BAD LANDS
AND FOUNDER OF THIS TOWN
THAT BEARS HIS NAME

ABOUT THE AUTHOR

Oakley Hall is a native Californian. Since 1967 he has divided his time between Squaw Valley, in the Sierra Nevada, and Irvine, in Southern California, where he is professor of English and a member of the staff of the Program in Writing at the University of California. He is the author of fifteen books, among them *Corpus of Joe Bailey*, and *The Downhill Racer*.

FREE
Fawcett Books Listing

There is Romance, Mystery, Suspense, and Adventure waiting for you inside the Fawcett Books Order Form. And it's yours to browse through and use to get all the books you've been wanting . . . but possibly couldn't find in your bookstore.

This easy-to-use order form is divided into categories and contains over 1500 titles by your favorite authors.

So don't delay—take advantage of this special opportunity to increase your reading pleasure.

Just send us your name and address and 35¢ (to help defray postage and handling costs).
